THE
ATTACHMENT

AN ELIZA GREY MYSTERY

JUDITH COSBY

This book is a work of fiction. Names, characters, businesses, organizations, places, events, and incidents either are the product of the author's imagination or are used fictitiously. Any resemblance to actual persons, living or dead, events, or locales is entirely coincidental.

Cover Design by Ana Grigoriu–Voicu, Books Design

Editing by Veronica Jorden

Proofreading by Kelly Hawkins

ISBN: 978-1-7341153-3-8 (Print Book – Paperback)

ISBN: 978-1-7341153-4-5 (Print Book – Hardcover)

ISBN: 978-1-7341153-5-2 (eBook)

1. Murder Mysteries 2. Woman Sleuths 3. Ghost Mysteries 5. Animal Mysteries 6. Suspense Thriller 7. Historical Fiction

First Edition

Visit my website at https://www.judithcosby.com/

I dedicate this book to my husband, Craig, who supported this project and became an integral part of the countless hours of chapter edits and proofing. Thank you for believing in me and my ability to write this book.

I thank my daughters, Sarah and Catherine, for all their love and support.

I thank my mother, Shirley, for reading the manuscript and loving the characters like I do.

To those who worked tirelessly to make *The Attachment* shine:
Thank you, Veronica, for believing in this book and helping to make it a reality!
Thank you, Kelly, for always being available for my many phone calls and texts. I appreciate your proofing prowess in keeping *The Attachment* grammatically correct!
Thank you, Ana, for creating a perfect book cover. You made the visual of Rosecliff Manor come to life!

A special thanks to Spiro M., who single-handedly saved *The Attachment* with his computer genius. The original manuscript would have been lost if it were not for your tech-savvy genius.

"I can call spirits from the vasty deep. Why so can I, or so can any man; But will they come when you do call for them?"

William Shakespeare Henry IV Part 1 Act 3 Scene 1

Prologue

Coventry-by-the-Sea, summer 1985

"ELIZA! FOLLOW ME! I found a cool path that leads to another beachside."

Hearing her brother Edmond's call, Eliza quickly tossed her coloring book and crayons into her toy bin and rushed to follow him. At seven, he was two years older than her and already several inches taller. Though their lightly freckled complexions were gifts from their mother, and matching green eyes gifts from their father, Edmond inherited their dad's adventurous spirit and devil-may-care twinkle in his eyes.

Edmond faced Eliza holding two pails, "Which one do you want, green or yellow?"

"Yellow," she replied with a huge grin. "But what are they for?"

"These are for us to hold the shells and sea glass we find."

Edmond grabbed her hand and pulled her toward a sandy path, almost hidden by overgrowth from the tall seagrasses, wild black gum trees, and scrub pines that shielded the trail.

Eliza stopped. "I don't know, Edmond, this feels scary. Shouldn't we ask Mom first?" Eliza worshipped her brother and rarely missed a chance to go off adventuring with him, but something about the path didn't feel right.

"El, it's fine. We'll be careful. Just wait until you see this place," Edmond said with confidence.

She followed closely on his heels along the thickly brambled, secluded path until they reached a break in the overgrowth that opened up to a private rocky shoreline.

Eliza spun around to search for the little white cottage with the pink door her parents rented for the summer. "I can't see the cottage, Edmond."

"We're almost there," Edmond said, running ahead. "It's just up here!"

Eliza could hear the melodious boom of the crashing waves beyond the opening. Bright sun pierced the dimly lit pathway as the two pushed their way under a thick green canopy of overgrowth. The sun showered a scattering of light through the gaps of leaves wavering above as they entered into a mysterious mecca.

Eliza's eyes widened, and she mouthed the word, "Wow!"

"Told ya!" Edmond replied, his chest puffed out slightly with the pride of his discovery.

Mesmerized by the view, Eliza could not contain her excitement. A fifty-foot cliff ran parallel to the water along the entire length of the secluded beach. Hundreds of scrub roses cascaded down its stony face dropping a shower of soft petals with every breeze and carpeting the shore in a sea of pink.

"It's so beautiful, Edmond. It is like a secret palace."

Edmond scrambled up a small outcrop of rocks and waved for Eliza to do the same. "Look at the tide pools. They're filled with hermit crabs and small fish."

Eliza clambered up after her brother and stared down into a deep, crystal-blue tide pool that rippled in the wind.

Edmond nudged her with his elbow and pointed up toward the edge of the cliff at the far end of the beach. "And it's even got its own haunted house."

Shielding her eyes from the bright sun, Eliza followed his gaze and took in the magnificent manor overlooking the shoreline.

"Whoa. I wonder whose home that is?"

"I have no idea, but it sure is spooky," Edmond replied.

Eliza nodded in agreement. But where her brother saw the possibility of something otherworldly, Eliza knew its reality. She could feel the rotting bones of the house's structure, decaying windows with their blank reflections, and the weary-looking oak door. She knew something not entirely human dwelled within that place.

Something secret.

"C'mon Eliza, let's get closer to the water and see what we can find."

Eliza gave the house one more glance, then followed her brother.

An abundance of sea glass sparkled in a band of damp sand, now visible due to the receding tide.

Eliza carefully hopped, rock to rock, past the tide pools to a stretch of uninterrupted sand in pursuit of the glittering droplets that sent a flood of rainbow-colored light diamonds dancing across the shoreline's wet surface. She sang the song her mother often hummed as she made her way toward the sparkling treasure, "By the sea, by the beautiful sea...."

Within seconds of her feet landing in the sand, she'd already added several larger pieces of sea glass to her pail. Spying two scallop shells as big as her fist, she hurried along the water's edge and knelt to snag them before a wave stole them back into the ocean. She dropped the shells into the bucket.

Out of the corner of her eye, a slight movement and a slender silhouette caught her attention. A beautiful woman with long dark hair and bright green eyes stood gazing out over the water. Her long dress rippling in the breeze like a princess in one of Eliza's favorite storybooks.

"H-hello," Eliza said.

The mysterious woman turned to face Eliza, smiled, and beckoned her closer.

Eliza's parents had forbidden her from approaching strangers, but she couldn't resist. Arching her chin over her shoulder in hopes of seeing Edmond, the magnetic draw of the woman's gaze cemented her in place.

"Eliza...," the woman whispered in a breathy, sing-song voice.

How does she know my name?

Eliza's heart thundered in her chest, and she stood transfixed as the young woman's appearance began to change.

The once beautiful figure and delicate features morphed into something hideous. The woman's vivid green eyes melted into lifeless black orbs, and her clothes grew wet and slimy. Her youthful face decayed into hollows and valleys until it became gaunt and sinewy. The former slender neck bent and strained until it held the unsightly head at a disturbing angle—the woman's kind expression now one of utter pain.

The ghastly woman pointed a finger directly at Eliza.

"Give me your hand, child." Her voice scratched and hissed as she spoke.

Eliza shivered and turned to run, but her feet remained firmly rooted in place.

Why can't I move?

Around her, the landscape changed. The vibrant pink of the roses and the austere home atop the cliff faded away. The sparkling multicolored sea glass and the scurrying hermit crabs hiding among the green seaweed disappeared in a thick mist of gray. A cold icy air descended, snuffing out the warmth of the bright yellow sun. Only the sound of the waves remained. Their violent collision with the shore grew louder and louder as salty water crawled up the shallow beach toward her, lapping at her ankles and covering her sneakers in chilly sea water.

Eliza struggled against the invisible forces that held her in place.

"Give me your hand," the woman repeated.

Eliza's arm, which only moments before had refused to move, now lifted as if it had a will of its own and reached out to the woman. She tried to scream, but no sound left her throat. The horrible stench of rotting flesh rose around her and made her gag.

The ghastly apparition grabbed Eliza's tiny hand, sending a surge of crackling electrical energy between them.

"You are mine from this day forward. You belong to me..."

A complete and penetrating cold invaded Eliza's entire body. She saw a small boy and a large man and then darkness. Helplessness and a supreme and never-ending sense of loss coursed through her as the inky black abyss stretched out further.

"You belong to me..."

"No! No, I don't belong to you!"

A bright light pierced the blackness, and a rush of emotion erupted from her throat.

"Let go of me!" Her hand slipped from the woman's slimy grip, and the coldness immediately began to ebb away.

"Our paths will cross again," the woman whispered with a crooked smile and vanished.

"Eliza! Eliza!" Edmond stood beside her, his hands gripping her shoulders. "Eliza Monroe! Answer me!"

Eliza blinked hard several times as the beach and her brother's angry face slowly came back into focus.

"What is wrong with you? Didn't you hear me? Mom is gonna kill us for getting our sneakers wet!"

Eliza's lips quivered as she started to cry.

"Edmond! I don't want to be here anymore. I want to go back to the cottage. I want to go back right now." She hugged him so tightly her tiny shoulders trembled.

"It's okay, Eliza. It's okay. I'll take you home."

Eliza's gaze darted up to the house on the cliff. She now *knew* it held a dark secret.

"Hurry, Edmond. Hurry, please."

Edmond carried Eliza piggy-back, toting both half-full pails, and retraced their steps through the same overgrown path, leaving the mysterious beach behind.

Once back within the sight of her parents' cottage, Eliza relaxed.

"You can put me down now, Edmond."

He obliged, placing her gently on a sunny patch of grass.

"What the heck scared you so much?" Edmond asked.

"Scared? I just didn't like that place," Eliza rebuffed, unsure if she should tell her brother what she'd seen.

"It's okay. You can tell me. What happened? I called your name a dozen times, but it's like you couldn't hear me."

Eliza didn't respond immediately. Instead, she untied her shoes and pulled off her wet socks, laying them out to dry in the sun. She glanced sideways at her brother, trying to decide if he would believe her if she told him the truth.

"Do you believe in ghosts?" she asked him.

"Ghosts?" He sat beside her to pull off his wet shoes and socks.

Eliza nodded. "That's what happened on the beach. I saw a ghost. A lady. A wet lady."

Edmond made a face, obviously skeptical but didn't contradict her.

"She grabbed my hand, told me I belonged to her. But I fought her; I didn't want to get lost in the darkness. I thought about you, Mom, and Dad, and the s'mores we're supposed to have tonight by the fire. And then I felt you touch my back and call my name. But she told me our paths would cross again."

"Have you seen her before?" Edmond asked.

Eliza couldn't be sure if his expression meant he believed her or not. She shrugged her shoulders.

"I don't know. But I think she died here. I think she haunts that abandoned house on the cliff."

1

THE 5 A.M. ALARM sliced through the quiet morning like a trumpet blast. Jason groaned.

"Why does the morning come so fast?" he rolled over to shut off the alarm.

Eliza eased out of bed, scurried across the cold hardwood floor, and headed downstairs to fix the coffee.

Less than forty-five minutes later, her dressed-but-half-awake husband had finished a cup of coffee, devoured two buttered slices of whole wheat toast, and now flitted from the counter to the table to the front foyer, gathering a leather-bound file folder and his cell phone.

"My, Mr. Grey, you do look handsome. Discombobulated, but still handsome."

He paused to give her an exasperated grin before disappearing down the hall, most likely to fetch a forgotten file from his office.

"I can't wait for you to join me on the next trip," he called from his office. "What's on your agenda for today?"

Eliza made herself a cup of tea, twisting the teabag around her spoon to get the last few drops of flavor. "Heading to *The Gazette* to meet with Art Cummings at nine to turn in my story on the history of Coventry-by-the-Sea's Waterfront District and to pitch my next piece. I am thinking of doing a series on the founding families for our town's upcoming 250th Jubilee. We've been here for so long, but I honestly can't say I know much about Coventry's history."

Jason reappeared in the foyer and added two files to his briefcase. He patted his pockets and looked at his cell phone.

"And then I'm going to head over to the spa for a full tar and feather treatment."

"Sounds great, honey," Jason said as he disappeared once again down the hall.

Eliza smiled and picked up her husband's favorite watch from the counter where he'd left it. He was handsome, funny, and a whiz at finding online deals, but organized for international travel, he was not.

She held it out and waited for him to return.

He emerged from his office a second time, another folder in hand. When he saw the watch, he closed his eyes and grinned. Taking a deep breath, he held out his arm and let Eliza slip the watch onto his wrist.

"Where would I be without you?" He kissed the top of her head. "Art is lucky to have you. Did you say 'tar and feathered?'"

Eliza fastened the clasp on his watch and wiped a smudge of butter from the corner of his lips.

"Ah, so you were listening. And yes, Art is lucky, but not nearly as lucky as you."

"The God's honest truth," he said.

"Travel safe, honey." She opened the front door and handed him his briefcase. "Your driver awaits. You better get going."

Outside, a man in a black suit stood beside a dark blue company limo.

Jason handed off two suitcases, then patted his pockets once more as if forgetting something.

She handed him the overcoat he'd left on the back of a kitchen chair.

He sighed and took the coat, then pulled her into his arms. "I'll call when I get settled. Three weeks away from you will feel like an eternity."

He kissed her, then darted out into the cool morning air.

As the limo pulled away, a profound feeling of loneliness grabbed hold of her heart like an unwanted visitor leaving a sting in its wake.

She wrapped her arms around her waist and shivered. A deep chill seeped into her bones, atypical for a mid-September morning in New England. The ominous biting cold made her shuffle her feet against the carpet and tie her robe tighter to retain her body heat. As she closed the door and moved back into the foyer, a gnawing in her stomach, spawned by the whispers of a brewing premonition, made her feel nauseous.

In her youth, these *knowing* sensations had helped to keep her and her brother out of danger, but they had also often been the precursor to horrific nightmares. As a child, she could sense and know things others could not, even when she didn't want to see them.

As a teenager, she'd learned to block most of them out, and thankfully, the creepy visions had disappeared almost entirely. But as the years passed, slowly, the *knowing* sensations returned, though more often for the better. They'd led her to accept the invitation to the party where she met her husband and to the market listing for Rosecliff, the house they now called home.

Sunlight streamed through the second-floor stained-glass window that looked down over the spacious foyer, one of her favorite rooms. Refracted colors sparkled across the wainscot panels that flanked the grand staircase. A spray of light danced along the polished mahogany rails and spindles as they curved up to the upper story. Eliza leaned in to let the light warm her face.

The fifteen years since they'd first crossed over the threshold as the new owners had passed by in the blink of an eye. Although in great need of repair when they'd put in an offer, she'd known that the bones of the old house held a sturdy foundation, one that physically and metaphorically would become the perfect place to raise a family. Rosecliff Manor, the house she feared as a child, called to her differently. For Jason, it checked all his boxes: size, location, and community. But for Eliza, it carried a distinct heft. She *knew* she belonged here. The echoes of her past memory did not haunt her the same, and the secrets within its four walls remained quiet.

A dark cloud moved over the sun, collapsing the rainbow-colored light display and casting the foyer into a grayish shadow. Almost instantly, the *knowing* sensation grew stronger. Flashes of darkness and a stabbing pain at the base of her spine made her reach for the rail to steady herself.

Seconds later, the cloud passed, and sunlight returned to her face. Immediately, the discomfort diminished, and the darkness behind her eyes dissipated.

Eliza took a deep breath, calming her mind.

"C'mon, Eliza, shake it off. It's probably just a storm brewing, nothing to fret about," she said aloud. "Get a move on. You've got things to do."

She rubbed her hands together for a little warmth, shook off her angst, and hurried upstairs to the promise of a long, hot shower.

As she passed her daughter's room, she paused and pushed open the door.

"Still empty," she said with a sigh.

Isabella, or Bella as she was called, meant the world to Eliza. But children, as they always do, grow up. A freshman at Salve Regina University in Newport, Rhode Island, her only child was a star student with a full scholarship to study business management and marketing. And as one of the only starting freshmen on the soccer team, Bella was a force on and off the field. Eliza couldn't be prouder of all her daughter's academic and athletic achievements. But she missed Bella's bright laughter and their morning talks before school.

She closed the door to Bella's room and entered the master bedroom. After the foyer, the ensuite bath came in as a close second to her favorite room in the house. Black and white honeycomb tile offered a modern contrast to the white wainscotting and soft blue walls. She pulled back the circular shower curtain around her clawfoot bathtub and turned the water on to warm.

Undressing, Eliza caught a glimpse of herself in the mirror. She ran a hand through her curly auburn hair and examined the growing number of fine lines at the edges of her round green eyes. Batting her thick, full eyelashes, she leaned in for a closer look.

"Welcome to the age of crow's feet."

Steam began to fog the mirror. Eliza abandoned the self-critique, stepped into the tub, turned the chrome knob to shower, and let the spray pulse against her face and chest.

When Jason initially broke the news about his trip – one necessary to establish the newest branch of his growing firm in the United Kingdom – she'd actually looked forward to the quiet and having more time to write. But with his absence and Bella away at school, she would be alone. Not just for the day but for three weeks. Twenty-one days and twenty nights entirely by herself. It had been years since she'd spent so much time without a husband or child to look after.

The gnawing in her gut returned, not as intense as before, but enough to make her catch her breath as it held constant. She rolled her neck and pressed her shoulders back, praying the feeling would pass. Moments of *knowing* came and went throughout her life, but she couldn't recall the last time the feeling had been so pronounced and prolonged. It wasn't a good sign.

Closing her eyes, she tried to visualize something that made her happy, a technique she'd mastered as a young girl to keep the *knowing* at bay. She pictured Bella on the beach. Warm sunshine. The sound of soothing waves crashing onto the shore.

A sudden yet crystal clear premonition passed through her mind's eye. The images of her daughter and the beach disappeared, replaced by darkness. A face appeared, a twisted haunting face she hadn't seen in years. The tortured eyes and anguished mouth loomed before her as the putrid stench of rotten flesh stung her nose. The portent of something ominous and familiar dominated her mind with fear.

The steam from the shower turned icy cold.

Eliza cried out and flipped the shower knob.

Down at her feet, water poured from the faucet, still hot and steaming.

"Get a hold of yourself, Eliza!"

Keeping her eyes open, she turned the knob once again. Under the renewed hot stream, she rinsed the shampoo out of her hair as quickly as possible, then wrapped herself in a fluffy white towel and hurried from the room.

She dressed in her usual casual style, a pair of slim-fitting jeans, a V-neck white t-shirt, and her favorite black suede boots.

The chilly hardwood floor, white caps rolling atop the sea, and waving tufts of seagrass meant she'd need to layer up.

She added a gray wool cardigan and a rose chenille scarf for an accent.

A quick scrunch of mousse to define her loose auburn curly hair, a bit of mascara, her favorite lip gloss, and the day was hers to conquer.

On her dresser, she spied her favorite gold necklace adorned with a sea glass pendant, a piece she found long ago on one of her many beach-combing jaunts. As she clasped it around her neck, a slow tingle made the hair on her nape stand up. She quickly scanned the room. Why did it feel like she was being watched?

The mantle clock chimed eight. She still had an hour to kill before heading to *The Gazette.*

"Just enough time for a cup of tea and a walk through the garden to steady my nerves."

A few minutes later, she pushed open her kitchen's French doors onto the slate terrace and stepped out into the cool sunshine, her favorite mermaid mug warm in her hands. She'd opted for an orange spice tea, and the scent of citrus, clove, and cinnamon was distinct against the brisk ocean breeze. Around her, mums bloomed in abundance. Their vibrant yellows and oranges offered a striking contrast to the patches of soft purple sedum and feathery September grass. No matter how hard a day ever got, this place was her peace, and the view always provided a sense of calm.

She followed a path of flagstones away from the house, across the lawn, and out to the cliff's edge, taking a sip of her tea as she glanced down at the crashing surf below. The glint of bits of sea glass sparkled on the narrow stretch of sand. Flashes of summer days collecting shells and bits of marine life with her brother made her smile.

It was from the same beach she recalled the first time she'd seen the house that would become her home. She turned to look around at the three-story Victorian with its gables and widow's walk. Its beautiful, whitewashed cedar siding and large windows lovingly replaced and restored along with nearly every other surface inside. Rosecliff Manor, as it was known, was a far cry from the dilapidated, haunting sentinel it had once been.

When Eliza first suggested they look for a home near Coventry-by-the-Sea, Jason had been delighted. The town's only realtor, the illustrious and somewhat infamous Althea Wickham, had insisted they see Rosecliff, despite Jason's initial misgivings. The renovations alone were enough to give him pause. He wanted new and turn-key and had shared his concerns about the pressure of home improvements while simultaneously building his new company. For Eliza, it wasn't Rosecliff's physical condition that had worried her. As a child, the house had always felt like it was hiding something. A past that was anything but happy, and she couldn't have ever imagined raising a family within its walls. She could not deny, though, that the 1790s home was beautiful and possessed a mysterious allure.

But its size and location were enough to entice Jason, and at Althea's continued insistence, they'd agreed to at least take the tour. Any wariness or concern she'd harbored about the place had melted away the moment she stepped across the threshold.

Now, deep down inside, Eliza believed it was Providence that she and Jason had purchased the old house and turned it into the home in which to raise their daughter. She took another sip of her tea and let her mind wander to the day of their house closing and the strange letter Althea left them with a basket of fruit and champagne.

Dear Grey family,

I am so happy you chose to keep Rosecliff Manor's name. It can now be restored to its original grandeur with your loving touch. May you find happiness within its old timbers.

Restore it with love, fill it with laughter, and heal the wounds from the past. Blessings to you and your family.

Althea Wickham

"Heal the wounds from the past."

That single line had struck a chord. They'd certainly filled its walls with love and laughter and, in doing so, transformed the house that had once seemed so dark and dismal.

A tingling sensation crawled up her arms and down her spine. The feeling that she was being watched returned.

A pair of seagulls crested over the cliff, cawing at her loudly before catching an updraft and swooping away.

Eliza...

She turned into the wind and, for a moment, thought she'd heard someone call her name.

Pressing her hand to her chest, a deep chill raced through her body, and she shivered. She'd heard her name, hadn't she?

Scanning the beach below one last time, she downed the last of her tea and headed back inside.

"Hardly two hours on your own, and you're already losing it."

Eliza pulled into a space in a public parking lot near *The Coventry Gazette* office building at ten minutes to nine. Housed in one of the oldest buildings on Main Street, the staff and workings of the local paper sat behind a wide bank of windows and an old oak door with glass inlay. The glass etching prominently read *The Coventry Gazette, Est. 1962.*

A bell rang from above the hinge as she entered. Inside, she was greeted with an unexpected combination of musty newsprint and the overpowering scent of a cloying perfume.

Lana Addison, the receptionist, wearer of said perfume, stood behind the front counter.

Eliza took a deep breath and approached the desk.

It wasn't that Eliza didn't like Lana; she did. Lana's dedication to *The Gazette* and her ability to dig for juicy tidbits for a story was second to none. Yet, the woman had a way of getting under Eliza's skin with her snarky comments and bossy demeanor.

"Good morning, Eliza," she said, her voice high and nasal. "I have something for you. It's on the printer, don't move."

Lana's kitten heels clicked on beige-speckled linoleum flooring as the short, curvy woman approached the printer and returned to her desk.

For more than twenty years, Lana had ruled *The Gazette* reception area in an officious manner, and there was no denying the woman had a distinct nose for snooping. Eliza referred to her type as a "curtain twitcher," one of those neighborhood busybodies who peered out behind their drapes, convinced they needed to know everyone else's business. She wore a trademark pair of black bedazzled cat-eye glasses, and her blunt-cut platinum blonde hair and thick false eyelashes were an obvious attempt to look younger than forty.

Eliza wasn't convinced it was working as well as Lana thought.

Lana handed the sheet of paper across the desk.

"Here are some suggestions from the locals about what they would like to read. Art thought you might find them useful."

"Thank you," Eliza said, scanning the list of topics: *Businesses we'd like to see in Coventry-by-the-Sea. Businesses we don't want to see in Coventry-by-the-Sea. Wine and local pastry pairings. Overwintering tips for local gardens.*

They were all perfectly fine ideas, but she was hoping for something with a little more history and intrigue.

"I've got an idea or two of my own for this next piece, but I'll keep this in mind for later."

Eliza nodded at the back office. The word "EDITOR," worn and faded, stood out from the 1960s frosted glass and tired-looking oak door. "Is Art ready for me? Staff meeting at nine, right?"

"Yeah, go on in," Lana said, sitting down at her computer.

It often struck Eliza funny that they referred to this little weekly update as a staff meeting when none of the other employees at *The Gazette* were included. Eliza had suggested the term "ideation meeting" once, but when Art gave her a deer-in-the-headlights look, she'd dropped the idea of calling it anything other than a staff meeting.

Eliza hesitated, then skirted around the front desk. One thing about working with Lana, she ran the office like a drill sergeant, which meant the staff meetings were always prompt and quick. The fact that she wasn't already in Art's office, pen in hand, waiting to begin caught Eliza off guard.

Eliza rapped lightly on the door before entering the office.

"Art, it's Eliza."

Behind a massive wooden desk, among a mess of typed pages and stacks of newspapers, sat Art Cummings, Editor-in-Chief. The third Editor to sit at that desk, and the longest-lasting staff member, beating Lana by two years. He motioned for her to enter.

"Come in, Eliza, come in," he said, gesturing for her to sit in a chair near his desk.

At fifty-three, Art still possessed a youthful face with a tight jawline, thick brown hair with touches of gray, and a mustache. He wore classic aviator double-bridged metal eyeglasses that made his eyes more prominent than necessary, but somehow it worked for him. No matter the day or occasion, his attire remained consistent: a traditional brown herringbone blazer, a crisp white button-down shirt, and a bowtie. Today's bowtie – a tartan pattern in red – screamed practical dresser. And Art was nothing if not practical.

Eliza sat down in the chair opposite Art's desk and smiled at him.

In the five years of working together, she'd known Art to be brilliant and funny but also socially awkward and uncomfortable around women. Whatever the task at hand, whether it be instructing young interns or helping customers at the front desk, the same man who had received first place in the Reader's Choice Awards for Small Town Newspaper Editors struggled to make eye contact with any member of the female persuasion. The same man who could pen a compelling, direct, and no-nonsense editorial would struggle to put two words together. Eliza had witnessed on many occasions how easily he interacted with men, with none of the nervousness.

Her journalistic inclination often made her wonder why he struggled. Still, she had long since decided any questions on the subject would likely make him uncomfortable, so instead, whenever they had a meeting, she did her best to make him as comfortable as possible.

True to form, a thin layer of sweat made Art's forehead shiny, and he busied himself straightening the papers on his desk to cover his lack of eye contact.

He cleared his throat and called out, "Lana?"

"I'm coming!" Lana bellowed in a sing-song voice from her desk.

Within seconds Eliza could hear the rapid clickity-clackity of her heels as Lana hurried into the office and plopped down in her regular seat, her reading glasses perched on her nose. She squirmed in her chair, pulling at the hem of her tightly fitted sweater dress. She folded her legs twice, alternating one leg over the other, causing her high heels to squeal against the flooring, before letting out a huff and pulling the pencil from behind her ear.

"Ready."

Art gave Lana a side-eye glance before clearing his throat once again and reading a few recaps from their last meeting. When he finished, his gaze darted up to Eliza and then back down at his desk.

Eliza took her cue and leaned forward to pitch the idea for her next article.

"I've got a proposal for a new series...a way to celebrate Coventry-by-the-Sea's 250th Jubilee. Between now and then, I'll pick several of our founding families to highlight, you know, ones who made a major impact on the growth of our community, and share interesting tidbits about them and how they contributed to our town. In addition, I would like to propose writing a piece for the week of Halloween about a haunting or ghostly family plot from Highgate Cemetery. I want to see if Coventry-by-the-Sea can snag some of the Halloween tourism from Salem or at least share some of it."

Salem, home of the infamous witch trials, was less than half an hour's drive away.

Art nodded, his eyes glancing up to Eliza again, then back to the stack of papers before him.

"I ...like it."

"I am planning to investigate the old gravesites at Highgate Cemetery. I would start in the mid-1700s and continue from there. But it may take a while to research and develop a story."

Another furtive glance up and back down. "What's your timeline?"

"I'd aim to have the first one to you by the beginning of October. And the follow-up story for the Halloween edition a couple of weeks after that. I was hoping Lana could give me a hand by pulling anything from the paper's earliest editions with keywords like 'ghost,' 'witch,' 'haunting,' or anything else from the realm of the paranormal."

Art sat up a little straighter, his head slowly nodding, his expression displaying as much interest and intrigue as she'd ever seen him convey.

Lana busily scribbled down her notes and mumbled, "Well, at least I will finally have some interesting research to do for a change."

A smirk slipped out of the side of Eliza's face.

That woman never minces words or hides her true feelings.

Art cleared his throat and made a covert side eye in Lana's direction. "Glad you approve."

Lana, mouth open and eyes wide, stuttered, "I-I didn't mean any disrespect, Art. Really. I merely expressed my excitement for the chance to do some real digging."

Art nodded and continued, "The Community section needs a little pizazz. We have the area towns, like Salem, that spin that. I agree; we could give *The Coventry Gazette* a leg up in that area."

Eliza smiled and stood. *The Coventry Gazette* was a small town paper, not exactly home to state-of-the-art equipment or salacious news reports. But she enjoyed its idiosyncrasies, and being part of the close-knit, eclectic team of local writers offered her a certain sense of pride. With its weekly gardening advice column and seasonal recipes, *The Gazette* represented everything that made Coventry-by-the-Sea the place she called home.

Eliza followed Lana out of the office and waited by the desk for her to log back on to her computer.

Lana looked up over the rim of her glasses and folded her arms. "I'll do a search of all of our scanned copies and microfiches and then print and organize everything. Founding Fathers of Yore meets the creepy factor, right?"

Part of Lana's job description included pulling archives and helping the staff conduct research, but usually, when Eliza asked for her help, she was met with loud huffs and eye rolls. But this, Lana seemed...happy about it.

"Yeah. I'd really appreciate that."

"I'm on it," she said, typing out a few lines before looking back up at Eliza. "I love all that paranormal stuff, and I happen to know for a fact this town's got some...skeletons in the closet." She laughed at her own joke and pushed her glasses up onto the bridge of her nose. "Give me a day or two, and I'll see what I can find."

"Appreciate it, Lana. Feel free to call or email me when you're done, and I'll swing by. Have a great day."

"Yeah, you too," she replied, her nose already back on her computer screen.

Eliza waited for the traffic light and made her way back to her car. Any apprehension she had about her time alone dissipated, now replaced with an excitement about her new storyline and the time to research and write.

In fact, maybe I should start some of that research right now.

Highgate Cemetery was just a couple of blocks away. The sun was bright; the gentle breeze was chilly but invigorating. It was the perfect kind of weather for some spooky investigating.

Turning from the parking lot, she walked through an alley to the closest cross-street and made her way to Highgate Cemetery, the town's oldest burial ground.

A ten-foot wrought iron archway lent a Gothic air to the cemetery entrance. Beyond the open metalwork, lush green lawns rolled through the heavily treed, hilly terrain that surrounded the abundant gravestones. Each stone representing a solemn remembrance for generations of local families.

Once inside the gate, Eliza followed the main roadway that meandered through different areas of the graveyard. The newest sections were nearest to the iron entrance, with its manicured lawn and neat rows of polished granite headstones.

While she could, and had, on more than one occasion, spent hours exploring the cemetery from front to back, Eliza made a beeline to the rear and oldest section. She much preferred the ramshackle layout of plots and the older headstones made of slate, limestone, marble, and sandstone, each one elaborately carved with designs, symbols, and poems. On any given day, these sections of the cemetery sated her inner researcher, but with her newest *Gazette* assignment, she was confident she would find the story she needed here. Somewhere among the elaborate artwork and lavishly detailed inscriptions, a story was waiting. When she found it, she trusted she would *know* that an immediate connection would occur. Honoring those who had passed so long ago, giving a new voice to who they were and the life they experienced, provided her with a sense of reverence for the past in a way she could hardly describe.

She read the names: *Spencer, Jones, Martin, Harris, Bergin, Sullivan, Fletcher, Miller.*

A crow landed on a cross-shaped stone and stared at her. An unearthly quiet settled around her. The sense of *knowing* rose inside of Eliza, sending her sixth sense into full alert. The feeling of being watched she'd felt that morning returned.

She scanned the cemetery.

As far as her eyes could see, grave markers and family mausoleums dotted the landscape. Along the cemetery's western edge, a massive hill gave rise to a stand of maples and oaks just starting to turn colors.

Movement near the base of the hill caught her attention.

A tall man's silhouette stood partially hidden by an old grove of trees. She recognized him immediately - Marty Evans, the Highgate Cemetery caretaker.

She raised her hand to wave, and he retreated into a thicker section of the trees. *That man gives me the creeps.*

Eliza had first met him briefly when she'd written a story about the history of the property of Highgate Cemetery a few months prior. She'd learned that his family served as caretakers of the property of Highgate for three generations and that he'd assumed that role in his late teens. Like his father and grandfather before him, he lived just outside the gates in a late 1940s bungalow that desperately needed updating and a new roof. The run-down abode was far from impressive, but Marty kept it neat. It paired perfectly with his 1958 white and powder blue Chevy pickup truck. If she'd learned nothing else, it was that he lived simply and without what he called the "burden" of most modern technology. This abhorrence of even a landline telephone had made her job of interviewing him difficult.

Truth be told, his disdain for present-day amenities and his quiet, distant nature made Eliza more than a little uncomfortable. She'd heard somewhere he'd been severely injured in a car accident as a teenager. The injury had left him with a permanent limp.

Despite his disability, Marty possessed rugged good looks, but his tall, lean body, prominent pointed nose, and strong jawline that stood out under the shadow of his Stetson hat reminded her of a scarecrow. His style was unusual for this area, to be sure, but his eyes unnerved her the most. Piercing and icy blue. Mysterious eyes that stared at her as if he could read her thoughts while holding fast to their own secrets. Had she just spotted him on the street, she might have considered him attractive, but his prickly exterior and awkward behavior left her feeling unsettled.

Ultimately, she'd chalked her sense of unease up to the enigma that likely engulfed anyone who worked around and dwelled with the dead. And despite her reservations, Marty had proved to be the best source of information about the cemetery and its inhabitants. If this series took off, she'd be spending quite a bit of time at Highgate. It would probably be better to engage his help now as it would likely save her some time.

She hurried toward the cluster of trees where she'd spotted him and found him pruning and clearing brush.

"Good morning, Mr. Evans. It's me, Eliza Grey, from *The Coventry Gazette*. I interviewed you a few months back."

Marty pushed his hat back on his head. He removed his work gloves, exposing large, veined hands.

"I-I know who you are, Miss Eliza," he stuttered in a low voice. He took a step toward her.

Eliza mirrored his action and took a step back, maintaining the distance between them while fighting to hide her growing discomfort.

"Okay, then. Um, I… I'm currently working on a storyline about our founding fathers. I'll be visiting Highgate often in the next several weeks to research the family plots."

She waited for his response, but Marty just stared. His blue eyes penetrating.

She swallowed hard and continued.

"So, um, what I mean is, I may need to be here frequently, and I wanted to make sure that's okay…with you? Also, if you could offer any cemetery records for my research, I would be very grateful."

After several long seconds, Marty nodded. "There are a lot of families here at Highgate that you could write about."

"Can you tell me about the family plots from the late 1700s? I'd like to start there if possible."

"Sure. Next time you come, I can show you the Lords down by the brook. Now that's a prominent family to start with if you are looking for old blood and wealth. You best be careful, though, Miss Eliza."

"Careful?"

"Yeah, some residents here have dark pasts. They can bring trouble."

Eliza stood quietly, trying to understand what Marty meant.

"Residents? Trouble-bringing dead residents? What are we talking about here? Zombies? *Night of the Living Dead*?" She laughed, hoping to break the tension.

Marty didn't even crack a smile. "Those who rest here eternally. I call them residents because you get to know them if you visit enough."

He held her gaze with those soul-piercing eyes of his, and a chill crawled up Eliza's back.

"Right. Okay, well, thank you, Marty, for letting me use the cemetery for my research and for any documentation you may be able to share. I...I gotta go." She gave him a short wave and practically jogged to the rear entrance of Highgate.

What the hell? Weird doesn't even begin to describe that conversation.

More than a little part of her wished there was another way to get the information she needed, but like Lana, Marty's input was a necessary means to an end.

A necessary evil.

2

O NCE OUTSIDE THE CEMETERY, Eliza slowed her pace and willed her nerves to calm.

As she turned onto a side street, a low, resonating wail made her stop in her tracks. The mournful cry called to her from deep within her soul.

First zombies, now this?

She followed the noise past the back entrance of a strip mall and its unpaved parking lot. Then, after passing through a grouping of Arborvitae bushes, she ended up in front of a white brick, flat-roofed building with a sign hanging between two azalea bushes that read *Coventry Animal Hospital*.

A low pleading howl bellowed from inside the building, leaking out onto the street through the screens of two large open windows. As if lured by an unseen force, Eliza followed the sound straight to the front door. Her hand reached for the knob.

What the hell are you doing? You cannot just walk in and demand to know what's making that sound.

A rapid wailing sound ramped up from inside, and before Eliza could stop herself, she burst through the door.

A filthy, white mammoth of a dog sat chained to a hook on the side of the front reception desk.

Spotting her, the dog immediately ceased its howling and sat. Its mouth curled in a smile, and its tail thumped wildly on the tile floor.

"What in the world happened to you?" Eliza asked, still standing in the doorway.

The sad pup was in poor physical shape. Its filthy fur was snarled and matted. Eliza even caught a glimpse of a space where a front tooth should have been.

"Hello? Is anyone here?"

A pretty young woman in blue scrubs appeared from behind a door marked "STAFF." She looked to be in her early twenties, with a slender frame and a kind face. She wore her long brunette hair back in a ponytail, a style that emphasized large, compassionate brown eyes with thick black lashes. Heart-shaped paw prints decorated her light blue scrubs. She offered Eliza a warm smile and a gentle wave.

"Can I help you?"

Eliza stood there, not quite sure what to say.

"Um, I was in the area, and I heard a strange howl, so I came to check it out."

Meredith pointed to the pleading-eyed dog tethered to the reception desk.

"I believe this big guy is your culprit."

The dog sat blinking at both women, wagging his tail. His heart-wrenching howling momentarily ceased.

"I really don't know why I am here except to satisfy my curiosity," Eliza said, shrugging her shoulders. "I heard that mournful commotion and–"

"Came to investigate?" The tech smiled and bent down to pet the disheveled pup. "It's sad but happens a little too often if I'm being honest. A woman surrendered him this morning just as I got out of my car. I reached for my coffee, and she appeared just before me, shoved his leash in my hand, rambling about how she rescued him for her mother. But, when they brought him off of transport from Texas, she didn't want him!" She looked down at the dog and sighed. "She had the nerve to complain that he smelled, barked, and his teeth were missing. I tried to talk to her, help her understand that with a bath and a little training, he would probably make an amazing companion, but she wasn't hearing any of it. She threatened to leave him on the side of the road if I didn't take him!"

"It amazes me how cruel people can be. What a horrible thing to say. What an awful thing to do...rescue a dog only to then turn right around and abandon it."

The tech stroked the dog's neck until he lay down on the floor and rested his head. "I brought him inside and gave him some kibble and water. He's loud, but he seems super sweet. Sometimes humans really suck."

"I can't disagree with that," Eliza said. "What will you do with him now?"

"I've been trying to track down his rescue, but she didn't exactly tell me where he came from. And he isn't microchipped, either. I am waiting for Dr. Jackson to come in and tell me what to do."

At that moment, the back door flung open, and a very handsome young veterinarian with an athletic build walked in, holding a bagel with his teeth as he struggled to put his left arm into the sleeve of his lab coat.

Lab coat in place, he took the bagel out of his mouth and smiled. "Good morning, Meredith," he said to the tech. "I see our first patient is here already and looks very calm." He smiled and extended his hand to Eliza. "I'm Dr. Jackson, and who do we have here?"

Eliza shook his hand. "Eliza Grey, but I'm not the owner. I am, um, just passing by."

Dr. Jackson's pleasant expression shifted into one of confusion, and he turned to Meredith.

"Let me fill you in on this big guy."

As Meredith went over the details of their new patient, Eliza knelt down next to the dog and patted his matted head.

"Good luck, big fella. You are in good hands here, I think."

She stood and turned to walk out the door, but the dog let out a booming bark and whimpered.

An indescribable longing warmed in her chest and pulled at her heart. This pitiful dog had come into her life for a reason. She could feel it. No, she *knew* it.

Before she could stop them, the words left her lips. "I might be interested in adopting him."

Meredith and Dr. Jackson stopped talking and looked at her.

"That is, if he is healthy and it's permitted."

Dr. Jackson scratched his head, glanced at Meredith, then back at Eliza, and then down at the dog and shrugged.

"Well, boy, this may be your lucky day," he said. "I don't see why you can't adopt him. I can do a full workup on him, give him his shots, and get the adoption process started if you are serious."

Eliza swallowed hard, and her mouth went dry.

What am I doing? I should tell him to forget it. I can't adopt a dog.

Big puppy dog eyes stared up at her, pleading.

"How can I say no to that face?" she asked. "Do whatever it is you need to do," she said, hardly believing she'd uttered the words aloud.

Meredith untethered the gentle giant, and Eliza followed Dr. Jackson into the exam room.

Forty-five minutes later, he gave Eliza the run down.

"Ms. Grey, it appears you have a Great Pyrenees; currently underweight, at ninety-eight lbs., heartworm negative, and he is not neutered. He needs his nails clipped, a bath, and a good grooming. We will book an appointment to have him fixed and microchipped and will give him his recommended shots for today: rabies, distemper, and bordetella to protect against kennel cough. That should get him up-to-date and ready to go home."

"Um...okay, great?" Eliza had no clue what half of what he'd just said meant, but he sounded confident, so she went along with his assessment. "How old do you think he is?"

"If I had to guess, I'd say he's between twelve to eighteen months."

Eliza gave the dog the once-over. She'd never have guessed he was so young. "I've never owned a dog before, a cat, yes, dog, no. I have no idea what I am doing," Eliza admitted.

Dr. Jackson put a hand on her shoulder. "Don't worry; we're always here if you have any questions. I'll have Meredith give you some information on the breed. They can be tough. The Great Pyrenees are guardian dogs, so they bark a lot. But they're an intelligent breed, though they tend to wander if you let them and can be stubborn. I have a saying about the Great Pyrenees."

"Oh yeah, what's that?" Eliza asked tentatively.

"What do you call a Great Pyrenees off-leash?"

Eliza shrugged. "I have no idea. What?"

"Gone!" Dr. Jackson let loose a full-throated belly laugh.

Meredith rolled her eyes, but, after a few moments, laughed along. She handed Eliza a sheet of paper.

"Gotta love a man who can laugh at his own jokes," she said. "Here's a list of dog obedience classes you may want to take. He seems fairly well-behaved, but with such a big dog, training is a must. I also have his rabies certificate and tag here to put on his collar."

"Oh boy." Eliza took a deep breath. "I am so not prepared for this. I don't even have a leash."

"It's okay; we can loan you one," Dr. Jackson smiled. "Before you go, there is one issue we need to clear up."

"Oh?" Eliza said nervously.

"He needs a name." Dr. Jackson used his pen to point to his clipboard. "To put on his chart."

"A name? Oh. Let me see." Eliza closed her eyes and thought.

She blurted out, "Murphy!"

"Murphy," Dr. Jackson wrote on the top of the chart. "I like it!"

"So, it's official? He's mine? What should I do next?"

The door opened, and a middle-aged woman and a young girl entered the clinic carrying a small calico kitten.

"Mrs. Pryne, come on in. I'll be right with you."

The pair took a seat in the chairs next to the window.

Dr. Jackson returned his attention to Eliza. "Well, since Meredith couldn't get the rescue's name or the woman who dropped him off, we can settle on his adoption here. Meredith, have Ms. Grey fill out one of our regular adoption forms and then send her home with a welcome kit. And if you have any questions, anything at all, just give us a call. This really is a win-win solution. We don't have to surrender him to a dog shelter; you get a companion, and he gets to have a home with you."

For a split second, Eliza debated calling the whole thing off. Some women bought sports cars or did major makeovers complete with plastic surgery, but she, apparently, went around adopting oversized abandoned canines.

I must be losing my mind.

Eliza glanced down at her first official dog.

Yup, my maiden voyage into canine ownership.

His large brown eyes stared straight into her soul.

Murphy opened his mouth into a broad grin, revealing his missing front tooth, and her doubts fell away.

Eliza stood and beamed down upon the pup who had roped her into adopting him.

Responding to her smile, Murphy rose and lumbered over towards her, sat, and hefted his front right paw, smacking hard and directly against her upper thigh.

Eliza's eyes widened. "Ouch!"

Dr. Jackson laughed. "That, Ms. Grey, is what is referred to as the 'Pyr Paw.' Read about it in your literature and learn to defend yourself against it."

"I think he knows he's going home," Meredith added.

"Let's set an appointment for a month to re-check Murphy and see how things have progressed," Dr. Jackson added. He offered Eliza his hand.

"Ms. Grey, it's been an absolute pleasure to meet you and Murphy today. They say there are no coincidences. I'd say it's a lucky day for you both."

"Mrs. Pryne, come on back."

"Good luck," he added, and Eliza thanked him before he disappeared back into the exam room.

As instructed, Meredith handed Eliza a clipboard with an adoption form and a folder containing information about vaccinations, food, and what to expect. She also handed her an itemized bill for Murphy's visit – a grand total of $400.

Eliza swiped her credit card and sighed.

Lucky, and $400 poorer.

When the adoption paperwork was complete, Meredith clipped a large collar around his neck, fastened on a worn leash, and handed the end to Eliza.

"You know, when that woman showed up this morning, never in a million years would I have thought the day would turn out like this!" she said, relieved.

Murphy wagged his tail. On all fours, he stood at Eliza's hip and looked massive next to her petite frame.

Meredith knelt beside him, rubbed the scruff of his chin, and offered him a treat. "You have a chance to have a good life, so don't mess it up, okay?" She stood and opened the door for Eliza. "Be a good boy, and we'll see you soon."

Eliza waved and led Murphy out onto the sidewalk, contemplating the best route back to her car. She glanced at her watch. It was close to noon. The morning had flown, and she hadn't written a word.

The quickest way would be to return through the cemetery, but she didn't relish the idea of running into Marty-of-the-undead-residents again.

"Well," she said, looking down at Murphy, "Main Street it is."

Murphy followed her lead, staying close to her side and not pulling at the leash as they crossed through the unpaved parking lot and down the side street that led to the main road. She followed along the outside of the wrought iron fencing of the east side of Highgate Cemetery.

As they passed the main entrance, Murphy tugged at his leash, pulling her inside the graveyard.

"No, boy. We aren't going in there today. I need a break from the strange and bizarre, at least for a few hours."

Murphy didn't fight her lead but looked back over his shoulder at the graveyard even as he followed her back out onto the street. It surprised her how well he walked on a leash and how fluid his movements were as they walked along. She imagined that with his massive size, he could drag her down the street if he wanted to.

She rounded the block and turned back onto Main Street. Together they made quite the visual, and Eliza could feel the stares from the drivers of the cars that went by. As they passed *The Coventry Gazette* office, Lana stood staring out of the front window, mouth agape. Beside her stood the town mayor, Graham Winthrop.

Eliza waved at them, and the mayor offered a hesitant wave in return.

A direct descendant of one of the richest and oldest families in Coventry-by-the-Sea, Mayor Winthrop's biggest claim to fame, besides being the youngest mayor on record, came from his family's wealth. His inheritance included the largest property in Coventry, the Brown family farm and estate, now called Harbordale Farm, as well as a considerable amount of money. He also held controlling interests in many of the town's most lucrative enterprises, including Winthrop Construction Company and the G.W. Real Estate Agency. A handsome man in his early forties with dark brown eyes and a full beard and mustache, Mayor Winthrop held a sensual magnetism that caught the attention of many local women making him the most sought-after eligible bachelor.

On the few occasions they had mingled in the same company – mostly at paper-sponsored events – despite his good looks, Eliza had found him a formidable man with a domineering and unpleasant personality.

With his re-election campaign in full swing, his name and picture on lawn signs and posters all over town, she guessed his visit to *The Gazette* involved some kind of publicity to secure another term as mayor.

Lana burst through the office door and onto the street, the mayor behind her.

"Oh, Eliza! What a beautiful dog! Is he yours?"

"Um, yeah, I guess so. I just adopted him from the veterinary office."

Lana knelt down, pressed her face between Murphy's big ears, and made several sounds resembling a cross between a goat and a hyena while repeating, "Aren't you just the cutest!"

Taken aback by a baby-talking Lana, Eliza stood silently by, trying hard not to laugh at the look on Murphy's face. His expression landed somewhere between distress and disgust.

Then as suddenly as this version of Lana had appeared, her slightly irritated business-like demeanor returned.

"What on earth possessed you to adopt a strange dog? You don't exactly come across as a dog person, Eliza."

"A dog person? Is that even a thing?"

"Well, I don't mean anything negative. It's just that you're so...," she looked Eliza up and down, "...neat. You don't exactly look like someone who would embrace a messy, smelly animal that could ruin furniture and dig in your gardens." Her tone was just light enough that Eliza couldn't tell if it was genuine concern or some kind of veiled insult.

Murphy nudged her hand with his head. She smiled at him. Maybe she didn't come across as a dog person, whatever that meant, but Murphy belonged to her, so for better or worse, she was one, regardless of what Lana thought.

"This sweet boy and I crossed paths rather serendipitously. We are a matched pair."

"Oh, I get it," Lana said, patting Eliza's arm.

Eliza looked at her in confusion. "Get what?"

"With your husband always traveling for business and your daughter away at school, it's not surprising you adopted a dog."

"It's not?" Eliza asked, still confused.

"Of course not. You're lonely."

Lana squished Murphy's ears and returned to her baby voice. "Maybe you are experiencing that empty nest syndrome, and this big fluff muffin is filling a void, isn't that right? Yes, she's just all kinds of lonely, isn't she boy?"

While Eliza couldn't argue that loneliness had undoubtedly reared its head earlier that morning, Lana's observation crawled under Eliza's skin like a splinter under a fingernail. And the woman's reputation as a gossip meant that she'd be painted all over town as a pitiful, forlorn, lonely housewife before she could even walk Murphy through the front door of her house.

Eliza glared at Lana and didn't bother to hide the sharp edge of her tone. "The big fluff muffin has a name. It's Murphy."

"Aww is this sugar plum fluff muffin named Murphy?"

To his credit, Murphy's tail wagged half-heartedly, which only egged Lana on.

"Lana," the mayor said, clearing his throat. "I need to go. Thank you for lunch."

Eliza didn't bother to hide the surprise on her face.

Lunch? The mayor and Lana are lunching now? Interesting.

"Oh, Grahammy, you work too hard." Lana reached out and straightened the mayor's tie. "You should let me come over and make you dinner."

"Raincheck?" the mayor asked. "I've got a council meeting, and then I'm meeting with my accountant."

Lana nodded.

If Eliza didn't know any better, she'd say the woman was pouting. Eliza caught the mayor's eye at that moment and saw his fleeting expression of indifference. She couldn't help but wonder if he was just being polite in putting Lana off.

"Ms. Grey, always a pleasure to see you," he added.

Eliza reached out with her free hand to shake his hand. "Mr. Mayor, same. Best of luck on your re-election."

The mayor smiled coolly. "I appreciate your support."

"Graham, Eliza is writing a series about our founding fathers for *The Coventry Gazette*. She should write about you and your family. Remind the people of this town who you are, how deep your roots are."

"Sounds intriguing. If it's good publicity, then feel free, Ms. Grey," Graham replied. He glanced down at Murphy, grimaced slightly, and hit a button on his key fob to unlock the convertible green Jaguar parked at the curb.

"Not making any promises, Mayor," Eliza whispered. She might be biased, but in her experience, anyone with that much money and that many pokers in the fire always had something to hide.

Lana waited until his car disappeared around the corner, then went back inside the office without even a goodbye.

Eliza waited for the light to change so she could cross to the public parking lot where she'd left her SUV.

"The mayor and Lana?" she questioned, looking down at Murphy. "Never in a million years would I have put the two of them together. Two bristly yet successful peas in a pod could make for the perfect couple."

Reaching her SUV, she opened the rear driver's side door, and unprompted, Murphy jumped into the car. Carefully tucking in the leash, she closed him safely inside.

When she opened the door to the front seat, she laughed out loud. Murphy sat in her seat, breathing heavily and smiling his missing-tooth grin.

"Murphy! What are you doing? Don't tell me you can drive."

He barked in reply, and she scratched behind his ear.

"Come on, move over! I'm pretty sure your legs won't reach the pedals, even if you are big."

Murphy made a mighty leap to the front passenger seat, and Eliza climbed in behind the wheel.

She fastened her seatbelt, then froze. The overwhelming acrid aroma of dirty dog filled her vehicle.

"Ew, Murphy, you stink." She covered her mouth and nose with her hand. "You need a bath!"

As she turned on the ignition, her stomach growled. It had been hours since the slice of toast she'd eaten with Jason.

"I bet you are hungry, too, aren't you, boy?"

Murphy responded with a loud bark.

"Alright, a quick stop for a snack, but then we're going to the pet store. And after that, it's home for a bath."

A minute later, she pulled into a parking spot in front of Murphy's Bakery.

"Be a good boy, wait here, and I'll be right back."

Inside the bakery, her best friend, Vanessa, a beautiful woman in her early forties with large brown eyes, olive skin, and glossy brunette hair, carefully carried a tray of lemon squares through the swinging door that led to the kitchen and placed them on the front counter. She immediately opened the display case and began strategically rearranging sweet bread slices and donuts to make room for the newest confection.

Eliza had met Vanessa the very first week she'd moved to Coventry-by-the-Sea, fifteen years ago. Despite her best efforts to organize the boxes for their move, Eliza had been unable to locate the coffee maker, and at Jason's very non-morning-person insistence, she'd ventured out into their new town in search of a coffee shop. She'd found one just off Main Street. Vanessa was her barista, and one macchiato and Americano later, Eliza had made a new friend.

Vanessa had taken the newly arrived Eliza under her wing and even became Auntie Vanessa to Bella. Then about a year after moving into Rosecliff, in the midst of renovating the downstairs, a fire broke out in the unfinished side of the kitchen. A good-looking fireman in his mid-twenties came to the rescue. He and Jason hit it off and became fast friends.

Eliza quickly realized Vanessa and Patrick were perfect for each other. It took a little convincing on Vanessa's end to accept Eliza's recommendation, but before long, Patrick and Vanessa were serious and, two years later, became Mr. and Mrs. Patrick Murphy. Vanessa eventually bought the coffee shop and turned it into Murphy's Bakery, and Patrick rose through the ranks at the firehouse and now served as Coventry-by-the-Sea's fire chief.

Vanessa slid the tray of lemon bars into the display case, then glanced up, noticed Eliza, and did a double take.

"Hey, El! What's wrong?" Her expression was a mixture of concern and curiosity.

"Wrong? Why would something be wrong?" Eliza asked, befuddled.

"Because it's nearly noon on a Monday, and you're standing in the door of my bakery. And because I'm your best friend, I can see something is troubling you."

Eliza smiled and shrugged. "I'm hungry. Can't a girl stop in for a snack from the best bakery in town?"

"Alright, we'll start there." Vanessa squinted and stared at Eliza for a second longer. "So, the usual? Jelly donut and vanilla chai?" Vanessa asked.

"To go, please. And make it two jelly donuts," Eliza said.

Vanessa's eyebrows shot up. "*Two* jelly donuts? You better tell me what's up."

"Well," Eliza said, sinking her hands into the pockets of her cardigan. "As it turns out, I have a friend in the car with me today."

Vanessa looked over Eliza's shoulder and through the large bakery window, and her eyes widened.

"Um, El. What the heck is that in your car?"

"It's my new dog. I just adopted him."

"You? Adopted a dog?" Vanessa flew around the counter and dragged Eliza by the elbow toward her regular table next to the window.

"Eliza, what the heck is going on? It took you a week to pick out the perfect toaster. Jason leaves, and suddenly you decide to adopt a dog?" Her eyes narrowed. "Or have you been secretly planning this and just didn't tell me?"

Eliza giggled. "No, this was totally unplanned. I am out of sorts, I guess. I was feeling a bit lonely after Jason left, and the poor dog was in a tough situation. You should see his sweet face. He's got these big eyes and a broken-toothed grin. I couldn't say no. It all happened so fast." Eliza leaned back in her seat. "Of course, no sooner had I made this monumental, life-changing decision, I ran into Lana. I introduced her to Murphy, and the next thing I knew, she was blathering on about how I am suffering some sort of lonely housewife mid-life crisis. That woman has a knack for getting under my skin."

Vanessa giggled. "As if she has any room to talk. Rumor has it she's got her eye on Mayor Winthrop."

"I'm guessing the rumors are true," Eliza said, dropping her voice to a loud whisper. "He was there with her at *The Gazette*. They had lunch together. She called him 'Grahammy.'"

Vanessa's mouth dropped open, and the two of them laughed.

"So, the dog's name is *Murphy*?" Vanessa asked.

Eliza looked a little sheepish. "It just came out at the vet clinic. I thought of Murphy's Bakery and how I love it here, and voilà. I got nervous; okay, there are worse things than having a dog named after you."

Vanessa shook her head. "Jason is going to freak. Don't get mad, but maybe Lana isn't wrong. Maybe you are a bit lonely and jumped into this whole dog thing without giving it some thought. I mean, Eliza, you aren't really a dog person. Maybe a cat person, but a dog?"

"Why does everyone keep saying that? I adopted a dog, so, therefore, I AM A DOG PERSON! Or, at the very least, I am that dog's person." She pointed out the window toward Murphy.

Some of the nearby patrons looked up and went silent for an uncomfortable moment.

Vanessa gave them a little wave and lowered her voice. "I get it, Eliza. I'm sorry if I didn't sound as supportive as I should. I just worry about you; you know that. What does Bella think?"

Eliza shrugged. "I haven't even had him for an hour yet. Besides the vet, his tech, Lana, and the mayor, you're the only other person who knows. But I can't imagine she'll be anything but happy."

The loud ding of the bell on the front counter rang. "I imagine you're right," Vanessa said, standing. "Be right back."

While Lana's assumption irritated her, Eliza trusted Vanessa. Maybe she had jumped the gun. In need of some reassurance, she stood and hurried outside to the car and used her phone to snap a picture of Murphy seated in the front passenger seat, head out the window, with a big wide grin on his face.

She scratched his head. "Be right back with your treat!"

Eliza sent the photo along with a quick text to Bella:

Eliza: You're a big sister, what do you think?

The phone buzzed a few seconds later.

Bella: We have a dog?! I love him!

Eliza headed back into the bakery and sat down at the same table. She texted briefly back and forth with Bella.

Eliza: Isn't he great? His name is Murphy. Can't wait for you to meet him. How are things there?

Bella: Having roommate issues. But don't worry. I'll get them figured out.

Eliza: You know you can come home anytime you want to.

Bella: I know. Can't this weekend. My group project is due Monday, and there is so much to do. Next weekend for sure. I'll try to find a ride home so I can meet Murphy. Gotta go. Talk soon. Love you.

Eliza sighed. She was happy that her daughter was finding her way, handling the pressures of young adulthood and school. But she'd be lying if she said it didn't hurt a little to no longer feel needed.

Vanessa returned and put a bag and the to-go cup in front of her.

"You okay, El? You look sad."

"I'm fine. I just have to accept that my daughter has her own life. It's everything I wanted for her; I just miss her. But everything has a season, right?"

Vanessa nodded. "Absolutely right. Spring, summer, college, dogs." She offered a sly smile.

Eliza smiled back. "At least I'll have the time to get to know Murphy and see if he likes living at Rosecliff as a Grey before Jason gets back."

"Can't wait to hear how it goes. Let's try to get together this weekend. Maybe you could come by and have dinner with Patrick and me. You can even bring your new friend," Vanessa said with a wink.

Eliza stood, hugged Vanessa, and picked up the bag of donuts and her cup. "I've got a new article series to get started on, but I'll call you," she said with a wave and headed back to Murphy.

Back in the SUV, seatbelt on, she took a sip of her chai before setting it in the cup holder. Placing the bag on her lap, Eliza opened it slowly, reaching in to pull out one of the soft, powdered-sugar donuts with her favorite raspberry jelly filling.

She took a bite, savoring one of the few sweet treats she allowed herself to indulge in. Vanessa might not be right about her being a dog person, but she certainly knew her way around a tasty donut.

In the seat beside her, Murphy stared at her intently. A large glob of drool hit the shift console, and more hung from his jowls. He let loose an anguished whine.

Jelly oozed out from the side of the donut, and she caught it with her finger. She offered it to him, allowing him to taste the sweet confection.

"Good boy! Now I am going to give you a piece of donut, but only if you promise to be gentle, okay?"

She tore off a bit of the sugary dough and offered it to him.

Murphy leaned forward, gently taking the offering from her hand. He chewed once and swallowed with a massive gulp, then licked his lips. His big brown eyes immediately implored her for another piece.

She laughed out loud, all at once delighted and surprised that the large beast already felt like an old friend, despite only having been in her life for a little more than an hour.

Sure, her car stunk, white clumps of fur covered her clothing, but it all just felt right.

"This is madness, Murphy. I have no idea what I'm doing, but we'll figure it out together."

He leaned over the center console and licked her face.

"I'll let you in on a secret. I don't share donuts with anyone, not Jason, not even Bella. You can ask her when she comes home. You must be doing something right."

He licked her lips and nose harder as she squirmed and squealed, trying to push away his large head.

"Gross!" She laughed and wiped her face of dog slobber.

"First things first, Murphy Grey. We need some supplies. You need it all big fella, shampoo, a new collar, a leash, a bed, food. And if you're good, we'll pick up some toys, too. You ready?"

Murphy's tail swiped back and forth against the seat.

"Alright, let's do this."

Eliza drove directly to the local pet store, and the two went shopping, picking out all the things Murphy would need.

A few patrons stared at them; one even gave a disapproving stink eye, presumably at Murphy's outward condition, but Eliza ignored the reaction and gave her gentle snowy beast carte blanche to choose the things that suited him best.

When they reached the toy aisle, he sniffed a number of dog toys hanging from their hooks on the display walls, but nothing drew much of a reaction until he came to the discount bin. There on top of the pile, sat a disheveled plush fox with a missing ear. Murphy grabbed that fox by its remaining ear and pranced about, showing it to any patron he could find.

"Well, Murphy, looks like you picked a kindred spirit. You are missing a tooth, and he's missing an ear."

She added his new toy to the already full cart. Inside were an extra-large dog bed, a variety of different canned and dry foods, treats, two extra-large bottles of doggie shampoo and conditioner, and a new leash and matching collar. Before checking out, she used a small, automated kiosk machine to engrave his name and address on a silver tag shaped like a bone.

She held it out for him to see. "What do you think?"

He sniffed the tag and licked her fingers.

"Alright then. Time to go home, Murphy Grey."

3

THE DRIVE HOME REQUIRED all the windows to be down to clear the car of the dirty dog scent. Murphy's head stayed permanently out of the passenger side window. He bellowed and snorted as he took in the sea air, his ears flapping against the breeze.

From the road, the view of the ocean was wide and clear. The water was blissfully peaceful. Waves lightly kissed the rocks and made minimal white splashes against the landscape's crags. Internally, Eliza mirrored the ocean. Calm and serene. She, too, inhaled the sweet, salty air in her lungs.

Eliza pulled into the driveway and reached across to pat Murphy's head. "Here we are, home at last."

As soon as Eliza opened the car door, Murphy leaped to the ground. She barely managed to grab his leash before he began exploring her front yard, sniffing every inch of space between the driveway and the front steps.

"Hang on a sec, Murph, we gotta get all of your goodies."

He followed her to the back of the SUV, and then with bags in both hands and the leash around her wrist, she led him up the steps to the front porch. She placed the bags near the door and sat down on the steps. Murphy joined her, his head several inches higher than hers. He tilted his big body close to her.

A warm wave of affection and comfort obliterated any remaining feelings of loneliness. Eliza now *knew*, without a doubt, that no matter how unusual or unsettling the events of the day had unfolded, bringing this dog here, bringing him home to Rosecliff, was destined to be. Their brief time together thus far had already cemented a bond between them that was difficult to articulate. His dirty and unkempt appearance did not overshadow his beautiful and kind disposition.

She placed her arm around his massive shoulders and patted his back.

"Welcome home, Murphy Grey."

Murphy turned his head and slapped a big wet tongue up the side of her face, and doggy smiled as if he fully understood what her words meant.

Eliza laughed and wiped the goopy spit off her cheek. "Let's go in. You need a bath."

She unlocked the door and stepped inside, Murphy tight to her heels. The jingling of his tags now hanging from his new collar echoed through the grand entry as he shook his head, and Eliza could not help but smile. She liked the noise. It somehow belonged here.

A buzz from her phone vibrated from her back pocket. It was a text from Jason.

Jason: Hi, honey. Arrived safely. Getting settled. I'll call you around 7:00 your time. Love you.

With her free hand, she quickly replied.

Eliza: Glad all went well. Love you more.

She dropped her keys in a cobalt blue glass dish on top of the antique mahogany console table that stood next to the door, then pulled the metal chain to turn on a Tiffany lamp. Soft light passed through the frosted glass lampshade painted with pink roses, white peonies, and green leaves.

She pointed at Murphy. "You sit right here and wait while I bring in all of your supplies."

Murphy sat at the base of the stairs, his pink tongue dangling from his gap-toothed smile.

Eliza fetched the three large bags of all the goodies they'd purchased at the pet store. She was now another $300 poorer, but she'd have happily spent more if it meant her new friend was comfortable and happy.

She kicked the door closed behind her. The entryway, where a large dirty white dog had sat just seconds before, was now empty.

"Murphy! Here boy!" she called.

She waited. Nothing.

She dropped the bags and hurried up the stairs. "Murphy!"

She checked Bella's room, then the guest room.

No sign of Murphy.

Down the hall, movement by her bed caught her eye.

From the doorway, she spotted him. Murphy sat by her side of the bed, his head resting on the cream-colored comforter, tail wagging.

"Murphy!" Eliza exclaimed. "What are you doing here, boy? I told you to sit and wait." She pointed toward the stairs. "Downstairs. In the foyer. Remember?"

His dark brown eyes stared tentatively, but his head remained stationary on the bed.

"Okay, listen up, buddy. I know all of this is new and that it's going to take some time for both of us to get used to each other, but first and foremost, I need you to stay by my side until we figure all this out, okay boy?"

Murphy's tail thumped at a steady pace against the floor.

She raised an eyebrow and pointed at him. "Let's try this again. You sit right there. I'm going to get your new shampoo, and then you and I have a date with the tub. Got it?"

She retrieved two of the bags with all of the necessary supplies and quickly returned to her room.

This time, Murphy followed her instruction and stayed where she'd left him.

"Good job, Murphy."

She unbagged the brown, oversized velour dog bed with gold cording, the only bed in stock at the pet store that was big enough for Murphy, and set it on the floor beside her bed.

"Come here, boy." She patted the soft cushiony interior. "This is your bed."

Murphy looked unimpressed, but after a few moments, climbed inside, circled around several times, and curled up on top of it.

She left him to rest there and went to draw his bath, stopping at the linen closet to dig out several old beach towels and a step stool.

Coercion and bribery finally landed a reluctant Murphy in the warm, soapy water. Eliza's lack of dog-washing abilities, combined with Murphy's subtle yet effective resistance to being scrubbed, made what likely should have been a ten-minute chore into a forty-five-minute ordeal. No amount of YouTube videos or Google searches could have prepared her for the dexterity or ingenuity needed to keep both the dog and water inside the tub. By the time Murphy's "spa treatment" had ended, Eliza and the entire bathroom floor were sopping wet.

She helped him out of the tub and reached for a towel.

"Now, we just need to get you dry and see what we can do about all these tangled mats in your fur."

Eliza used his new brush and her hairdryer to do the best she could. Murphy, for the most part, cooperated with her efforts. He bit at the invisible steam of warm air as Eliza dried his face. Upon completion, Murphy's coat was beautiful—white, fluffy, and mat-free.

Eliza smiled. "Murphy, you clean up rather nicely. What a handsome boy you are."

Murphy wagged his tail and appeared very pleased with himself.

"Let me change into something a little less soggy, and we'll go get some dinner."

Together they returned downstairs, with Murphy now a much thinner and definitively less smelly dog. Grabbing the last bag of their pet store haul on the way, she led Murphy into the kitchen. She made a selection from his dinner options, scooped it into a bowl, and presented it to him.

He gave the sniff of approval and devoured his food.

As he ate, Eliza rummaged through the cabinets for a treat canister and found a large empty Ball jelly jar.

"Perfect!"

Filling dog biscuits to the brim, she watched as Murphy's eyes brightened at the sound of them clanking against the glass.

"This, sir, is your treat jar. You toe the line here, you get one of these babies!" She put the jar on the counter next to her flour and sugar canisters, then put the tea kettle on to boil.

For her supper, she settled on leftovers from the night before and warmed them in the microwave. With her dinner and a cup of her favorite orange spice tea in hand, she sat down at the kitchen island to eat.

Murphy stood near his bowl, watching her.

Their first meal together had gone better than expected. And once again, despite the newness of his presence, there was a familiarity between them as if he'd always been a part of her life.

"Well, it looks like you are moving in, Mr. Murphy Grey. What do you think?"

Murphy laid down and rolled onto his back.

Eliza bent down and gave him a belly rub. "I'll take it you approve."

Murphy stood and barked.

Eliza laughed. "Alright then, let's get everything settled and unpack the rest of these goodies. What do you think, should we hang your leash by the front door?"

Murphy gave her a resounding, "Woof."

The clock in the family room chimed six p.m.

"You know what that means," Eliza said, as she hung the leash on the coat stand in the foyer. "Jason will be calling soon from England."

Eliza bit her lip and took a deep breath. Normally, she looked forward to hearing her husband's voice and talking, but tonight she would have to explain her rash decision to adopt Murphy. Jason loved animals, but at this stage of his life, he didn't want to be tied to one. They'd discussed getting a pet, often at Bella's request, but the timing had just never seemed right.

The apprehension and worry only grew as she cleaned up the kitchen and introduced Murphy to his fenced-in backyard. The white scalloped picket fence served mainly as a decorative feature showcasing the native pink roses, now in full bloom, as they cascaded over the wooden slats.

"Go on, Murphy, explore your new territory. I pray that fence is high enough to keep you from escaping."

She watched as he sniffed from tree to tree, bush to bush, looking for the perfect spot.

Maybe I am having some kind of mid-life crisis or empty nest syndrome psychosis. The fact that Lana and Vanessa had both suggested as much gave her pause.

She stared out at the ocean, reflecting on her daily decisions. The waves rolled in succession, blasting the shoreline with a roaring force beneath a dramatic orange and pink sky.

Head down and tail wagging, Murphy explored his new domain, pausing to urinate on every tree and bush.

What am I going to do if Jason says no to this?

There was one person in her life she could trust to always tell her the hard truth, even if she didn't want to hear it—her brother Edmond.

"C'mon, Murphy, let's go back in the house."

Murphy immediately ceased his exploration and bounded across the yard to her side.

The fact that he came when called surprised her. He had obviously had some training. She scratched behind his ear. "Where did you come from, Murphy? I wish you could tell me."

In the living room, Eliza flipped the switch, and the gas fireplace ignited, creating a warm, cozy glow.

At the marble bar in the corner of the room, she took a stemmed glass from the shelf and filled it with her favorite cabernet. "Wine, why yes, I'd love a glass," she said as she sunk into the warmth of her favorite chair and pulled the cranberry-colored chenille throw blanket over her lap.

Murphy stood in the door between two white confederate-style oak columns, original to the house, his tail wagging.

"Come here, Murphy; it's okay."

Murphy complied, circling around on the area rug in front of the fire. He settled down and quickly fell asleep. His gentle snoring steady and constant.

"Poor thing," Eliza whispered. "What a day you've had. What a day *we've* had." She took a healthy sip, then another, and another. She could feel her face begin to warm from the alcohol.

She set her wine glass on the antique pie table and pulled out her phone. Her brother, Edmond, was her first go-to whenever she needed advice.

She found his name in her recent contacts and pressed dial.

Within seconds she heard Edmond's warm voice, "Hey, Eliza."

"Hi Edmond. How are you?"

"Oh, you know, crazy busy with never enough hours in the day, but busy is good, right?"

"You sound just like Mom, but yes, I would have to agree busy is good. And Leah?" Leah was her brother's second wife, but Eliza was sure she'd be his last.

Smart, beautiful, and matching tenacity and drive made her Edmond's perfect better half.

"Well, funny you should ask, she just found out that they're making her a full partner. It will likely mean she'll be burning the candle at both ends even more than she is now, so it looks like I'll be seeing less and less of my beautiful bride, at least for a bit. But she's excited, and I couldn't be prouder. How about you? How are things with the Grey clan?"

"Nothing much new," Eliza hedged. "Jason is traveling, Bella's at school, and I'm working on a new story, two stories really, for *The Gazette*. Something to hopefully pull in some Halloween tourism and interest in the Jubilee." She sighed. "Like you said, busy is good."

"Uh-huh. Except it doesn't sound like everything is good. What's up? Are you okay?"

"Oh yeah, I'm fine, but I need to talk to you about something. I'm kind of hoping you can help me sort it out before I tell Jason."

"This sounds serious," Edmond said, his voice edged with concern. "Okay, lay it on me."

"I...I might have done something a little impulsive."

"That certainly doesn't sound like you. Tell me more."

"It's just that I needed to follow my heart, you know? Don't get me wrong, I love being a wife and a full-time mom, but it's time I take care of me and my needs. I'm not getting any younger."

Eliza reached for her wine. "I've been lonely, there I said it. Very lonely, and frankly a tad unhappy. Jason's off caravanning across England, Bella's away at school, and well, I didn't plan to do it, but he came into my life, and I just couldn't say no. I mean, how could I say no? He needed me."

"Eliza—" Edmond said, but she cut him off.

"Ed, it was an immediate attraction, like nothing I've ever experienced before. And if I'm being honest, I fell madly in love with him at first sight. And now, I'm second-guessing myself, and I have no idea what Jason is going to think."

An audible silence lingered on the other end of the line.

"Are you there? Do you understand what I'm saying? What am I going to do?"

Her brother cleared his throat. "I didn't know you and Jason were having problems. Have you thought about counseling? God, Eliza, what the hell happened? I thought you guys were solid."

"I don't understand," Eliza said, confused. "No, we haven't been to counseling; this just happened. I mean, he's off growing a company and doing all sorts of amazing things in jolly ol' England, and I'm sitting here drinking wine with our beautiful new dog, nervous as hell that he'll tell me I've gone crazy and that we can't keep him. But other than that, we're perfectly fine. Why would you even ask that?"

She glanced over at Murphy, entirely befuddled.

"You just said you'd done something impulsive, told me you met someone and fell in love. Did I miss something? What am I supposed to think?"

"Met someone?" Eliza asked, puzzled. A moment of clarity broke through the growing fog and warmth of the wine. "Oh my gosh, Edmond. I'm talking about a *dog*. I adopted a dog. I fell in love with the sweetest semi-gigantic uber-fluffy *dog*."

Another audible silence between them filled the line, and then her brother's laughter sounded through the phone.

"Damn! You scared me for a minute there."

"I hope you know me better than that. This is how rumors get started, you know. Seriously, you actually thought I'm capable of an affair?"

Edmond launched into another round of laughter. And Eliza couldn't help but join him.

"No, Sis, I would never have imagined you would," Edmond said after a few seconds. "And thank God for that. So, a dog, huh? Interesting."

"I know. I can't explain it. But this dog is perfect for me, and we clicked right away. When I saw him, I just *knew*."

"Ahh, now it's starting to make sense. Far be it for me to question the things you just *know*. But I'm guessing you don't think Jason's going to be on board with this decision?"

Eliza bit her thumbnail. "Exactly. I mean, I know he wants us to travel more, and having a dog kind of puts a kink in that, but I promise you, there is something about this dog. Murphy belongs here with me at Rosecliff."

"Sis, all I can say is that I have no doubt you'll figure it out. Promise Jason you will kennel the dog when need be so that you can still travel. He loves you and knows you are alone a lot. I believe if Jason thinks about it, sharing your bed with some big fluffy dog while he's away is better than sharing it with some random guy, right?"

"Seriously? You're not going to let me live this down, are you?"

"Nope, not for a while anyway."

"Well, thanks for nothing. Glad I could entertain you."

A beep sounded in her ear. She looked at the phone screen. It was Jason.

"Hey, that's Jason on the other line. Gotta go. Have a good night, and give Leah my love. Tell her I said congrats and not to work too hard."

"Will do. Night, El."

"Good night."

Eliza swallowed the last of her wine and clicked over to Jason's call.

Here we go.

"Hey, honey! How's England?"

Jason's warm and welcoming voice soothed her angst.

"It's chilly, but I'm glad to finally be here. How was your day? Things go well at *The Gazette*? Tar and feathering a success?"

Eliza laughed. "Complete success. Art gave me the thumbs up, and I've already started researching."

"I'm glad to hear that. Have you heard from Bella?"

"We spoke briefly today through text. She's having some roommate issues and has a big project due on Monday, but I think she's doing well."

"Good," Jason replied. "And you're doing okay, home alone?"

Eliza took a deep breath. Her brain buzzed pleasantly from the wine.

"I won't lie; it is a little lonely here without the two of you. It's so good to hear your voice, Jason. I miss you."

"I miss you too. I can't wait for you to come out the next time I am here."

"Um, about that, I need to tell you something."

"Oookay. Should I be worried?"

Just tell him, Eliza. Just rip off the band-aid.

"I rescued a dog today. A beautiful Great Pyrenees. He's amazing. He is next to me, sleeping beside the fireplace. It's like he has always been here."

Silence permeated another phone conversation.

"So...um...can we keep him?"

Eliza heard a sigh.

"Are you mad? Don't be mad."

"I'm not mad; I'm just a little surprised you would make such a big decision without talking to me first. We've discussed this before, and the timing isn't right. I'm traveling frequently, and I thought with Bella away at school, you'd be up for coming with me more often. How's that going to work if we have a dog?"

Eliza felt frustration begin to bubble in her chest. "Look, I didn't set out to adopt a dog today. It happened by accident, sort of. It's complicated, but you'll understand how perfect he is when you meet him."

"You accidentally adopted him? How does that work?" Jason asked, his tone short and clipped.

"You travel a lot, as you mentioned, and not just overseas. It makes me feel good to have him here, a little less lonely. A little safer." The last part wasn't entirely true. She'd never actually felt unsafe at Rosecliff, but if a little guilt helped her case, so be it. She played with a loose strand from the blanket in her lap. "I know I should have talked to you about this first, but it's done now. So..." She took a breath and tried to calm her voice. "Can I keep him? Please?"

For a moment, Jason remained silent. Then he asked, "Did you name him yet?"

"Yes," Eliza said coyly.

"You could have at least given that to me."

She could hear the smile in his voice.

"The vet needed a name for his chart, so I had to decide on the spot. I named him Murphy."

"Murphy? Sounds like he may resemble a donut at your favorite bakery. Hopefully, you treated him to one."

"Maybe. There is a good chance I did." Eliza laughed.

"Does Bella know?"

"Yes. And Edmond. And Vanessa, of course. And pretty much anyone in the vicinity of downtown this morning."

"I see." His tone simmered, and Eliza wondered if the idea of a dog living at Rosecliff had actually received his seal of approval.

"Well, I should let you get ready for bed," he said, his voice sounding tired. "It's already after midnight here, and I need to try to get a little sleep, or the jet lag will be kicking my ass by the time I get to the office. Enjoy your evening with our new addition, and we can catch up tomorrow."

"Thank you," Eliza said softly. "I love you, you know."

"I do. And I love you too."

Eliza hung up the phone with a sense of relief. Of course, there would be some adjustments to their life now, but they would figure it out. They always did.

4

THE NEXT MORNING, ELIZA measured out the grounds for coffee and flipped the coffee maker to brew. She rolled her neck and watched as the dark liquid dripped ever so slowly into the pot. She would need at least two cups – one to combat the wine hangover and one to compensate for her poor night's sleep.

After her call with Jason, she'd poured herself another glass of wine. It had helped her to relax, and not long after, she'd gone to bed. But she'd tossed and turned all night, the same dream on repeat: she entered a dark room where she could hear loud, angry voices shouting at each other. A woman was trembling, and Eliza could feel her fear, but the image was cloudy, like she was looking through a pane of leaded glass. Then, with startling clarity, a gaunt face with dark eyes and slimy skin would rush toward her out of the darkness, sharp and menacing. Every time, at this exact point in the dream, she would startle from her sleep and sit up gasping for air, her heart racing in her chest. An hour later, the same dream, the same fear, the same terrifying face.

Murphy sat at her feet, his cold nose nudging her hand for some attention.

"Good morning, Murph. How'd you sleep? Better than me, I hope."

Jason wasn't exactly happy that she'd adopted a dog without discussing it with him, but she had no doubt that once he saw Murphy's sweet face, he'd agree that she'd made the right decision in bringing him home.

She reached into the glass treat jar, retrieved a small dog bone for Murphy, and tossed it at him.

Murphy opened his mammoth mouth and caught it, then chewed and swallowed the treat down in two gulps.

"You just need to be on your best behavior when he comes home."

Murphy barked, and Eliza pressed her fingers to her temple. "Not so loud, okay? And next time, maybe warn me about drinking so much, huh?"

She poured a cup of coffee and popped an English muffin into the toaster, then opened the back door to let Murphy out.

Murphy dashed out into the sunlight like a bull out to pasture and bounded across the soft green grass to the first tree on the right.

The morning air stung her face and hands, an even colder temperature than the day before. Not unusual for Coventry, especially so close to the ocean, but still much colder than she would have expected at this time of year.

She rubbed her arms to stave off the chill and headed back inside to prepare Murphy's breakfast. As soon as she set the bowl down, now filled with a chunky dog-worthy mix of beef, rice, and peas, a large black nose pressed against the glass.

She opened the door but stepped in front of him to prevent his immediate entry.

"Hey, Murphy! Let's make a deal. You keep your wet nose and paws off my French door, and I will keep the treats flowing!"

He bent his head and licked her knee.

"I'll take that as a 'yes, ma'am.'"

She stepped aside, and Murphy flew past her directly to his bowl and devoured its contents.

After her second cup of coffee, a couple of aspirins, and a quick shower, Eliza's head finally stopped pounding. She sat for a bit and watched a morning talk show on TV. A weather warning banner scrolled across the bottom of the screen. A severe storm front would blow through later that afternoon.

Hmm, well, that would explain this sudden cold temperature change.

She didn't doubt the forecast, but the current view through her family room windows offered nothing but clear skies and sunshine in full force. Some fresh air would probably do her some good.

"How would you feel about a walk, Murph?" she asked. "A little exploring at Highgate, perhaps before this storm rolls in?"

Murphy responded with a bounding leap. He barked and wagged his tail.

"What? Did I say the magic word? Walk?"

He repeated his antics, and Eliza laughed.

Together they fetched his new leash from the hook in the entry, and Murphy jumped and pranced around the foyer as she pulled on a black fleece jacket, a white knit headband, and a matching scarf. Last but not least, she added a pair of leather gloves.

Murphy wiggled like a fish out of water as she tried to clip on his leash. "Hold still," she said, laughing. Finally managing to clip it onto his collar, they headed out the door.

A blast of a crisp autumn wind took her breath away.

The view from the porch screamed fall in New England. Beyond the edge of the cliff that gave her home its name, the Atlantic Ocean stretched out toward the horizon, crashing in spurts against the sandy shoreline.

Eliza couldn't contain her smile. She loved New England no matter the time of year, but fall checked all her boxes.

She led Murphy along Rosecliff Avenue, then crossed the road onto Shore Drive. They meandered their way along the semi-busy thoroughfare to the traffic light and crosswalk that led onto Main Street. There was a bustle of activity as cars beeped and drivers waved to Eliza and Murphy as they passed. She'd never really paid much attention to it before, but many of the businesses and shops in downtown Coventry-by-the-Sea were dog friendly. Water bowls and baskets of treats welcomed dog owners and their four-legged friends. Though she knew this had been the community practice well before they'd moved here, Eliza took it as a sign adopting Murphy really was meant to be.

To Eliza's surprise, many of the storefront owners greeted Murphy as they walked by, offering more than a quick pat on the head. Treats of all kinds were part of the package.

"Murphy, if we don't curb your snacking, I see a major diet in your future!" Eliza lectured.

And although the storefronts in her little seaport town were pet friendly, Murphy's reaction to the bakery made Eliza certain it was his favorite.

"Come on, Murphy, in we go," Eliza said as she held the door to the shop.

Vanessa greeted them with a smile and finished with her customer.

"Hey, guys! Come on over!" Vanessa urged as she rounded the counter.

"I am here for my usual vanilla chai, but can you make it a cranberry muffin today?"

"Coming up!" She leaned over the counter and waved at Murphy. "It just so happens that because of our 'little' namesake, I have decided to do a doggie donut!" Vanessa pointed to the blackboard behind the counter.

The top of the board featured a giant chalk paw outline with the words *New Special – Murphy Grey Donut Hole* printed inside.

"Really? You created something, especially for Murphy?"

Vanessa patted him, "And you will be my first recipient."

"And it's okay for dogs?"

Vanessa gave her a perplexed look. "Of course. You're not the only one who knows how to do a little research. It's a small plain wheat donut hole filled with either peanut butter or pumpkin. Totally safe for dogs."

"Well, you, my friend, just amaze me! We will order one Murphy Grey for the road!"

Vanessa hustled around to the display case to prepare their order.

"Where are you two headed today?"

"I thought we would walk through Highgate. It's for the research for my story."

"Sounds creepy. You'd best keep an eye on the weather. We are in for a doozy of a storm today."

"I heard, but you wouldn't know it right now," Eliza said, pointing to the blue sky. "I plan to be home well before it breaks."

Vanessa set a brown bag and a to-go cup on the counter in front of her. "Here you go, vanilla chai, cranberry muffin, and a Murphy Grey to go!"

"Thanks, Van. You are the best. Talk later," Eliza said, holding the bag and chai in one hand and Murphy's leash in the other.

After a few more meet-and-greets along Main Street, Eliza sat on a bench just outside of Highgate and finished off her muffin and chai. Murphy ate his namesake donut in one bite and sat staring at Eliza as she ate, his big eyes pleading for a bite of hers.

"Nope, I told you, I don't share," she teased him. "Your first day was special, but you've had yours; this is mine."

When she'd finished, she tossed the bag and her empty cup in a nearby trash can and brushed the crumbs off her shirt.

"Ready for a little research?" she asked as she led Murphy through the wrought iron gates of Highgate. As soon as they reached the line of rose bushes that separated the older sections from the new, Eliza released Murphy from his leash to roam freely.

She paused by the gravestone of a Revolutionary War hero, Lemuel Caine. She'd found his gravesite on previous jaunts through the cemetery when writing the Highgate article. She'd been drawn to his grave, not because of elaborate markings or words, but mainly because it stood alone instead of being one stone in a small cluster of family as was common. He had died on the battlefield and been put to rest far from his home, and here he would lay for eternity. She bent and plucked the last of the purple and yellow wildflowers that grew near the edge of the path and placed them on his headstone.

A sharp cawing sounded from a maple tree in a stand of trees, one of many that defined the back terrain of Highgate. Eliza spotted the dark feathers of a crow perched on one of the highest branches. Another crow landed on top of an elaborate gravestone. Another followed, and another, and another until dozens of them littered the ground near the base of the path that disappeared into the hilly, rocky terrain.

Murphy spotted the birds and gave chase.

All at once, the murder of crows took flight. Eliza watched, bewildered by the multitude of dark feathers and wings climbing into the cerulean sky, calling to something unknown.

A blustery wind tugged at her scarf, and she tucked it deeper into the collar of her jacket.

Storm must be on its way.

Murphy jumped and barked, his attention fixed firmly on the swirling flock of birds undulating in the wind.

"That's enough, Murphy. Come on, let's go this way."

Murphy didn't respond to her command. He continued to bark, clearly agitated by the constant cawing.

Clapping her hands, Eliza called to him again.

"Murphy Grey, I said enough. Come. Come here."

This time, Murphy complied. He pranced up the path to her side, giving her his snaggle-toothed grin as if he hadn't a care in the world.

"You let those birds alone."

Murphy's head and tail remained erect, and his gaze snapped back up to the sky, but he didn't bark. As she led to another section of the cemetery, he remained at her side; a low growl periodically rose from his throat, his eyes vigilantly glued to the skyline.

Together, they climbed the path to the top of a hill where a bench stood next to a small plot of gravestones. From this vantage point, stretched an endless horizon of ocean and shore and a nearly bird's-eye view of the town below with bursts of yellows, reds, and oranges from the fall foliage erupting between slate and shingled rooftops and the bright white church steeple. Tilted grave markers covered in moss and hard to read jutted out from uneven terrain next to the bench.

The quiet solitude of this hallowed area, combined with the view of the ocean, was a reminder of just how vast the world was and how short life was in the grand scheme of things.

The quiet shattered with a loud *caw-caw.* The flock of crows had returned and swirled overhead, swooping and twisting until, one by one, they landed in the leaf-covered branches of a nearby tree. Their cacophonous chorus reaching an uncomfortable pitch.

Murphy charged toward the tree, standing on hind legs, paws on the trunk, barking up through the branches.

Eliza hurried after him but tripped over a cluster of roots and fell to her knees. As she returned to her feet, the wind sent a swirl of leaves and dirt into the air around her. She covered her face, her eyes already watering from the debris.

Pain shot through her head, and Eliza felt her vision begin to fade, darkness creeping into her periphery. A voice whispered in her ear.

You belong to me...

Eliza felt a scream rising up in her throat.

Almost as quickly as the wind had surged, it died away. Eliza sank back down to the ground, her heart racing. She'd heard that voice before, but it had been years. Her childhood memory of that day on the beach flooded her mind. A beautiful woman had called to her, then transformed into a horrible, twisted figure. The experience had thoroughly terrified her. She'd refused to go anywhere alone for weeks, and nightmares plagued her sleep. With time, the dreams and visitations stopped, and as she got older, the memories faded. But that voice...those words. She'd heard them before.

"C'mon, Eliza, pull it together. Happy thoughts. Happy thoughts."

She rubbed her eyes and called for Murphy.

"Murphy! Come here, boy! Murphy!"

Nothing. Not a collar jangle or a bark.

She scanned the area around her, then the tree where she'd last seen him.

"Murphy! Please come!"

Still nothing.

She took a deep breath and fought to bring her breathing under control. Despite the cool air, sweat beaded on her brow.

"Stay calm; he's here somewhere. I just need to find him."

Frustration and a growing sense of apprehension added an urgency to her steps despite the pain in her knees from her fall. She moved as quickly as she could back down the path towards a larger section of gravestones from the late 1700s to early 1800s, calling and whistling for him.

Maybe if I were a dog person, I'd know what to do.

She couldn't recall how far back the cemetery went, but it turned out that Dr. Jackson was right. A Great Pyrenees off-leash was nothing short of gone. Only it wasn't nearly as funny as the vet had made it out to be.

She stopped short in front of an old stone cemetery fence about thigh-high that bordered the rear perimeter of the cemetery. It appeared to surround a family plot.

Whoa! How have I never seen this section before?

A wrought iron archway and gate, completely overgrown with thorns and bramble, marked the entrance but stood nearly impassable. Beyond it lay a dense overgrowth of thorny shrubs and weeds that filled the area around a small group of headstones, barely visible from Eliza's viewpoint. A large barren oak tree stood in the middle of the brush, gnarled and disfigured.

A muffled growl and then a bark sounded from within the overgrowth.

Eliza raised her arm to protect her face, pushed into the thick underbrush, and spotted Murphy ten paces ahead.

"Oh, for the love of Pete! Murphy! Come here!"

But Murphy kept barking and ran deeper into the thicket.

Eliza continued to tramp across the undergrowth, her scarf snagging on prickers as she went.

"Murphy Grey! It won't be pretty when I get my hands on you."

As she stepped through the dense outer thicket, she found herself in the center of what appeared to be a small family burial plot. It surprised her to find the underbrush almost non-existent. Stranger still, the air inside the secluded spot was calm and noticeably warmer.

Murphy sat in the corner of the tiny graveyard, wagging his tail like a broom sweeping the ground. The small unkept site with varying-sized brown headstones lay under the large oak tree. She took a moment to brush off her jeans and pull bits of leaves from her hair.

"Murphy! Come here! I am so mad at you right now!"

But Murphy didn't move. He remained fixed in place, playing sentry to a brown weathered headstone as if guarding the grave's occupant.

"Fine, stay there, then," Eliza said, still trying to catch her breath. She leaned down to rub her knees.

Near the center of the family plot, directly in front of the great oak tree, stood a large headstone that dwarfed the others. Eliza moved closer so she could read the epitaph: *Elijah Simon Brown, died in 1840, aged sixty.* A medium-sized headstone and two small flat markers flanked Elijah Brown's grave. She read the next inscription: *Anne Brown, Wife of Elijah Brown, died in 1822, aged thirty-two.* The flat markers bore just a single name and a date: *Daughter, Esther, 1815,* and *Daughter, Hannah, 1817.* She'd seen many graves like this throughout the cemetery for children who had died in infancy.

Eliza made her way to Murphy and squatted down to examine the headstone he guarded. Tree roots had shifted the stone, making it hard to read. She pulled a thick layer of ivy from the stone and brushed away the dirt so she could read the entire epitaph. At the top was a skull with angel wings. Etched willow tree branches flowed down either side. The words read:

Here Lyes The Body Of Levi Ashley Brown
Beloved Son
Who Departed This Life
October 1 1808 Aged 8 Years
May He Rest In Peace
Sleep On My Son And Take Thy Rest
To Call You Home, God Saw It Best
For God Has Made You Now His Own
For Thou Dwells In Heaven, This Is Known

To lose a child was unfathomable. She couldn't imagine what it would feel like to never see Bella's face again, to hear her voice or her laughter. Eliza pushed to her feet, fished her cell phone out of her pocket, and texted Bella.

Eliza: Hope the group project is going well. Love you.

Out of the corner of her eye, she spotted another grave, this one obscured by brambles and resting just outside the cemetery wall. The reddish slate marker stood out amongst the brush that encompassed it. The top of the headstone bore a face with angel wings surrounded by flourishing flowers and leaves.

Carefully climbing over the four-foot-high cemetery wall and using her feet to compact and move the brush, she knelt to uncover the intricate etchings. The body of the stone bore a sizeable etched heart with the epitaph written inside.

Here Lyes The Body Of Mrs. Honor Temperance Brown
The Wife Of Elijah Brown
Who Departed This Life
October 1 1808 Aged 26
Behold And Read A Mournful Tale
A Mother's Pain So Great
She Could Not Live Without Her Son
Thy Life Was Thrown To Fate

Eliza stood, glanced back at the family plot, then down at the grave before her, puzzled. So many questions raced through her mind. Why the separation of Honor Brown's grave from the rest of the family? Is Levi her son? They passed on the same day? What did Honor do to be cast outside the family plot? Is this grave even on Highgate property?

"Murph, I think I've found my story," she said, reaching out to touch the angel wings at the top of the stone.

As her hand touched the cold stone, an electric shock stung her fingers, and she cried out as a surge of frozen electricity rushed through her body. She hunched over at the waist, trying to quell the sudden wave of nausea.

Behind her, Murphy barked ferociously, his paws up on the edge of the wall.

Desperate to balance herself, Eliza reached for the wall and pulled herself to the other side. Dizziness made her legs weak as she sat down on the ground.

What is happening to me?

Eliza's heart pounded, and she tried to calm herself with large deep breaths.

Murphy licked her face.

Almost immediately, the dizziness faded.

The sound of snapping branches broke the silence, and Eliza turned around to face the entrance.

Murphy did not bark but moved in front of Eliza to block whatever or whoever was coming their way.

"Miss Eliza! What are you doin' in there? You okay?"

Marty Evans leaned over the cemetery fence, his worn beige barn jacket open to display a red plaid shirt neatly tucked into a pair of blue jeans.

"I...I...I chased my temperamental dog back here, and then I don't know what happened. I guess I just got a little dizzy."

She had no intention of telling him about the wind or the voice she'd heard. Weird or not, the last thing she needed was anyone else thinking she was losing her mind in the middle of some kind of mid-life crisis.

Eliza stood slowly, waiting to see if the ground would stay constant, then clipped the leash onto Murphy's collar and made her way back to the edge of the stone fence.

"Marty, I'm sorry for the intrusion. Murphy took off on me, and I found him here."

Marty smiled a crooked smile that warmed his face and said, "No problem. You want me to help get him out of there?"

Eliza smiled. "If you could help him navigate his way back out while I prepare to do battle with these thorns and thicket again, I'd appreciate it."

Eliza grabbed Murphy by the collar, whispered, "Go with Marty, and don't give him a hard time." She handed Marty the leash, then began her laborious trudge through the prickly brush and ungraceful climb over the stone fence. She immediately found herself back in the windy corridor of the graveyard.

Marty stood waiting, leash in hand, a concerned look on his face.

"Here you go, Miss Eliza," he said, passing her the leash. "You know, it's been a long while since anyone visited these particular graves."

"Thank you for helping me with this guy," she said, taking the leash and dusting the dirt and leaves from her pant legs. "If it hadn't been for Murphy, I'd never have seen it. And, as you know, I've visited many graves in this cemetery. Why is this area so overgrown and unkept?"

"Hard to say, other than that my father said Elijah Brown possessed a dark past. He used to tell me not to bother over here, that nothing but weeds would grow."

He stopped, scratched his head, and continued, "That, and it attracted a whole lotta crows. It seems as if they like it around here."

Eliza pulled her scarf tight around her neck, a chill inching up her spine.

Yes, they most certainly do.

"Marty, I think I might like to know more about this family. I feel like there's a story here. Is there anything else you can tell me about the Browns? More about this dark past?"

Marty shuffled his feet on the pebbled path and looked over to the oak tree and the gravestones beneath it.

"Well, Honor, his first wife, died under mysterious circumstances. You know, her death caused a lot of questions. Some say she killed herself. Flung herself over the cliff of her home by the sea. They say the grief of losing her only son was more than she could bear." He took his hat off and held it between both hands.

"Some speculate that her husband pushed her, but it was never proven. His second wife died young, too, as did their daughters. Really tragic."

"Incredibly tragic," Eliza agreed. "Honor's gravesite is beyond the stone wall. I wonder why she is there. Is it because she possibly committed suicide?"

"I'm not entirely sure." He put his hat back on his head. "Could be. Folks were funny about stuff like that back then."

"And the gravestone closest to her was her son, then?

"Yes, that is her son Levi. He died real young. Just a boy."

"I can't even imagine." Eliza glanced at her phone. No reply from Bella. Not that she had expected one.

She turned to take in the small family burial plot once more. She'd promised Art something juicy for *The Gazette's* Halloween edition. The Brown's family tragedy had all the makings for a compelling piece. It might not have the paranormal pull of Salem's witches, but a grieving mother dying under suspicious circumstances was intriguing. There was something more here; she could feel it. Better still, she *knew* it.

"Marty, would you be interested in sitting with me and talking about that section and what you know? It would be a great piece for *The Gazette*."

Marty looked down at his feet. "Um, I don't know, Miss Eliza. I am not much into talking about stuff here. I just care for the grounds like my father did before me."

"Maybe think about it? Like I mentioned yesterday, I'll be making regular visits as part of my research. Maybe we can talk again the next time I'm here?"

"Sure," he said and offered her a shy smile.

"Thanks again for your help with Murphy."

He nodded and tipped his hat to her.

Eliza watched him walk away. Marty always creeped her out, but not for reasons she could put into words. He unnerved her deeply. Their few brief encounters left her sensing he had his own secrets, and he could discern she held one herself.

Regardless of this feeling, he did help us. And Murphy certainly didn't mind going to him.

Eliza glanced up to the sky and noticed the dappled dark clouds had closed in and were blanketing out any sight of blue.

"Time for us to get a move on Murph."

Eliza started to walk down the path to the side exit. In the short time they'd been here, the temperature had dropped at least five degrees. She was already looking forward to a warm bath, a cup of tea, and a completely boring and uneventful rest of her day. When they reached the line of rose bushes and passed into the newer part of the cemetery, she heard Marty call out to her.

"Miss Eliza!"

She turned around and waited for him to catch up to her.

He moved remarkably fast for a man with a bum leg. When Marty was close enough to talk without yelling, he paused for a moment to catch his breath.

"The cemetery doesn't have many people who visit it and appreciate her beauty. But I know you like it here."

Eliza wasn't quite sure how to respond. She would never have admitted out loud that she liked visiting the cemetery, but he wasn't wrong.

Is that creepy? Oh God, am I going to start referring to the deceased as residents, too?

Marty continued. "What I mean to say, is that sometimes it calls special people, you know. Sometimes it has things it wants to say. That's why I like it here. I respect it and those who rest here. I get a sense that you do too. You and Murphy are always welcome."

Marty was hitting just a little too close to home. There was no way he could know about her ability to *know* things, and if he had somehow figured it out, he would need to keep that to himself.

"I appreciate that, but I just like looking at the headstones. I don't feel any call other than an appreciation for history." Even she could hear how terrible of a liar she was.

"I understand," Marty replied. His tone suggested he could see right through her. "You best get home, Miss Eliza. There's a storm brewing. I think it's gonna be a rough one."

With that, he turned, and limped back the way he'd come.

Again, Eliza glanced up at the sky. The weather had changed drastically since her discovery of the gravesite. Dark grey clouds were moving in at a steady pace, blown in by a northerly wind.

That's one angry sky.

By the time they turned back onto Rosecliff Drive, a storm raged on the horizon. A biting wind blasted the shoreline. The whistling and whipping of the sand and sea was just a hint of what was to come.

"C'mon Murph, let's hurry inside."

5

ELIZA SCURRIED THROUGH THE front door, the warmth of her home replacing the icy blast of ocean air behind her. Outside, angry gusts of wind howled, and driving rain pelted against the windows and the front door's glass inlay. The house creaked and moaned around them.

"We made it just in time, Murph," Eliza said, removing his leash, tossing her house keys in the glass bowl on the front table, and setting her cell phone beside it. She caught sight of herself in the hall mirror as she took off her scarf and jacket. Her face was red, her hair a tangled mess. Not unexpected considering the morning's events. But she looked exhausted, too.

Eliza Grey, you better not be getting sick.

Murphy shook hard in the middle of the entryway, then lumbered straight toward the kitchen, his nails tapping on the hardwood floor as he headed to his water bowl. His collar tags clanged against the metal bowl. He paused and turned to look at her.

"Why yes, Murphy Grey, I am hungry. What's that? A cup of tea? Sounds delightful. I think I will."

She joined him in the kitchen and put the kettle on to boil.

Murphy returned his attention to the bowl and lapped his water with great fervor.

"Slow down, boy! You'll make yourself sick."

He lifted his head. A significant glob of drool dripped onto the hardwood floor.

She tossed Murphy a treat, then fetched her mermaid mug from the cabinet, opened a pack of her favorite crackers, and fixed her tea. From the foyer, she heard a buzz from her cell phone.

Once in hand, Eliza beamed when she saw the name on the screen—Bella.

"Hey, Bella! How's it going?"

"Hey, Mom. Things are okay. Just checking in. I just got a weather alert on my phone. Looks like there is a bad storm brewing in your area. We are in preparation for high winds here at school."

"Oh, it's more than brewing; it's already raging. Murphy and I had just made it back home before the worst hit. You should see it. The ocean is a sea of white caps!"

A flash of blue light and a crack of thunder rattled the glass in the French doors. The lights flickered.

"Whoa, I heard that," Bella said. "You should get some candles and a flashlight ready, just in case."

"Hey, kid. This isn't my first storm, you know."

Eliza opened the old wooden pantry and fumbled for her flashlight and a couple of candles.

A violent gust of wind shook the side of the house, and the lights flickered again before going out entirely.

"Storm is picking up," Eliza said, flipping on the flashlight. "I need to go around and make sure everything is secure."

"Well, at least you can snuggle with Murphy tonight. Hopefully, the storm doesn't get too bad. Are you going to be alright?" Bella asked.

"I'll be fine, don't worry. Already got my flashlight and candles."

"Love you, Mom. Talk tomorrow?"

"Love you too, honey. Talk to you tomorrow. Bye."

Eliza put the cell phone on the counter and lit one of the candles. Then with the flashlight in one hand and her tea and crackers in the other, moved into the living room. With its large east-facing windows, she had a wide view of the incoming storm.

Dark, fast-moving clouds made the late afternoon sky look like night. Savage bolts of lightning ripped across the sky. Strong winds bent the trees in her yard. She could hear the branches creaking, leaves shuddering as gale winds howled. Heavy, pelting rain drenched every inch of the house and yard.

"*Eliza...*"

Eliza spun, searching around the entire room, finding nothing but its regular inhabitants – an oversized couch, her favorite chair, and the bar in the far corner.

She let out the breath she'd been holding.

"Nope, nobody here," she said aloud, trying to reassure herself. "It's just the wind."

She glanced at Murphy, looking for any reaction from him. He had settled on the area rug next to the fireplace, his bulbous head placed neatly between his two large paws, his eyes tightly shut.

"See, nothing to worry about. If Murphy's not worried, I'm not worried."

Eliza returned to the window and watched the storm as she finished her tea and crackers. Returning to the kitchen, she rinsed her cup and set it next to the sink.

Across the room, the pantry door creaked open.

She turned slowly, her heart racing, her breath hitched as she crept across the room, instinctively reaching for the flashlight, and raised it above her head, ready to strike should something come rushing out towards her.

She paused next to the door and listened, straining to hear any sound that would alert her to whatever had pushed the door open, but all she could hear was the wind and rain.

Slowly, she pulled the pantry door all the way open and peered into the darkness inside.

She directed the flashlight beam into the pantry and scanned from corner to corner and along each shelf, noting nothing but packs of paper towels, dry goods, and several cases of water bottles.

"This old house," Eliza mused. "The outside air pressure from the strong winds must have pulled the door open. I swear, I've turned into a regular wuss, scared of the wind."

For some reason, the antiquated pantry, original to the house, held an allure that Eliza couldn't explain. Jason didn't understand. The renovation contractor didn't understand either. They both wanted it demolished and rebuilt with more modern amenities, but Eliza didn't care. She loved the old worm holes in the wood and the pungent herbal smell that permeated the space. It represented the heart of the old house to Eliza, so she kept it in its original form.

But right about now, I'm rethinking that decision.

Her eyes settled on the red emergency box they kept on a back shelf. Inside, were two small flashlights, a set of backup batteries, matches, and a few extra emergency candles.

"Probably should get that out, too, just in case."

She took several steps into the pantry and reached back to grab it.

Inside, the pantry felt cold. *Too cold.*

In the narrow beam of light from the flashlight, she could see her breath. Thunder boomed, and the flashlight flickered, dimmed, and went dark. A bitter taste rose up in her throat as a round of nausea bent her over in the gloom of the tight space.

She moved backward toward the open door, then felt herself falling. She sprawled out on the kitchen floor, the emergency box making a loud bang as it hit the hardwood, the flashlight spinning away out of reach.

Scrambling on the floor to grab her only source of light, she turned and settled the beam back toward the darkness that filled the pantry door to see what caused her to trip.

The light reflected back from a set of eyes.

And then a pink tongue materialized.

"Murphy! You scared the hell out of me!"

Eliza pushed herself up from her seated position on the floor and grabbed the box.

Murphy came to sit beside her, leaning onto her side, staring at her with a quizzical look.

"Oh no, don't you say it. I am not overreacting!"

He licked her cheek.

The tension she'd been holding melted away, and she laughed. "Just do me a favor, don't tell anyone what a magnificent klutz I've become, okay? This is the second time today I've ended up on the ground."

He whined and licked her face again.

Eliza winced as she climbed to her feet. Unlike the dirt and grass at the cemetery, the hardwood floors were unforgiving, and she'd likely have a glorious bruise as a prize for tripping over her own feet.

As early evening set in, the storm raged on around them, with no indication that it would be finished any time soon.

"Well, Murph, I should probably try to get some work done. C'mon, let's go sit in the dining room."

She took the candle and her cell phone from the counter and grabbed a notebook and pen from the office.

Once settled at the table, she began recording the events of the day, including the discovery at Highgate and the things Marty had shared with her about Elijah and Honor Brown. Even though the power was out, the signal on her phone still read five bars. She did a quick search for the Brown family in Coventry-by-the-Sea. The irony of writing by candlelight while researching on her phone wasn't lost on her.

Shakespeare, eat your heart out.

One of the first search entries mentioned the town archives. Eliza clicked the link and scanned the article from a book titled *Notable Families of Sussex County from 1673 - 1912.*

Elijah Brown, 1780 - 1840, (md. Honor Lord, 1798) was the son of a prominent farming family that owned the largest piece of farmland in Coventry-by-the-Sea. His ability to produce a vast amount of corn brought immense wealth to their family and made them a significant player in the merchant trade with England. Elijah Brown was one of the first farmers to use small fish as fertilizer to help increase crop production. Although he held entrepreneurship qualities when it came to farming, he was careless and viewed as a risk taker when it came to the Lord Shipyard.

Honor Brown, née Lord, 1782 – 1808, was the daughter of the wealthy and successful shipping merchant, Ashley Lord. He and his family sailed to America in 1784 from Liverpool, England. The Lord Shipyard, based out of Salem, MA, played a vital role in the Sumatra pepper trade, bringing spices, gin, and pepper to America by way of his ships, the *Trade Winds*, and the *Zephyr.* When the two families merged, their farming and shipping successes were unrivaled by many in the New England area. Although their families acquired wealth and prominence, illness took its toll on the Brown family. Elijah and Honor Brown lost their only child, Levi Brown, to pneumonia in 1808. Honor Brown committed suicide hours after the passing of her son, Levi. Although family members questioned her manner of death, her death was ruled a suicide upon the findings of the Coroner's Court.

Eliza made a note to research more about the Lord family. Marty had known enough of them to mention them. Two prominent families joined by marriage for back-to-back articles in *The Gazette* made sense.

For the next hour, Eliza continued her research, reading several articles about both the Lord and Brown families, making notes, and compiling a list of questions and ideas for how to best frame the story for *The Gazette*.

Murphy, who had slept at her feet, now sat upright, his paw on the arm of her chair, whimpering and glancing at the kitchen.

She checked the time. Six o'clock.

"Alright, let's figure out dinner. We've had one hell of a day."

At the mention of the word "dinner," Murphy's tail began to wag.

"Oh, so you know that word too. You're a pretty smart dog, Murphy Grey."

Eliza gathered her notes, carrying them along with the candle back to the kitchen.

"Let's see, chicken, carrots, and cranberries? Or salmon, brown rice, and green beans?" she asked, showing Murphy both cans.

He sniffed each one but licked the can of salmon.

"Wonderful selection, sir. I'll have the chef prepare her finest at once."

She fixed herself a peanut butter and jelly sandwich and another cup of tea.

Once they'd both been fed, Eliza let Murphy out, feeling slightly guilty as she watched him dash across the rain-soaked yard from inside the warm, dry house.

Though the rain wasn't as heavy as before, it was still substantial, and the winds continued to howl.

A boom of thunder crashed in the distance.

Murphy disappeared behind a small stand of trees, and Eliza watched the spot, trying to see through the darkness.

A few seconds later, Murphy burst out of the underbrush and rushed back towards the door.

Lightning flashed, and the sky illuminated in stark blue whiteness.

The rain suddenly returned in full force, sending sheets of water slanted sideways across the stone patio.

The wind whipped her face, hair, and clothing as Eliza opened the door to let him back inside.

Murphy raced through the opening like a battering ram. Soaking wet, he galloped onto the wooden floor and gave two mighty shakes.

Eliza pushed the atrium door closed with all her might as the driving rain poured horizontally into the sunroom. She locked the latch and zig-zagged over paw-shaped puddles back into the kitchen.

In the middle of the room, leaning against the island, Murphy stood, looking dejected, dripping from head to toe.

"Aww, Murphy, you look miserable. Wait right there."

Taking the flashlight, she grabbed a folded bath towel off the shelf in the laundry room and hurried back to the kitchen.

When she returned, her notebook was on the floor, pages ripped out and scattered all over the kitchen.

She glared at Murphy. "Did you do this?"

Anger flared as she tossed the towel onto the counter and began to snatch papers from the floor. Many of the pages were drenched, the ink running. She laid them out on the granite countertop.

"Seriously, Murphy," she held out her arms in frustration. "This is hours of work ruined."

Murphy hung his head.

Eliza meticulously rearranged the pages to see what could be salvaged. As she carefully peeled a page from the cold granite, she paused and examined the edge of the paper. It was a clean tear, perfectly straight where the paper had given way at the perforation. Hardly what she'd expect if a dog had used her notebook as a chew toy.

But it must have been him. How else could this have happened?

She glanced back down at Murphy. Water dripped down his head and off his nose into a puddle.

She reached for the towel and knelt down, and rubbed his head.

"Let's get you dried off, and then I say we call it an early night." She rubbed his back and dried his legs and tail before tossing the towel back into the laundry room.

As they made their way upstairs, the power returned. Eliza turned off the flashlight and set it on the mantle of her bedroom fireplace. She flipped on the bathroom's overhead light, and a soft, warm glow spilled out into the bedroom.

She crossed to the window and stared out at the blackness over the ocean's horizon. Sporadic flashes of white electric zigzags illuminated the skyline as the soft rumble of thunder ebbed away in the distance.

"Thank goodness that's over," she said looking over at Murphy who had settled into his bed. He was far from dry, but he looked less pathetic.

His sad eyes and drooped head crushed her heart a bit.

She sat down on her bed and called him.

"Come here, Murphy. I'm not angry with you. I don't know how my notes ended up on the floor, but I'm sorry I yelled at you. How about we move your bed over here and start a fire so you can dry out and warm up?"

She pulled his bed next to the brick hearth and started the fire, then sat beside him, stroking his head until he fell asleep.

Her cell phone buzzed. It was Jason.

She took the phone into the bathroom while simultaneously grabbing a bath towel from the cabinet.

"Hey, honey."

"Hey El, how are you? I'm struggling with jetlag and have been lying awake in bed for hours and thought I'd give you a quick call."

"Things here are good, well, kind of. A real tempest just blew through. Took the power out and everything. It's back on now, so all is well." She debated telling him about her fall in the kitchen and the weird things that had happened at Highgate. "It's been an…interesting day."

"Oh yeah? Did you hang out with Murphy?"

"Yep. We took a walk into town so I could start researching a local family for my founding family feature. We almost got caught in the rain, and then poor Murphy got drenched when I let him out after dinner. He's in his bed next to the fire."

"How's the research for your story going?"

"Interesting, you should ask. I took Murphy to Highgate and made the mistake of unleashing him while we were walking around. He ran off, and while I was looking for him, I ended up in a part of the cemetery I'd never seen before. It's one of the oldest parts, secluded and hidden by a ton of overgrowth and prickers. How he even got in there, I have no idea, but that's where I found him, next to a family plot. And then I ran into Marty Evans, you know, the caretaker there at Highgate? He told me a story about a woman who was interred outside the cemetery wall. The historical record says she threw herself off a cliff, but Marty said some people think her husband might have pushed her off."

"So, your rescue dog ran away, found a grave, and the town recluse regaled you with stories of murderous bygone times?" Jason snickered.

"He's not exactly a recluse; at least, I don't think he is. But I won't argue that he's a bit odd."

"El, can I be honest with you? I'm really not sure how I'm feeling about this dog thing. If he can't behave and goes running off, maybe this isn't meant to be. And, recluse or not, the idea of you hanging around Marty Evans isn't giving me the warm fuzzies either. He gives off crazy stalker-murderer vibes, like something from a horror movie."

"I think you might be overreacting a bit. He may be strange, but he also seems to have a kind side. He helped me with Murphy, and he is a treasure trove of information about the residents of Highgate.

"Residents?" Jason asked. "You mean dead people?"

Oh Lord, I can't believe I just said that.

"Look, I promise to be safe, okay? I won't take Murphy off leash again, so I won't have that problem. And Marty is harmless, you have to trust me on this. How about you just congratulate me on finding the story?"

"Of course, honey. Congratulations. I can't wait to read it," he said, his tone soft and conciliatory.

"How are things there?" Eliza asked, changing the subject.

"Pretty good. I think we've secured some strong accounts. I hired a new assistant. She'll be helping with the influx of new business."

"That's great! I'm glad to hear things are going so well. Any chance you'll be headed home sooner than you thought?"

"Actually, yeah. Things are progressing much faster than I anticipated. I'm finishing up a few loose ends, then turning the reins over to Kent. It may take another week or so, but nowhere near the three weeks we thought it would."

Kent Jenkins was Jason's British counterpart. He'd done the bulk of the work securing the location and building for the new branch. While she'd never met him, from everything Jason had told her about the man, he was exceptionally capable and had been a big part of the expansion abroad.

"That might be the best news I've heard in a while. You know I love this house, but it is awfully lonely here without you and Bella."

"I know, El." He paused. "I'm sorry about what I said about Murphy. Truth is, I'm actually kind of glad you found a dog. It's probably a little less lonely with him there. And at least I know you've got a partner in crime as you go skulking through graveyards."

Eliza laughed. "I'm glad you think so. It is comforting to have him with me. We're like Sherlock and Watson, and we've already become a bit of a sensation in this little town."

"No doubt," Jason said, sounding amused.

"By the way, I had a chance to chat with Bella briefly before the storm moved in. She sounds like she might be a little overwhelmed. Maybe text her and let her know you're thinking about her?"

"I'll do that," he said. "Do you think Bella's rethinking her choice of school?"

Eliza shook her head. "No, I think she just needs to figure it out and spread her wings. She'll be fine; it's just hard to hear her struggling, you know? I'm hoping to get her home next weekend. Or maybe, after you return and have a few days to settle, we could visit her at school?"

"Sounds like a plan. A long weekend together. We need some family time."

"I agree." Eliza yawned. "Now, if you don't mind, Mr. Grey. After today's adventures, I'm beat, and you need to get some sleep. There's a soon-to-be drawn bath calling my name for a good long soak followed by seven solid hours of sleep."

"Promise me you'll be careful, El," Jason said softly.

"I promise. Love you."

She set the phone on the bathroom counter and pulled back the curtain around the tub. She adjusted the hot and cold water until it reached the perfect temperature and dropped the stopper in the drain. Steam began to rise from the running water. She poured a capful of lavender oil into the bath, letting it swirl as she inhaled its aroma and undressed. Before stepping into the tub, she opened the bathroom door wide enough to keep an eye on Murphy. He was still sleeping in his bed next to the fire.

With a sigh, she slipped into the steamy warmth and let the water and floral scent envelop her.

Closing her eyes, she laid back and took several slow, deep breaths. She could feel the tension in her shoulders and back begin to melt away. In her mind, she reviewed the day's events, both at home and at Highgate. Something was off; she'd felt it yesterday morning and then again when she touched Honor's gravestone. She'd heard something call her name. And the partial destruction of her notebook.

The more she thought about it, the more she was certain Murphy couldn't have done it.

Maybe it was the wind? Or maybe some wild animal found its way down from the rafters. It's an old house with a lot of crawl spaces. But wouldn't Murphy have barked or given chase?

She let out a breath, shook her head to clear the thought, and sank down further into the water. The bath was hot and soothing, but she still felt cold.

She opened her eyes briefly and glanced out toward the dimly lit bedroom, relieved that Murphy lay just feet away. A slight swooshing sounded in her ear, and the sensation of air blew over her face, the lavender oil masked briefly by a briny pungent scent.

Relax. Think happy thoughts. You have a dog.

The gentle dripping from the faucet drew her focus.

Drip...drip...drip.

Regular and steady, its soft rhythm hypnotizing.

Drip...drip...drip.

In her mind's eye, she was back in the family plot. Elijah Brown's large headstone in front of her. She remembered the odd arrangement of all the tombstones around it.

Her memory drifted over each of the gravestones, stopping on the oak tree and its strange placement, and then landing upon the lonely grave beyond the cemetery wall. She drew closer, trying to remember the epitaph.

Drifting deeper into her thoughts, the image of the strange sanctuary within the stone wall faded and, in its place, an ethereal vision of a beautiful woman with long dark hair. She appeared in 18th-century clothing, effortlessly floating towards her. Closer and closer until the woman's face grew so near that Eliza could feel her breath.

She felt her body jerk, pressed back against the porcelain tub, but the woman pushed closer still, then whispered in her ear:

"The night is my protectress; I yearn to breathe your breath. To tell my truth."

The beautiful face transformed into a ghoulish figure with remorseful eyes and long, stringy wet hair. Her gown tightened around a gaunt body, and a pair of bony hands reached for Eliza's neck.

Eliza recognized the woman immediately.

No, no, not again! You're not real! You can't be real!

Eliza felt the bony fingers close around her throat, and she sat up, sending water splashing from the tub.

Her eyes flew open, and she screamed.

Murphy howled and pushed the door open wider, racing to her side. His white face with his dark, wet nose and concerned-looking brown eyes watched her. He leaned his head over the tub's rim, resting his chin just inches from her face.

"Oh, Murphy!" She hugged his furry neck tightly. "Thank goodness you're here!"

She waited until her heartbeat returned to a normal rhythm before climbing out of the tub. Then pulled a nightgown over her head and wrapped herself in a warm, fuzzy robe.

Her eyes landed on her phone, and she debated calling Edmond. He'd always been her confidant when the nightmares woke her in the middle of the night as a child. But what would she say? Hey Ed, remember that crazy scary ghost lady I thought I saw as a kid? Yeah, well, she's back.

He'd think she'd lost her mind.

"No, no. I refuse," she said firmly, aloud. "This isn't real. I'm just stressed, tired."

Murphy sat at the foot of her bed. His head tilted one way then the other as if he was trying to assess if she was okay.

"Some tea and then sleep. Yes, that's exactly what I need. Thanks for the suggestion, Murph."

Downstairs in the kitchen, she tossed him a treat and put the kettle on again. She thought of checking the pantry for the culprit who had destroyed her notebook, but when she touched the knob, decided against it. Instead, she pushed against the old door to make sure it was closed all the way. If there was an animal of some sort in there, it could wait until morning. If she were lucky, it would make its way out the same way it had gotten in.

A few minutes later, she sipped on a cup of chamomile tea as she made the rounds, checking to ensure the doors and windows were locked.

By the time she'd finished, her nerves had settled a bit.

"Okay, Murphy, now it is absolutely time to call it a night."

The grandfather clock chimed the half hour. It was only half past nine, but it felt like well after midnight.

Halfway up the stairs, the hairs on the back of her neck rose. The sensation of something walking behind her made her skin crawl. Through the foyer window she caught sight of the moon. Clouds raced across the bright disc as the tail end of the storm broke apart.

She turned and scanned the lower level, half expecting to see something, entirely thankful the power had come back on. Nothing except all of the things she was used to seeing in her foyer.

Ahead of her, Murphy sat on the landing first, his attention fully locked on her.

She took two more steps, stopped, and heard the stairs creak behind her once again.

"Nope, I'm just freaked out because of the storm and this crazy, weird day."

She continued up the next four steps. The creak of the stairs behind her continued.

She felt her breath quicken. Goosebumps danced up both arms and down her legs.

Eliza hurried to her bedroom and closed the door tightly behind her.

Deep breaths, calm down. It's nothing, just the wind or your suddenly overactive and irritatingly spooky imagination.

Murphy let out a low growl, his attention focused on the bedroom door.

"What is it, boy?"

A shadow darkened the space beneath the door.

Murphy stalked forward, growling as he approached.

The shadow disappeared, and Murphy turned to her, his ears cocked on alert but his tail wagging.

Eliza hurried over and locked her bedroom door.

"It's nothing, just a shadow. The cloud floating in front of the moon." She'd said the words aloud and did her best to believe them.

Murphy settled back into his bed, and Eliza allowed his renewed calm demeanor to stave off the edginess that made her insides quiver. Too anxious to sleep, she climbed into bed and tried to read until exhaustion finally took hold of her and made staying awake impossible.

Eyes closed, she quickly fell asleep, drifting in and out of a new and cryptic dream. She was outside, running away from the house. Something or someone was chasing her. She could feel the grass under her feet, the cold night air on her skin, and the sting of her breath as it rushed from her lungs. Then she was at the cliff's edge, staring down at the rocks and crashing waves. A devastating pain stabbed her heart. Deep sobs rose within her chest as she called out for help.

She tried to scream, but her voice was muffled. She strained to see through the inky mist and identify who or what pursued her.

In her ear, a low guttural growl made her shiver.

A thunderous boom like a cymbal crash yanked Eliza from her sleep. She sat up in bed and opened her eyes, her heart pounding. A brilliant flash from a lightning bolt cast an eerie green glow to the inside of her room, illuminating a horrific dark figure at the foot of her bed.

Eliza sat frozen with disbelieving eyes. Her nightmare no longer hidden in her dreams.

The Wet Lady stood, pointing at her.

The same fierce growling from her dreams reverberated through the room.

Murphy, highlighted by the light of the fire, stood in a protective stance, fur raised, teeth showing.

The hideous figure hovered closer, staring with pulsing yellow-green eyes, the air thick with the stench of rotting seaweed. Eliza's breath escaped in tiny puffs of mist, the air unforgivingly cold around her.

Out of the corner of her eye, Eliza could see Murphy, his lips curled in a snarl. He crept toward the bed, then lunged.

The Wet Lady disappeared.

Eliza reached out, her breath intense and shallow. She could barely utter the words.

"Murphy, come."

Her protective companion leaped onto the bed and rested his head on her shoulder. She leaned over and held him tight.

"Thank you, Murphy."

She wasn't losing her mind; Murphy had seen her too.

Terror gnawed like a wild animal in her gut.

There was no denying it any longer.

The Wet Lady had returned.

6

ELIZA SAT IN FRONT of her computer, reviewing her notes. The rain-soaked pages had dried out overnight, and she'd been able to reconstruct those sections marred by running ink.

Despite the horrible visitation that plagued both her dreams and waking moments, with Murphy's calming presence next to her for the rest of the night, she'd managed to get several hours of deep sleep. She'd woken early, found some additional online resources highlighting each family through several generations, and began compiling the information she'd need for her articles.

William and Abigail Brown were the first of the Brown family to settle in Coventry and amassed a considerable fortune through large-scale farming. Their main trading crop, corn, elevated them to a significant player in the Salem mercantile shipping trade with England. The Browns owned the largest acreage in Coventry-by-the-Sea, and as a prudent farmer and businessman, William and his sons secured a profitable deal with Ashley Lord, owner of the Lord Shipyard, becoming a major producer of trade crops to ship overseas. The marriage of Honor Lord and Elijah Brown linked these two families together in what could be described as a social and financial windfall: power, wealth, prestige, and success.

Satisfied that the two families would make for interesting features, she copied several links about each, including one mentioning Honor's death, and pasted them into an email to Art.

Art,

I found the first family to feature. The Lord family contributed greatly to the wealth and prestige of Coventry-by-the-Sea. The Brown family

will be the spotlight in my Halloween piece. A tragic death of mother
and child and rumors of murder. More to follow.
-Eliza

She hit "send."

While some of the town's history and portions of the archives had been
scanned and were available online, Eliza's past experience had proved to her that
there was no better source of information than the people who had grown up in
Coventry. And there was one woman in particular who had been a godsend of
historical information – the town historian, Ginny Burke.

Eliza scrolled through her phone until she found Ginny's number.

Ginny, a descendant of another founding family of Coventry-by-the-Sea, had
dedicated her adult life as the full-time town historian, as well as a part-time
member of the historical preservation society. At seventy-two years old, she had
lived through many of the changes of the last century and was a treasure trove
of information for the hundreds of years of town history before that. The first
time they'd met, Eliza had been impressed and delighted by the older woman – a
petite, thin figure with delicate youthful features, shoulder-length silver hair, and
soulful grey-blue eyes. Ginny Burke radiated an ageless beauty.

She dialed the number, and within seconds she heard Ginny's sweet voice on
the line.

"Hello?"

"Hi, Ginny. This is Eliza Grey. How have you been?"

"Oh, I'm trying to stay busy, you know. It's been a little quiet around here, but
my daughters have been visiting often, and I've been spending more time reading.
And, of course, there's my book club on Wednesday and lunch with old friends
every Friday."

Alexander Burke, Ginny's husband of fifty-two years, had passed away from a
stroke in early spring. It was good to hear that Ginny was staying busy.

"I am hoping you might be up for some company today. I'm working on a new
article for *The Gazette*, a founding families feature, and need some help from you.

"Oh, of course, Eliza. You know I'm always up to talking about town history. Why don't you come by this afternoon for a cup of tea, and we can chat about it all then. Shall we say one o'clock?"

"One o'clock it is! Thank you, Ginny! See you then."

Eliza checked her watch. She had a couple of hours to kill before meeting with Ginny.

"Hey Murphy, how about a walk? You haven't been down to the beach yet."

Bright sunshine made the waves sparkle. Save an abundance of seaweed on the shoreline no evidence remained of the tempest that had swept in the night before. And while still cool, it was considerably warmer than the past few days.

Once they'd reached the flat expanse of sand that sat at the base of the cliff, Eliza allowed Murphy to explore, but she kept him on a leash.

One lost dog adventure is more than enough for me.

Murphy's tail wagged as he sniffed one rock and then another. A tiny crab skirted out into the open, and Murphy chased behind it, obviously curious.

"Let that poor crab be, Murphy," Eliza said, smiling. "Let's go over here." She led him to a spot that she and Bella had deemed their "special place," where they would come to find periwinkles, hermit crabs, seashells, and sea glass when Bella was a child.

Eliza cautiously hopped between the sand and large rocks, trying not to slip on the slick surface covered in slime.

Murphy followed her, surprisingly agile for such a big dog.

Eliza leaned over to look down into one of the main tide pools. Temporarily separated from the sea during low tide, the water teemed with small sea creatures. She caught her reflection on the still surface, Murphy's face beside her.

Murphy let out a low growl.

"Oh, sweet boy, nothing to worry about," she said, stooping to scratch behind his ear. "It's just our reflections."

She pointed to the ripples that spread across the small pool, obscuring a solid picture of their reflections from above.

A gust of wind blew throughout the tiny inlet, and small specks of sand stung her face. Within its swirl of chilly air came a whisper, *Eliza, Eliza Grey.*

Her back arched, and that familiar chill raced down her arms and clung to her spine. She turned her head in either direction to see if someone was nearby. Murphy leaned his head closer to the water, his nose almost touching the surface, and made a deep threatening growl.

She glanced back at the tide pool, now completely still and glass-like. The once shallow water appearing fathomless and dark.

Instead of her reflection, the beautiful woman she met on this very beach as a child appeared on the water's surface, eyes glassy and lifeless, staring above to something unknown. Her long, dark hair spread out around her, fluidly swirling over her shoulders. Closed full lips, icy blue, permanently holding her final words.

Murphy continued to growl.

Could he see her too?

Eliza swallowed hard as she watched the woman's listless face.

This can't be.

The woman blinked, then opened her eyes and began to mouth words Eliza couldn't hear or understand. As the wind picked up, ripples expanded across the water, sending an expression of fear over the woman's delicate features, morphing them into an all too familiar and terrifying form.

Murphy snarled and erupted into a menacing bark.

The Wet Lady stared up at her with such intensity that Eliza screamed and jumped backward. She turned to run, but the slick green algae on the rocks offered little traction, and she fell backward. Her head smacking against a large rock.

Eliza rolled onto her side and sat up, a growing darkness threatening the periphery of her vision.

Her fingers tentatively probed the back of her head. No blood, but pain pounded in her skull.

Murphy stopped barking and ran to Eliza's side. He whined as he licked her face.

"It's okay; I'm okay," Eliza said, patting his head to calm him. "But maybe we should head home?"

She carefully rose to her feet and stood.

Murphy picked up the end of his leash and held it for her to take.

In the warmth of her kitchen, Eliza took a couple of ibuprofen tablets while holding an icepack to the developing goose egg on the back of her head.

The growing regularity of the Wet Lady's appearance had her worried. It was one thing to call it a nightmare, but she'd seen her in broad daylight. And the scare had sent her crashing backward into a rock.

What if the fall had knocked me out? How long would I have laid on the beach before someone found me?

On her phone, she scrolled through her recent contacts for Vanessa's number and dialed. It went to voicemail.

"Hey Vanessa, it's me. Give me a call later if you can," she sighed. "I need your opinion about something."

She hung up.

I need your opinion on whether or not I'm going crazy.

An hour later, most of the pain had subsided, and Eliza gathered her notes and computer, readying herself to see Ginny.

As she pulled on a jacket, Murphy nudged his leash where it hung from the hook in the foyer.

"Sorry, buddy, but I must go solo for this visit. I won't be gone long, I promise."

Murphy let out a slow whine but let go of the leash and lay down on the floor.

It was a short drive into the historic district of Coventry-by-the-Sea, where Ginny Burke lived. She'd visited the town historian on more than one occasion for previous articles. However, as she pulled into the driveway, she marveled at the beautiful Cape Cod-style house, with its cedar shake siding and white painted steps leading to a wide front porch. Two inviting white rocking chairs moved ever so slightly in the gusts of September winds.

Eliza prepared to knock on the glassed-in screen door, but before she made contact, Ginny appeared with a warm smile. Then, holding the door open, she beckoned Eliza into her home.

"So good to see you again, Eliza! Come on in. I put some tea and scones in the breakfast nook. I thought we might sit there and enjoy the view."

Eliza stepped inside and smiled as she took in the homey décor.

"Thank you for making time for me today," she said, pulling off her jacket.

"No trouble at all," Ginny said, taking the coat and hanging it from a hook on an antique hall tree.

Eliza followed Ginny through a large, warm living room into a hallway that led to the kitchen. Windows adorned with soft yellow valances allowed the bright sunlight to cast an early afternoon glow across the rich wood tone of the kitchen. Ginny led her to a cozy built-in nook around a lovely oak farm table.

On the table sat two blue Wedgewood teacups with matching teapot. Beside them was a plate of scones, sugar and creamer bowls, and a tiny ornamental dish of raspberry jam.

"I hope you like lemon poppyseed," Ginny said as she took the teakettle from the stove and filled the teapot on the table. "They were my husband's favorite. I made them this morning."

Returning the kettle to the burner, she sat at the table and motioned for Eliza to join her.

Eliza reached for a scone and broke it in two. She placed half on the saucer beneath her teacup, spread a layer of jam on the other, and took a bite.

"Ginny, this is magnificent. Maybe the best scone I've ever had."

Ginny beamed. "It's my mother's recipe. The jam too. That batch is the last of my raspberry crop." She pointed out the window to her garden and a line of bushes that ran along the fence line. "Alexander planted those raspberry bushes back in the '70s. That man loved my raspberry jam, and to this day, I make the jam as if I am making it for him."

A moment of sadness slipped through her grey-blue eyes, but she immediately brightened, as she returned her gaze on Eliza.

"So, tell me more about your next article. How can I help?"

Eliza pulled out her notebook and relayed how she'd found the overgrown and unkept burial site of Elijah Brown and his family, including Honor and Levi.

"The two of them died on the same day. I've only just begun my research, but I know Honor was born Honor Lord, daughter of another prominent Coventry founding family."

A slow smile spread over Ginny's face as she nodded. "Boy, do I have something for you. Wait right here."

Ginny shimmied out of the nook and disappeared into the front room, returning a few minutes later with a sizeable leather-bound book about four inches thick, with gold-rimmed pages and a metal clasp holding it shut.

Eliza moved the scones and teapot out of the way, and Ginny placed the book on the table.

"This, my dear, is my greatest treasure," she said, putting on a pair of reading glasses. "It is a Bible with a written history of my family, captured by my ancestors for many generations."

Ginny struggled momentarily to unlock the clasp but soon succeeded and opened the book, turning a few pages before carefully pulling out a much longer, folded page with an elaborate family tree. Though the paper was well-creased, there was no denying the beauty of the artwork or the delicately flourished penmanship.

Ginny ran a finger along the page until she found what she sought. After a moment, she looked up at Eliza with a broad smile.

"Honor Brown, or as she is recorded here, Honor Lord, is a member of my family. Niles Lord, Honor's younger brother, was my fourth great-grandfather. He married a woman named Charlotte. The family was very wealthy; I believe they owned two successful trade ships." Her eyes narrowed as she paused in thought. "The *Trade Winds* and the *Zephyr* I believe. They traded in spices and pepper, if I'm not mistaken."

"Is there more?" Eliza asked, excitedly, nodding toward the book.

Ginny readjusted her glasses and continued. "On September 26, 1782, in Leek, Staffordshire, England, Ashley and Mary Lord welcomed their first child, a daughter, Honor Temperance Lord, a beautiful girl with sea-green eyes and thick ebony hair. In the year 1784, the Lord family set sail, bound for America.

They made port at Ipswich, Massachusetts on October 12, 1784. On November 1, 1784, Mary Lord gave birth to their second child, a son, Niles Edward Lord."

"That's incredible," Eliza said, adding that information to her notes about the Lord family.

"I barely know my family history beyond just a couple of generations. And your family has been here, in Coventry, for hundreds of years."

Ginny turned the book so Eliza could see and pointed to Honor Lord's name, date of birth, marriage, and death. Next to Honor's name, in the adjacent box in intricate cursive writing, was the name Elijah Brown. Below was the name of their only child, Levi.

"Shall I read more?" Ginny asked.

Eliza nodded. "Yes, please. I'm fascinated by all of this. That we can sit here, in the day and age of computers and cell phones, and read about this family, your family, in their own words, in their own handwriting. It's nothing short of remarkable."

Ginny turned a page and scanned several passages.

"It says here that in 1799, Ashley Lord acquired a trade deal importing Sumatra pepper. Included with the acquisition was a ship, The *Trade Winds*." Ginny glanced up and tapped her temple. "Glad to see this old brain is still holding onto the details." She smiled and returned her attention to the book.

"Though small in comparison to the pepper fleets that sailed out of the Salem Harbor, the Lord fleet, including his first ship, the *Trade Winds,* was highly successful, turned a substantial profit within just a few years, and somehow remained unscathed by the pirate attacks that plagued the larger ships."

Eliza jotted down notes as Ginny spoke. "In one of the articles I wrote last year, I remember reading about how pirate attacks on the open seas caused a significant issue for many of the merchant ships at that time. The pirates would capture the ships, plunder the cargo, and kidnap or kill their crews."

Ginny nodded and continued. "The Lord Shipyard grew and added several larger ships over the next few years. By 1806, they were credited with bringing more than 500 tons of pepper into the colonies."

"An amazing feat. Is there anything more, anything about Honor, about what happened to her?"

Ginny adjusted her reading glasses and flipped the page, then read:

"Elijah Simon Brown wed Honor Temperance Lord July 24, 1798. The grand celebration of the nuptial, hosted by the Ashley Lord family at the estate of Lord Manor, became the talk of Coventry-by-the-Sea. The food, décor, and grounds made for an auspicious occasion. The couple will reside in the grand home, built by Elijah Brown, on the north side of town above the cliff of cascading roses, henceforth named Rosecliff Manor."

Eliza couldn't hide her surprise.

"Elijah and Honor lived at Rosecliff?"

"I'd say so," Ginny replied. "Elijah built it."

Eliza leaned over the table to reread the passage. *Rosecliff Manor!*

Ginny patted her hand. "What a remarkable find, my dear. And what an amazing coincidence that you would decide to write about this particular family, this particular couple."

Eliza did a quick calculation. "She was only seventeen when she married him. Do you think she loved him?"

Ginny leaned back. "Hard to say. Most marriages at that time were contractual, made by families to protect their wealth, and in many cases to secure alliances and connections that would grow their affluence."

A sharp pain fired from the back of Eliza's head. She squeezed her eyes shut, willing it to pass.

"Are you all right?" Ginny asked.

"Oh, I'm fine. Just a bit of a headache, but please, continue. I want to hear more about Honor and her family."

Ginny nodded and gave her a wide smile. "Very well, let's see what else we can find."

Eliza pressed back in her seat. Her head throbbed. She closed her eyes and tried to focus on Ginny's soft voice, the images of a time long gone coalescing in her mind.

August 1797

The carriage creaked, and the sway of the bench seats made Honor feel a little queasy, but it did not dampen her mood. She watched the green terrain of the passing countryside through the carriage window as they made their way to the Pierce estate where her dearest friend, Patience Winifred Carlyle, would marry the handsome Thomas Pierce, son of Coventry's most prominent banker, Isaac Pierce. Patience was the first of her friends to be married. At sixteen, Honor understood that such an occasion would soon be in her own future. Whom she would marry, she could not say, but she prayed he would be as kind and handsome as Thomas.

"Be careful of the dust, Honor, dear. Keep your head inside, please," her mother ordered over the constant clomping of the horse hooves.

"Yes, Mother," Honor replied, sitting back in her seat, turning her gaze from the window to her mother. Mary Lord wore a beautiful silvery-blue silk gown. The color nearly matching her eyes. Large pearls dangled from her ears, and a matching pearl necklace around her neck. To Honor, her mother looked like royalty.

"You look beautiful, Mother," Honor said softly.

Mary Lord's face softened, and she smiled. "Thank you, my sweet. Nothing like a wedding for putting on one's finest and enjoying the day."

Honor couldn't disagree. She wore a new dress in the latest fashion. The light blue taffeta gown practically shimmered in the sunlight. A cream-colored sash cinched at her waist, and she wore a pair of gold and pearl earrings, a gift from her father. Their maid had coiffed Honor's long ebony hair up into an intricate arrangement with loose curls cascading down her back.

As the carriage pulled up in front of the Pierce family home, Honor ignored her mother's previous instruction and leaned out to take in the splendor. Tables adorned with lanterns and flowers in a variety of colors covered the lawn.

"Mother, look at how beautiful everything is!"

The carriage lurched to a stop, and the driver stepped down from his seat and came around to open the door.

Mary Lord was the first to exit. Behind her, Honor, being careful not to catch the hem of her mother's skirt, tried to contain her glee. When offered, she took the driver's hand and climbed down from the carriage, quickly straightening her gown, flattening it out around her waist, allowing the moderate-cut front to emphasize her now budding bosom.

"Come, Honor; I see your father and brother waiting by the tables."

As friends of the Pierce family, her father and brother had been invited to be groomsmen and had arrived much earlier in the day.

Honor raised a hand and waved to her brother, Niles.

She followed her mother through the growing group of attendees. At a table on the outskirts of the lawn, a tall, muscular young man caught her attention. Mysterious brown eyes held her gaze. He wore a navy blue satin coat and a waistcoat that accentuated the broadness of his shoulders. The delicate lace collar of his shirt emphasized a strong jawline and full lips. His long thick hair was pulled back in a satin ribbon.

"Honor," her mother whispered sternly.

The magic of the moment broke, and Honor felt color warm her cheeks.

"Handsome he may be, but that man is to be avoided."

"Why? Who is he?"

"His name is Elijah, son of William and Abigail Brown. His mother is kind enough, but his father has a reputation that, by all accounts, has rubbed off on his son. Mind your attentions, Honor. I'll not soon see you associate with him or his father if I can help it." Her mother took her hand and pulled her along.

Honor dared a glance back across the lawn, but Elijah had turned and was deep in conversation with another guest.

After the ceremony, Honor stood with her mother, congratulating the happy couple.

"This is such a lovely celebration. We wish you a lifetime of happiness and many children to fill your home." Mary Lord beamed.

The ceremony included a lovely exchange of vows that nearly brought Honor to tears. That she might find a love like Patience had would be her newest and most fervent dream.

Honor nodded and hugged her friend. "You look beautiful, Patience; you make a lovely bride."

"Soon, it will be you, Honor." Patience said. "And it will be me congratulating you on your nuptials and beauty. Pray tell, is there a certain gentleman who's caught your eye?"

Mary interjected. "Mr. Lord and I are very particular about who shall wed our Honor, and I am not eager just yet; she is still very young."

Honor felt the blush of color return to her face. But in truth, until this day, she had possessed no desire to become a lady of a household or a wife. It was upon seeing her friend's joy and the look of love between the newlywed couple that changed her way of thinking. That, and the sensual attraction to the mysterious young man whom her mother so ardently disapproved of.

An older woman with brown hair, a ruddy complexion, and dressed in a yellow gown approached, with a young man in tow, offering her own well wishes to Patience and Thomas.

"Forgive my interruption," she said. "I could not wait a moment longer to give my deepest wishes for a happy and fruitful marriage to this charming couple."

She embraced Patience. "Such a beautiful bride, my dear."

The woman turned and addressed Mary. "Good afternoon, Mrs. Lord."

"Good afternoon, Mrs. Brown. Always lovely to see you. And you as well, Master Samuel," Mary Lord replied. "Allow me to introduce my daughter, Honor. Honor, this is Mrs. Abigail Brown, and her son, Samuel."

Honor worked to hide the growing interest and excitement in her voice.

"Lovely to meet you both," she said. "Are you enjoying the celebration?"

"Oh, yes, quite, my dear. Though I must say, I am not as able to enjoy all the excitement as I once did in my youth." She flipped open a fan and fluttered it in front of her face. "My Elijah is off with his father and your father to see what we might do to hurry along the musicians so that we might have some dancing. Do you enjoy dancing, dear?"

At the mention of Elijah's name, Honor glanced at her mother.

Mary gave her the same stern expression as before.

"Yes," she said, offering both Browns a smile. "I dare say I do enjoy dancing."

Abigail Brown turned to look over the lawn and pointed.

"There, it would seem they have been successful. I hear the first notes of a reel."

Honor followed her gaze to see her father, flanked by two other men, approaching them. One of whom she assumed was the ill-reputed Mr. Willliam Brown and the other, the handsome Elijah.

As they approached, she felt Elijah's smoldering stare. Good manners required her to look away, but she held his gaze.

"Come, Honor," her mother said. "We cannot monopolize all of Patience's time; she has so many other guests to greet."

"Once again, well wishes to you both," she said to Patience and Thomas. "So good to see you, Mrs. Brown, Master Samuel," she said, taking Honor's arm and leading her away.

Nearby, several long tables draped in white linen and adorned with wildflowers in vases and sprigs of greenery were set with countless trays and dishes of food. Honor immediately identified roasted pigeons, salmon, trout, and multiple loaves of bread. Further down, an entire table had been dedicated to dessert with various tarts, apple cakes, gooseberry pies, and sage cheeses.

"I beg you to remember my warning," Mary said under her breath as they each selected from the many offerings laid out in a lavish display of savory and sweet dishes. "For some, a pretty exterior hides a tendency toward dishonesty and sin," she said.

"Of course, Mother," Honor said, glancing back at Patience and Thomas conversing with Abigail Brown. Elijah stood beside his brother and mother, smiling and shaking Thomas' hand.

Mary Lord was a pious woman who believed in God and doing charitable works. However, she showed no tolerance for gossip or demeaning qualities. That she would offer any ill-begotten words about anyone was both a surprise and a testament to her warning. But it did little to quell Honor's growing desire to meet Mr. Brown and his handsome son.

Honor followed her mother to a table where her father and Niles were seated.

Niles snatched a petite pie from Honor's plate.

Mary shot him a stern glance. "Niles, behave yourself."

He winked at her. "Always."

Honor stifled a giggle, and the two of them were soon laughing in unison.

"That table reminds me of the story you read to me once about the girl who goes into the woods and finds a magical party with fancy foods, wood sprites, and music. Remember?" Niles asked.

Honor nodded and smiled.

"How do you find this celebration?" Honor asked her father.

"It's lovely, of course. Nothing short of what I might expect from such an affluent family." He narrowed his eyes. "Enjoy yourself, but don't let it into that pretty head of yours that your wedding will be half as extravagant as this."

"Mr. Lord," Mary interrupted. "Our Honor is just sixteen. Let us do away with any talk of her wedding." She glanced at Honor. "Besides, you have several years yet. With the recent addition of The Zephyr to your fleet, you may yet make a fortune befitting of such a celebration as this."

Honor caught the twinkle in her mother's eye.

Yes, and Father allowed me to choose the name of his newest ship. The Zephyr may promise more than a west wind. Maybe a grand wedding to the handsome Elijah Brown, Honor mused to herself.

"Excuse me, Mr. Lord?"

Honor took a quick breath. Elijah stood behind her father, his eyes on her.

"Elijah," Ashley Lord said, standing and offering him a hand.

Elijah shook and smiled. "I was hoping you might introduce me to your lovely daughter so that I might ask her to dance."

"Of course," Ashley Lord said, motioning for Honor to come and join him.

"Master Elijah Brown, allow me to introduce my daughter, Mistress Honor Lord."

Honor curtsied. Elijah bowed in return.

"Now that we are properly introduced, might I have the next dance, Mistress Honor?

Honor looked at her mother. Mary Lord wore an expression Honor could not quite decipher. Was it disdain or fear?

"Of course, a single dance, then return her to us, safe and sound, yes, Master Brown?"

"By all means, Mrs. Lord," Elijah replied.

Mary nodded, and Honor took Elijah's offered arm.

As the music began, Honor allowed herself to drift into the dreamy nature of the movement. Elijah was an able dancer, his deep brown eyes all the more mesmerizing up close.

As promised, he returned her to her parents' table once the dance was done.

"A privilege and an honor to have danced even one dance with one as beautiful as you," he said, bending to place a tender kiss on the back of Honor's hand.

Honor was aware of her mother's disapproving scowl, but she didn't care. Elijah Brown held her fancy. Any woman would consider herself lucky to attract the attention of a man as handsome and wealthy as he.

Abigail Brown sauntered over and stood beside her son.

"What a handsome couple my Elijah and your Honor make, do they not?" She took her son's arm. "Perhaps you will be the next to host a wedding."

"Perhaps," Mary said through tight lips.

"Come, Mother," Elijah said. "You must take a turn about the floor with me next."

Once they had gone, Mary leaned over and whispered to her husband.

"Are you sure, my dear? It is early yet," Ashley responded.

Honor couldn't hide her disappointment. "Must we go? So soon? The dancing has hardly begun."

Mary looked at her husband. "Feel free to stay, as I am sure Mr. Pierce will expect it. But I am taking our children home. Now."

"All right, my dear. I'll fetch the carriage. We'll all go."

Honor's heart sank. She didn't want to go home. The sun setting cast a warm and romantic glow as servants in red and gold jackets began lighting lanterns around the lawn.

Honor climbed back inside the carriage and sat next to her brother. Honor faced her father, who looked displeased about something. She adored her father, and he rarely showed unhappiness in her presence. She looked at her mother, who stared defiantly out the coach window.

They rode home in silence.

Later that night, unable to rid her mind of the events of the day, Honor heard her parents talking in the parlor below her bedroom.

Quietly, she tiptoed from her room and sat listening at the top of the stairs. Her parents rarely argued, and she could not help but feel their current disagreement had something to do with her.

"Mary, it would be a good union. Why is this so upsetting? I discussed it with William Brown. He, too, feels Elijah is a perfect match for our family. I spoke with the young man myself, and he is very astute. He has aspirations that would benefit all, particularly Honor."

"What aspirations? He is pompous and boastful, like his father—two qualities I do not respect and would hate to see portrayed in any way by our daughter. There is something behind his eyes, something in his manner. I swear the boy lacks a soul."

"Mary! That is a strong allegation! Elijah Brown possesses great knowledge in regard to farming and is eager to learn the shipping business. They are attracted to one another, creating a strong union."

"Elijah Brown provides only lofty ideas. Why not pursue the younger brother, Samuel? He is Honor's age and comes from the same Brown wealth. His moral standing is most evident."

"Samuel is not as formidable as Elijah. I do not see him as a strong asset for the shipyard."

Mary huffed.

"My dear," Ashley coaxed. "Will you not trust me on this? You have no knowledge of the boy except for your feelings, feelings that I am sure will change when you get to know him. He is very personable, bright, entertaining, charming even. And by all accounts, Honor was taken with him. You can't deny that."

"She's a girl who doesn't know the way of the world yet."

"He has been given the finest part of the Brown land, a fitting place to build a home. He is eager to learn the shipping business."

"My mind will not be changed."

Honor could hear the growing frustration in her father's voice.

"Mary, we both knew this day would come. I treasure our Honor as you do. And as her father, I want nothing short of what is best for her. I do not share your reservations, but I am trying to respect and understand them. All I ask is that you have a little faith in me. Allow him to court her. Get to know the boy and see if your mind will be changed by his good nature. That is a benefit to us all. I was fortunate

in my betrothal to you. I loved you from the moment I saw you. I want that for our daughter as well."

"As you wish. I will agree, not because of your sugary words, but because I will respect your decision. But if I am right, you must not allow Elijah to marry our daughter."

"I promise, if he proves unworthy, I will sever all ties and be glad to do so."

Honor smiled to herself and went back to bed, her head and her dreams filled with broad shoulders and mysterious brown eyes.

Eliza heard a rush of wind and opened her eyes, blinking rapidly. The vision of Honor and her family faded.

Ginny sat looking at her expectantly.

"I'm sorry, what was that?"

"I said, isn't this fascinating?"

"Oh, yes," she said, offering a smile. "It's all quite fascinating."

Ginny gave her a sly grin. "You're humoring me; I've read nearly ten pages. Not exactly riveting stuff, this," she said, tapping the book.

"Not at all," Eliza replied, her mind still foggy. "You know me; I love a good jaunt into the historical records of this town." She looked at the time on her phone. "But I've probably bothered you enough for today." She gathered her notes. "Okay if I call you with any questions that come up?"

"Of course, of course. Call any time."

Ginny stood and escorted Eliza back to the living room on their way to the front door.

Eliza pressed a hand to her forehead. The pain throbbed with growing intensity. In her mind, a vision as clear as day inside Rosecliff Manor. A woman she could only guess to be Honor, beautiful but frail, descended the grand staircase with a small child holding her hand. Behind her, the brooding face of a man Eliza knew had to be Elijah. His arms folded, and a scowl on his face.

A wave of panic and fear raced through her gut. Mary had been right to warn Honor. He was dangerous.

"Eliza? Eliza? Are you okay?"

She could hear Ginny's voice, but she sounded far away.

"I'm fine; I just need to warn her," Eliza replied, hardly recognizing the sound of her own voice. She opened her eyes a crack and saw the concern on Ginny's face before the room turned to blackness.

7

A BRIGHT LIGHT DANCED back and forth, and Eliza squinted as she opened her eyes and tried to focus on the serious face of the young paramedic. He held a finger up in front of her. "Follow the movement of my finger," he instructed.

"Do you know what year it is, Ms. Grey?" he asked.

"What? Yes, of course, I do." She moved to sit up. Pain raced through her skull and down to her shoulders.

"Lie back, please. I need to get your blood pressure."

"What is going on?"

Ginny Burke appeared at her side. "Oh, Eliza! You passed out on me. I called an ambulance."

Eliza sighed. "Ginny, I am so sorry. I have no idea what's wrong with me."

"Please, don't be sorry. I'm just glad you're all right." She handed Eliza her phone. "After I called the ambulance, I tried to call Jason, but he didn't pick up. So I called Bella. She's on her way."

Eliza squeezed her eyes shut. "Jason is in England. I should call Bella back and tell her not to come. I just need to go home and rest."

The EMT removed the blood pressure cuff. "Ms. Grey, have you had any other issues lately? Any falls or injuries I should know about?"

"I fell earlier today, bumping my head on rocks on the shore by my house. It's nothing."

The paramedic gently felt the back of her head. Even his light touch exacerbated the pain.

Eliza winced.

"That's a nasty bump."

"I'm sure it's nothing."

"I'm sure it's a reason to be concerned, especially since you passed out. I recommend we take you to the hospital. You could have a concussion."

Ginny took Eliza's hand. "Go dear, go get checked out. Better safe than sorry. I'll call Bella and let her know you're on your way to the hospital."

Eliza sighed. "Okay, you're right."

Inside the ambulance, Eliza struggled to keep her eyes open.

"C'mon now, stay with me for just a little bit longer, Ms. Grey," the paramedic said. "No sleeping until after the doctor assesses you."

Before long, they arrived at Mercy Medical Center. Eliza held a hand over her eyes to block out the bright lights as she was ushered into a hospital room. She could hear the sound of machines beeping as they moved her from the gurney to the bed. Time grew ambiguous as people rushed around her. She felt the prick of an IV and a woman's voice, a nurse, more than likely, telling her they were taking her upstairs for a CT scan.

Minutes or hours later, Eliza wasn't sure, a doctor stood at her bedside, her chart in his hands.

"I ran a series of tests, and the CT scan doesn't show anything abnormal. I believe you have suffered a mild concussion. While it could be worse, you shouldn't brush this off as insignificant. We'll give you a little something for the pain and send you home. My recommendation is bed rest for the next few days."

"Just so long as I can go home, I'll do whatever you say."

"Glad to hear it." He pulled a pen from his breast pocket and clicked it open. He wrote something on her chart and handed it to a nurse. "Let's give her something to help get rid of the headache and send her home." He turned back to Eliza. "You should call someone to pick you up. This medication will make you a little drowsy. And if I were you, I'd avoid driving for a couple of days or until you no longer have any pain." He paused a moment to acknowledge Eliza's faint nod.

"I'll be right back with your prescription," the doctor said and patted her leg. "Follow up with your primary care in a few days but come back and see us if the pain gets any worse."

He waited for Eliza to agree, then put the pen back in his pocket and disappeared out into the hall.

She watched as the nurse emptied a syringe of fluid into her IV.

Eliza's cell phone buzzed from the bedside table; Edmond's name appeared on the screen.

"It's my brother," she said, reaching for it and wincing.

The nurse handed it to her.

Eliza swiped to answer her phone.

"Hey, Ed."

"Eliza! It's good to hear your voice. Are you okay? Are you still in the hospital? What happened?"

"I'm fine. It's a mild concussion. Doctor just gave me the thumbs up to head home. Let me get home, and I'll call you back and tell you everything, I promise." She wanted to tell him about seeing the Wet Lady right then, but it could wait. The last thing she needed was a medical professional overhearing her talking about seeing ghosts.

The door to her room opened, and a second nurse escorted a very nervous-looking Bella inside. Still in her soccer uniform, the color drained from her face; Eliza could tell she'd been crying.

"Ed, Bella just came in. I'll call you when I get home."

"Okay, Sis, call me later."

Eliza hung up the phone and reached out to her daughter.

"Mom! Oh my God, are you okay?"

Bella took her hand and sat beside her on the bed.

"Seriously, Mom, that might have been the scariest phone call of my life. One of my coaches drove, and we got here as soon as we could. Poor Mrs. Burke could barely speak. What happened? How are you feeling?"

"I am fine," Eliza repeated. "I just had a little fall and –"

Before she could finish, an exasperated Vanessa burst into the room.

"Eliza! Holy Moses, woman. Ginny Burke called me; she told me they took you off in an ambulance. Something about a fall and a concussion?"

Eliza sighed. The medication was already taking the edge off her pain, but it did little to squelch her growing frustration at having so many people fawn over her. "I'm fine," she said. "Why are you here? Not that I am not glad to see you, but you really didn't need to come all the way down here. You either," she said to Bella.

"Ginny called me at the bakery and told me what happened. She mentioned that your car was at her house, so I had one of my regulars drop me off there and I drove it here so I could bring you home."

"You're a good friend, you know that?" A pleasant buzzy warmth spreading through Eliza's body as the medication took full effect.

"Yeah, well, you might change your mind when you find out who that regular was."

Eliza smiled lazily. "Never. You're my best friend, no matter what."

Vanessa blew out a breath. "So, when I tell you that when Ginny called that Lana was in the bakery picking up something for the mayor's office..."

Eliza's grin faltered. "You didn't. Please tell me Lana doesn't know about this."

"See, I told you." Vanessa took one of Eliza's hands in her own. "In the moment, it seemed like the right thing to do."

Eliza smirked, any inkling of anger dissipating as the medication took full effect. "Whatever, Lana can kiss my–"

"Whoa!" Vanessa smiled at Bella. "I think your mom is feeling A-okay right now."

Eliza giggled, and Bella laughed. "I think you're right."

The doctor returned with a script for a stronger Tylenol if her headache worsened. Bella took it from him.

"But I suspect the medication we gave her will get her through the night."

"Can my mom go home?" Bella asked.

"Yes, I just put in for her to be discharged. Ms. Grey, do you have any questions for me?"

"Nope, you've been a great help," she said and held out her hand. "I'll leave a five-star review for your wonderful customer service."

The doctor chuckled. "I see they've already given you the pain meds." He pointed to the paper in Bella's hand. "That will help over the next couple of days, but please remind your mom to take it easy."

"Hello, I'm right here." Eliza waved her hands. "I'm going to go home and rest. Doctor's orders." She gave him a half-hearted salute.

"We'll make sure she takes it easy," Vanessa promised.

Bella pushed Eliza's wheelchair down to the emergency room exit while Vanessa pulled the car around.

Vanessa hopped out to help Eliza into the front passenger seat.

"I can drive," Bella said. "Drop you off at the bakery."

Vanessa held out the keys. "That would be great. I left in such a hurry. I need to do a proper closing and prep for tomorrow."

They drove the twenty minutes to the bakery mostly in silence, making a quick stop en route to pick up Eliza's prescription from the drugstore.

Bella slowed the vehicle and pulled along the curb in front of Murphy's Bakery.

Vanessa exited out of the back seat and came to the passenger side window.

"Rest well tonight, my friend. We'll talk tomorrow. You're in good hands with Bella."

She gave Eliza a light kiss on the forehead.

"I meant what I said," Eliza murmured, feeling only slightly less loopy than she had at the hospital. "You're a good friend and I forgive you for telling Lana, even if she is my arch nemesis and is probably sleeping with the mayor."

Vanessa's eyes grew wide, and she laughed. "Your arch nemesis? Go home and sleep this off. Bella, bring your mom by tomorrow and the jelly donuts are on the house."

"Deal," Bella said.

As Bella pulled out onto Main Street and turned toward Rosecliff Manor, she glanced over at her mom.

"You doing okay?"

Eliza nodded gently. "I'm so glad to be heading home. Murphy must be beside himself. It was the first time I've left him home alone. I promised him I wouldn't be gone long."

"Mom, what happened today?"

"It was nothing. I just slipped on some algae, a clumsy accident. Murphy and I decided to walk along the shore, and the next thing I knew, I slipped and hit my head. It's no big deal. I iced the bump and figured it would be tender for a bit."

"I am glad it isn't serious. And I'm glad Murphy was with you."

Somewhere in the fog of her thoughts, Eliza didn't feel right hiding the truth from Bella. She'd grown up well aware of Eliza's ability to just *know* things, but Eliza had never shared anything about the Wet Lady with her daughter. Now wasn't the time, and she didn't want to scare Bella.

Bella helped Eliza from the car and up the porch steps. A large white head appeared with worried eyes staring at them from the living room window. A low woof sounded from inside the house and quickly became a booming bark!

Bella unlocked the door, and Murphy jumped up, his paws resting on her shoulders. His long pink tongue licked Bella's face.

"Murphy! Oh, my goodness! So good to meet you, boy."

Murphy danced around them, wiggling his overly large rump this way and that, tail wagging.

"Murphy Grey, easy boy!" Eliza said as sternly as she could, holding herself against the door frame for support.

Murphy promptly sat, his tail still wagging, but his large body stilled.

"He came trained, too? Mom, he's great. I love him already."

Bella bent down and rubbed her two hands across his large flat ears.

"Sorry, Murph, for the long day," Eliza said, making her way inside and closing the door.

"Let's get you something to eat and then into bed." Bella offered her arm. "I'll feed Murphy and let him out. You need to rest like the doctor ordered."

Eliza smiled and took Bella's arm. This caring, nurturing side of her daughter was one she rarely saw.

"I'd like to take a shower if that's okay. It's been a long day."

"All right, you shower, and I'll fix dinner and get Murphy taken care of. Do you need my help up the stairs?"

"No, no, I'll be fine. I'll be down in a bit."

Bella waited at the bottom of the stairs until Eliza waved her off.

Twenty minutes later, Eliza sat in the living room, a TV tray in front of her with a bowl of tomato soup and a grilled cheese sandwich.

"I know it's not a gourmet meal," Bella said apologetically, but this was what you always fixed for me when I wasn't feeling well. Seemed like just the right food for tonight."

Eliza sipped a spoonful. "It's perfect. Thank you for taking such good care of me."

Bella smiled and flipped the switch to the gas fireplace.

"Dad called while you were in the shower and I filled him in about your accident. I told him you were okay and he said for you to rest and he would call in the morning."

"Thank you, honey. I'm sorry I missed Dad's call. I appreciate you doing that for me."

When she finished her supper, Eliza asked Bella to fetch her cell phone.

"I promised your uncle I'd call."

"While you chat, I've got some homework to work on," Bella said. "You going to be okay in here by yourself?"

Eliza shot her daughter a look.

"Okay, okay, just call me if you need something. I'll be in the kitchen. I mean it, Mom, I'm here; let me help."

Eliza smiled and dialed Edmond's number.

"Hey, Edmond, I'm home," she said when he answered the phone.

"Hey, Sis, how is the noggin?"

"A little sore but doing fine. I'm resting. Bella is here, made me dinner and everything."

"You gave us all a scare, you know."

"I know; I'm sorry. I've been meaning to call. I need to tell you something."

Eliza recounted the strange events of the past couple of days, starting with finding the Brown family plot and the crows.

"Cemeteries always creep me out," Edmond said. "But something tells me there's more."

Eliza took a deep breath. "I'm having nightmares, no, not just nightmares; I'm seeing the Wet Lady again. The same one from when I was a child. She's back."

"The Wet Lady? Eliza, I haven't heard you talk about her in years, not since we were kids."

"I know, but I've been seeing her in my dreams, and I saw her this morning, or her reflection at least, in a tide pool while I was walking Murphy. It was almost in the same place where I first saw her that summer when we came to the beach, remember?"

"I do remember," Edmond replied, his voice filled with concern. "I recall how terrified you were that day and all the nights' sleep lost to nightmares and visions of her."

Eliza hesitated for a moment and then changed the tenor of her voice. "Edmond, the Wet Lady is real; she must be. I've seen her several times now. She scares the crap out of me, but I get a sense there is something she wants me to do."

"How is that connected with hitting your head?"

"I told you; I saw her in a tide pool. I got a little freaked out and slipped on the rocks. I hit my head when I fell. But you want to know something bizarre? I think Murphy saw her too. He was barking like crazy."

"Have you spoken to Jason yet today? Does he know about any of this?"

"No, I haven't. You, of all people, know he doesn't give much credence to my...well, my ability to *know* things."

When they were first married, the topic of Eliza's special gift had come up at a family dinner. Jason laughed it off and insisted the stories she shared highlighted nothing more than coincidence. It was Edmond who reminded her that the family had all been a bit skeptical at first, but had seen Eliza prove her ability too many times to doubt it. "He'll come around," he'd told her. "Just be patient with him."

Eliza heard her brother sigh on the other end of the line.

"No, I guess not," he said softly.

"I will tell him, eventually, just not yet."

"I'll trust your judgment, but El, be careful. And please call me if you need anything. It would take some doing, but if you need me, I can be on the road and there in half a day. Long Island isn't that far."

"Thanks, Edmond. I appreciate that. Please don't worry. Bella is taking good care of me, and honestly, the more I think about it, the more I believe Murphy is here for a reason. I can't explain it, but he has an energy about him. He's my protector, and he arrived just when I needed him."

"So, what you're saying is, your big brother has been replaced by a dog."

"Hardly. Well, maybe." Eliza laughed. "Never. Thanks for listening, by the way. And for checking on me."

"You bet. And I'm always here. Rest, and we will talk tomorrow."

As soon as Eliza hung up the phone, Murphy dashed into the room from the kitchen, Bella on his tail.

"He's been fed and been outside. Give me another thirty minutes or so, and we can watch a movie if you're up for it."

"Sounds good."

Bella headed back to the kitchen, and Eliza watched Murphy circle in front of the fire and lie down on what was fast becoming his usual spot.

Despite the pain and grogginess, Eliza was content, happy even. Bella was home, Murphy was here, and she had the makings of an excellent story for *The Gazette*.

"Except for this concussion and that nasty old Wet Lady, things aren't so bad, are they, Murph?"

Murphy let out a half-hearted whine, and Eliza swore he rolled his eyes at her before he put his head down and fell asleep.

8

T HE NEXT MORNING, ELIZA opened the French doors and released Murphy into the dimly lit backyard. He let out a joyful bark and dashed to the closest tree.

"Shhh, Murphy, no barking this morning, okay?"

Murphy looked back at her, his tail wagging, but stayed quiet. He put his nose to the ground and sniffed hard, then followed some unseen trail farther into the yard.

Eliza's head pounded. She pulled her robe closer to her body and returned to the kitchen for her coffee and a couple of extra-strength Tylenol. The time on her cell phone read 6:14 a.m.

The phone buzzed in her hand. Jason.

Eliza took a deep breath, exhaled, and answered.

"Hey, Jason."

"Hey, you. It's good to hear your voice. Did I wake you?"

"No, I woke up early. Came down to let Murphy out."

"How are you feeling? I spoke to Bella last night while you were in the shower. She filled me in about what happened. She said you fell and got a concussion. My God, Eliza, you scared us all. Are you in pain? A head injury is serious stuff."

"Well, I've got a nasty bump on my head, and it's just a mild concussion; nothing too serious."

"Bella didn't seem to think it was nothing. She was pretty freaked out. What exactly happened?"

"Murphy and I decided to walk among the tide pools at low tide. He went one way and I the other. I tripped over him and banged my head on some rocks." Eliza felt bad lying, worse for making Murphy the scapegoat, but she wasn't ready to tell Jason about the Wet Lady. Not yet.

"El, that's twice this dog has been an issue and put your safety at risk. Maybe he's just not the right dog."

"This dog is perfect. And with every passing day, I couldn't be more sure that I made the right decision to bring him home." Eliza retorted.

"El –"

"No, I mean it. I know everyone is upset because I hit my head. But the truth is, I go down to the shore all the time. I could just have easily been alone when I fell. He makes me feel safe."

She waited for a moment and continued, working to ease the aggravation from her voice.

"How about we discuss this more when you get home? After you've met him?"

"Fine," Jason said, his voice tight. "But will you promise to be careful until I do get home?"

"I promise to be as careful as I always am," she said. "Now, how are things there? Is the new office everything you thought it would be?"

Jason sighed. "I wish you could be here. I would love to introduce you to everyone. I am heading over tomorrow morning to see the new office space in person. It's in Staffordshire and exactly the kind of place I know you'd love. Castles, cobblestone streets, old churches," he said, his tone now light.

"Did you say Staffordshire?" Eliza asked, spying her bag on the kitchen table and pulling out her notes from Ginny's.

"Yeah, it's the perfect place. Kent found it. He'd gone to visit some family there and happened to drive by the building on his way. It checks off all our boxes."

Eliza scanned her notes. *Yep, there it is. The Lord family was from Staffordshire.*

"Want to hear a weird coincidence?" she said, opening the door to let Murphy back inside.

"Sure," Jason said tentatively.

"One of the families that came up in my research, the Lord family, traced their origins back to England. More specifically, to Staffordshire. I've got it right here in my notes."

"Must be a sign," Jason teased. "Now you'll have to agree to come with me next time."

"Without a doubt. Could you take some pictures for me when you go to see the office, I mean of Staffordshire?"

"Yeah, not a problem. That is a weird coincidence. I'll have to tell Kent. What was the name of the family? The Lords? Maybe he's heard of them."

"I'll take any information you can find, but don't stress. Focus on setting up the office."

"Speaking of which, I've got to run. More meetings and then a dinner out tonight with Kent and the rest of the office. If it's not too late when we return I'll call you back. Otherwise, tomorrow?"

"I'll be waiting by the phone."

Eliza ended her call and tossed Murphy a treat before turning on the coffee pot. Jason joked that it was a sign, but he wasn't wrong. The connection between his location and the Lord family felt intentional. As if something or someone was trying to make her pay attention.

Bella shuffled into the kitchen. "Morning, Mom," she said with a yawn. "I should have been the one to get Murphy out and make you some breakfast. I can't believe I slept so hard."

"No worries, honey. Grab yourself a mug."

"How are you feeling?"

"Better, I guess. Bit of a headache, but the medication is helping." Eliza hugged Bella. "Do you see the lengths I must go to, to get my girl home?" Eliza winked and poured the coffee.

"After we get dressed, do you want to head over to the bakery? Vanessa said we had some jelly donuts waiting for us."

"Awesome, Mom. Let me get my running clothes on, and maybe I can show Murphy the town, Bella-style."

"Oh, honey. Murphy is a powerhouse, but I'm not sure he's a runner. Maybe start slow. Stay on Main Street and test his stamina."

Bella looked over at Murphy and smiled. "No, pressure, Murph. We will go at your pace."

Bella pulled into an on-street parking spot right in front of the bakery. Eliza climbed out, and Bella opened the rear driver door and clipped Murphy's leash onto his collar.

"You ready, boy?"

Murphy leaped down, his tags swinging back and forth.

"Go inside and catch up with Aunt Vanessa," she said, bending down to re-tie her running shoes. "I'll be back in a bit. Need to stretch my legs a little. I'm gonna see if this big boy can run."

"Just be careful."

Eliza watched as Bella jogged to the corner, Murphy keeping pace at her side. Bella jogged in place as she waited for the traffic light to change.

A pair of teenagers exited the bakery, coffee cups in hand. The scent of coffee and freshly baked goodies wafted out, strong enough to lure her inside.

Vanessa stood behind the counter, pouring a latte with one hand and grabbing a Danish with the other. After handing off the contents to the customer in front of her, she smiled and waved.

"Good morning. How are you feeling?"

"Like I fell and hit my head."

"Ahh, so we're back to our regular snarky self. I'd say that's good news. So, your usual then?"

"A chai and a jelly donut, that's me. Oh, and one for Bella to go, and a Murphy special too. She took him out for a run."

"Got it," Vanessa said and nodded toward the window. "Speaking of running, don't look now, but your arch nemesis is on her way in."

"My what?" Eliza turned and spied Lana, cat-eye glasses, determined expression and all, crossing the busy street like a woman on a mission.

"Oh great. Can't I just hide in the back or something?"

Vanessa snickered and handed Eliza a sheet of parchment paper wrapped around her regular jelly donut. "Oh no, people pay good money for this kind of drama, and I've got a front-row seat."

Groaning, Eliza snatched the donut and went to sit at her regular table. She took out her cell phone and pretended to be deeply intrigued by something on the screen. Maybe if she kept her head down and pretended like she was busy, Lana wouldn't see her.

Out of the corner of her eye, Eliza watched Lana stop briefly to wave to Bella and Murphy as they jogged down the street before making the kind of entrance that only Lana could pull off as she beelined right for her table.

The heavy scent of perfume overpowered the aroma of baked goods and coffee.

"Eliza Grey! Have we been worried about you!"

Eliza cringed but offered Lana a half-hearted smile. "Well, thank you, Lana. I appreciate your concern. It's just a little bump. I'm fine."

"A little bump?" Lana squealed loud enough for the whole bakery to hear.

"Yep, just a little bump."

"If you'd have heard the call come over the police scanner, you'd have thought you died! I'm just glad poor Ginny Burke didn't have a heart attack from all the commotion."

Vanessa cleared her throat and set a chai and a bakery bag on the table in front of Eliza. "I stopped by Ginny's house on my way home last night. She's doing just fine, told me to tell you she's up for more research as soon as you're feeling better," Vanessa said before turning to Lana.

"How about a chocolate croissant or a slice of banana bread?"

Eliza licked her lips to hide a smile. Vanessa really was a good friend. Nothing like distracting the enemy with the promise of carb-heavy baked goods.

"No, thank you," Lana replied and tossed the thick folder in her hand onto the table. "I'm watching my figure. I saw Eliza pull into the bakery and figured I'd be nice and bring this over. These are some of the archived files you wanted me to locate about eerie happenings here in Coventry over the years. It's been sitting on my desk, taking up room. Figured you probably weren't going to stop in, what with your head injury and all."

Eliza resisted the urge to roll her eyes. "I'd have been happy to stop in for it; next time, just send me an email. But thanks, I appreciate it."

"Just a little FYI," Lana said, leaning in closer. "Art is thrilled with the direction you are going with the founding family idea and all and loves that you have chosen the Lords for your first article and the Browns as your focus for the haunted edition. I overheard him talking to the mayor about it. Graham's pretty happy about it, too, seeing as he's a descendant of the Brown family."

The news that the mayor was related to the Browns came as a surprise to Eliza, but she wasn't about to let Lana know that. "Well, so long as the mayor's happy," Eliza said, with just a tinge of sarcasm.

Unaffected, Lana sat down, her hand on the table. "Any chance you could send me a draft so I can share it with him before we go to print?"

"Oh, that's right, I heard you and the mayor were a thing," Vanessa said, breaking into the conversation.

Lana pivoted to focus her full attention on Vanessa. Her eyes narrowed for a split second, then she stood and pushed her glasses up on her nose. "Graham and I are just friends. We enjoy each other's company now and then." She looked around the bakery, glancing from one customer to another as if trying to identify who might have overheard. "The rumor mill in this town is just awful. Everybody worried about everybody else's business."

The woman's lack of self-awareness nearly made Eliza laugh out loud.

"I appreciate all your hard work putting this together for me," Eliza said, tapping the folder. "But the mayor will have to wait to read my story when it comes out in *The Gazette*, just like everybody else."

"As long as you keep it factual and positive. After all, this is an election year for Graham, and he wants to be seen in a favorable light."

Even the slightest inference that she would be anything other than factual irritated Eliza.

"Lana, I spend a great deal of time researching and re-checking my facts. I do not write gossip pieces. My intent with this story is to provide an interesting glimpse at the history of Coventry and the families who live here. I would never do a hit piece on the mayor."

"Heaven's sake. Don't get defensive; I'm just sharing a little friendly advice or advice on the part of a friend, I should say. I've got to get back to work. Take care of our girl; she has a way of finding trouble everywhere she goes," she said to Vanessa and made her way out of the bakery door, the cloud of perfume trailing in her wake.

"Yeah, I can see it now. Arch nemesis totally fits. And I think you're right. She's definitely sleeping with the mayor."

Eliza swatted Vanessa's hand. "If she ever finds out I'm the one that told you that, heaven help me."

They laughed and watched Lana strut back across the street and into *The Gazette*.

"But seriously, how are you feeling today?"

"I feel better, just a bit tender in one spot. Jason called this morning." Eliza took a sip of her chai. "He was rightfully concerned about me, and I did something I'm not proud of. I threw poor Murphy under the bus and told him it was Murphy's fault I fell."

"Was it his fault?" Vanessa asked.

"No, not at all. Murphy is completely innocent. And now Jason is rethinking his agreement to let me keep him."

"Okay, I'm confused. Why would you blame Murphy?"

Eliza looked out the window and spotted her new favorite furry beast strutting by with Bella in a slow jog.

"Remember how I told you about how I used to see things when I was little? How I've had this sixth sense about things?"

"Yeah, of course. Hello," Vanessa said, holding up her left hand and pointing to her wedding ring. "This only happened because you knew Patrick and I were destined for each other."

"Yeah, well, Jason isn't exactly a fan. He thinks anything and everything can either be explained scientifically or chalked up to pure coincidence."

"Okay," Vanessa said, frowning. "But what does all of this have to do with the bump on your head?"

"I've been feeling off lately like I can just tell something's up. The other day, in the cemetery, I found an old family plot, the Brown family. There's this man, Elijah Brown, and his wife and kids, but then I discovered this other grave. Honor Brown, his first wife. She's buried outside the cemetery wall, and then I found out there's a possibility that she was murdered by her husband, but it was made to look like a suicide. On my property, nonetheless. This man who potentially, probably, murdered his wife built my house. Can you believe it?"

Vanessa let out a low whistle. "Wow. I had no idea Coventry had such a shady past."

"I know," Eliza said and continued. "Something in my gut is telling me there is more to this story. I've been having these dreams, visions really, of a woman I think might be Honor Brown. And then there's the Wet Lady."

Vanessa shook her head. "Wait, who's the Wet Lady?"

"It's this woman, this terrifying, scary woman who haunted me as a child. She's the reason I fell at the beach. I saw her reflection in a tide pool, and it scared me. I lost my footing, and you know the rest."

"The rest where you end up in the hospital and throw an innocent dog under the bus? Remind me to never get on your bad side."

Eliza shot her a look. "I think Honor might have some unresolved business, and she's reaching out to me for help. She's connected to the Wet Lady, I think; I'm just not sure how."

"What are you going to do about it?" Vanessa asked.

"I'm not sure. I guess I'll keep researching and see what else I can find."

Bella tapped on the window and waved, then pointed at Murphy and gave the thumbs up before opening the back passenger door of their SUV.

Murphy jumped inside.

"I should get going. I promised Bella I'd take it easy today. I'm running her back up to school in the morning. Thanks for the chai and the donuts." She stood and picked up her cup and the bag. "Let me settle up with you."

"Oh, no, it's on the house. After the scare all of you had, you deserve a little something sweet."

Eliza wrapped her arms around Vanessa and squeezed.

"You know you're the best, right?"

"How was your run?" Eliza asked her daughter as she climbed into the passenger's seat.

"Great. He's so good on a leash. And he knows all the places to stop for treats. He's a regular celebrity on Main Street."

Eliza turned to look in the back seat. "He's a celebrity, all right, gets free donuts and everything."

She reached into the bag, pulled out the donut Vanessa had included for Murphy, and offered it to him.

Per usual, he swallowed it in a single gulp.

"Vanessa put one in here for you, too," Eliza added, handing Bella the bag.

"Yum, these are my favorite."

"Mind if we make a quick stop at the library before we head home? I need to look up a few more resources on the Brown family for this article. I'll just be a few minutes."

"Yeah, sure. Consider me your chauffeur for the day."

A few minutes later, they pulled into the library parking lot.

Eliza made her way up the sidewalk to the front door. The fall air was cool but not unpleasantly so. Tall trees, their leaves nearly completely turned, made a spectacular backdrop for the modern, glass-front building that housed the county library.

Eliza waved as she passed the front desk. Lily Campbell, the librarian for the past ten years, waved back.

She descended the stairs toward the resource room and knew exactly where to find her materials in the archive section. There she'd find what she was looking for: books on the town's history and origins.

She made a quick scan and selected several books, including one that detailed five prominent families that contributed to the success of Coventry-by-the-Sea from the mid-1700s to the late 1800s. Written in the early 1940s by town historian Edwin Lynd, Ginny's predecessor, the book featured many first-hand accounts of town events along with pictures and personal documentation.

Eliza flipped through the musty pages and stopped when she found an image of a hand-drawn family tree. In the first few pages, she recognized the names of Honor, Elijah, and Levi Brown, as well as his second wife and two daughters. As she had seen in Highgate, all of his children had passed in childhood, except there was also an annotation of a surviving son, David Abbott, though there was no mention of the boy's mother.

"Interesting. Why would he have a different last name?" Eliza mumbled to herself.

Eliza turned a page to follow the descendants of David Abbott. Near the bottom, another familiar name, Winthrop, caught her attention.

"This must be the connection to the mayor."

Several pages later, Honor's name jumped out at her.

SALEM GAZETTE
OCTOBER 12, 1808

Tragedy at Rosecliff Manor in Coventry-by-the-Sea. The prominent family of Elijah S. Brown, shipping and trade mogul of the Lord Shipyard, suffered a terrible tragedy. In the early morning of October 1, Levi Brown, age eight, the only child of Elijah and Honor Brown, succumbed to pneumonia. His wife, Honor Temperance Brown, daughter of the shipping magnate Ashley Lord, took her own life hours later. It is said that Mrs. Brown, overcome with grief, threw herself from the cliff of their home, Rosecliff Manor. Members of the Lord family are questioning the manner of Ms. Brown's death. One member alleges foul play. At present, there is no evidence to support those allegations. Elijah Brown has requested his need for privacy as he grieves for his family.

"Holy cow! Honor's death made the Salem paper! And it appears there wasn't a love fest between Elijah and the Lords."

Flipping the page, she found a copy of the Coroner's Court findings.

Honor Temperance Brown's cause of death was a broken neck. It was determined to be self-inflicted. Signed this day, 20th October 1808. James McMann, Coroner, Sussex County.

"Well, that coroner's statement put to bed any questions of foul play or investigations into her death."

She climbed the stairs to the research desk and set the small stack of books in front of Lily Campbell.

"Lily, I know you don't usually let folks check out books from the archive section, but I'm working on a series for *The Gazette* about the town's founding families. Any chance I could borrow these for a few days if I promise to be extra careful?"

"Throw in a promise to convince Art to make the library's donation drive ad a full page in the spring, and I might see a way to let you 'borrow' these."

Eliza didn't know what to say. She hesitated, then said, "I mean, I can try. You know Art, he's kind of a stickler when it comes to layout."

Lily smirked, then laughed. "Eliza, I'm kidding. Given this is our 250th Town Jubilee and how impressed I was with your last article, I think I can trust you to borrow these for...two weeks. Will that be enough time?"

Eliza smiled. "More than enough time, thank you. And I'll see what I can do about that ad."

Eliza exited the building and headed for the car with a spring in her step.

"Did you find what you needed?" Bella asked as Eliza climbed back in the car.

"Did I ever."

9

THE LUMP ON HER head had reduced significantly, and after a restful night's sleep, Eliza felt almost as good as new. It had taken a bit of convincing on her part to assure Bella she was fine. Eliza had been happy to have her home, but she knew it put undue stress on her daughter. Bella finally agreed and after breakfast the two headed back to Salve Regina.

"I promise, if anything changes or anything else happens, I'll call," she'd said, hugging Bella before watching her walk to the front door of her dorm.

As the stony grey clouds played peek-a-boo with the sun on the drive back from Salve Regina, Eliza felt a renewed sense of vigor. The crisp September air enlivened her senses and she heeded its call. She needed to be outside with Murphy.

She pulled into the driveway and hurried inside to grab Murphy's leash.

"Feel like a walk to Highgate?" she asked.

Murphy pranced and ran back towards the front door with a look of pure excitement.

As she opened the door, he released a mighty snort and trotted briskly down the stairs.

"Just need to grab some shears first," she said, leading him to the side yard and her potting shed. She needed pictures of the gravestones for her article but didn't relish the idea of making her way through the overgrown prickers again.

She found a pair of gardening gloves and the small pruning shears and put them in her coat pocket.

"Off we go!"

Several car horns beeped and drivers waved as they approached the main road. Eliza smiled. Murphy brought an element to her life she never knew she was missing.

"We're like Holmes and Watson, Cagney and Lacey, Murph. Jason will see that, I promise."

They reached the steep road leading to the graveyard's back entrance. The gate lay open, and they made their way through. Once inside, Murphy looked up at her and took his leash in his mouth.

"Oh no, buddy, we are not repeating that mistake. You're staying on leash and right by my side."

Murphy let go of the strap and pulled her along at a quicker pace.

"How is it you know where I want to go?"

He barked, and she shook her head, allowing him to lead the way.

Eliza spotted the stone cemetery fence and the overgrown iron gate that marked the entrance to the Brown family plot.

Pulling out her gardening gloves and shears from her coat pocket, Eliza carefully pulled back the brush, clipping just enough to open a small pathway through the entrance. "A little elbow grease, and we'll have a clear passage with no more thorns and scratches," she said, placing Murphy's leash on the ground.

Less than twenty minutes later, and with a sizable pile of severed underbrush, she'd completed her task of clearing the opening.

Eliza quickly stepped into the obscure little burial plot with Murphy by her side. The gnarled oak tree shaded the area, its roots large and woody upon the surface of barren dirt. High above, hidden by the branches, she could hear a crow cawing.

Eliza carefully stepped over the rutted ground until she reached the headstone of Levi Brown. She reread the epitaph and ran her hand along the edge of the weathered stone before stepping back to take a photo with her phone.

Murphy sat next to the boy's headstone.

Eliza snapped another picture, this time with Murphy.

She crawled over the other side of the cemetery wall to where Honor's grave remained hidden among the brush. She snipped several vines and branches, then knelt and began to brush the lichen and moss away with gloved hands. Finally, she stopped and read the words etched into the tombstone, running her fingers along the grooves.

She snapped multiple pictures at different angles, trying to capture the words on the epitaph. It was severely damaged, and the letters difficult to read in her photos.

"I'll have to come back and do a rubbing," she said, half to Murphy but mostly to herself.

A gust of icy wind sent dust and bits of dried leaves swirling around the thicket and undergrowth. Murphy barked, then took a defensive posture, growling and staring into the oak tree above Levi's grave.

She turned to follow his line of sight. A wave of vertigo brought her to her knees. She put her hands on the wall, trying to still the growing sense of nausea.

Murphy continued to growl.

Several crows landed on the lower branches of the oak tree. Their incessant cawing growing louder and louder.

The world around her began to spin. A sense of doom and anguish filled her entire being. And grief, overwhelming grief. Tears welled in her eyes.

What is happening to me?

"Mur...Mur..." She tried calling Murphy, but the words stuck in her throat.

I've got to get out of here.

Eliza pulled herself over the stone wall and sat on the ground, her heart pounding in her chest. Another wave of nausea traveled like a ripple through her abdomen, causing her to gag.

Murphy charged at the tree, jumping up and snarling at the crows.

"Hey now," came a voice from outside the family plot.

In an instant, the crows quieted and took to wing. Murphy stopped barking and cocked his head, then bounded toward the gate.

A few moments later, a face in a familiar Stetson hat appeared under the wrought iron archway.

Eliza had never been so happy to see Marty Evans.

"Miss Eliza, you okay?" Marty squatting down beside her, his face was awash with concern.

Eliza took a deep breath. The worst of the nausea had dissipated.

Marty offered her a hand.

The gesture surprised her, but she accepted his help. His callous palm rough but warm.

"No, I just had a little mishap climbing over the wall." She cleared her throat and smiled. "Seems I've become a bit of a klutz lately."

"You sure? I can call someone. I heard about your fall from Mrs. Burke. She was here yesterday visiting her husband, told me what happened. Best to not be taking any chances when it comes to head injuries."

"No, I'm fine. My foot caught on some of the underbrush," she lied. "I came to snap a picture of Honor and Levi Brown's headstones for my article." She opened the screen and turned her phone to show him. "Honor's is pretty damaged though; I'll have to come back and do a rubbing if that's okay?"

Marty smiled and pushed his hat back slightly. "Yeah, I'd say that's okay." He turned and looked back at the narrow path she'd cleared. "You know, Miss Eliza, if you are considering visiting here often, I could clean this spot up for your story. Make it neater and easier to access. Unless you're looking for a job and want to tackle the rest of this yourself? I can always use the help." Eliza felt a pang of pity for the man. Sure, he was a bit strange, weird even, but he had to be lonely.

"I think this kind of thing is best left to the professionals," she said. "But if you have the time to make this a bit more passable, I'd appreciate it."

Marty gave her a toothy smile. "Give me a couple of days, and you won't even recognize the place. It would be nice to have this old plot return to a respectable site, especially since they are a part of my extended family, after all."

"Your family?" Eliza asked.

He adjusted his hat and sank his hands into his pockets. "I can trace my lineage back to Samuel Brown, Elijah's brother."

"Marty, that's incredible. Now you have to let me interview you again; I mean if you're willing to share more about your family. I'm writing two articles for *The Gazette*, one about Honor's family, the Lords, and another about the Browns."

She smiled brightly at him. "The roots of this town are long and tangled. Did you happen to know that Elijah built Rosecliff, the house I live in, for Honor?"

Marty nodded somberly. "Yes, and that's where she died."

Eliza's smile faltered. "Yes, so I've just learned."

Wonder what else he knows that he's not telling me.

"I should get going," she said, brightening. "But thank you for your help."

He guided the way back through the gate and onto the pebbled path that led to the back part of the cemetery.

"You know, there's no shame in coming by and talking to them. They are all lonely. I talk to them sometimes too. Nothing wrong with it. Nothing at all."

"I'm sorry, talk to who?" Eliza asked, worried and feigning confusion.

Marty turned and looked at her directly.

"Sometimes spirits reach out and want you to help them. It's no coincidence that this place called you. That you live at Rosecliff. We," he pointed back and forth between them, "we're special."

"Marty, I told you, I came here to do some research for my article." She held up her phone. "Pictures, remember? Gonna come back and do a rubbing? This is research. That's all."

"You can't hide your gift from others who have a similar inclination. You've got it, I've got it, and I suspect Murphy is special too. He sees things most people can't and protects you from the unseen."

Eliza bit her lip, her mind racing. He *knew*. He understood what had compelled her to come back to this plot and that despite her deadline, the founding father story somehow didn't seem to matter as much as finding out the truth of what had happened to this woman.

"Just a word of advice," he said. "Best be careful. Once we open certain doors, we can't close them."

She was just about to insist that everyone needed to stop telling her to be careful when her phone rang. She pulled it from her pocket. It was Bella.

My darling daughter, your timing is impeccable.

"Excuse me, Marty; I have to take this call," she said, hoping he couldn't sense the mix of frustration and relief in her voice.

"Take care," he said and waved, then turned and walked in the opposite direction, whistling to himself.

Eliza took Murphy's leash and led him back to the rear entrance of the cemetery as she answered her phone.

"Hey, my girl. What's up?"

"Hi, Mom! You okay? You sound out of breath."

"I'm fine, just out on a walk with Murphy."

"So, you're still feeling okay?"

"No different than this morning. Practically perfect. No pain today at all."

"Good, that's good," Bella said, her voice deflated.

"Hey, what's wrong? You sound upset."

"Nothing, nothing really. I'm just homesick. Getting to come home and take care of you the past couple of days made me realize how much I miss being at home. Plus, I know I just met him, but I already miss Murphy."

"Oh, honey, I get that. I've been missing you too, and with your dad gone, I'm in that big house all alone."

"When is Dad coming home?"

"Hopefully soon. He believes he will be able to finish up earlier than he thought, plus, I think this whole head injury thing spooked him a bit."

"If it's okay with you, after Dad gets back, I could come home again. Have a family weekend?"

"You know, I made that same suggestion the last time your dad and I spoke."

"Okay, then it's a date. Give Murphy a hug for me, and take care of yourself, okay, Mom?"

"I promise. Love you."

"Love you too."

On the way home, Eliza slowed their pace, loosened the leash, and let Murphy sniff what was likely every tree between town and home. Though the nausea was gone, there was a heaviness in Eliza's gut that lingered. The sun shone brightly above the horizon as they made their way home to Rosecliff. The farther she got away from Highgate, the better she felt. When they reached the path down to the small beach cove at the edge of Rosecliff property, Eliza knelt and looked Murphy in the eyes. "If I let you off for a bit, do you promise to behave and not disappear?"

Murphy's tail wagged.

"And come back immediately when I call you?"

He pressed down on his front paws, rear end in the air, then jumped and pranced around. Eliza laughed at his obvious anticipation and released him from his leash. He barked and took off in a blur towards a flock of seagulls hunkered in the sand.

She smiled as she watched Murphy romp about on the shore chasing invisible prey.

Eliza couldn't help but think of Honor. This view must have been the same one Honor had seen every day of her married life.

Maybe she stood on this rocky sand in the same spot I now stand. There is more to Honor's story, but what?

She whistled for Murphy. He came running at full speed, passing her to race up the rocky slope, across the lawn and up the porch steps.

A white cloth tote bag rested on one of her porch rocking chairs. Next to the chair on the wicker side table was a plate of mini blueberry muffins covered in plastic wrap and a tiny jar of raspberry jam, an envelope neatly placed beside it.

"What do we have here, Murphy?"

Murphy was quick to investigate the muffins.

"Oh, no, you don't!" Eliza chuckled as she whisked the plate away.

She opened the front door and ushered Murphy in, returning to grab the bag, jelly, and note.

"I have a feeling I know who paid us a surprise visit!"

Eliza placed her goodies on the dining room table and peeked inside the tote. A large rectangular item, wrapped in a protective cotton cloth, lay inside.

She quickly opened the envelope and retrieved a beautiful ivory note card with a gold monogram letter B on the front.

Eliza,

I thought you might like to read through my family Bible and the Lord/Brown history at your leisure. I added a few little treats to add to your enjoyment! Take your time with your research.

Ginny

"No way!" Eliza pulled the heavy book from the bag and carefully unwrapped it. The gilded edges of Ginny's family Bible, the same one she'd read from on their last visit, glistened in the late afternoon light like a chest of gold.

Eliza smiled, grabbed her cell, scrolled for Ginny Burke's number, and hit "call."

After several rings, it went to voicemail.

"Hi, Ginny. It's Eliza. Sorry I missed you. Thanks for loaning me the Bible and for the yummy treats. I can't wait to dig into both. I'll be in touch." Eliza ended the call and turned to Murphy.

"Well, Murph, looks like Christmas came early!"

Even after dinner and a hot cup of tea, the chill of the day still ached in Eliza's bones.

"Come on, boy. Let's head upstairs." As she passed through the dining room, she retrieved Ginny's Bible. "I need a hot shower, a comfy robe, and some reading time."

Murphy hefted his tired body with a moan and followed Eliza reluctantly up the stairs.

Sitting on the edge of the bed, she placed the book beside her and gently opened it. An overwhelming sense of its historical significance made her breath catch in her chest as she trailed her fingers over the inside cover. Feeling the pages as they fluttered in her hand was like opening a portal to the past with its colorful embellished drawings, gold-rimmed pages, and beautiful flourished handwriting.

"I can't wait to really delve in and see what treasures I can unearth. What do you think we'll find, Murph?" She glanced toward the fireplace. He had all but collapsed into his bed. She watched the slight rise and fall of his body deep in sleep and smiled. It had been great to have Bella home, and in her absence, Murphy was a good, if not more slobbery, prone-to-snoring substitute.

She closed Ginny's Bible and pushed it away from the edge of the bed. Through the window, the inky blues and purples of the night sky swirled with clouds. She caught a glimpse of a waning moon as she moved closer to the window, its bright light reflected in the white caps far out at sea. Once again, she thought of Honor. Had she stood in this same window staring out across the ocean? Had she been happy here?

Eliza rubbed her arms, then drew the drapes closed. She flipped the switch, igniting the fireplace, and headed to the bathroom and the promise of a hot shower.

Disrobing, she drew the shower curtain back and turned both porcelain knobs, feeling for the perfect temperature. She waited for a healthy cloud of steam to rise up before entering into the pulsing spray.

As she stepped into the tub, her skin prickled, and an overwhelming sense of *knowing* washed over her, turning her stomach, but she pushed it away. It had been a long day, and right now, all she wanted was some quiet. Closing her eyes, she let the heat and gentle pressure of the shower penetrate and relax her mind.

A sharp pain ripped through her side, and this time there was no denying the power rushing through her. In her mind's eye, shadows dipped and rose, coalescing into a darkened landscape. A voice, anguished and wailing, filled her ears. A woman stood on unsteady legs near the edge of the cliff, looking out towards a great rock half-buried within the ocean's depths. The waves roared against the side of the cliff, crashing full force against the stone in a frothy swirl before retreating, only to strike again and again in a never-ending battle. The wind howled as it lashed at the craggy shoreline. The woman's beautiful long dark hair whipped around her in the wind. A white nightdress clung tight to her body, pressed against her curves by the unrelenting sea breeze. A piercing, grief-stricken scream broke through the darkness of her vision.

Another shadow took shape, this time a man, his face shrouded in darkness. He stormed toward the cliff, his enormous bloody hands reaching out for the woman, grabbing her. He jerked her slight frame, her strength no match for his as she struggled to pull away from him.

Eliza reached out to steady herself, bending over to grab the edges of the tub, her body rigid and tight. She could feel the man's grip on her arms, her voice strangling in her throat. A scream sat just behind her lips, her heart galloping in her chest.

All at once, the vision grew softer, the sound of the waves ebbing away.

Eliza gasped for breath. She stood up straight and turned her face to the warm stream of water. The image had been so clear. Like she had been standing beside the woman at the cliff's edge. No, like she had *been* that woman. She'd felt the woman's fear, her agony. Even now, the echo of pain throbbed in her arms where the man had grabbed her.

She forced herself to fill her lungs, taking long, slow, deep breaths. The water cascaded over her body and with it, relief from the fear. She let her shoulders sag and dropped her head back.

A cold flutter kissed her neck, and her body grew rigid once again.

"Eliza..."

She snatched the shower curtain open and peered through the steam that enveloped the room.

"Who's there?"

Through the mist, a set of vacant eyes appeared in the vanity mirror. She blinked hard, her body shaking as she stepped out of the tub to wipe the mirror, to then find nothing but her own reflection.

Out of the corner of her eye, a dark form walked in front of the firelight and moved toward her bed.

Any residual heat from the shower evaporated as gooseflesh covered her entire body. She reached for a towel from the rack and wrapped it around her as she crept toward the bedroom.

It took a moment for her eyes to adjust to the dim light, her body tense, ready to fight or flee. Murphy stood in the corner of the room, hackles raised, growling. Ginny's Bible sat precariously close to the edge of the bed, and though she'd carefully and intentionally closed it, it now sat open to the back cover.

She forced herself to slowly scan the room. But other than Murphy and her furniture, the room was empty. The shadow she had seen – and she had seen it, hadn't she – was gone.

Or maybe I really am losing my mind?

As she entered the room, a shimmer of light near the floor caught her attention. She moved to catch the dancing firelight just right.

A trail of wet human footprints circled around her bed.

Eliza tried to rationalize what she was seeing. She hadn't left the bathroom, so whose footprints were these?

She flicked on the bedroom's overhead light and inched toward the bed. Slowly, she bent to touch the watery trail. Their dampness was icy cold against her fingertips.

"I don't understand. Who are you? What do you want from me?" she said aloud.

No response followed, not that she'd really expected one.

Murphy moved to her side and sniffed at the footprints, growling low in his throat for a moment, then he nudged her hand with his nose and licked her palm.

At the same moment, the room felt lighter, brighter, even.

She scratched his head and sat at the end of the bed, willing the churning in her gut to ease. With shaking hands, she pulled Ginny's Bible toward her. At first glance, the book appeared intact and no worse for wear. As she lifted the heavy bible onto her lap, she noticed a slight elevation in the decorative paper lining the back cover. She ran her fingers along the seam, leaning down to examine it more closely. Yes, there was something underneath. Gently, she lifted the corner of the interior lining and pinched the sheet of yellowed paper hidden beneath. With a gentle tug, it pulled free.

Carefully, she unfolded the sheet to find a small journal page with a slightly torn edge. The delicate handwriting faded with time. She turned on a bedside lamp and held the page in the light.

October 10, 1808

My most beloved husband, Niles, is beside himself with grief over the loss of his dear sister, Honor. Although I have tried with great zeal to ease his broken heart over the deaths of Honor and our nephew, Levi, it is to no avail. He cannot accept that his sister would take her own life and leave her soul to damnation. He swiftly changes from deep sadness to terrible anger at this situation. Niles shared with me that he believes that his sister did not kill herself and that he suspects it is the work of Elijah. I have begged him not to utter such words aloud, but he is full of rage.

Mary and Ashley Lord are inconsolable. Mary shared with me in private that she, too, feels that Honor suffered at the hands of Elijah's terrible anger. I cannot help but bear some form of guilt for my dear sister-in-law as she confided in me often of her fear of Elijah and what he may do. I pray that the Lord our God will aid us with our grief.

Eliza stared hard at the paper. What would cause them to believe Honor may have been murdered at the hands of her husband? Everything she'd been told and read clearly noted that the devastated, grief-stricken woman had taken her own life.

A familiar feeling made Eliza's stomach tighten. Running her finger along the sentence describing Elijah's terrible anger, she nodded.

Honor hadn't taken her own life. That she *knew*.

"Is this the truth you want me to find? But how?" she asked aloud. Once again, there was no response.

Eliza carefully refolded the letter. Honor Brown lived and died on her property more than two hundred years ago. How on earth would she ever prove that the circumstances of her death were different from what history had recorded?

She glanced over at Murphy. "Any ideas?"

Murphy sneezed.

"I'll take that as a no."

10

ELIZA WIPED HER KNIFE clean and dumped the celery and onions she'd chopped into the roasting pan. True to his word, Jason had finished his business trip early and was at that moment somewhere over the Atlantic. In just over six hours, he'd be home.

She rinsed and dried several potatoes and sliced them as she contemplated the next steps for her article. Once she'd begun to dig deeper into the Lord and Brown family history, she'd been further convinced that there was more to the story. But, wanting to remain good on her promise to both Jason and Bella, she'd taken it easy and spent most of her time over the last week close to home. She'd taken Murphy down to the beach every day, staying clear of the tide pools and any further mishaps. She'd even done her best to examine the pantry and found nothing amiss. A fact that was both reassuring and unsettling.

The photos she'd taken of headstones on her last outing to Highgate would be sufficient for the paper, but she wanted to include a transcription of each, and Honor's was nearly impossible to read. She added the sliced potatoes to the pan and checked her watch. She had just enough time to dash to Highgate for the rubbing she needed, get cleaned up, and put dinner in the oven.

She pulled a trimmed pot roast from the refrigerator and settled it on top of her vegetables, and seasoned the meat liberally with salt, pepper, garlic, and thyme before adding beef stock and a generous pour of red wine to the pan.

She put the entire roasting dish into the refrigerator, washed her hands, and hurried to the foyer to put on a jacket.

Murphy sat by the front door, looking back and forth between her and his leash.

"Sorry, Murph," she said, pulling on a hat and grabbing her keys.

"I have to be quick. You'll hardly even know I was gone."

He whined and laid down.

"Don't forget, best behavior tonight. Jason will be here, and he's going to love you."

He has to love you.

Murphy rolled over.

Eliza eyed him. Dramatic and a bit snarky. How could anyone question that he was her dog?

Ten minutes later, she'd parked near the rear entrance to Highgate and made her way to the Brown family plot with a roll of paper and a small pack of charcoal in her pocket. She expected to see the familiar overgrown mess of bramble and weeds but instead found the area neat and manicured.

The stone cemetery fence stood out, prominent, revealing its beautiful workmanship. The wild shrubbery and scrub pines had been cut back and pruned. Eliza paused to take it all in. With just a simple clean up, the spot had transformed entirely. The ornate artistry of the intricately designed wrought iron archway, with its large scrollwork B, provided an austere entrance to the once dilapidated family burial ground.

"Well done, Marty. And so fast!" she said aloud, amazed at the transformation.

"It cleaned up rather good, didn't it?" a voice behind her asked.

Eliza turned to find Marty standing behind her, smiling.

"Morning, Miss Eliza. I just got back from the hardware store and saw your car; thought I'd come by and see what you thought of the plot."

"Very nice. Thank you for getting to it so quickly."

"My pleasure," he said. "I tried not to make it look too kept for fear it would ruin the pictures for your piece."

"Thank you, Marty. I appreciate that. I just stopped by to get that rubbing I mentioned when I was here last."

Marty nodded. "I figured as much." He moved forward and opened the gate to let her into the family plot.

"Miss Eliza, I hope you don't mind me saying this, but I'm glad you found this place and made me clean it up. People in this town, they don't appreciate what's here." He held his arms wide to indicate the expanse of Highgate around them.

"Well, at least not until someone they love passes. I know plenty of people in town think I'm odd, that a cemetery is a strange place to make a living." He glanced at her. "I really don't blame them. I keep to myself and don't really go out of my way to change what they think, but it is nice to have someone who sees this place in a good light anyway."

Eliza smiled softly. She recognized his loneliness and, for her own assumptions about the man, felt more than a little ashamed. He wasn't a great conversationalist, but his work spoke for itself. She could see how much this place meant to him with each carefully trimmed hedge and every inch of the well-manicured lawns.

"I hope you don't mind *me* saying that I appreciate you and your work here. You keep the grounds impeccable, and your respect for those who rest here is admirable. We should all be lucky enough to have a place as beautiful and well-cared for as this when our time comes to be laid to rest."

Marty beamed. She liked how his eyes creased in the corners when his face softened.

Eliza thought back to the article she'd written last year about the cemetery and the three generations of caretakers. "I am sure your father and your grandfather would be very proud of the work you continue to do here."

"Yeah, I suppose they would, though Grandpa Brown never had to worry about all the fancy lawn care. But my dad, Lucien Evans, had a vision, and I'd like to think I'm honoring him by taking care of this place. He wasn't a Brown, of course, but after he married my mother, my grandfather took him under his wing, taught him what he needed to know to take care of Highgate. He was meticulous, knew every acre of this place, every tree, every bush." Marty glanced over at stones marking the Brown family's final resting place. "But he always had a real aversion to this plot here. He rarely would say a good word about any member of that part of the family. It wasn't until I grew older that I understood why."

As they approached the cemetery wall, Eliza was surprised to find all of the underbrush around Honor's grave had been cleared allowing easy access to her headstone.

Eliza climbed over the wall with Marty following close behind. Kneeling beside Honor's grave, Eliza placed a sheet of paper against the marker. Marty held the top edges of the paper against the slate as she rubbed the charcoal over the surface until the image grew dark enough to read.

"Marty, do you have records of the individuals in the Lord and Brown burial plots? Maybe original documents that I could look through some time?"

"I'm sure we do. I have some boxes of records from that period in the main office dating back a hundred years or more."

"Would you mind if I came by at the end of the week and glanced over them?"

"Um, sure. What with the weather getting colder, I don't have as much work to do. Wanna say tomorrow morning? I'll dig out what I can find and…" His voice trailed off, and he looked at her, his eyes narrowing as if trying to decide what to say.

"And?" Eliza prompted.

Marty hesitated, but finally said, "And I'll find what I can, but I don't think the answers you're looking for will be there. Better to just sit by their graves and listen. You can learn a lot that way. They usually tell you what they want you to know."

Eliza swallowed hard and gave an uncomfortable nod.

She stood, brushing the dirt from her knees, and carefully held onto the rubbing in her right hand. Marty rose and climbed back over the wall. He turned and offered his hand and gently pulled Eliza over.

"I've got some fertilizer to unload," he said. "You okay here by yourself?"

Eliza forced a smile. "Of course. Not much to trip over now. I just want to do a couple more rubbings, then I have to hurry home. Jason's back from England tonight."

"All right, I'll leave you to it." He took several steps then turned back. "Hey Miss Eliza, make sure you close the gate behind you so nothing follows you home."

"Okay, got it, close the gate." She was thankful for the long sleeves of her jacket so he couldn't see the goosebumps crawling up her arms.

She waited until she couldn't hear his footsteps on the graveled path, then proceeded to take a rubbing of Elijah's and his second wife's gravestones. Once that task was completed she turned her attention to Levi's grave. She carefully avoided the tree roots, knelt over Levi's resting place, caressing the coldness of the slate, letting her fingers drift over the clumps of moss and lichen that covered much of the old lettering. A deep and penetrating sadness grew heavy in her chest, along with a yearning to know about this little boy. She'd caught a glimpse of his form and sweet face in her dreams.

Before leaving, she turned to gaze upon Honor's grave and thought about Marty's words.

They usually tell you what they want you to know.

Her heart ached for Honor and what she must have endured in losing her only child.

"I give you permission, Honor Brown, to visit me and tell me your secrets," Eliza whispered.

The rest of the afternoon passed in a flash, and the late day sun soon sank behind the sherbet-colored horizon. After a hot shower, a heated self-debate over what to wear, half an hour brushing Murphy's coat, and dinner prep, she'd barely poured the wine when she heard the *beep-beep* of a vehicle in the driveway.

She'd missed Jason terribly. The original plan for three full weeks in England had, in actuality, been seventeen days, with Jason finishing his work earlier than expected. So much had happened since they'd said goodbye.

Murphy lay on the kitchen floor in front of the French doors, fluffy and magnificent. Would Jason fall in love with him as she had? Would he believe her when she told him why it was so important to keep him? Did she dare tell him about the Wet Lady and the visions she's had about Honor Brown? When and if to tell him any of it or all of it would remain to be seen.

Just take it one minute at a time.

She ducked into the half bath to check her appearance one last time in the mirror. After trying on several options, she'd decided to pair comfort with a little sex appeal. Her mother had instilled in her the old adage that the way to a man's heart was through his stomach, but some confidence and a little skin didn't hurt either. A pair of tight-fitting jeans hugged her curves perfectly, and a maroon cashmere sweater revealed a bare shoulder. Her long auburn curls lay loose around her head.

Nothing like beef, potatoes, and perfume to butter a man up before you try to convince him you're not crazy.

She darted back to the kitchen to pull the pot roast from the oven and light the candles.

The front door opened, and she heard the soft plops of luggage being placed on the floor.

"I'm home," Jason announced from the foyer.

Before Eliza could react, Murphy raced through the kitchen.

"Whoa! Slow down! Who released the hound?" Jason exclaimed.

In the foyer, Murphy danced around him, stopping to sniff him, then licking his hand until Jason knelt and gave him a hearty scratch.

Eliza leaned seductively in the kitchen doorway and smiled.

"Welcome home, Mr. Grey."

Jason smiled and moved to her side.

She melted against him. The scent of his cologne and the warmth of his skin dissolved any remaining nerves.

"God, I missed you," he said, nuzzling her neck before pressing into her, kissing her hard on the lips.

"It's so good to have you home," she said. "How was the flight?"

"Long, but I'm glad it was on time. I checked the weather before I left. There's a line of storms moving through tonight. If I had missed my connection, I might not have made it home until sometime tomorrow."

Murphy huffed and moved closer to Jason. He raised his paw and placed it against Jason's leg.

Jason looked down at him.

"Someone wants a formal introduction," Eliza said, smiling.

Jason bent to rub Murphy's giant head.

"Well, hello there, Murphy. I have heard a lot about you. You are so much bigger than I anticipated." He looked up at Eliza. "I guess it's a good thing we have a big house."

"So, does that mean I can keep him?" She batted her eyelashes at him.

Jason laughed. "Sweetheart," he said, pulling her back into his arms.

"Yes, darling?"

"I'm starving, and something smells amazing. Feed me, and you can have anything you want."

Perfume down, beef and potatoes up next.

"Well then, Mr. Grey, let's get you fed. You've got a long night ahead of you."

She took a step toward the kitchen, then offered him a coy smile over her shoulder.

Together, the two caught up on Bella, England, and Murphy's full and complete adoption story.

After dinner, they held hands and settled on the couch by the fire in the living room. Jason stretched his legs out in front of him.

"I'll need to go back for the grand opening of the office in about two weeks. I'd really like you to be there with me. It won't be long, I promise, maybe five days—a week, tops."

Eliza's heart sank, and she looked at Murphy. She hated to leave him, and there was still work to be done on her article for *The Gazette*. But she'd promised him she'd go.

Eliza smiled. "Of course. I'll call the vet's office and get their help making arrangements for Murphy while we're gone. I would like to see Staffordshire with my own eyes."

"Speaking of which—" Jason took out his phone—"here are the photos I promised."

Eliza took his phone and swiped through several images of a quaint English town. There were others of wide-open pastures and tall, aged trees.

"How's the article coming?"

"It's going well. Come, let me show you what I've got so far."

She pulled him to his feet and led him back into the dining room, where she'd left her notes and the recent rubbings.

Eliza spread out the rubbings on the table in front of Jason. She watched as he read the epitaphs.

"Elijah Brown, based on my research, really didn't have a happy life. His entire family perished before him. And this woman," she pointed at the rubbing of Honor's gravestone. "She was his first wife. Her death was recorded as a suicide, but I'm beginning to think that might not be the case." She showed him Ginny's family Bible and the letter she'd found. "By all accounts, Elijah had a temper, and Honor was afraid of him."

"And you think he had something to do with her death?" Jason asked.

"My gut is screaming that he did. I think there may have been foul play. I feel like something terrible happened to Honor, but her death was made to look like suicide."

"That's pretty heavy. But this happened over 200 years ago. It's going to be almost impossible to prove."

"I know, but I want to try. Honor is buried outside Highgate Cemetery for a reason. Suicide was seen as a mortal sin back then. It breaks my heart to even think about it. What if instead of killing herself, it turned out to be murder? It would change everything, wouldn't it?"

"I suppose it would."

"Oh, and I forgot to tell you. She lived here. They both did. Elijah built this house for her when they got married."

Jason gave her a curious look. "You're kidding?"

"Nope, I was just as surprised as you are. There was a passage in Ginny's book, and then Marty confirmed it."

"Marty?" Jason asked, his tone sounded irritated.

Eliza brushed off his concern. "He's a good soul. An odd duck, sure, but accommodating. And as it turns out, a part of the Brown family. Through Elijah's brother, Samuel."

"Accommodating, huh?" Jason put his arms around her waist, his eyes narrowing but an unmistakable teasing tone in his voice. "How accommodating are we talking here?"

Eliza laughed. "Why? Jealous? I mean, what's a wife to do when her husband goes off galivanting half a world away? I have to stay entertained somehow."

"Very funny," he said, his expression now more serious as he tucked a wayward curl behind her ear. "I'm not thrilled with you hanging out in graveyards with some guy I've never met, but I do like the idea that you will have a large dog to keep you safe."

She looked over at Murphy, who had followed them into the dining room and then promptly laid down and gone to sleep.

"Me too."

She reached out and ran her fingers along the rubbing of Honor's tombstone. "I can't help but feel the heart-wrenching sadness of this tragic family. To lose a child? How devastating that would be."

"Well, I can imagine that the fact she lived here on our property has some allure to it."

"Obviously. Aren't you a little curious? I mean, they lived right here. She died out there." Eliza pointed through the window at the darkened view of the cliff.

"You've definitely piqued my interest." He turned his head and yawned.

She unbuttoned the top button of his shirt. "Does this pique your interest?" she asked, unbuttoning another button.

Jason smiled. "Maybe we should continue this investigation upstairs?"

"Lead the way, Mr. Grey."

11

Eliza watched Jason's chest rise and fall. He now slept soundly, jet lag taking its full effect. Tossing and turning, she'd tried for over an hour to drift off, but thoughts of Honor rattled around in her head. Had she sat in this room grieving for her son?

Unable to find a comfortable position or quiet her mind, Eliza rose and pulled on a robe. Murphy slept soundly in his bed, and she moved quietly out into the hall, a cup of tea and another review of her notes calling to her. She flipped on the foyer light. Outside, she could hear the rumblings of a storm, rain already tapping against the roof and windows.

Halfway down the stairs, she paused. A woman with long dark hair, stood in the foyer, peering into an ornate mirror on the wall.

"Honor?" Eliza whispered.

The woman turned and glanced up at her and smiled, then returned her attention to her reflection.

Eliza reached the foyer and stood behind her, looking over her shoulder at a reflection of delicate features and a calm expression. Honor took a step back, and the two became one.

Vertigo made the edges of her vision blurry. Eliza closed her eyes until the nausea passed. When she opened her eyes, she saw herself in the mirror. Sunlight poured through the windows. Her robe replaced with a long ivory silk gown; her hair arranged in an updo with cascading curls. Around her neck lay an emerald necklace with intricate gold filigree. She touched the jewels; they felt cool against her skin.

At her side, a small boy with clear blue eyes smiled sweetly at her and tugged on her sleeve.

Eliza knelt and squeezed his hand.

"Levi?" she said softly, opening her arms to embrace him.

He was slight and frail in her arms, but she could feel the strength of his love.

Without warning, the room darkened, and a sinister, pulsing energy circled around them. A man she could only assume was Elijah stood behind her, his voice sharp and angry. His hands grabbed her shoulders and spun her around.

He glared at her, yelling, but she couldn't understand his words. He reached for Levi, and she pushed the boy behind her. Elijah's face grew red with rage, and he raised a fist.

Fear crawled up Eliza's throat. She opened her mouth to scream.

All at once the room around her changed again.

She stood alone in the foyer. Her dress now heavy and black. The front door stood open. She could see the sea, hear the waves as they crashed against the cliff.

Four somber-faced men descended the stairs carrying a small coffin. They carried it outside and placed it in the back of a horse-drawn cart.

An uncontrollable and overwhelming sense of grief and loss sent Eliza to her knees. Elijah appeared in the doorway, his rage replaced with contempt and disgust.

The cart pulled away, out of view, and she climbed to her feet and rushed to the door.

Outside, an inky blackness filled the night sky. A biting wind and rain whipped against her skin. Her nightdress clung to her, cold and wet. She could barely see more than a foot in front of her, but she had to run. Panic pushed her faster and faster into the night. Lightning flashed. The edge of the cliff was close, but she couldn't stop.

She reached the edge, but hands grabbed her shoulders and pulled her back. She clawed at his face, her nails scraping against his stubbled jaw before she stumbled.

Her knee slipped off the cliff's rocky precipice, but she flattened to the ground and pulled herself back onto the grass.

Arms wrapped around her waist, heaving her toward him.

"You killed her, and you killed Levi," she screamed, punching his chest. "You're a monster!"

She struggled against him, her arms turning to jelly as she struck his solid chest.

Then all went quiet, and a feeling of falling enveloped her. An inky void swirled around her, and for a moment, she was suspended in both time and space.

The Wet Lady's face crackled into focus, just inches in front of her own.

You belong to me...

A penetrating cold stabbed her body. Her muscles shivered in protest, her teeth chattering in her jaw.

A man's voice called to her.

"Eliza..."

You belong to me...

"No," she screamed and reached out into the darkness. Something grabbed her hands.

She yanked them free and in her mind, pushed against the darkness. She was back on the beach. She thought of the pink door of her parents' cottage. Of her brother. And then there was Jason and Bella. She saw the day she was married and the day her daughter was born.

The visions melded together, a spiral of sound and emotion. The loud roar of the crashing surf below pulled her from the dark place. Cold rain pelted her skin. The ground beneath her felt wet and slimy, and a strong salty taste rose in her throat.

Her instinct was to swing her arms, to fight off the man who held her so tight around her wrists. A deep, menacing guttural growl reverberated in her ear.

"Eliza...please, wake up. Wake up!"

A pulse of electricity made her body jerk. A rush of wind sounded in her ears, and she opened her eyes.

Jason held her against his bare chest, his hair dripping wet.

"Jason?" She struggled to focus on his face.

"Don't fight me; we need to get inside."

She nodded and wrapped her hands around his neck as he lifted her from the ground and carried her up the stairs and inside the house.

He set her gently on the couch in the family room and flipped the switch to ignite the fire.

"I don't understand what's happening," she said, her body beginning to shake from the cold. She'd been in the foyer, seen Levi, Elijah. The images came hard and fast. He'd chased her outside. She'd run for the cliff.

Oh God, she'd run for the cliff!

"That makes two of us," Jason said curtly. "Stay there. I need to get us some towels and some dry clothes."

Again, she nodded, her teeth chattering. Her heart raced, and her head pounded.

Murphy sat at her feet, staring at her.

She reached out and patted his head. He leaned forward and licked her face.

Jason returned and helped her to stand, then pulled off her wet robe and nightgown, dried her and pulled a sweatshirt over her head, and sat her down to help her into a pair of flannel leggings. He wrapped a blanket around her, then stripped off his own wet clothes for a pair of pajama pants and a sweatshirt of his own.

"Jason?"

He shook his head. "Not yet. I need a minute to calm down." He pointed at her. "Stay right there. I'm going to make us some tea."

She struggled to read his expression. He was concerned, but he was angry, too. She rubbed at her temples and pulled her legs up under her on the couch.

Jason returned a few minutes later and handed her a steaming mug. He set his own cup on the coffee table and positioned the ottoman in front of her so he could sit and face her.

"What the hell just happened, Eliza?"

She reached out to touch a set of red scratches on his cheek.

He winced and pulled back.

She wrapped both hands around her mug, her mind racing to form an explanation he would understand. "I don't really know. I couldn't sleep, so I came down to look at my notes. I think I was dreaming; I saw Honor, I saw Levi's coffin, and then I was running. He was going to kill me...kill her. I could feel her fear. And then I was looking up at you."

"Maybe I should take you to the hospital. Maybe the concussion was worse than they thought."

"What? No, I mean, my head hurts, but I'm okay. I just..."

"What, Eliza? You just what? Do you even know what happened out there?" he shouted at her.

Tears flooded her eyes.

"You almost died." He stood and raked his hand through his damp hair. "I don't even know what I would have done." His eyes darted back and forth, his shoulders tense. He took a deep breath and sat down on the ottoman. He placed his hands around hers.

"Murphy woke me up barking like a demon dog. You weren't in bed, so I followed him downstairs. The front door was open, and he raced outside.

"Thank God for the storm." His voice hitched in his throat. "I only saw you because of the lightning." He closed his eyes. "You were running right at the cliff. Honestly, I don't even know how I got to you in time.

"I called to you, Eliza. You looked right at me, but it was like you didn't know who I was."

The moment came back to her in a rush.

"I said something to you."

"Yes." Jason nodded and opened his eyes to look at her. "Your exact words? 'You're a monster!'"

"Jason, I'm sorry. I wasn't myself."

He released her hands and rubbed his face.

"If Murphy hadn't woken me up in time." He reached out and scratched Murphy's ear. "I really think we should go back to see the doctor. Maybe a concussion can cause sleepwalking."

Eliza swallowed hard. Her heart ached to have caused him so much pain. She needed to tell him, but would he believe her?

"Jason, I must tell you something, and I need you to try to hear me, really hear me, okay?"

He watched her for a moment and took a long deep breath. "Okay, I'm listening."

"This wasn't because of the concussion, and it wasn't sleepwalking. It was a vision."

"A vision? Like a hallucination?"

She shook her head gently. "No, a vision. A sixth-sense kind of a knowing."

His expression flattened. There was no denying the skepticism in his eyes, but she continued.

"When I was five, my family and I vacationed here in Coventry-by-the-Sea. I actually played on the shores of Rosecliff Manor, though I didn't know the house's name or history back then, of course. Edmond and I went down to the beach alone, and while we were there, I had my first vision. I saw a woman in period clothing standing along the rock jetties at the far point of the shore. She was beautiful at first, green eyes, long dark hair, but then she changed, she turned into this awful version of a woman, and it terrified me. She claimed me that day and told me our paths would cross again. And now they have. That first night after you left, I saw her again for the first time in years. I believe she is tied to this land somehow, and she might even be mixed up in whatever happened to Honor Brown."

Jason's eyes narrowed and he stood up abruptly to pace in front of the fireplace.

"Eliza, I don't even know what to say to that." He searched her face. "I can see that you believe this, but it sounds…" He exhaled slowly. "It sounds crazy. I mean, what are you saying? You see ghosts?"

"Yeah," she said simply. "And I sometimes get a feeling about people or places. I just *know* things. I know things that I shouldn't know, but I do."

She stood and moved close to him, taking his hands, and drawing them up under her chin. "Would you believe me if I told you that I got a feeling about you the first time I met you?"

The edges of his mouth turned up in a shallow smile. "I'm not sure that counts. I had a similar feeling about you."

"What if I told you that I knew that you and I would buy this house and that we would raise our daughter here?"

"Hard to disprove since that actually happened. Is it possible you feel that way because we actually did those things?"

Eliza shook her head. "No, I knew I would live in this house. The second I saw the listing, I had a vision, a clear picture of our life here together. I knew we would buy it and raise Bella here."

He was quiet for a moment, and she could see his doubt begin to crack. He tucked a strand of her hair behind her ear. "El, I want to believe you. It's just so incredible. Like something out of a fiction novel or a movie. I mean, I just don't believe in this kind of stuff."

Eliza turned her face and kissed his palm. "I wish there was a way I could prove it to you. I'll figure out a way to help you understand, but maybe for now, you can just trust me?"

He leaned in and kissed her lips. "I'll trust you if you can promise that you'll be safe and there will never be a repeat of what happened tonight."

Eliza nodded and wrapped her arms around him, her head resting on his shoulder as she hugged him tightly, knowing full well she couldn't promise any such thing.

12

T HE NEXT MORNING, ELIZA awoke on the couch in the living room, her head pounding. Although she couldn't quite make out his conversation, she could hear Jason in the kitchen. The aroma of brewing coffee and bacon was enough to get her on her feet and headed in his direction.

Jason smiled at her and flipped eggs, then pointed at his earbuds. He mouthed the word "work" and sank two split English muffins into the toaster.

The scratches on his face had calmed, but he looked tired.

"Yes," he said into the phone, pouring a cup of coffee. "Reschedule all of my afternoon meetings." He set the cup on the counter and pointed at it and then at her.

Eliza sat down at the massive granite island, wrapped her hands around the mug, trying to absorb some warmth, and took a sip.

A white blur ran by the atrium glass doors and then back again. Then a large black nose pressed against the glass-paned door.

Eliza opened the French doors to let him in.

He nuzzled her hand, and she bent down to snuggle his neck.

Jason set two plates of bacon and eggs on the island and tapped his earbuds to end his call.

"How are you feeling this morning?"

"Much better, you?"

"A little jet-lagged but feeling good." He took a large sip of coffee.

"Thank you for this," she said, finishing off a piece of bacon. "Apparently, I was starving." She smiled at him, but his expression remained serious.

"What's wrong?"

"Do you think you should book an appointment with the doctor for a re-check?"

She wiped her mouth with a napkin. "I told you, there's nothing the doctor can do about this. And I'd really rather not have to explain it to another skeptic, at least not this early in the morning."

He leaned against the counter. "I think you should go get checked."

"Well, I don't." Her voice was tight and defensive.

"Fine, then why don't you just take a few days off from writing the article?"

"I appreciate your concern and love you for it, but I just can't take the time right now. I'm on to something. I can feel it."

Jason's lips pursed. "Humor me, please?"

"And if I asked you to take time off from your work for no reason other than that I was concerned about you, would you do it?"

"I guess that would depend on whether I agreed with your assessment."

"Well," she said, pushing her plate away, no longer hungry. "There you have it. I don't agree with your assessment."

Jason dropped his fork on his plate. "It's not the same. My job and this casual writing gig you've got at the paper. They are not the same. I work to pay the bills; you write for fun."

The second the words left his mouth, his expression changed.

"El, I didn't mean that."

She crossed her arms and glared at him. On the counter, her cell phone buzzed. She snatched it up. Ginny Burke's name and number flashed on the screen.

She held a finger up at Jason to stop his protest and answered the call.

"Good morning, Ginny."

Jason sighed and sat down, stabbing his eggs with his fork.

Ginny's warm voice was excited and animated on the other end of the line.

"Eliza, I wanted to call you first thing. I've been reviewing my family records and those books and journals I have collected through the years, and you will never guess what I found!"

"I can't imagine," Eliza said, leaning back in her chair.

"It's actually quite unbelievable. I was hoping you could stop by. I promise it will be worth it."

Eliza glanced at the time on the microwave. It was already almost eight-thirty. "Can I swing by around ten?"

Ginny agreed. "See you then."

"Everything okay?" Jason asked.

"Yep. Ginny is actually *helping* me with my *fun* little article and has some new bits of information she would like me to have."

"El, don't be mad. I'm sorry. It was a rough night. I'm tired and grumpy."

"As am I, and I'm entitled to feel how I feel," she said. Her expression and tone softened. He was right; they were both tired and out of sorts. She took a bite of her English muffin. "But it won't last. I think we both just need some time to think."

They sat side by side, eating breakfast in silence.

After several minutes, Jason cleared his throat.

"I need to go to Boston for a few hours this morning to check on things at the office. I'm wiped from my trip and our hellish night. I don't plan to put in a full day unless issues arise."

"We can talk when you get back, then?"

He nodded without making eye contact and put his plate in the sink before heading upstairs, leaving her alone in the kitchen.

Eliza pulled into Ginny's driveway a few minutes before ten. Vivid red burning bushes ignited a brilliant display along her driveway. A tall maple that towered over the house had already begun to drop its colorful leaves onto her lawn. It was the first week of October, and fall was in full force with all of its vibrant glory.

Ginny waited for her on the front porch and waved.

"Good morning," she said as Eliza climbed the porch steps and was quick to offer a hug. "It's so good to see you. I've been so worried. You're feeling well?"

"Yes, I'm feeling just fine. And I promise, I won't leave your house in an ambulance this time."

Ginny gave her a wide grin and ushered her inside, through her living room and into the warm and inviting kitchen.

"I've just taken some muffins from the oven. Shall I get you one and a cup of tea?" Ginny offered.

Eliza took a deep breath as she sat down in the cozy breakfast nook. The kitchen smelled of oranges and cardamom. "Oh, yes, please."

Ginny plucked a muffin from the pan cooling on the counter and set it on a plate, then set the dish in front of Eliza. She put the kettle on the stove and disappeared for a moment into the living room, then came to sit with Eliza, an old book that looked like a Bible in her hand.

"I could hardly wait until you got here. The storm woke me in the middle of the night. The wind was so strong, it blew open my French doors." She pointed across the room to a set of double doors that led out into the backyard from her dining room.

Memories of what had nearly happened the night before, of Jason's face when she'd told him the truth, made a slight heat crawl up her neck. "Yes, the storm was quite a tempest."

"That's the proper word for it, a tempest. The wind blew over a stack of books I'd retrieved from the attic earlier in the evening. I knew I had more information about the founding families somewhere, and these are but a few of many. To be honest, I wasn't even sure what I had would be useful." She pointed to the stack of books. "These were in an old cedar chest that appeared to be from the right time period, so I brought down as many as I could carry."

The kettle whistled on the stove, and Ginny stood and poured the hot water over two matching mugs, each with a tea bag dangling on the rim.

"The wind howled like a banshee, the doors flailing about, and there were books and pages everywhere. After I finally managed to close the doors, I was surprised to find that nothing was wet and except for a few torn pages here and there, there was hardly any damage to the books at all."

"That is strange, though I'm glad to hear it," Eliza said, taking a sip of the hot Earl Grey.

I'm guessing Ginny doesn't have a wild animal roaming the rafter either.

"But that's not even the best part." Ginny tapped the book in her hands. "When I picked this one up from the floor, these fell out." She opened the small brown leather Bible and took out two folded letters. "When I saw the inscription, I knew they were important." Ginny turned the book for Eliza to see.

To our beloved Honor on her wedding day, July 24, 1798. May God bless and keep you this day and always. Mother and Father

Eliza looked up at Ginny. "This belonged to Honor? What an incredible coincidence. Did you know you had this?"

Ginny shook her head. "I didn't, though I suppose it's not a great surprise. It may have been returned to her family after her death, and her brother, my ancestor, must have kept it. To think that it's been among the old books and furniture passed down from that generation to mine for two centuries." Ginny shifted slightly in her seat to turn to look at Eliza.

"You'll probably think I'm a daft old woman after this, but to find this now...I can't help but believe those letters and her Bible, well, they were meant to be found! I sound crazy, don't I?"

Eliza offered a sympathetic smile. "Not at all. May I?" She pointed at the letters.

Ginny smiled back and slid them carefully across the table. "Of course. I couldn't wait for you to see them. The handwriting is exquisite. It really is a gem of a find."

Eliza cautiously unfolded the first letter and stared at the intricate handwriting.

September 27, 1808

To my dearest Charlotte,

I am relaying my intentions to you in fear for my life and my dear son Levi. The events of late have caused me great concern. I believe that we are in mortal danger and must plan our escape from this house. I do not know what has come over my husband, Elijah, but he is no longer the man I married. I believe he is a monster plotting to harm us and take over the Lord Shipyard. I will write to you in the coming days about my plan. I know you are with child and in a delicate situation, and I will do my best not to cause you distress. You have been my confidant and trusted friend, and I know I can rely on you when the time comes.

With heartfelt love,

Honor

Eliza looked up at Ginny, her eyes wide with surprise.

"Honor wanted to leave Elijah. She was afraid of him."

Ginny nodded. "Read the following letter. It, too, is very telling of the terror she lived with during her years at Rosecliff."

Eliza opened the second one and read out loud.

September 27, 1808

My dearest Mother,

I pray you read this letter with the utmost haste. I have no other choice but to protect the life of my dear Levi. We can no longer safely remain at Rosecliff. Upon the first opportunity we have to leave this forsaken house, we will be coming directly to your home. Please receive us.

Your beloved daughter,

Honor

"I can't imagine having to write letters like this. Honor must have been truly terrified. And for her family to find out how bad it really was for her, only after her death, when it was too late to intervene. Heartbreaking," Eliza said.

"As you know, divorce was rare, if even possible, for women at that time. To contemplate leaving him would have meant scandal and a considerable amount of shame for her and her son," Ginny added.

Eliza recalled Levi's face, the feel of his embrace. "I have to figure out how to work this into my story. These letters describe a woman and a child clearly being abused."

"I would agree. It gives a whole new side to Honor Brown, who has been viewed for so long as a tragic figure who took her own life."

"Yes, well, I'm beginning to think that may not be true. A lie that keeps them separated, even now."

"Oh, that reminds me," Ginny said and took a sip of her tea. "I spoke to Marty Evans the day before yesterday on my weekly visit with my dear Alexander."

Eliza gave Ginny's hand a quick squeeze. Despite his occasional hard-headedness, she couldn't imagine not being able to see Jason, talk to him. His recent trip had been just shy of three weeks and had felt like forever.

Ginny continued. "Well, I spotted him and Mayor Winthrop in a rather heated discussion outside the Highgate office. Marty looked upset, so I made it my business to check on him. When I got within earshot, the mayor gave me a nasty look and hurried off. I asked Marty what it was all about, but he wouldn't tell me."

"Mayor Winthrop has never been one of my favorite people. He strikes me as a bit of a bully. And he's got too many connections and special interests in our little town."

"Yes, I suppose so. While I was there Marty showed me the Brown family plot. I don't recall ever having seen it before."

"I'm guessing not. Marty mentioned that his father stopped caring for the plot some time ago. It was only after I discovered it and started researching Honor that it's been cleared of all the brush and scrub trees. Marty has been very helpful, and he did a nice job cleaning up the area. And he agreed to show me some of the documentation he has in his office regarding the Brown and Lord plots. I think I'm going to stop by when we're done here, see if he's found anything."

The two chatted a bit longer, Ginny showed her several other books with short passages and copies of newspaper articles about the Lord and Brown family businesses. She gathered them in a canvas bag and offered it to Eliza.

"I look forward to reading your article, Eliza," Ginny said as she walked her to the front door. "You breathe new life into that old rag."

"I promise I won't tell Art you said that."

Ginny waved her off. "You're the best writer he's had in ages, and he knows it."

Eliza drove directly to Highgate. She parked in the back and made her way to the Brown plot. She closed her eyes and thought of Honor and Levi, then hurried along the pebbled path to the Highgate office. She found Marty blowing leaves from the walkway.

"Ah-ha, *I* found *you* for once," she said after he'd turned the leaf blower off.

"Good afternoon, Miss Eliza." He stood and pulled a handkerchief from his pocket to wipe his hands. "C'mon in; I found a few of the documents I mentioned."

"A few? Are there more somewhere?" she asked. It felt like such an innocuous question, but she watched the easy manner in which he had greeted her shift into discomfort.

Marty shuffled from foot to foot and glanced at her and then at the ground by his feet. "I'm sure there are more; I just haven't been able to locate them."

"That's all right. I'll take whatever you can find, but could you show me something else first? I'd like to see where the Lord family is buried. Ashley and Mary Lord, and their son, Niles, and his wife Charlotte, if that's possible. I'd like to include a picture with my article on the Lords."

"Sure," Marty responded, scratching underneath his signature hat. "But I thought you were researching the Browns."

"Oh, I am; they're up next. Not quite finished with that article yet. I can't help but think I'm close to figuring out what really happened to Honor. I don't believe she jumped off that cliff of her own accord."

Marty nodded, pushing his hat back on his head, but didn't say anything.

She followed him toward the older section of the cemetery. He made a hard right after the row of arborvitae and led her to a plush lawn surrounded by beautiful pine trees. A small brook ran along the outer edge.

He pointed to two large granite headstones and a stone ledger covering the entire grave.

"These are the remains of Ashley and Mary Lord," Marty stated, pointing to the area. "If I recall, a storm took down a tree, and it fell on her stone when I was a kid." Mary Lord's ledger marker had indeed suffered some damage. A significant crack had splintered it into two parts requiring considerable repair.

Then Marty pointed over to two intricate grave markers adorned with an urn and willow branches.

"And here is Niles and Charlotte Lord's final resting place. They have a daughter, Temperance, I think. But she isn't buried here."

Eliza noted that these grave markers seemed more ornate and prominent than the Brown's plot. She took out her phone and snapped pictures of all four.

"This area seems more prestigious than where Honor is buried."

"Yup. True. The Lord family held a high level of importance in our town. Wealthy, successful, and from what I understand, good faithful citizens."

"Thank you for showing me. How about I grab those records and get out of your hair?"

Marty nodded and led her back the way they'd come.

"Just so you know, I looked through some of the documentation I found to make sure it was what you needed. There is a note about why they buried Honor the way they did and about poor Levi. And some information about the conflict between Elijah and his brother Samuel."

"I will take whatever you have, Marty. Thank you."

The two moved at a steady clip towards the office together. Once again, his speed surprised her despite his irregular gate. When they reached the office, he bent and rubbed his left knee.

"Sorry to make you walk so far."

"I'll be right out, Miss Eliza. The cold sometimes makes this arthritic knee ache."

Marty entered the old red brick building. Two worn windows with peeling trim flanked either side of the front door. Directly above the entrance, a large brick bore a stamp: *Est. 1862.* The aged green wooden door, weathered and in desperate need of a coat of paint, creaked as Marty unlocked and opened it.

"Wait here; I'll bring the paperwork out to you."

Eliza nodded and checked the time on her phone as she waited. She'd spent longer than she'd anticipated with Ginny, and her schedule was growing tighter by the minute.

Behind her, a single crow cawed. Then another. The ruckus grew louder, followed by the sound of dozens of wings flapping around her. She scanned the trees surrounding the old building as their branches grew heavy with the clicking and squawking of the roosting brood. Eliza covered her ears and inched toward the door. She reached out for the knob just as it flew open.

Marty stepped outside, manilla envelope in hand. Instantly, the horrible din stopped.

His eyes followed the murder of crows as they took to flight in one large feathery group and converged on another part of the cemetery.

"Damn birds," Marty said with disgust.

He offered her the envelope.

"These are all originals, Miss Eliza. They mustn't get damaged or lost. I'm not implying anything, just that I am responsible for them as caretaker of the cemetery."

It took a moment for Eliza to find her voice. *Had he not heard the crows? How was he so unaffected?*

She cleared her throat and reached for the envelope. "I understand. I promise to look at them, scan the ones I need and return them promptly."

Marty nodded. "No hurry. Take your time. And I'll keep looking to see what else I can find."

13

RUNNING THROUGH THE DOOR with the documentation from Ginny and Marty, Eliza, determined to solve the mysteries unfolding before her, became a woman on a mission. She wanted to combine all her research to finish her first submission, "The Lord Founding Family," for *The Gazette*.

Murphy greeted her in the foyer, his tail wagging.

"Hey, Murphy! Need to go out?" She stepped to the side and opened the door wide for him.

He galloped across the grass to bark at a seagull riding the air current above the cliff line, inspected half a dozen trees to do his business, then raced back through the French doors.

Eliza hurried to the kitchen, tossed him a treat, made herself a cup of tea, and with the new books from Ginny, settled at the dining room table with the remainder of her research.

She reread the letters Ginny had given her and scanned several other books; a few included additional information on the Lords' and Browns' estates and how the two families had made their money. Along with the information from the library, she pulled together the prestigious history of the Lord family, from their arrival to America to the prosperity they brought into their town by the shipping trade with England. The Lords certainly had put Coventry on the map.

An hour and a half later, she gave the article a final once-over and attached it and the photos she'd taken that morning to an email.

Hi Art,

Attached, please find my story on the Ashley Lord family, the first of the founding families' series, including pictures of their gravesites at

Highgate, as well as an old picture of the Lord Shipyard taken in the late 1800s before it was razed. Feel free to contact me with any questions or concerns.

Eliza

As soon as she hit "send," a huge relief flooded over her. She'd completed the first piece in record time. Now she was free to pursue the mystery of the Brown family, in particular Honor.

Two hours later, Eliza had just finished putting together a salad to go with the lasagna bubbling in the oven when her phone buzzed. It was her mother.

"Hey, Mom," she said, answering the phone. "Everything okay?"

"Hi, dear! Of course, everything's fine. Is that how you answer all of your calls? Assuming something must be wrong on the other end?"

At sixty-eight, Jane Monroe was as sharp and sassy as ever. There was no question that Eliza inherited her quick wit and was very much her mother's daughter.

Meticulous when given a project to tackle and wholeheartedly dedicated to her family and home, Jane held the title of matriarch of the Monroe family with pride.

"Sorry, Mom. It's been a long week. What's up?"

"Dad and I want to invite you kids up for this weekend. Leah and Edmond are free as well and I thought it would be nice to spend some time together."

"Okay, but I'll need to check with Jason." Still irritated by their earlier argument, she wondered if she really wanted to spend a weekend away with him. "He just got back and I don't know if he's free," she said, her tone doing a poor job of hiding her irritation.

"Uh-oh. Sounds like something's up between you two."

"No, I mean, yes, but it'll pass. We had a little argument this morning. And I'm not done being angry with him yet."

"Ah, well, I suspect you both need some time away then. And Bella too."

Eliza smiled. "Yes, I'm sure she'd love to get away for the weekend. She's been working so –"

The sound of Murphy racing to the foyer interrupted their conversation and reminded Eliza that her mother was unaware of their new family addition. "Mom, I don't know if you've heard, but we adopted a dog. So, he'll need to come too, if that's okay."

"A dog? Eliza what on earth –"

"His name is Murphy, and he's amazing. You'll love him."

Murphy barked from the entryway, his paws scratching at the window.

"I promise, Mom. He's a great dog. And I don't have anywhere else for him to go right now."

"If that's the only way I can get you here, bring the dog," Jane said.

"Thanks, Mom. Looks like Jason is home. I'll talk to him and let you know."

Eliza hung up the phone and made her way back to the kitchen. She pulled two wine glasses from the cabinet and decanted a bottle of Cabernet.

"Smells great!" Jason called from the foyer. "Hey Murphy, hey boy."

She heard him drop his keys in the bowl and open the front closet.

"What's for dinner?" he asked when he'd joined her in the kitchen.

"Lasagna. I had a craving," she said.

Jason grabbed a piece of Italian bread from the counter and dipped it in the pot of leftover sauce on the stovetop.

"My mother always told me I'd be a happy man if I married a woman who could cook!"

Eliza crossed her arms and leaned against the island. "How did it go at the office?"

"Great." He grabbed another piece of bread to dunk. "How about your story? Are you done?"

Eliza stared at him for a long minute, waiting for him to apologize. She wasn't nearly as hot as she had been, but she still felt entitled to an apology.

"I am," she said tentatively. "Ahead of schedule too, for this first article. Which is good because there's still more research I want to do on the Brown family. There's more to Honor's story. Wait until you see the letters Ginny found."

When his expression went flat she knew there was something more he wanted to say, and her temper flared. She watched him dip another piece of bread into the sauce. "If you continue to eat bread, you won't have an appetite for lasagna."

When he finally met her gaze, he cleared his throat. "I can see that you're still mad at me. And rightfully so. I'm sorry about this morning. I didn't mean to imply that my work is more important than yours. I've been stressed with all of the company expansion stuff. And worried about you if I'm being honest."

"I get that. I understand why the concussion worried you and how things just got heated. Let's just chalk up last night's incident and this morning's argument to jet lag and a bad night's sleep and pretend it never happened, okay?"

The muscles in Jason's jaw clenched, and he shook his head. "Last night's incident? Eliza, I found you outside in the rain in the middle of the night, running full speed toward the edge of the cliff. I don't think I can just forget it."

She reached out to touch him, but he shrugged her off. "No, I've been thinking about it all day. I don't like fighting with you, but this isn't something we can just sweep under the rug. I must have called your name a dozen times last night, and you didn't respond. Hell, you didn't even look like you when you spoke to me."

"What?" She uncrossed her arms. "I didn't look like me? What does that even mean?"

He pursed his lips and hesitated before continuing. "I don't know how to explain it, but you looked different. I almost didn't recognize you at first." He ran his hand through his hair, then took a step toward her and squeezed her shoulders.

His voice softened and cracked. "If it weren't for Murphy waking me up and bringing me to you...I don't even want to think about what might have happened. He saved your life."

Eliza opened her mouth to speak, but Jason continued.

"I am all for you finding your niche and writing for *The Gazette*, but if this is what happens when you get too deep into a story, then I'm sorry, but I think you should quit. I love you, but all of this talk about murder and suicide and you traipsing all over a cemetery like it's some kind of amusement park, I'm just not down for it."

"You're not down for it?!" Eliza's temper reignited. "I'm sorry, I didn't know I needed your approval or that I needed to clear my writing assignments with you first. Sure, let's run that by Art. 'Hey Art, I'm totally on board to write for the paper, but you need to run all my assignments by my husband first.'" She placed her palms on the island. "Good grief, it's like I hit my head and woke up in the early 1900s."

"You know that is not what I mean. In the two and a half weeks I was gone, the same two and a half weeks you've been working on this story, something's changed."

Silence hung between them.

He wasn't wrong. She'd told him about the visions, but he didn't believe her. So, what now?

The oven timer sounded, and Eliza turned from him. She grabbed two plates down from the cabinet and slammed them hard on the granite island, the clanging of the stoneware echoing her displeasure.

Without a word, she pulled the lasagna from the oven and placed it on the hot pads next to the stove. She sliced more Italian bread, slashing through the soft texture with a bread knife.

Count to ten or you will say something you wish you hadn't.

She glanced over at Murphy, whose ears drooped against his jowls. His pensive eyes following Eliza's every move while keeping his head perfectly still.

Inhale. Exhale. Count to ten.

She slowly turned around to face Jason.

"Let's call a truce. I know my temper gets the better of me. I will take into consideration your concern for my well-being. I can't deny that things have been out of the ordinary with this assignment. I'll make a point to be more careful and you can make a point to be more supportive of my career and my desire to solve this mystery. Deal?"

"Alright," he said, his shoulders pressing back as he took a deep breath. "For the record, I do respect your career." He offered her a sad smile. "I'm sorry, El. I really am."

She wrapped her arms around his waist. "Me too," she said.

He rested his forehead against hers. "Now, I am starved. Can we please eat?"

Eliza smirked, "I see your stomach knows a good deal when it hears one."

Jason patted his stomach. "Hasn't let me down to date."

14

ELIZA TUCKED SEVERAL COPIES of *The Coventry Gazette* into her purse, along with the last of her toiletries. "The Lord Founding Family" article had already received glowing reviews, with nearly two dozen comments posted online in less than twenty-four hours.

She gave herself a once-over in the floor-length mirror. She'd gone for casual chic in off-white jeans, a teal sweater, and a multicolored silk scarf. She checked her makeup and methodically pulled her hair back into a loose knot at the nape of her neck.

She needed this weekend away. They all did. She and Jason had called a truce, but truth be told, his comments still picked at her brain. He'd equated her cemetery research to "traipsing through an amusement park." He'd tried to make peace with her, however she couldn't help but feel he didn't respect her work. And it stung. And something about this trip just didn't sit right with her. She *knew* something was off, but not why.

She grabbed her purse and headed downstairs.

Jason stood by the door, their luggage beside him. He turned and looked up at her.

"I think that's everything," she said. "Just my purse and Murphy's bag from the kitchen."

"Wait right there, for a second," Jason said, smiling up at her.

"Why? What's wrong?"

"Nothing. Watching you come down the stairs like that, I just remembered seeing you for the first time at the clambake in Jamestown. You took my breath away then, and you still do."

She should have smiled but complimenting her wasn't enough to make her forget the things he'd said.

"You do remember our first meeting, right?" Jason asked, teasing when she didn't respond.

"Of course I do. You were the guy with the wild curly hair wearing a Metallica t-shirt," she said as she hurried down the remaining stairs. Her tone was shorter and more curt than she'd intended.

"Hey," he said, head cocked to one side. "We okay?"

She sighed. "Honestly? I'm still a little irritated about our argument. I know we called a truce, but you think my research and writing is equivalent to 'traipsing through a graveyard like an amusement park.'" She made air quotes to remind him that those were his exact words. "That hardly screams respect. I've always respected what you do for work. I want you to do the same for me."

Jason came closer and took her hands. "El, I am so sorry. I really am. I do respect you and your work."

She looked away, unable to hide a smile.

He tipped her chin up. "You're an incredible writer, and I'm very proud of you. Forgive me?"

Eliza's resentment ebbed slightly.

You are good Jason Grey. I'm feeling a little like the Wicked Witch of the West in The Wizard of Oz after she's been doused with water.

"Alright, if I must," she replied with another sigh, and he kissed her firmly.

"Why don't you grab Murphy's bowls and food while I load this stuff up, and we'll get out of here."

"Alright. Meet you outside in five."

Murphy watched her intently as she gave his bowls a quick rinse before adding them to the bag of food and treats she'd packed the night before.

"Don't worry; you'll like it there. And Bella will be there."

Murphy barked and followed her out to the car.

Jason took the bag from her and added it to the back with the others.

"Ready?" he asked.

"Yes, but can we make a quick stop at the bakery? I texted Vanessa with an order for some Danishes and lemon squares for my dad. You know how he loves those lemon squares."

He took her hand and brought it to his lips. "Anything for you."

Jason pulled into a parking spot right in front of the bakery.

Eliza undid her seatbelt and opened the car door. "I'll be right out."

As always, the bakery was filled with the delectable scent of coffee and baked goods.

Vanessa stood at the front counter, helping a customer, but soon waved her over.

"Got your order all ready to go, heavy on the lemon squares for my biggest fan." She held up a handled paper bag with the bakery logo on the front.

"Did I ever tell you that you're just the best!"

Vanessa laughed, "Maybe a few times. Can I get you anything else?"

"Yeah, maybe just keep your fingers crossed that Jason and I can get through this weekend without another blowup."

"Yikes. You wanna talk about it?"

"I'm a little peeved right now. He gets to travel around the world for work, and I have to accept that, but for some reason, he's got it in his head that my work at *The Gazette* is just a lame hobby."

Vanessa's eyes went wide. "He said your job is lame?"

"Well, maybe not in those words, but pretty much. He thinks my storyline is dangerous, and he doesn't support me digging any further into the Honor Brown mystery."

"I'm sure he didn't mean it. We all say things we don't mean when we're angry."

"Yeah, I know. I just want him to respect what I do and support me. This story... it's important to me. Maybe more than any other piece I've written."

"Does he know about the Wet Lady? And the rest of it?"

Eliza shrugged. "I told him the basics of it anyway, but he doesn't really believe me. He just doesn't understand."

Vanessa came around from behind the counter and hugged Eliza.

"I'm sorry you're feeling this way, but I know that man would move heaven and earth for you. Maybe give him some time?"

Eliza smiled.

"Thank you for listening to me and being such a good friend."

"Go and have a good time with Bella and the rest of your family. You deserve this!"

Eliza nodded and took a deep breath. "You're right. I do. We do."

"Wait, I forgot one little thing." Vanessa raced back to the other side of the counter and dropped a Murphy Grey donut hole into a bag, and handed it to her.

"Thank you. He'd have never forgiven me if I came back to the car without it."

"Be safe and try to have a good time. Oh, and I love this new hairdo, by the way. Looks good on you."

Another customer stepped up to the counter, and Vanessa took his order.

Eliza reached up to touch her hair. *New hairdo? It's just a bun.*

She quickly ran next door to Rinaldi's convenience store to grab one extra copy of *The Coventry Gazette.*

Tony Rinaldi, store manager, handed over Eliza's change, "Great piece, Eliza!"

"Thanks, Tony. I appreciate the feedback."

"I'm not the only one! Mayor Winthrop bought the first copy I sold. You've got fans in high places." He winked.

Eliza nodded and smiled.

Mayor Winthrop? A fan of mine? Not too sure about that.

On the drive to Newport to pick up Bella, Eliza's mind wandered as she watched the fall foliage fly by, her emotions as varied as the colors of the leaves. The farther they got from home, the stronger her sense of unease.

When they turned off Bellevue Avenue and onto Ruggles Avenue, they spotted Bella talking with a group of friends.

Jason beeped the horn as he pulled up to the curb.

Bella grabbed her backpack, waved goodbye to her friends, and hurried towards the SUV.

She crossed in front and leaned in to hug Jason through the driver's side window.

"Hey, Dad"

"Hey, my girl!"

Bella scurried around to the other side, stuck her head in the window to kiss Eliza's cheek. Then she opened the rear, flung her backpack inside, and nudged Murphy over to settle in the back seat.

"Hey, big guy!"

Murphy laid down and put his head in her lap.

An hour later, the Greys pulled up in front of the Monroes' lovely home.

A cloud of grey smoke billowed from the massive stone chimney. Quaint, green, slatted shutters flanked the paned windows. Yellow mums, ornamental cabbage, and gourds filled out the window boxes. Festive cornstalks lined the front porch with an array of orange and white pumpkins, leaving little doubt of the season. Jane Monroe's annual ornamental corn arrangement embellished with a crisp maroon bow hung on the front door.

Her parents' house still felt like home to her.

The front door opened, and Jane appeared on the porch. Right behind her followed Eliza's dad, Charles Monroe. He waved.

Bella climbed out of the car and raced up the steps into the loving arms of her grandparents.

Jason opened the trunk to fetch their bags, and Eliza grabbed Murphy's leash as he jumped out of the vehicle.

"Oh, my goodness, Eliza," her mother said. "He's the size of a bear!"

"Hi, Mom." Eliza leaned in to give her mom a side hug. "Meet Murphy, the newest Grey."

Jane shook her head. "Eliza, I am not sure we have room in the house for him. He must shed something terrible."

"He's big, but he's generally well-behaved. I'll make sure I vacuum before we leave."

"Gram, he is the sweetest guy," Bella added, kneeling down to hug his neck.

Jason leaned in and kissed Jane on the cheek. "I was skeptical at first, but Eliza's right. He really is a great dog. And you know if I accepted him, he has to be cool."

Jane squirmed a bit.

Eliza patted her mother's arm. Her mother liked dogs, but only from afar.

Jane reluctantly placed her hand on Murphy's head, robotically patted him, and then wiped her hand with the corner of her plaid apron.

Charles' expression was one of concern, but Eliza caught the amusement in his eyes. He always got a kick out of watching his wife's over-the-top reactions.

"Let's get you all inside," he said and offered Jane his arm.

Jason followed with their luggage, then Bella, then Eliza with Murphy in tow. Inside, not much had changed since Eliza was a girl. To their right, a beige and blue oriental rug spanned the living room atop a honeyed tone wide-planked pine floor. A sofa and loveseat in a shabby chic cabbage rose pattern gave the room a rustic charm. A large ornate mirror hung over a stone fireplace where a warm, bright fire burned softly. The other rooms held a similar style of homey farmhouse décor. There were vintage signs and a large clock on the dining room wall. A tall, slightly rusted milk tin served as an umbrella holder near the door. The old staircase with its white wooden banister stood tight against the wall to the left, with a small-paned window at the first landing giving a peek into the side yard.

A slim figure seated in an embroidered armchair under the window in the living room corner, raised a mug with a welcoming grin. Edmond. His sandy brown hair, thick and wavy, still complemented his rugged good looks.

My brother. He always looks like he walked out of an L.L. Bean catalog.

"Hello, Grey family!"

Edmond rose and shook Jason's hand, then hugged Eliza, then Bella.

"I've missed you!" Bella said.

"Ah, Bella, it is so good to see my favorite niece. Have you conquered the world yet?"

"Working on it."

Edmond looked down at Murphy.

"So, this is the other man?"

Eliza let out a laugh. "Behave yourself," she said, pointing at her brother.

"Too soon?" Edmond asked, a smirk on his face.

Murphy made the rounds of pats on his head and then went over to the base of the large stone fireplace hearth and laid down. Once the massive white body finally got comfortable, he let out a large sigh and closed his eyes.

Jane took their coats and hung them inside the hall closet just under the staircase.

"Something smells good," Jason said, rubbing his stomach.

"Let me guess," Bella said, inhaling deeply. "I smell...pot roast with all the fixings!"

Jane smiled. "You got it. Popovers too!"

"And a freshly baked apple pie for dessert," Leah, Edmond's wife, added as she descended the staircase.

Leah, a tall, slender woman, wore a powder blue sweater and tan linen pants. Her long blonde hair perfectly coiffed, fell neatly around her face, making her blue eyes sparkle. She wore her trademark silver hoop earrings and plain silver cross necklace.

"Leah! I am so happy you could get away." Eliza hugged her sister-in-law. "Edmond told me about your new partnership. Congratulations."

Leah beamed. "Yeah, it's been a long time coming, and there is so much more work, but it's good to get away. Not that we had much of a choice," she teased, looking at her husband.

"Here, let me help you take those upstairs," Charles said to Jason, reaching to take one of the suitcases and making a beeline for the staircase.

Jason leaned in and planted a kiss on Eliza's cheek. "Be right back."

"That looks amazing, Grandma!" Bella exclaimed.

Jane shuttled between the kitchen and dining room, first carrying in a bowl of mashed potatoes, then the pot roast and veggies on a large ceramic platter. She set them beside a festive centerpiece of orange mums and miniature gooseneck gourds.

"Bet your college food doesn't compare to Gram's home cooking," Edmond teased.

"Ooh my, I forgot the butter for the popovers!" Jane said just as she sat down.

"I'll get it, Mom, stay. Is there anything else you need?" Eliza asked warmly.

"Maybe grab the extra bowl of potatoes; they seem to be going fast!"

"And extra gravy," Edmond added, pouring a healthy amount onto the heap of mashed potatoes on his plate.

"Pace yourself, big guy," Leah said, pointing at her husband. "I'll grab the gravy and butter if you grab the potatoes," Leah said to Eliza, standing up from the table.

"I am so glad we were able to get together this weekend. Aren't you?" Leah asked when they reached the kitchen. "When Edmond told me Jason called, that he'd planned this whole weekend to give you a chance to rest and recover after your concussion, there was no way we could say no." She rubbed Eliza's arm. "He was really worried about you. Wouldn't take no for an answer." She laughed. "I imagine it's a skill that serves him well in his business."

Eliza's fingers clenched the bowl of potatoes.

"Wait. What? I thought this weekend was Mom's idea?"

"Oh, no, this was all Jason's doing. I think he wanted to surprise you. Not that it took much cajoling on his part to get Jane to agree." She wiped the edge of a second gravy boat with a paper towel. "Shall we?" she asked, holding the French door into the dining room open for Eliza.

Eliza stared directly at Jason as she set the bowl of potatoes on the table.

Any casual conversation at the table ceased. Jason sat for a moment, a deer-in-the-headlights expression on his face as he wiped his mouth with his napkin.

"Care to explain how this weekend came to be?" she demanded, standing across the table.

He held up his hands. "Eliza, it's not what you think. We talked about a family weekend while I was in England," Jason said defensively.

"And my mother just happened to call and invite us all up right after you started insisting I take time off from the paper?" Eliza shook her head. "It was all way too coincidental; I should have known better."

She then turned her attention toward her mother.

"Mom, so you're in on this, too?"

Jane pursed her lips. "Eliza Mae, you're overreacting. Jason called, told me you were having a tough time after your accident, and asked if we'd be willing to host this little family gathering. Bella was free, and Edmond and Leah had the weekend available. Simple as that. Why are you making a bigger deal of this?"

"This isn't about family; it's about all of you thinking I'm not well or impaired somehow. And about you," she pointed at Jason, "not listening to me. And instead of just talking to me, you had to stage this...this intervention?"

Charles moved to stand next to his wife. "Come on, Ellie girl, come sit down. Let's eat and talk this out."

Edmond gave Eliza a soft look, "Come on, Sis. Don't do this."

"Eliza, I didn't mean to upset you," Leah said. "When Jason explained about the concussion and how the storyline may be affecting you, well, we wanted to help. Please don't be angry. We love you."

Bella rose from her seat and hugged her mom. "I'm sorry, Mom. We just love you so much."

Eliza closed her eyes and took a long, cleansing breath. An eruption of tears grew behind her eyelids. That he'd felt it necessary pricked her pride right to the core, but regardless of his motivations, she was here, surrounded by a family that loved and cared about her.

"Heaven forbid I let a pot roast go to waste," she said with a half-smile. She looked at Jason. "You and I need to talk this out more, but for now, let's eat."

Edmond and her father did their best to lighten the mood with funny stories from their family history. Still, the damage had been done, and a lingering tension prevented Eliza from truly enjoying the meal.

When everyone had eaten their fill, the table had been cleared, and the dishes done, Bella, Eliza, and Leah took Murphy out for a walk.

"You want to come, Mom?" Eliza asked.

Jane waved her off. "No, I still need to make sure all the rooms have towels and everything is ready for the lot of you. You girls go on ahead."

"We won't be long," Leah said. "It's getting cold out."

Eliza did her best to shrug off her sour mood. They chatted about Bella's love life, and both she and Leah reminisced and laughed at their own teenage crushes and failed romances as they made a loop around her parents' small neighborhood. The early evening air was brisk enough to make her wish she'd brought some gloves.

"I'm going upstairs to unpack," Bella said as they approached the steps to the back door.

"I'll go with you," Leah said to Bella. "I was going through my closet the other day and brought a few things I thought you might like."

The instant Murphy was off his leash, he followed the two women upstairs. Eliza hung his leash over the back of a chair in the breakfast nook before bending to pick up Murphy's water bowl to refill it.

She found her father, a few minutes later, fast asleep in his usual spot on the couch, partaking in his regular after-meal catnap. Her mother was likely still upstairs.

She needed to find Jason. There was no sense delaying the conversation any longer. Best to get it over with and try to clear the air.

She headed for the den and the promise of a finger or two of her father's favorite scotch whiskey to bolster her courage and calm her nerves but stopped just short of the door when she heard her brother's voice.

"Eliza is special. She has always had an empathic way about her. She absorbs the feelings of everyone around her. Maybe the story grabbed hold of her because she related to this family, this woman, in some way. With Bella away at school, you traveling, and nothing for company save that big old house, maybe she just immersed herself into the story more than she should have."

"I agree," Jason replied. "That is why I am here. To get her back to feeling part of a large group again, remind her that we're all still here for her. I never imagined in a million years she'd react like she did today. I chatted with Bella a couple of days ago, and she's even noticed that something's off. It's silly, but I feel like she has changed. I mean, she's even wearing her hair differently. I go away for two weeks, and it's like I've come home to someone else."

Eliza touched her hair. *Now he has a problem with my hair? What the hell?*

"Do you think it could be the head injury that is causing the difference?" Edmond asked, sounding concerned.

"I have no idea, maybe, probably. The night on the cliff convinced me she is off. Ed, when I tell you I've never been that scared in my life, I mean it. She didn't even look like herself. And worse, if there could be something worse, she looked at me like she hated me. Like she wished I was dead. She has never looked at me like that, not even when she's angry. It's like it wasn't even her looking back at me."

"I can't and won't even begin to think about what might have happened if you hadn't been there," Edmond said. "But I know this: Eliza adores you. Whatever this is, it will work itself out."

Jason's tone grew frantic. "She adopted the dog without even thinking to ask me how I'd feel about it. She's off running through the cemetery, hanging out with this creepy caretaker guy. And then, to top it all off, the night she almost threw herself over a cliff, she tells me she sees ghosts and that there's one she first saw as a child who's come back to haunt her. I mean, what am I supposed to do with that?"

"The Wet Lady?" Edmond asked. "She told you about her?"

Jason continued. "Yeah. Why? You know about this, whatever, lady? Don't tell me you buy that ghost story. Do you really believe that she can see and hear dead people?"

Eliza stiffened. She had a momentary urge to bust through the door and give them both a piece of her mind.

"Eliza," her mother called from upstairs.

The conversation in the den ended without hesitation, and she heard the two men rise out of their chairs.

Eliza hurried to the refrigerator and gently opened the door, pretending to be rummaging for a bottle of water.

"I didn't know you all were back," Jason said, leaning against the doorframe.

Eliza stared at him. Part of her could understand and empathize with his concern especially after hearing the things he was worried about. The other part of her was furious that not only did he not believe her, but he hadn't had the courage to talk to her about it before complaining to her brother.

"Where is everyone?" Edmond asked.

As if on cue, Murphy bounded down the stairs, Jane, Bella, and Leah behind him.

"There you are," Jane said to Eliza. "Ready for dessert?"

"Sure, Mom," Eliza said, thankful for the distraction. She'd been ready to have it out with Jason, but now, she needed some time to think, to prepare what she was going to say. "What's on the menu again?"

"Apple pie and ice cream," Jane replied. "Who wants the first slice?"

Later in the evening, Eliza excused herself from the kitchen table where they'd gathered to play a game of cards.

She slipped away up the old stairs of her family home. The third step up from the second landing still creaked, and she lightly stepped over it as she had done as a child. She came to the top of the stairs and the familiar hallway that led to her room, the last room on the left.

The three-paneled white wood door moaned softly on its hinges as she opened it. She turned on the bedside lamp and took stock of her old room. The striped rose wallpaper she'd picked out on her sixth birthday had been replaced by a fresh coat of grey paint that lightened the room. The two dormer windows and the lovely window seat beneath them, painted a crisp white, continued to be the room's star attraction.

The double bed, bureau, and small pine desk remained a tangible part of Eliza's childhood memories, along with the traumatizing visitations from the Wet Lady.

She sat on the window seat and let her head rest against the cold glass, recalling the countless times she'd sat at this very spot reading or daydreaming.

A soft knock sounded at the door.

Edmond stood in the doorway. "Okay if I come in?"

She nodded, and he took a seat on the bed so he could face her. The old mattress squeaked under his weight.

"How are you doing?"

"I've been better, but I've been worse. Why do you ask?" She was curious if he'd come to beg Jason's case.

"You seem different. Preoccupied. Tense, maybe, I don't know."

"And is this your opinion of me, or are you coming by this information second-hand?"

Edmond held up his hands. "Don't shoot the messenger, Sis. Jason's worried about you. And after talking to him, I can't say as I blame him."

"Yeah, so I heard."

Edmond's eyebrows shot up. "You heard?"

Eliza sighed and crossed her arms. "I didn't mean to eavesdrop when you two were in the den, but I'm not sorry I did. He's worried, but he doesn't believe me. He doesn't trust me, and now he's sent you up here to talk to me instead of facing me himself."

"Come on, Eliza. Cut the guy a break. You know he loves you. You have to admit, laying the Wet Lady stuff on him is a lot. And then there's the dog and your trip to the hospital. And that night where you almost jumped off a cliff."

Eliza looked away and stared out the window. "I don't know what's happening. I know it's a lot, but it's like he doesn't really want to hear any of it." She turned back to face her brother. "The truth is, I don't know how I ended up at the cliff that night. It was like I became someone else. I've been working on this story for *The Gazette*, and I stumbled on this place in the cemetery. This woman, Honor Brown, she lost her son and then, by all accounts, threw herself off that very same cliff, but I think there's more to it."

"I'm all for having passion about what you do, but to hear Jason tell it, you've become a little obsessed," Edmond said firmly.

"Obsessed? Hardly. Intrigued, genuinely curious, for sure. I guess, it's on my mind a lot. There's a reason all of this is happening; I just don't know what it is yet."

"Okay. So, it is becoming a smidge unhealthy, maybe?" Edmond delivered the last word gently.

"Unhealthy would be me refusing to eat or not taking care of my other responsibilities. That's not what's happening here."

"Alright, then tell me about it. Tell me your side of things."

Eliza shared everything with her brother. She recounted the strange happenings at the cemetery, the nightmares, the vision at the beach that had resulted in her concussion.

"The worst are the dreams, but the fact that this woman, Honor Brown, died on my property, that she lived in that house, it's got to be connected. I think she needs my help to prove that her husband pushed her off that cliff."

Edmond leaned forward, elbows resting on his thighs. He stared down at his hands neatly folded between his knees.

"Throughout our childhood and beyond, I have always believed in your ability to see things I couldn't. I remembered that day at the beach, and the nights you couldn't sleep because the Wet Lady haunted your dreams. I never told you that I believed you, but I did. And I do."

"Thank you for that," Eliza said quietly.

"Edmond, I told you she came in my dreams, but that wasn't entirely true. She wasn't in my dreams; she was there, in my room. I'd wake up freezing. I could see my breath; that's how cold it was. My nightlight would start to flicker, and then she'd be there, at the end of my bed, just staring at me. Sometimes, if I refused to look, she'd hover above my bed, floating over me, her hair dripping on my face."

Edmond's pained expression made Eliza wish she hadn't revealed that truth.

"My turn to confess something I never told you. Maybe because I didn't want to believe it, or maybe I was scared, I don't know. One night when you were six, I think, you came into my room in the middle of the night. There was a bad storm, and you begged me to let you sleep at the end of the bed."

"I think I remember that night. That was the storm that took down the old oak tree across the street, right?"

He nodded. "You were crying, you dreamt the Wet Lady was floating over your bed, and you were cold. I'd never seen you that scared. After I patted your back, you fell right to sleep under a blanket at the foot of the bed. I started to fall asleep, but it suddenly got so cold. Even though the storm ended, bright flashes of lightning continued, randomly brightening my room. I looked down at you, and that's when I saw her hovering directly above you, glowing drips of water falling from her hair, your breath turning to mist. I didn't want her to see me, but she cricked her neck and looked directly at me. I freaked and covered my face with my blanket. It felt like an eternity, but when I pulled the blanket off my face, she was directly over me. Her bulging eyes staring at me. I froze. She put a finger to her lips and whispered, 'Shh,' and then she disappeared."

Eliza leaned forward and grabbed her brother's shoulder. "Edmond! You saw her?"

"I think I did. I mean, it was so long ago, and you stopped talking about her much after that. I tried to convince myself she wasn't real, but deep down, I knew I'd seen her."

"So, you really do believe me."

"Let's just say I've always known you were different. Knew that you *knew* things, things I didn't understand. But now, even if all of this is true, let's say this woman is reaching out to you from beyond the grave. To what end? What will it accomplish if you continue to investigate? And will it be worth it if it causes this rift between you and Jason to get any worse?"

Tears welled up in Eliza's eyes. She shrugged.

"I will always be here to help you through anything you need. Just think about this a little bit. Try to see it from Jason's point of view. He's scared, El. Scared that he'll wake up one night and not make it to the cliff in time. It's a lot to ask."

Eliza reached out her hand, and Edmond took it and squeezed.

"Thank you for listening to me and for making me hear his side of things. I will give it some thought. I promise," she said.

Edmond stood. In the doorway, he turned back. "By the way, for what it's worth, I like the new hairdo. When I first saw you this afternoon, I thought you looked different, but sometimes change is good. I like it."

When she could no longer hear his footsteps on the stairs, Eliza stood and stared at herself in the bedroom mirror. She usually wore her hair down in curls or soft waves that often hid some of her face. But for some reason, that morning, she'd twisted it in a loose bun at the nape of her neck. Several pieces of hair had pulled loose and framed her face. It was a bit old-fashioned, but she wasn't unhappy with the look. It made her neck appear long and slender and drew attention to her face.

The change didn't upset her so much as the fact that she couldn't remember making the conscious decision to try a new style. Maybe Jason and Bella were right to be concerned.

The anger that had simmered for most of the evening began to wane. She gave her room a last once over and switched off the light before returning downstairs.

The rest of the family, including Murphy, had migrated to the living room and sat around a blazing fire in the room's stone fireplace.

Leah offered Eliza a glass of Moscato.

Eliza sat on the floor next to Murphy as he placed his head on her lap.

"Eliza, I have to admit, that dog does love you," her mother said. "Even though he is a bit big, he is a good dog."

"Yeah, he is," she said and bent to kiss the top of Murphy's head.

Jason sat in the armchair nearest to the fireplace. She caught his eye and gave him a soft smile.

He smiled back.

Charles stood at the small bar in the corner of the room, poured two glasses of Oban, and handed one to Jason and Edmond before returning to the bar to pour one for himself.

Eliza cleared her throat. "I wanted to apologize to all of you for my outburst at dinner." She looked at Jason. "I'm really happy to be here. It wasn't my idea, but in hindsight, I absolutely needed some time to unwind and get away. I've been working hard on my latest article for *The Gazette*. And I know you've all been worried about me. The concussion wasn't on my bucket list for this year, to be sure, but I promise I'm fine, and I appreciate you all making time to be here. And I'm incredibly grateful that we could all come here, Bella and Murphy, too."

Bella came over and sat beside her mom, and hugged her.

"Speaking of your article. I just finished reading your latest," Leah said, holding up a copy of *The Gazette*. "I'm no history buff, but it was really interesting to read about the Lord family and the history of Coventry. Will you be writing about other families too?"

"As a matter of fact, I'm currently working on a similar piece about the Brown family for the Halloween edition," Eliza replied excitedly.

"Edmond tells me you have found a family with an interesting past. Something about foul play, a murder made to look like suicide? Is that the Brown family, then?"

"Anybody in the mood for a snack?" Jason asked abruptly. He stood and drained his drink. "I think I need something to munch on." He made his way out of the room and headed to the kitchen.

Eliza made eye contact with Edmond.

"I'll go help him," he said and followed Jason to the kitchen.

Eliza took a breath and let the excitement of what she'd discovered so far take over. "I don't know what happened yet, not exactly, but yes, there are definitely some hints of foul play. The possible murderer involved is a man named Elijah Brown. The man was married twice, and both of his wives and all of his children died before him. Well, all but one child who is listed as his descendant but whose mother isn't listed in the family tree."

"A bastard son? How scandalous," Leah said. "Tell me more."

"His first wife, a woman named Honor Brown, is rumored to have thrown herself off a cliff after her son died, but now I'm not so sure that's true. They died on the same day. Poor woman is buried outside of the family plot and cemetery. There is very little information on the family, but between the town archives and my work with the town historian, I'm sure we'll be able to find the truth of her death.

"Oh, and I haven't even told you the best part. All of this, the suicide or murder, whichever it turns out to be, it all happened at Rosecliff. Elijah Brown built our house for Honor."

"You're kidding," Jane said. "The cliff at your house is where she..."

Eliza nodded. "Yes. It's incredibly sad. Hard to believe that some place so beautiful could be a scene of such tragedy."

When Jason and Edmond came back, she allowed her brother to change the topic of conversation and boast about how proud he was of Leah.

Jason returned to his seat but didn't say much; his gaze fixed on the glass in his hand.

Before long, one by one, the family members headed off for bed, leaving her and Jason alone with Murphy.

Eliza straightened the throw pillows and gathered the empty glasses to take to the kitchen.

She loaded the glasses into the dishwasher in silence, then grabbed her fleece jacket from the back of a chair where she'd left it from their earlier walk. "If you want to head up to bed, I'll be there in a minute. I want to let Murphy out one more time," Eliza said to Jason, zipping up her jacket.

"If it's alright, I'll join you."

"Sure. Murphy's usually quick."

Outside, the cool night sky was crystal clear, and a full harvest moon illuminated the leaf-covered back yard. Between the trees, countless stars glittered above. The sounds of scuffing and crunching dried leaves broke the quiet as they followed Murphy to the big maple tree in the center of the yard.

Jason broke the silence. "I think Leah is really rubbing off on your brother. He made a pretty good case arguing that I haven't been very understanding about your feelings." He gave her a sad smile and put his hands in his pockets. "I wish I could take back the things I said; I never meant to hurt you or make you feel like I wouldn't give you the moon. I never meant to make you feel like I don't respect what you do. I really am proud of you, and I want you to be happy."

"So proud you had to leave the room when I started talking about it?"

"I didn't leave because I didn't care. I think, in that moment, listening to you talk made me realize how important it is to you. How I'd tried to diminish that for you. I was so angry with myself; I needed a moment to think. But don't worry, Edmond read me the riot act. I get it, though; I can see you're just as fulfilled with writing and research as I am with investments and profits."

Eliza leaned into him and nudged him with her elbow. "Yeah, he's a good big brother, always has been. But I don't need him to fight my fights, you know. We've known each other too long for you not to come to me with your concerns. I don't get it; why did you feel the need to involve my family in all of this?"

He turned to face her. "El, I need you to hear me when I tell you, you scared me. Really, really scared me. That night at the cliff. It's been on my mind ever since. I wake up in a cold sweat at night, terrified you won't be in the bed beside me. We have been married for a long time, and you talk about this thing where you see ghosts like it's no big deal. But if you've always been this way, why am I just hearing about it now?"

Eliza looked down at her feet. "It's not something I go around telling everyone. And I've wanted to tell you, but I knew how you felt about this kind of stuff." She glanced up at him.

He reached out and touched her face.

"I don't know how I feel about it," he said. "I don't know if I actually believe in any of it. But I trust you, and if you say that's what's happening, then I promise to give you the benefit of the doubt moving forward."

She wrapped her fingers around his hand.

Jason pulled her close to him, and she buried her head in his coat.

"Don't stop trying to keep me safe. No matter how much I fight you."

"I promise." He kissed the top of her head.

Murphy let out a whine, and they both turned to look at him.

He sat in the yard, not more than five feet away, just looking at them.

"How long have you been there eavesdropping?" Eliza asked.

Jason chuckled. "A dog that doesn't respect our privacy. I don't know, you sure you want to keep him?"

Eliza punched his arm playfully. "No doubt whatsoever."

Murphy wedged himself between them, pressing his head against their thighs.

"Why Mrs. Grey, I do believe something has come between us."

15

A THICK MIST SETTLED about Coventry-by-the-Sea, making visibility across the ocean almost impossible. Eliza stood looking out the French doors at the thick swirling fog. The gloom seeped within the walls of Rosecliff, giving Eliza a reason to stay inside and hunker down. Their trip to see her parents had started out less than desirable, but in the end, she'd appreciated that chance to see her brother and her parents. And she and Jason had come to a more definitive truce, even if he was still skeptical of her abilities. They'd left late Sunday afternoon, dropped Bella back at school, returned home and gone to bed early; the tension between them greatly eased. With a new week in front of them, Jason had risen early for a long day at the office, allowing her time to dig into her research and flesh out her article about the Brown family.

Murphy sat at her feet, looking from her to the outside. He made a small whine and pawed at the door.

"Murphy, sorry, today is an indoor day."

He huffed, and Eliza scratched his head. "I know, but such is life, my friend."

Pouring some tea to stave off the chill of the early morning, Eliza sat at the dining room table, her notes laid out in piles. She examined the Lord and Brown family trees, denoting how they intersected, and sorted through the information she found in Ginny's family Bible.

Finding nothing new, she pulled the book on family histories written by Edwin Lynd from the stack of books she'd borrowed from the library and turned to the index. Eliza flipped to the first page listing of the Brown family and read.

There was mention of the family's wealth tied to trade and devastating losses due to rash business deals and poor investments. Several pages later, a section about a lawsuit in the early 1900s made her sit up straighter in her chair.

According to the book, in the summer of 1904, the Brown estate became the center of a lawsuit after a lost heir was discovered in the Brown family lineage.

The book included an image of an old newspaper clipping.

January 4, 1904

FOUND HEIR!

The missing heir of Elijah Brown (deceased), the wealthy owner of the Lord Shipyard in Salem, Massachusetts, and landowner of Rosecliff Manor and Brown Farm, has been found after many years, pulling the entire Brown estate into question.

Town historian, Mr. Winston Winthrop of Coventry-by-the-Sea, shared news that he discovered the missing heir of Elijah Brown after months of tedious and meticulous research. Through the stipulations written in Elijah Brown's last will and testament, the entirety of his estate was to pass to his illegitimate son, David Abbott. However, at the time of Mr. Brown's death, the boy had never been found, and subsequently, the estate had passed to Mr. Samuel Brown, the decedent's brother.

"It was a delight and a surprise to find the true heir to the Brown fortune was living just a few towns away," Winthrop stated. "That the great-granddaughter of David Abbott, Nellie Smith, should now be recognized and given the benefit of this inheritance seems only fair."

The current Brown family, descendants of Samuel Brown, have secured legal counsel and announced their intention to fight the claim.

The family's attorney professes to "have in our possession irrefutable evidence that would prove the claim to be faulty." The court case is set to begin in the early fall.

Eliza skimmed the next few paragraphs, the sensation of uncovering another layer of the Brown mystery driving her to read faster. Included on the following page was a copy of Elijah Brown's last will and testament.

May 5, 1840

As I am of ill health and do not expect to see another summer, I write this, my last will and testament. I have acquired status and wealth in my lifetime, both desired aspirations. I leave this world with ownership of the Brown Farm and Rosecliff Manor.

Both my wives have predeceased me, as have my three children.

I have no legitimate heir but will now lay claim to the product of a union made outside of the bonds of holy matrimony while married to my first wife, a son named David Abbott. To keep my secret and maintain my social standing, I paid my mistress, Ms. Adelaide Abbott, a handsome sum to leave town and care for the boy. I know not where they have gone.

But, as he is the last of my children to survive me, I have instructed my attorney, the honorable Horatio Adams, to make every effort to find him. And to him, David Abbott, and his line in perpetuity, I leave the entirety of my estate. There must be every attempt to locate my son by my lawyer. If he is not found, the estate will be bequeathed to my brother, Samuel Brown, with the expectation that he will do what he must to keep the estate in good standing.

Elijah Brown

Further reading revealed more information about the descendant of David Abbott. Nellie (née Abbott) Smith, a woman from Gloucester, Massachusetts, recently widowed, and mother to a young son provided documentation of lineage, including birth certificates, to secure her claim to Elijah Brown's estate. Winston Winthrop, town historian, assisted Nellie with her claim, successfully suing the estate, and establishing herself as great-granddaughter to David Abbott and legal and rightful heir to the Brown fortune.

"Winston Winthrop? As in Mayor Winthrop? But how does this all connect? What say you, Watson?" Eliza asked, looking down at Murphy.

He lifted his head and woofed.

"I don't get it either. How does this town historian play into the story?" She sifted through her notes and located a more recent version of the Brown family tree she'd downloaded and printed out from the town archives.

Eliza adjusted her reading glasses and examined the pages carefully. She followed the line of descendants of David Abbott and found the connection she'd been looking for.

The town historian, Winston Winthrop, married Nellie (Abbott) Smith and adopted her son, Wendell, as his own. Wendell went on to have a child, Barclay, who fathered a son, Graham Winthrop.

"So, the town historian who solved the mystery of the missing heir was the mayor's adoptive great-grandfather, and his great-grandmother was the found heir to the Brown family fortune."

Knowing the court case angle would make for a sensational read in *The Gazette*, she googled the town archives for more information. There was little documentation beyond another article that covered the same information annotated in the book. There was, however, another article published shortly after the case was settled, an interview with the family attorney in March of 1905. It made mention of the fact that a great flood had delayed the case for several months and that Benjamin Brown, Samuel Brown's grandson, had insisted that claims made by the widow were bogus but he died of a sudden heart attack while shoring up his home during the flooding in the fall of 1904. The lawyer continued to say that Benjamin Brown decided to hide the evidence after someone ransacked his home. Based on family testimony, it is believed he hid the documents of proof at his current residence, somewhere within Rosecliff Manor. Due to his untimely death, the family had no idea where he'd hidden the evidence but vowed that they would continue to search and return to court when it was found.

She reread the second to last line, "hid documents...somewhere in Rosecliff Manor." Documents that would prove that the historian had it wrong? The realization that Samuel Brown's family had lived at Rosecliff until the courts awarded it to the mayor's great-grandmother, Nellie Abbott, left her puzzled. Why had the Winthrop family not kept Rosecliff, such a prime piece of property, as part of the estate?

Dissatisfied with the information in the archives, Eliza wondered if the courthouse would still have records from the proceedings.

"Hey, Murph," she said, looking down at the sleeping dog at her feet. "You up for a little ride into town?"

Twenty minutes later, Eliza pulled up in front of the courthouse. She left a window cracked for Murphy and hurried up the marble steps of the building, out of the cold air, and headed directly to the office of records.

A young clerk, a woman in her thirties, sat at the desk.

"Can I help you?"

"Good afternoon. My name is Eliza Grey. I'm a reporter for *The Coventry Gazette*, and I'm looking for records from a court case, Brown vs. Abbott, a family inheritance case from 1904. Any chance records from that case have been archived as part of public record and are available for review?"

The clerk smiled warmly and nodded.

"Yes, we have court case documents all the way back to the 1800s. It may take me a few days to find and prepare those files. Not everything has been digitized yet. I think we've only managed to capture cases back to around 1950." The clerk pushed a pad of paper and a pen across the desk. "If you'll leave your name and number, I can call you when they're ready."

Eliza scribbled her contact info onto the pad and gave it back to the clerk. "I'll look forward to your call."

Returning to her car, Eliza smiled. For the first time in a long time, she felt a sense of purpose. How or if this had anything to do with Honor's death, she wasn't certain, but like a bloodhound on a scent, she was definitely on to something.

16

E LIZA'S FINGER HOVERED OVER the "send" button. She'd finished the
article on the Brown family, but part of her couldn't help but feel it was
unfinished. "Secrets from the Grave: The Dark History of the Elijah Brown
Family" gave a detailed recount of Elijah and Honor Brown and the tragedy that
surrounded their ill-fated marriage. Eliza wove a story around Elijah's repeated
risky business ventures and the eventual severing of ties with the Lord Shipyard
after Honor's death. She balanced the accounts of deadly and costly pirate attacks
and seedy contracts with the more human Honor, her heartbreak over losing her
beloved Levi, and the undeniably cruel and abusive conditions she'd lived under.
She'd provided pictures of a family plot making mention of the fact that Honor's
grave lay outside of the cemetery wall. And she'd finalized the story asking the
reader to imagine a mother in the ultimate despair running towards the cliff's edge
at Rosecliff. She'd left it open, refusing to say one way or the other how Honor
had died.

*It is alleged that Honor Lord Brown threw herself from the cliff of her home that
stormy October night, but one never knows what truly pushes an individual to the
brink of a deadly outcome. Some say her husband may have had a hand in her
death, but after two hundred years, the truth is murky at best. Did Honor Brown, a
God-fearing Christian woman, willingly throw herself over the cliff's edge? Or did
someone push her?*

She was close to figuring out the truth of it all; that she was sure of. But until
she had that proof in her hands, this was the best she could do. It might not have
the allure of hanging or pressing witches like Salem, but there was still enough
scandal and intrigue to get the town talking. Or at least she hoped so.

"Fingers crossed you'll think so too, Art," she said out loud and finally sent it off. "I suppose I'll find out soon enough," she added and headed upstairs to get dressed for the weekly staff meeting at *The Gazette*.

Arriving early at *The Gazette*, she was surprised to find Lana and Mayor Winthrop huddled together in the corner of the office, deep in conversation. As Eliza passed, her eyes met the mayor's. He gave her a short nod, and Eliza returned the acknowledgment with a polite smile.

Lana didn't seem to notice that she'd lost the mayor's full attention and carried on with her conversation, hands waving as she spoke.

Art's door was half open, and she knocked softly.

"Come in, Eliza," Art said.

"Hey, Art." She sat in her regular seat and set her bag on the floor next to the chair. "Any chance you've had time to peruse the file I sent you this morning? I'm anxious to hear what you think."

Art glanced at the clock on the wall, held up a finger, and leaned over his desk to peer out into the main office.

Lana and the mayor hadn't moved from where Eliza had seen them when she'd come in.

"This has become a regular occurrence around here. I'm thinking of letting the mayor run the meetings at *The Gazette*," Art said with a snicker.

Eliza couldn't hide her surprise or her amusement, and she chuckled.

Hell must have frozen over. Did Art just make a joke?

"Ms. Addison, will you be joining us?" Art asked, once again surprising Eliza with his unusually curt tone.

As if suddenly aware that her job wasn't to schmooze with town politicians on the Gazette's dime, Lana gave him a startled look and broke away from her conversation.

She snagged a notepad and pen from her desk and turned back to wave at Graham.

The mayor, however, was already outside, the door closing behind him.

"Sorry about that, but Graham, uh, Mayor Winthrop was just providing details about the upcoming 250th Jubilee announcements, as well as dates for specific publicity ads for his campaign. Important people require our utmost attention."

Art waited for Lana to take a seat, then cleared his throat and began the meeting.

"Eliza and I were just discussing her most recent submission on the Brown family." Art looked down at his desk at what Eliza could only assume was a printed copy of her article. "I did a first run-through before you arrived, and it's great writing. Your ending captivated me. It feels as if there may be a follow-up in the future?"

"I hope so. If you'll allow me, I'd like to spend a little more time investigating Honor's death. I can't tell you when it'll be done, but I've been diligently researching and feel like there's more to discover."

Lana leaned over closer to Eliza, tapping her pen on her notepad. "I'm sure Graham would give his blessing to learn more about the Brown family. Any chance you could work in something about him being related?"

Art cleared his throat and began to fidget with his bow tie, clearly unhappy with her comment.

"What?" Lana said, her head snapping in Art's direction. "That man has done a lot for this town, his family too. Nothing wrong with giving a little credit where credit is due, is there?"

Eliza looked at Lana for a moment considering how to proceed.

"How about I write the article first, and if it makes sense to mention that our illustrious mayor is part of that family, I will. By all accounts, some of the Browns in this town have a notorious history." She pointed to the article on the desk. "For all I know, the mayor may not appreciate me associating his name with some of it."

Lana's eyes narrowed above her eyeglasses now resting on the tip of her nose.

"Anything you care to share?"

"Not at the present," Eliza said, staring her down.

The front door buzzer rang, sending Lana straight out of her seat in a single leap.

"Be right back."

Eliza waited for Lana to pass, then stood. "If there's nothing else for me, I'll head out."

Art made work of straightening the already neat pile of folders on his desk and nodded. He glanced up at her. "I'll keep an eye out for that follow-up."

Eliza closed his office door behind her and stopped short when she spotted Lana near the front door, furiously whispering once again with Graham Winthrop.

Lana glanced back and held up a pair of leather gloves.

"The mayor left his driving gloves, and they are his favorite pair."

The mayor took the gloves then addressed Eliza.

"I hear your research on the founding families is going well. I read the piece you wrote last year about Highgate Cemetery and your recent article on the Lord family. You've done the history of our little town some justice."

"Thank you," Eliza said, reaching into her bag for her car fob. "The Highgate Cemetery piece and this series on the founding families has allowed me to shine a light on our prestigious heritage." Her eyes narrowed slightly. "And our questionable past."

Graham's brow furrowed.

"Eliza, you should give us the inside scoop on your latest article, the one about the mayor's family, the Brown family," Lana said, inching closer to Graham.

Eliza hesitated, but the chance to see the mayor's reaction to some of what she'd uncovered was irresistible. "Well, there is certainly the lion's share of mystery and intrigue. A little murder made to look like suicide, lost family heirs, stolen family fortunes, you know, all the juicy skeletons in the closet kind of stuff." She made eye contact with the mayor. "Nothing incriminating, of course."

The mayor sneered. "I'm not afraid of a scandal! I have been a lifelong politician and dedicated to the betterment of our town. Every family has its secrets, mine's no different, but public record will show my family has also been pillars of morality and generosity."

"Do you associate much with the rest of the Brown family, Mayor? Marty Evans, for example?"

The mayor offered her a slow smile that didn't quite reach his eyes. "Ms. Grey, it's no secret that my extended family isn't as close as some families often are. Hardly any scandal in that."

"No, I suppose not, though the rift is hardly unexpected since the Brown family descendants alleged to have evidence that your great-grandmother's claim to the Brown estate was bogus. I've requested the court records from the archives, to see if I can shed any light on what that evidence may suggest. Any thoughts on what you think it might be?"

The mayor's smile disappeared. "Do your worst, or your best Ms. Grey. I've nothing to hide. It's been over a hundred years since the courts recognized my family's right to their inheritance. Any evidence to the contrary would surely have been found by now if, in fact, such a thing actually exists. Interesting, though, the direction you are taking. I'm surprised Art Cummings is okay with turning *The Gazette* into a gossip rag by doing hit pieces on prominent members of society. Now, if you'll excuse me."

He stepped around them and moved quickly toward the door.

"Mayor, how about an interview then?" Eliza asked, keeping her temper in check. He was trying to bait her, but two could play this game. "I could share a bit of the Brown family history you think this town needs to know."

He turned and licked his lips, his eyes narrowed. "You know, Ms. Grey, I think you've got all the information you need. Sure, there are some shadows and bumps in my family tree, but there's no denying the good I and my family have done for this town. Feel free to quote me on that."

He pushed through the door, letting it slam behind him.

Lana looked at Eliza and frowned. She quickly ran to the door and yelled out to the mayor as he stormed across the street: "Lunch tomorrow?"

Graham turned, almost annoyed. "I have a meeting."

Lana stomped back toward Eliza. "You better do right by Mayor Winthrop! He's a good man, and he works hard for this town!"

"Yeah, so he says."

"I mean it, Eliza. That man works hard, day and night, to make this little community of ours better. Don't go running him through the mud just because you think it will sell more papers."

Lana stormed off to the storage room where they kept the boxes of paper and toner.

Eliza wanted to laugh, but she'd heard genuine concern in Lana's voice. *Poor woman. She's falling hard for our illustrious mayor, but my gut tells me he doesn't feel the same.*

As she made her way back to her SUV, Eliza's phone rang.

She answered. "Hey Jason, just got done with my staff meeting. Everything okay?"

"Everything's great. What did Art think of your piece?"

"So far so good. And he gave me the thumbs up to do a follow-up on Honor, if I find any new evidence about the circumstance of her death, that is."

She waited, half expecting Jason to try to dissuade her, but to his credit, he offered her a bit of encouragement instead. "If it's out there to be found, I'm sure you'll find it. Which kind of leads me to the reason I called. I am headed back to Staffordshire next week for the office grand opening and am hoping you're still up for going with me."

Eliza pressed the crosswalk button at the corner. "Of course," she said, trying to hide the trepidation in her voice. The chance to see where Honor was born, from whence the Lord family originated, would be a great addition to her body of research, but there was Murphy to consider.

"Great. We leave on Sunday and will be back the following Monday. That will give me plenty of time to finish up what I need to and give us a few days to take in the sights."

"Okay, I'll start packing," she said with a nervous laugh as she crossed the street and climbed into her SUV.

"I should be out of here by six. Love you."

"Love you too."

Eliza hung up the phone and turned on the ignition, and circled around the block to the veterinary clinic. With any luck, they'd have an idea of some place to board Murphy with such short notice. Otherwise, she'd have to tell Jason she wouldn't be going with him, and she didn't need a sixth sense to know how that would go.

17

URPHY WATCHED ELIZA CLOSELY as she packed his bed, his toy fox, and his jar of treats into a bag.

"Don't look at me like that, Murphy; you're killing me with those sad eyes."

As it turned out, stopping by the veterinary clinic after her staff meeting at *The Gazette* had been the right thing to do. Meredith, the same vet tech who had saved Murphy from being dumped on the side of the road, had only the week before finally convinced the doctor to allow her to board animals in their facility.

"We've got the room, and I've got the time," she'd said. "Funny you should stop in; I haven't even had a chance to email our patient list or put up any flyers."

Eliza had shrugged it off to luck, but of course, something in her gut had told her what to do. That he would be in such good, caring hands gave Eliza some peace, but the thought of going even a single day without seeing his big ol' fluffy face made her sad. Their bond had grown deep and fast over the last month, and the separation made her edgy. Her worst fear was that Murphy would think she was abandoning him, like his previous owner.

"How about a walk before we go?"

There was still a lot to do, odds and ends to finish with her own packing, but she needed to spend some time with him.

She grabbed her coat, gloves, and Murphy's leash. As a last-minute thought, she grabbed a plastic baggie from the drawer in the kitchen island and filled it with birdseed from a large bag she kept in her pantry. She added the baggie to one of her coat pockets and two small suet blocks from the bottom shelf in the other pocket.

Might as well give the birds something to nibble on before the winter sets in.

As Eliza stepped out onto the massive porch, her face warmed by the sun and her senses invigorated by the cool salty air, her anxiety lessened a bit.

She held the door and let Murphy out. He trotted down the steep front lawn, across the dead-end street, and onto the sandy beach. He ran briefly onto the sand and chased a seagull, then stopped to sniff a mound of dried seaweed that had washed up on the shore.

Eliza strolled along the road and, when she reached the corner, patted her thigh, and called out to Murphy, who raced to her side and sat until she'd leashed him. Together, they turned off from Rosecliff Avenue and made their way towards town and the entrance to Highgate. It was already the middle of October and although some of the trees had shed their leaves en masse, the scenery looked glorious. She unzipped her jacket and let the sun warm her body. A V-shaped flock of geese honked as they flew overhead.

They followed the main road through the cemetery to the Brown family plot.

Eliza smiled. *Marty has done such a great job keeping this gravesite well cared for.*

She navigated around to the back and squatted down in front of Honor's resting place. She cleared some leaves and vines from Honor's headstone and lightly touched the letters of the epitaph.

"I'm headed to England—Staffordshire, if you can believe it," she said, wiping away a bit of moss. "I will stand where your family once stood and think of you."

She sat on the stone wall and swung her legs over to kneel by Levi's stone.

"Sweet boy, someday I hope to find out what happened to you and your mom."

Then she stood up and pulled a small bag of birdseed from her coat pocket. Eliza lightly sprinkled the fruit and seed mixture on the tops of the stone wall. Then she opened the two blocks of suet feeders and strategically hung them from the gnarled old tree over Levi and near Honor.

"There you go. Now that looks so much better."

"Hello, Miss Eliza."

"Hello, Marty," she said, smiling.

He never misses a chance to sneak up on me.

"Putting out a little bird seed, I see," Marty said, pointing to the hanging suet feeders.

"Yes, is that okay to do? This place needed a little life, no pun intended."

Marty stared at her for one long second before breaking out into a smile.

Eliza let out a little breath in relief. She knew he took his work and the "residents" of Highgate seriously, and she'd meant no disrespect.

"It's fine, Miss Eliza. I think it is nice. It feels more welcoming here. Much more pleasant for the living to pay their respects. The dead, or spirits, don't mind either way; they just want you to remember them."

"I suppose that makes sense."

"Have you figured out what she wants from you yet?"

Eliza hesitated. It was one thing to *know* things, to share her gift with a limited few, but to chat about the things she'd seen as if it were nothing more than passing conversation was a first for her.

"I suspect, as you do," he continued, "that she didn't throw herself off that cliff like they say she did. Is that it? Does she want you to set things right so she can be with her boy again?" He turned to look over at Levi's headstone.

Eliza took a breath and nodded slowly. "Yes, I think that's exactly what she wants. I'm just not sure how or why yet. But there are definitely bigger forces at play here: me adopting Murphy who helped me find this place and the fact that I live at Rosecliff, the same place she lived and died. There's no denying that I've been brought here, in this time and place for a reason."

"And now that you know that, that you've acknowledged that, the answers will come, I'm sure."

Sharing her truth with him gave her an unexpected sense of relief. He hadn't looked at her sideways, hadn't expressed any doubt or disbelief. She considered his words and hoped he was right. She wanted to find the answers, for Honor's sake, if not her own.

"Marty," she said, "on a slightly different topic, I was hoping I might ask you about something I read in my research. Did you know that the Brown family estate was taken from your family and given to the great-granddaughter of Elijah's illegitimate son?"

Marty nodded. "Sure. I mean, I wasn't alive back then, of course, but my grandfather talked about it. My great-grandfather, Benjamin Brown, was the man they sued. His son, my grandfather, was a teenager at the time and took the job as the caretaker of Highgate after they stripped away the estate." He held out his arms. "We've been here ever since."

"I'm so sorry, Marty. I read that Benjamin died of a heart attack during the trial?"

"Yes, to hear my granddad tell it, he died angry and brokenhearted." Marty rubbed his neck. "Said his father told him that he knew the case was built on lies and that he had proof, but the old man didn't trust those around him and hid whatever it was that would prove they were lying so the lawyer could use it in court. Never sick a day in his life, the family believes the stress of the trial and the flood damage to some of his businesses took its toll. He died of a massive heart attack at Rosecliff, where he was living at the time."

"I don't suppose you have any idea what it was he hid or where he may have hidden it?"

"I really don't, Miss Eliza. My family hadn't lived there for years by the time I was born. I've never even been inside. But whatever it is, it could still very well be somewhere in that house or on the grounds."

"Maybe one of Highgate's residents will do me a favor and point me in the right direction," She laughed, still a little uncomfortable talking about her gifts out loud.

"Maybe so. If they mention anything to me, I'll let you know," he said, smiling.

"Listen, I'm headed out of town for a week, but when we get back, you should come by. We'll make dinner and you can see the house. Maybe seeing the inside will jog a memory, something your grandfather may have mentioned?"

"Thank you, Miss Eliza. That's really nice of you. I'd be honored to come. Are you headed out on vacation?"

Eliza shook her head. "No, well, not really. Jason and I are headed back to England. He's opening a new office there, but I hope we'll have some time to take in the sights. We'll be in Staffordshire, where the Lords are from."

"Well, isn't that another happy coincidence."

Eliza grinned. "I suppose it is. Poor Murphy here will be staying at Dr. Jackson's kennel, however. I just hope he doesn't think I'm abandoning him there."

Marty bent down and rubbed Murphy's ears.

"I'd be happy to stop in and see him while you're gone. Maybe taking him out for a walk or two. I don't mingle well with people or most animals really, but Murphy's different. I like him."

"That's very nice of you to offer. I will let the vet know that it is okay with me if you come to walk him. Murphy likes it here, and he likes you, too."

Eliza wasn't lying. It was evident in the way they interacted that the affection between Marty and Murphy was mutual. In their short time together, Eliza had learned to trust Murphy's reaction to people. Strange as he may be, Marty was a good person and posed no threat. Of that, she was sure.

"I appreciate that, Miss Eliza. Thank you for trusting me and treating me nicely. Not many in this town do."

By the time they made it back to Rosecliff, Jason's car was in the driveway. They found him in the kitchen, making a sandwich.

"How are you?" he asked. Eliza hadn't been coy about her trepidation over leaving Murphy.

"I'm doing okay; I'm just going to miss him so much."

Jason moved around the counter and pulled her into a hug. "Everything is going to be fine. The vet will take good care of him; you said so yourself."

Eliza's eyes welled up with tears.

"Jason, this is harder than I thought it would be. I feel so bad."

"It's okay. How about instead of thinking about how it will feel to leave him, start thinking about how excited he'll be to see you when we get back?"

Eliza sniffed and nodded. "Yeah, okay. That's a good idea."

Just before five o'clock, they loaded into the car with Murphy's supplies for the five-minute drive to the veterinary clinic. Rather than the stress of trying to drop him off in the morning, Dr. Jackson had suggested they drop him off the night before departure.

Jason pulled into the parking lot and put the SUV into park.

"Want me to go in with you?"

"No, that's okay. I can do this."

Eliza climbed out and opened the rear hatch to grab Murphy's bag, then opened the car door and took Murphy's leash.

Murphy jumped down and walked with her up the steps. The bell over the door rang as they stepped inside.

Murphy pressed his thick torso against Eliza's thigh.

Meredith came out from behind the counter.

"Well, hello, Murphy! Look at you, handsome. You have been groomed and well-fed. Wow!" She looked up at Eliza, and her expression changed. "Don't worry; he's going to be fine. The doc and I will take good care of him."

"I know. I'm just going to miss him, and I know he doesn't understand."

Dr. Jackson poked his head around the corner.

"Good afternoon Ms. Grey. Hello Murphy! Glad you could join us."

Meredith touched her arm. "We have so many activities planned for him; he won't have time to be sad. And you'll be back, and everything will be just fine again."

Eliza handed over Murphy's bag. "You have my number if anything happens. Call day or night. Oh, and Marty Evans may stop by to see Murphy, take him for a walk. I'm totally fine with that."

"Marty Evans? The cemetery caretaker?" Dr. Jackson asked.

"Yep, one and the same."

"Interesting; we'll make a note in his file," the doctor replied.

"Ready to see your new digs, Murphy?" Meredith asked, taking his leash.

Eliza bent down and held Murphy's head between her hands. She leaned in, kissed him and whispered in his ear: "Murphy, I promise you I'll only be gone for a week. After that, I will come back to you. I am not like your other owner. I love you, Murphy Grey."

She wiped at her tears and gave him one last hug.

Murphy looked devastated. He let out a soft whimper, then tried to sit on her, blocking her from the door.

Meredith tugged gently on his leash. "I know it's hard, but he'll be better once you've gone. Dogs are really empathetic creatures. He's feeding off your emotions, making it more difficult for him. His goal is to ensure you are okay, and right now, he senses that you are not."

Eliza wiped her face and nodded. "That makes sense. I'll go. Thank you for everything."

Without looking back, she hurried outside. "Be good, Murphy. See you soon!" she said and let the door close behind her.

Almost instantly, she heard the same wailful howling that had drawn the two of them together on the day she'd adopted him.

Eliza hurried to the car, quickly wrapped the seat belt around herself, and clicked it into the buckle.

"Hurry, let's go. If I sit here any longer listening to him howl, I'll change my mind about going."

Jason reached over and squeezed her hand, then threw the vehicle in drive and headed home. When he pulled into the driveway, he asked, "You okay?"

She nodded. "Yeah. I'll be fine. You know me, I cried when we took Bella to kindergarten on her first day. And when we dropped her off at the dorm. This will pass."

Inside, the house felt overwhelmingly empty. Murphy's presence in her life had touched her in a way she'd never expected. Now more than ever, she knew their paths had crossed for a reason.

The next morning was a rush of last-minute packing. Jason took out the garbage, and Eliza did one last run through the house, checking the windows and doors. While waiting for the coffee to brew, she texted Bella.

Eliza: Getting ready to leave. Will text when we land in England.
Bella: Have fun! I wish I could go with you!

For a moment, Eliza imagined being able to tour England with Bella, and her angst then briefly alleviated. At ten minutes to seven, as Eliza finished putting on earrings and checked for the umpteenth time that their passports were in her purse, she heard the horn beep from the driver as he pulled into their driveway.

She'd slept poorly, her thoughts of Murphy making it difficult to relax, but in the flurry of preparation between the alarm clock and now, she could feel her excitement growing. She'd be there to see Jason open his new office and meet his English co-workers, all the faces and places he'd been talking about since his last trip. But there was something more fueling her enthusiasm. Inside her briefcase were several document copies of her research on the Lord family with as much as she could find about their original home in Staffordshire, England. Jason's new assistant, Katherine, had done additional research locally and promised to share what she'd found along with directions to the Lord estate once they arrived.

Marty had warned her about opening doors and digging into secrets, but she *knew* there was something greater at stake than just her curiosity. Between the unexpected discovery of the Brown family plot, Ginny's connection and treasure trove of information on the history of the Lords and Browns, and now the opportunity to physically visit the birthplace of Honor, this story had coalesced into something beyond mere coincidence. She had no idea if this trip would provide any additional clues in clarifying the circumstances of Honor's death. But there was little doubt that treading the land where the woman's family had once lived would further root her in her purpose and give Honor the peace she deserved.

The horn blared again, and Jason called up to her from the bottom of the grand staircase.

"Eliza, it's time to go."

Grabbing her handbag and doing one last check of her appearance, she joined him in the foyer.

"Mrs. Grey, you never fail to take my breath away."

Eliza smiled. While he had not yet acknowledged her ability to *know* things and remained skeptical of ghosts, he had gone out of his way to show her that he loved and supported her. Any lingering tension between them had faded, and the thought of spending an entire week abroad with him at her side made her almost giddy.

Jason opened the front door and ushered his wife onto the landing. The driver, already outside waiting by the limo, opened the rear passenger door.

Before she knew it, the Logan Airport departure terminal loomed ahead of them.

Their trans-Atlantic flight on British Airways was smooth and uneventful. At Heathrow Airport, London, Jason picked up the keys for the rental car, and they were on their way. Through the window, Eliza caught a glimpse of the city as it gave way to fewer buildings and more trees and pastures. The soft glow of interior lights from homes and businesses cast a splattering of illumination, dotting the countryside as they sped past on their way to the flat Jason had rented not far from the office in Staffordshire.

She leaned her head on Jason's shoulder and covered a yawn. "I'm so tired. I can't wait for a cup of tea and a comfy couch."

"Won't be too much longer, another hour tops. Why don't you close your eyes for a bit."

"Alright, if you insist," she said through another yawn.

When Jason nudged her awake, they sat in front of a charming red brick apartment building. The two-story flat held a classic English charm, with its Tudor-style windows and curtain of ivy nearly covering the exterior.

Jason unlocked the large white wooden door with a brass number 28 affixed just below the peephole. He stepped aside and allowed her to enter first, following behind with their bags. They climbed a tight creaky staircase until they reached a tiny landing at the top of the stairs.

The light above them, a utility bulb encased in a metal cage, cast a dim yellow glow. The entire space smelled of old rugs and cedar, much like her mother's hallway closet.

Jason opened the door marked "2B" and flicked on the entry light. The room inside was small and homey, a far cry from their grand home in Coventry-by-the-Sea. The sparse furniture and sterile décor lacked warmth, but there were hints of a vintage cottagey charm.

"What do you think?"

"It's sweet, but it could use a little color, a little something to make it feel like home."

"Yes, I suppose it does." He dropped the suitcases near the door and kissed her. "Have I told you how happy I am that you're here?"

She smiled and leaned into him, her head resting on his shoulder.

"I know it's a bit low-key," Jason said, wrapping his arms around her. "Kent helped me find it. I am renting through one of his family members. It's a fair price and very convenient to the office. They've agreed to a long-term rental for the first year, so we can come and go as necessary, so feel free to let your inner interior decorator loose and give it your best shot."

Eliza stepped farther into the room and ran a finger over the slender sofa table and the back of a floral-patterned couch.

"Dusty. Don't suppose this place comes with room service."

Jason pulled her back into his embrace.

"I have other ideas when it comes to room service. Now, if the lady would be so kind as to allow me, I'd very much like to show her the bedroom."

Eliza laughed. "Lead the way, my good man."

18

ELIZA FOUND SLEEP EASILY and awoke to bright sunshine and the scent of coffee. She checked the time on her phone. It was nearly seven o'clock local time. She followed the earthy aroma and the sounds of clinking dishes through the bedroom door and directly into the kitchen.

"There she is," Jason said. He motioned to a small table and chairs under the kitchen window. "I ran down the street and picked up a couple of scones and clotted cream. The coffee is just about ready."

Eliza stood behind him and wrapped her arms around his waist.

"You ran out already, and I didn't hear you? I must have been unconscious."

"Jet lag is no joke. Besides, you looked so peaceful; I didn't want to disturb you. The bakery is right on the corner. So, it's an easy walk. But, unfortunately, there isn't much else in the way of food here, so we will have to do a little shopping later."

Eliza slipped around him, sat at the table, and selected a scone from the box. She lifted it to her nose. Lemon poppy seed, perhaps? She added a generous dollop of clotted cream to the top of the warm scone.

Jason poured the coffee and set two cups on the table before sitting down across from her.

"So, what's on the agenda for today? Are we heading to the office?" she asked.

"Yes," Jason said, pulling a scone from the box. "I'd like you to come down with me. We won't be there long, but I'd love you to see the place. Meet the staff, Kent and Katherine."

"Of course. It'll be nice to put a face with a name. Then maybe we can take in a little bit of the town. Grab some groceries. Maybe a few knickknacks to spiff this place up a bit?" She pointed at a corner fireplace. "Does it work?" she asked.

"Yeah, I believe so. Kent said as much when he showed me the flat."

"If you like, we could invite Kent and Katherine over for dinner. I mean, I'm sure I could whip up something easy."

"Are you sure?" he asked, pausing mid-bite, the scone hovering in front of his mouth. "I didn't whisk you across the Atlantic so you could become a taskmaster in the kitchen. We can go out if you like."

"No, I think I'd like to stay in. Nothing makes a new place feel like home more than sharing it with friends."

"I adore you, you know," he said and then took a gigantic bite of his breakfast.

"If you love me even half as much as that scone, then I'll consider myself lucky."

On the drive into the office, Eliza had a much better view of the beautiful and peaceful countryside. The temperature was cold and raw, but the sun shone through breaks in the stony-colored clouds.

Grey Financial Investments' newest office was housed in a modest-sized building with beautiful, Tudor-style beveled leaded glass windows that emphasized the building's charm. The entry vestibule was both professional and welcoming. As they passed through the large glass doors into the lobby, a woman in her mid-forties stood from behind a small mahogany desk and greeted them.

"Mr. Grey, it's good to see you again. This must be your lovely wife we've all heard so much about."

Jason introduced them. "Eliza, this is Katherine, our office manager. Katherine, this is indeed my infamous wife, Eliza."

Eliza shook Katherine's hand. The woman was of medium height and build and wore a pretty charcoal grey sweater and black pants that complemented her coloring. Her shoulder-length champagne blond hair showcased deep brown eyes and an ivory complexion.

"How very nice to meet you. I hope you have had a chance to settle in a bit. Such a long flight."

Eliza nodded. "Too long, but worth it," she said. "I'm so happy to finally see this place and meet all of you."

A tall man with fair skin and blue-green eyes appeared from one of the offices. His wavy ginger hair and prominent side part emphasized his high, unlined forehead.

"Ahoy, the captain of this fair ship has returned."

Jason offered him a handshake.

"Eliza, this is Kent."

The tall man turned and offered his hand.

"Eliza, it is so nice to finally meet you. I hope you slept well and found the flat comfortable?"

"Yes. It's very comfortable, thank you. Thank you for everything, really, finding this place and helping my husband."

"Not at all; I'm quite chuffed to be a part of this new team. I've no doubt the level of success we'll achieve here will exceed our expectations."

Jason turned to Katherine. "If you don't mind, will you show Eliza to the conference room?" he said, taking Eliza's hands. "There are just a few things I need to go over with Kent before we head out and take all of the Staffordshire retail establishments by storm. Half an hour, tops. You okay to wait?"

Eliza nodded, "Of course, take your time."

Jason and Kent disappeared into Kent's office, and she followed Katherine to a glass-walled conference room with a window overlooking a cobblestone street and a grass-covered field beyond. The table that anchored the room was long and narrow with a live edge and a magnificent shine. Eliza paused to admire the artwork that adorned the walls – black and white photos of castles and strongholds that had weathered with time.

"Can I get you anything? A cup of tea? Water?" Katherine offered.

"Oh, no, thank you. I am content to simply sit and admire the view and enjoy the quiet."

"Mr. Grey tells me you are quite the writer. He mentioned that you are currently writing about a family that had roots here in Staffordshire?"

Eliza nodded. "Yes, the Lord family originated here and migrated to America in 1784."

"What a coincidence to find yourself researching this connection only to have this new office in the same place."

"Yes, undoubtedly a coincidence."

Or purposeful direction by forces unseen.

"Well, I'll leave you to the quiet then, but if you need help researching anything, my cousin Sarah works at the Civic Centre. She may be able to lend a hand with old records. I'd be happy to give her a call if you are interested. She's such a good soul; I'm sure she'd be happy to help."

"Thank you. I appreciate that very much."

"Just say the word." Katherine gave her a little wave then went back to her desk.

Eliza settled into one of the conference room chairs and turned to face the window. The last couple of days had been a flurry of goodbyes, packing, and traveling, and she hadn't felt even a tingle of *knowing*. She'd slept so deeply last night that not a single dream had broken through. Maybe coming to this place was exactly what she'd been meant to do.

She let her mind wander, trying to recall the layout of the flat and imagining what kind of pieces she wanted to look for to make it feel more like home.

She'd just finished picturing how she would rearrange the furniture and where she'd add spots of color, a throw rug here, a colorful blanket and scented candles there, when Jason tapped on the glass door behind her.

"All set. Ready to go get your shop on?"

"You have no idea," Eliza said, laughing and taking his arm.

"Katherine, I will be at your disposal tomorrow. Eliza and I will be taking in the sights for today. Text me if you have any questions about the Crawford account. I'll be meeting with them tomorrow morning. I emailed you the presentation."

"Will do, Mr. Grey."

Eliza and Jason spent the late morning shopping and enjoying their time together in the English countryside. Her vision for the flat still clear in her mind, Eliza bought some throw pillows, blankets, framed artwork, candles, and a bouquet of fresh flowers.

"These treasures will make that little flat more of a home," Eliza said, holding two pictures of the English landscape.

Jason looked at the two framed pictures and shrugged. "I will have to trust that you know what you're doing," he said and took the two frames from her and added them to the stash of items already occupying the trunk of the car. "Shall we hit up the market for supplies to stock the kitchen?"

"Yes, and all the things we'll need for dinner. Will any guests be joining us?"

"Kent, yes. He said, and I quote, 'I'm hardly the kind of man to deny myself a home-cooked meal.'"

Eliza giggled at Jason's terrible English accent. "And Katherine?"

"Unfortunately, no. Her daughter is in a school play this evening, but she made me promise that the next time you're in town, we'll accept an invitation to dinner at her house."

"How kind of her. Well, let's not disappoint the man in need of a home-cooked meal; lead the way."

By five-thirty that evening, Eliza had made Jason a believer. Her purchases had transformed the stark interior of their rented flat into a cozy hideaway, perfect for short-term travel and entertaining friends. She pulled a tube of lip gloss from her purse and applied, then lit the candles and turned the vase of fresh flowers on the counter just so. The kitchen was too small to host their dinner, but with some assistance from Jason, she'd pushed the coffee table in the living room against the wall and positioned the kitchen table in its place. Borrowing a painted wooden chair from the bedroom, she'd set an eclectic but inviting table with the mismatched dishes and silverware she'd pillaged from the kitchen cabinets.

The delectable smell of spaghetti bolognese simmering in the pot filled the tiny apartment.

Jason lifted the lid to the sauce and inhaled deeply.

Eliza pointed to the counter where a cutting board and a knife sat, surrounded by a small crop of fresh vegetables. "Would you mind washing and cutting the veggies for the salad while I finish up dessert?"

Jason got to work standing beside her in the kitchen.

Eliza stirred the pot of Bolognese, then fished around in the kitchen drawers until she found the beaters for a hand-held mixer and set about turning a pint of heavy cream into whipped cream for their dessert.

"I'm glad you decided to come with me," Jason said, opening his mouth to taste the fingerful of whipped cream she offered him. "Can you imagine if you hadn't? I'd be here, holed up in this stark little flat, eating take-out, not having to rearrange furniture or chop any vegetables. Not sure I could have survived."

Eliza raised an eyebrow. "Okay, have your fun, Jason, but you know as well as I do that you'd be miserable without me."

He kissed her forehead. "That is undeniably true."

"I want you to know how incredibly proud I am of you," she said, her tone turning slightly more serious. "I know I got a little wound up in my research, and even though it was hard to leave Murphy, I have to admit, it feels good to get away. I've been a bit distracted and, if I'm being honest, a little lonely with Bella gone and you traveling. This was a great reminder that there are so many experiences just waiting for us to go out and find them."

"I'm really glad you like it here. I know my business takes a lot of my attention, and I was worried that maybe we were drifting apart," Jason said with honest relief.

"I guess we both need to be a little more aware, huh?" she asked, tasting a bit of the whipped cream herself.

"I will if you will," he said.

"Then I'd say we have a deal, Mr. Grey." She offered him her hand, and he shook it, then lifted it to his lips.

"Oh no," she said, giving him a pointed look. "I know that look. We've got company coming. Get to chopping, mister."

He laughed and finished slicing the last of the carrots and added them to the bowl of chopped celery and lettuce. Eliza added some pickled beets and a bit of feta cheese before placing the salad in the refrigerator next to freshly whipped cream and the mini trifles made with pound cake and fresh berries she'd prepared for dessert.

"Now, all we need to do is slice the bread when Kent arrives."

Their guest arrived shortly after six o'clock with bottles of red and white wine.

"Welcome," Eliza said with her arms outstretched.

"Wow," he said, taking in the changes she'd made. "I hardly recognize this place."

Eliza took the wine; Jason took his coat.

"I told you I had a remarkable wife," Jason teased. "Give her a week, and the entire building will get a make-over."

"No, but seriously," Kent said, "you've worked a special kind of magic here. Thank you so much for the invite. I've been working so much lately; I can't remember the last time my dinner didn't come in a delivery bag."

"My pleasure," Eliza said and led him to their makeshift dining room. Jason lit the tiny fireplace while Eliza fetched three wine glasses from the kitchen.

Kent uncorked the red and poured three generous glasses of wine.

As they ate, they conversed about business and local news.

Kent finished his plate and had seconds. "I've forgotten how good real food can be," he said, wiping his mouth with his napkin. "I'm packed to the gills but a happy, happy man. This was quite delicious. And, I have a little surprise for our lovely hostess."

"A surprise? For me?" Eliza asked, looking from Kent to Jason and back again.

"Don't look at me," Jason said with a shrug.

"When your husband mentioned that you were writing about a family who had once called Staffordshire home, I asked him to send me the article after it was published and then took it upon myself to do a little research of my own, with Katherine's help, and her cousin's, of course."

Kent rubbed his hands together before pulling several sheets of folded paper from his jacket pocket. He opened them and handed the stack to Eliza.

"On top is a map of places nearby I think you'll find of interest. The location of the Lord estate, though there's not much of the original home left standing. There's also a church they likely attended and some other locations related to their business and trade. I thought maybe the day after tomorrow, when the dog and pony show is all done, I could take you both around, show you these places. Thought you might find it enlightening to see the lay of the land and visit where they came from."

Eliza examined the map. "Thank you, this is better than anything I could have expected."

Kent sipped his wine. "Additionally, there are some copies of old documents, birth and marriage registries with Ashley and Mary Lord listed."

"Anything with Honor Lord?" Eliza asked, turning to the second page.

"There is," Kent affirmed, reaching across to take the papers and sort through them, flipping one page over, and putting it on top before handing the stack back to Eliza.

"It's not much, just a small record detailing the passenger list from the *Friendship*, the boat she sailed on from Liverpool to Ipswich. I found it in the records in one of our parish registers in the local archives. But unfortunately, there wasn't much else and certainly not anything you don't already know."

"This is amazing. Thank you for taking the time. I can't tell you how much I appreciate it."

"And there's one more thing," he said, draining the last of his wine and wiping the edges of his mouth with his napkin. "No one was more surprised than I at this final bit of information. On the last couple of papers in your stack..." He waited as she sorted through the pages and ended on a family tree with a genealogy of the Lord family starting from 1695 to the present.

She skimmed over the names and noticed a highlighted line under Ashley Lord's only sibling, Thomas Lord, born in 1762. Thomas's descendants were many. The highlighted line continued off the end of the first page and down the next until it ended at the bottom of the third page, where the last name listed was circled. *Kent Edward Jenkins, June 1, 1988.*

"As you can see, I inadvertently unearthed an interesting tidbit of my own history while looking up yours. Thomas Lord is my sixth-great-grandfather on my mother's side."

Eliza stared at him, wide-eyed, waiting for him to crack a smile and have a laugh at her expense as part of some elaborate joke, but the serious look on his face said otherwise.

"Hold up a sec," Jason said, laying his napkin on the table. "Are you saying you are related to the family Eliza is investigating back home?"

Kent nodded. "It's remarkably coincidental, but yes. I read and reread everything I could find, even called my aunt, who is nothing short of the expert in our family history, and she confirmed it."

Eliza handed the stack of papers to her husband so he could see for himself.

Jason scanned the page, then sat back and sighed, his gaze focused on Eliza. "Remarkably fortuitous."

Kent leaned his elbows on the table, a Cheshire cat grin. "It's almost like we were destined to meet, the three of us. Don't you think?"

Jason's expression grew almost imperceptibly darker, but he covered it with a smile and raised his glass. "To happy coincidences and new beginnings."

Kent and Eliza raised their glasses in a toast.

Later that evening, after they'd finished dessert and sent Kent off with a small dish of leftover pasta for his lunch the following day, Eliza washed the dishes.

Jason stood beside her, towel in hand, to dry them. He dried three forks and put them back in the drawer. "Well, tonight sure was full of surprises. Though I'm guessing you *just knew* something like this might happen."

Eliza stopped scrubbing the pan in the sink and stared at him. His tone was difficult to interpret.

"And if I had an inkling that something interesting was going to happen, would that be such a bad thing?"

Jason leaned his hip into the counter. "No, I guess not. I mean, what are the chances that the guy I partner with from another country would be a distant cousin of the family you've been researching? Part of me wants to just chalk it up to coincidence, but I'm trying to see things as you do. Does this mean something? Do I need to dead bolt the door to keep you from running out into the street or jumping into the ocean?"

Eliza bit her tongue, her gaze falling to the floor.

"That came out harsher than I intended." Jason touched her cheek. "I love you, and I worry because I don't understand. I just need to know that everything is going to be okay."

She let him wrap his arms around her. "For what it's worth, I do think there is some higher force at work here, leading me to the Lord and Brown families and you to Kent and this place." She leaned back so she could look him in the eye. "But I don't think there is any reason to be worried. I haven't had a nightmare in several days, and I feel at peace in this place. I can't really explain it other than I think we were meant to come to England so the spirits, or whatever force is at play here, are happy, and they're leaving me alone. For now, anyway." She gave him a weak smile.

"Okay," Jason said and reached over and pulled the pan she'd cleaned from the dishwater. "Happy spirits, happy wife, happy life—I can work with that."

"Do you want a refill, El?" Jason asked, holding up the pot of coffee.

"No thanks. What a dreary day. I hope it clears by tonight."

Eliza pulled her robe tighter around her. Sitting by the window, she watched through rain-splattered glass as an umbrella-clad passerby dodged wide puddles on the street. Sheets of water pelted against the black pavement in synchronized movements with the increasing wind gusts.

"It should lighten up by this afternoon. I hope you'll be okay on your own for a bit today. Kent and I will be busy getting ready for our big night tonight. Katherine's planning on leaving early to pick up the appetizers and wine."

"Is there anything I can do to help? Pick up flowers? Make a dessert?" Eliza stood and pulled him closer so she could fix his tie.

"No need. Katherine ordered all of that in advance for tonight's shindig. She's a dream, very organized. I feel like she's got half the task done before I even ask."

Eliza finished straightening his tie and flatting his cowlick. "Then I'm sure tonight will be a hit."

"With you by my side, how can I lose?"

Jason smiled and kissed her forehead. "What's on the agenda for today? Sightseeing?"

"Actually, I really want to go through Kent's paperwork from last night. That family tree is extensive! I plan on spending the day here, nice and dry. Plus, I have to make sure I am dressed to the nines for tonight. Glamour takes time, sweetheart."

"You could show up in a potato sack, and you'd still look amazing."

She rolled her eyes at him. "Go, get out of here. Let me be with my research and my primping."

He laughed and kissed her lightly on the lips. "I'll be back around 4:00 to freshen up and change. We can head back over about 5:30. Guests should start arriving around 6:00."

"I'll be ready."

She worked through lunch, reading over the papers Kent had given her more thoroughly, making notes, and searching online for additional information. After she finished, she allowed herself a 45-minute nap, then took a long, hot shower.

She dug her hairdryer out of her suitcase. She couldn't help but think of Murphy and the disaster that had been his first bath on the day she'd adopted him. There had been as much water on the floor as in the tub, but he'd sat so patiently and allowed her to dry and detangle his thick fur.

She was happy to be here with Jason, to see his success with her own eyes, but she missed Murphy. The clock on the bedside table read 3:28 p.m. Jason would be back in about thirty minutes. She had just enough time for a quick call home.

She reached for her phone and scrolled until she found Coventry Animal Hospital. Sitting on the edge of the bed, she typed in the necessary exchange and waited for the connection to go through.

"Good morning, Coventry Animal Hospital, Meredith speaking. How can I help you?"

"Hi, Meredith. It's Eliza Grey. How are you?"

"Ms. Grey! We're doing just fine; how is your trip going?"

"Wonderfully, I'm so glad I came. But I'm missing Murphy and just wanted to check on him."

"Aww, he's doing great. He's quite the celebrity here. Doc lets him walk around with us, and he's fast becoming our resident ambassador to the animals that come in. You'll probably be surprised but happy to know that Marty Evans stopped by yesterday to take Murphy for his walk. And promised to come back today."

"That does make me happy; thank you for letting me know." Eliza smiled to herself. She was glad that Murphy had a familiar face to keep him company. And she was also happy that Marty was leaning into the connection, even if it was with a dog.

"Oh, sure. Mr. Evans comes in all shy but lights up when Murphy greets him. I've never seen his smile before, but he really brightens up. That's the power of an animal for you."

"And Murphy's sleeping and eating okay?" Eliza asked. "No more howling and carrying on like that first day?"

As if on cue, a long mournful howl sounded in the background.

"That dog might just be too smart for his own good. I don't know how, but he must know it's you on the phone. Did you want to say something to him?"

"Yes!" Eliza said excitedly.

"Hey Murphy, come here. There's someone on the phone for you. Go ahead," Meredith said. "I'll put the phone down by his ear."

"Hey, Murphy! How is my beautiful boy? I can't wait to see you. I will be home soon. I promise!"

She heard a significant amount of sniffing and moaning through the phone and laughed.

"Aww, his tail is wagging like crazy," Meredith said, coming back on the line.

Her voice trailed for a moment, and Eliza overheard Meredith telling Murphy what a good boy he was.

"So, as you can hear, he's alive and well."

"Thank you so much for letting me check in with him, Meredith. And for taking such great care of him. I'll see you both next week."

"Perfect, Ms. Grey. Enjoy the rest of your vacation."

The call ended, and Eliza sat on the edge of the bed, a stabbing pain in her chest and the pangs of homesickness in her gut.

"Everything okay?"

Eliza jumped off the bed and dropped her phone. "Jason! When did you get home? I didn't hear you come in!"

"Evidently not. But who could blame you? Sounds like you were deep in conversation." A wide smirk played on his lips, his blue eyes staring at her adoringly.

"Don't tease me; I'm already a wreck about it. I miss him so much."

Jason came and sat next to her on the bed. "I figured that might be it. What did the vet have to say?"

"That he misses me," Eliza said, wiping away a tear.

"I'm sure that's true." He put an arm around her shoulders. "You'll see him soon. How is the big guy, by the way?"

"Meredith said he's doing just fine. Made himself at home there, apparently. She also mentioned that Marty Evans had stopped by to take him for a walk. Actually, coming back today, too."

"Seriously? Well, now I *know* that dog is special."

Eliza laughed and shoved his shoulder. "I've been telling you that since the day I brought him home."

"So, you have. Sorry it's taken me so long to see it."

Jason's custom-tailored Italian wool suit fit him perfectly. Eliza admired him from the doorway of their bedroom. With a crisp white French cuff shirt and silk tie, he was every part of the successful investment broker and the man she loved. He held his gold and onyx cufflinks in his hand. "Can a guy get a little help?"

Eliza smiled, "Of course." She attached them to his sleeves and removed a small thread from his shoulder, then slowly circled him, inspecting every inch of his suit. "Perfection."

"A requirement if I'm to walk in with you on my arm."

"What, this old thing?" Eliza said. She wore a short, fitted black cocktail dress with bell sleeves and moderate cut scoop neck, and black pumps. She handed Jason her diamond pendant. "Can a girl get a little help?"

She lifted her long auburn curls and turned her back to him. He pressed up close behind her, put the chain over her head, and fastened the clasp.

He spun her around and beamed, "You look beautiful. I can't wait to introduce you to our clients." He leaned in and whispered in her ear, "The sooner you meet them all, the sooner I can bring you back here and see if that dress looks half as good on the floor."

"Get my coat; the clock is ticking," Eliza said with a coy smile.

Jason parked in front of the building. Eliza waited for him to open her passenger door.

"The office looks amazing at night. The lighting is just beautiful," she said, taking his hand and stepping out of the car.

The silver Grey Financial Investment sign was illuminated by a spotlight above the leaded glass door. Inside, the glow from the elaborate chandeliers sparkled with soft, yellow light. Jason offered Eliza his arm and ushered her inside. Seasonal flower arrangements had been placed sporadically around the large office space. A massive round table in the center of the room held a spread of cheese and fruit and a variety of mini canapés. Instrumental music softly played in the background. Kent waved from across the room, where he consulted with a bartender standing ready behind an antique wooden buffet sporting a generous selection of wines. Katherine set a large floral arrangement between the bottles of wine and the stemmed glassware.

"Looks great!" Jason beamed.

"You both have outdone yourselves. What a wonderful transformation," Eliza added.

"I believe I may have missed my calling as a party planner." Katherine giggled. "This is so much fun."

The buzzer rang from behind the group, and they turned in unison. "Ah, mates, looks like the guests are arriving," Kent said, moving forward to open the door.

Jason stopped him briefly.

"Everything we've worked for, it starts now, tonight. I couldn't have done it without you."

Kent offered him a hand, and Jason shook it.

Jason gave a nod towards the door. "Now, how about we get this party started?"

By the time they made it back to the flat, Eliza's feet screamed to be released from her shoes. She must have met at least two dozen prospective investors, each one excited about working with Grey Financial Investments. She'd watched Jason and Kent maneuver like pros.

"If I never wear heels again, it'll be too soon," she said, flopping down onto the bed.

"Kent said he'd be here around ten tomorrow," Jason remarked, taking off his jacket and kneeling down beside her. "He's almost as excited to show you around this town as he was about the party tonight, I think."

She groaned slightly when Jason pulled off the offending heels and began rubbing her feet. Eliza popped up on her elbows and looked down at him. "I'm so proud of you, honey. You've worked so hard. I know this office was the right move."

He kissed the top of her foot and then her shin. "Far be it for me to ever doubt what my wife *knows*," he said, kissing her knee.

"Know what else I know," she said, slightly breathless.

"What's that?"

"This dress unzips in the back."

As promised, Kent arrived just before ten, and using the map, he had so kindly drafted, he took them through Cannock Chase and beyond into the beautiful British countryside. While the early morning had threatened rain, the clouds had burned off, leaving a gloriously clear brisk day for their adventures through Staffordshire.

"I thought we would stop to see the remnants of the Lord estate and then drive out to the Roaches, the best Gritstone Crag in the UK. They're imposing but a must-see."

As the roads rolled on, the beautiful unspoiled ancient heather heartland of Cannock Chase took Eliza's breath away. The soft brown grass and bits of purple heather stretched out between a mix of old and modern buildings. In a way, it reminded her of Coventry, a mix of old and new, but everything felt as if it belonged. Eliza couldn't shake a sense of déjà vu. The edges of her vision began to go fuzzy. Kent and Jason sat in the front seat talking about work, but their voices grew hollow like they were underwater and growing farther and farther away. Her eyes grew heavy, and she gave in to the vision.

May 17, 1784

A young mother and father sat on a tufted sofa, heads close together, talking about going to America. Beside them, a dark-haired toddler sat on the floor, playing with a quilted doll. The woman leaned back and put her hands on her pregnant belly—a concerned look on her face.

"I've made all the arrangements," the husband said lovingly. "It will take several weeks, but I've secured a private cabin." He placed a hand on his wife's belly. "We'll be there before the baby comes, together in a new place where nothing but opportunity awaits." He turned his attention to his young daughter, where she sat on the floor. "What say you, Honor? Shall we sail away on an adventure?" The girl smiled up at him before climbing to her feet and into his lap.

Eliza felt the warmth of his hug as he embraced the girl. He smiled, his lips moving, but she could no longer hear his voice. The image of the family faded, and she opened her eyes to find Kent and Jason staring at her.

"Eliza? Are you okay?" Jason reached into the back seat and touched her face.

Eliza concentrated on the words, fighting against the wooziness. "Yes, I...I am just feeling a bit car sick...need some fresh air."

Her car door opened, and Jason knelt at her side. "Take my hand; let's get you on your feet."

She took his hand and held onto him as the world came back into focus. She took a deep breath, the cool air settling her stomach.

"So sorry, Eliza. These country roads can be a bit windy," Kent apologized, smoothing the hair on the back of his head. "Maybe you should sit up front for the remainder of the day?"

"I think that's a good idea," Jason said, rubbing her back. He leaned in to whisper in her ear, "Are you really all right?"

Eliza recognized the fright in his eyes. Though not as intense, she could see his fear. She'd seen a similar expression the night of the cliff incident.

She gave him a small smile and nodded. "Yes, I promise." She held his gaze until his expression softened.

He kissed her forehead and helped her settle in the front seat.

A few minutes later, Kent pulled off onto an unpaved road, parked, and led them down the pathway on foot to an old stone wall about a quarter mile from the roadside. Beyond the divide, a beautiful heathered glen stretched out before them.

"According to the town records, this is the original stone fencing of the property once belonging to the Lord family. Based on this expanse of land, I believe they left for America with a bit of wealth."

Kent pulled two neatly folded pieces of paper out of his back pocket and opened up a diagram.

"The home stood about here. According to this, Ashley Lord frequented Liverpool to conduct business with the merchant ships. He may very well have been initiating his sea trade business."

"It's really lovely, don't you think?" Eliza asked, taking Jason's hand. "Do the records mention what happened to the estate once they'd departed?"

Kent nodded. "I believe it stayed in the family for a while, but I imagine the upkeep required a pretty penny. It wasn't uncommon for large-family homes such as this to fall into disrepair. Brings new meaning to house-rich cash-poor if you know what I mean."

Kent pointed out remnants of outer buildings, one that was most likely a stable, another that had probably been where the house laundry had been cleaned.

"It really is too bad that none of this has survived," Eliza said. "But there is still something magical about standing here and taking in the same view that they did all that time ago."

While Kent drove to the Roaches, Eliza studied his diagram of the Lord estate. There was no question the family had been wealthy, even before setting out for America and growing their fortune at sea. She wondered why they had decided to leave it all behind. Had Ashely Lord simply been a man who craved adventure? Or had he wanted more? A chance to prove himself and grasp the opportunity to test himself?

The same thoughts danced in her mind as she watched her husband when they reached the crags. He climbed up and stood leaning into the wind. Much like Ashley Lord, he saw the opportunity of distant shores. His desire to challenge himself had led him to start his own company to begin with. And now, they stood across the same ocean that had led the Lords to Coventry, looking for connection and a chance to expand their wealth and security. She climbed up to stand beside him.

"Thank you for bringing me here," she said, squeezing his hand. "I didn't know how much I needed to see this place, be here, in this place. Hard to explain, but it feels almost familiar."

Jason lifted her hands to his lips. "Don't take this the wrong way, but I know what you mean. It's like part of us belongs here. The more I think about it, the more I know that opening this office was the right decision."

"Be careful, Mr. Grey. Your intuition is showing."

He raised an eyebrow, his expression stern at first, then he chuckled. "Just don't tell anyone. I've got a stiff-backed skeptical reputation to uphold."

The rest of the afternoon was spent checking off all the spots of interest from Kent's map.

"After all this sightseeing, I don't know about the two of you," Kent said as he adjusted the rearview mirror, "but I'm famished. Can I take you back to town for dinner and a pint at my favorite pub?"

"Yes, please," Jason said in agreement. "I'm starving."

"The perfect ending to a wonderful day if ever there was one," Eliza added.

"Very well, off we go." Kent put the car into gear and headed back toward Staffordshire.

They arrived an hour later at The Copper Fox. The wooden sign out front, with a fox on hind legs and a top hat and cane, made Eliza smile.

The interior was warm and cozy, with rich dark woods and the heady aroma of stale beer and cheese. They sat at a high-top table near one of nearly a dozen diamond-paned leaded glass windows that ran the length of the small establishment.

Kent ordered three pints of stout and recommended a pub favorite.

"They make an incredible ploughman's dinner here. It's a bit of a smorgasbord of nibbles and bits – bread, cheese, and ham served with savory delicacies like Scotch eggs and pork pies. It's really quite good."

"One for each of us, then?" Eliza suggested, and Jason agreed.

After two pints and her dinner eaten, Eliza wiped her eyes with the corner of her napkin. "I haven't laughed this hard in so long!"

Kent wrapped his hands around his beer. "Ah, Eliza, now you know my secrets and checkered past. Although I can't quite picture Jason with a scruffy face, curly hair, and dressed in a Metallica T-shirt."

Jason laughed out loud. "There was a time in my life when I never met a microwave burrito or an economic predictive equation I didn't like."

Eliza reached out and took his hand. "I promise you, he stood out in a crowd even then, but he's only gotten more handsome since."

"And you?" Kent asked, focused on Eliza. "Now we know your husband was all about long hair, microwave Mexican food, and metal bands, information that will be highly coveted for any future social gatherings, but what about you? I now know all about this Honor Brown and her egotistical husband. But have you always been interested in the dead, or is it strictly a result of your recent work? Most people I know would not feel at home visiting a cemetery."

Eliza laughed.

"I wouldn't say an interest, but rather a calling. Interesting stories and people just seem to find me. As for the cemeteries, that was absolutely due to my work, but truth be told, I can't help but be fascinated. Every person has a story, I guess."

Kent looked thoughtfully at Eliza and nodded. "I'm not sure I believe in coincidences, but there must be a reason you found that little graveyard, and now you've got a 200-year-old mystery to solve. I must admit, it's very intriguing."

"Coincidences have become rather repeatedly coincidental as of late," Jason said.

Eliza caught his eye but couldn't quite make out the emotion he was working to hide. Frustration? Fear?

Kent took the last sip of his stout and hailed for the check.

"I've got this, mates. It's been great seeing my countryside again. I have not done that in so long. Funny how we often take for granted the things that are right in front of us."

The ride back to the flat was mostly silent. Kent dropped them off and wished them a good night.

"You okay?" Eliza asked as they climbed the narrow staircase to their apartment.

"Yes, why?"

"You seemed quiet at the end of this evening and on the way home."

"Tired, I guess," he said as he pushed open the door.

Eliza moved closer to Jason and ran her finger along the outline of his face.

"Thank you for a lovely day, for taking the time to go and see all things Lord today. It means a lot to me."

He pulled her close. "You know I'd do just about anything to make you happy."

She nodded. "I know. I've *known* it from the moment I first met you."

Eliza's mind rolled back in time, a flashback to a clam boil in Jamestown, Rhode Island, shortly after her college graduation. Lindsay, her college roommate, had organized the event with the intention of setting Eliza up with one of her guy friends. Dreading the party, she almost backed out, but *something* told her to go. When she arrived at the beach, a throng of tanned, toned bodies stood around a large sand mound with seaweed spread beneath a giant stock pot. The scent of clams, corn, potatoes, and hot dogs hung in the salty ocean air. She'd spotted the handsome guy with tanned skin, thick wavy brown hair, and a black Metallica t-shirt almost immediately. Their eyes met, and at that moment, she'd *known* she would spend the rest of her life with him.

Jason yawned. "I'm beat. And I need to be in the office tomorrow morning for a meeting. You okay if I jump in the shower? Or do you need help with any zippers?"

Eliza smiled and rolled her eyes. "Go shower. I want to check my email. Meet you in the bedroom in, say, ten minutes?"

"Make it five," he said and planted a quick peck on her lips.

After pulling off her shoes, Eliza sank into one of the armchairs and fished her cell phone out of her purse. She was a little disappointed that there were no texts from Bella, but there was an email from Vanessa.

El,

I hope your trip is going well! Thought I'd share a little of the news since you've been gone. The courthouse's archive storage office burnt to the ground the night you left. There was some really nasty weather and at first, they thought lightning might have been the culprit. Patrick and his crew battled the fire well into the night. He came home exhausted and hinted that someone may have deliberately set the fire. But the next morning, the mayor held a press conference and declared the cause to be faulty wiring and spouted some "if re-elected" promise that he would ensure the town's oldest buildings would be inspected and brought up to code to prevent future mishaps.

Patrick has no idea what to think and can't imagine why he would fabricate the story about faulty wiring. I don't have your abilities, but even I know something's off about this whole thing. My only question now is what was in that building the mayor doesn't want anyone to see?

I'll keep you posted if anything changes. Travel safely and hurry home, my friend. I miss you!

V

Eliza rolled her neck and leaned back in the chair. Regardless of Jason's inclination to believe that coincidences were nothing of consequence, the fire couldn't just be an unlucky occurrence. That the building had burned down after she'd requested copies of the Brown family court case, and the fact that she'd revealed as much to the mayor, only made her more certain that it was arson rather than lightning or faulty wiring. The only question was, had the clerk managed to find the records in time, or was the evidence now nothing more than char and ash?

19

O N THEIR LAST FULL day in England, Eliza was left on her own to explore at will as Jason and Kent met with clients and finalized any loose ends before Jason's return to the States. She spent the morning at the Civic Centre with Katherine and her cousin, Sarah, examining the Lord family records as well as several business contracts, land purchases, and last will and testaments for several members of the family. As they worked, she shared the circumstances of her research and how she suspected that Honor had come to an untimely end at the hands of her husband.

"How cruel and utterly heartbreaking," Katherine remarked.

"It's why I'm so keen to understand her and her family better. I can't help but feel like the move to America may have been fortuitous for her family, but slightly less so for Honor. What might her life have looked like had they stayed here?"

"So hard to imagine what could have been, isn't it?" Katherine asked.

Unfortunately, likely due to her young age, the rest of their research revealed only limited information about Honor. However, they were able to find out more about Mary Lord, Honor's mother. Born into a wealthy aristocratic family from Liverpool by the surname of Seymour, her marriage came with an abundant dowry that aided in the financial success of Ashley Lord's business endeavors. All in all, it gave Eliza a clearer picture of the life the Lord family enjoyed before emigrating to America.

"Thank you, for helping me with these," Eliza said, as they walked to their cars. "I have a much better understanding of the woman I'm writing about. It'll allow me to give my readers a much broader sense of who she was and where she came from."

"It was my pleasure. Nothing like a little mystery to keep the day interesting," Katherine said with a wink. "I'm headed back to the office. Where are you off to?"

"Back to see where the old Lord's homestead used to be. I forgot to take pictures when we were there before."

"Enjoy your day and as I don't think we'll see each other again on this trip, safe travels back to America."

Eliza hugged Katherine and said her goodbyes.

A short drive later, Eliza pulled onto the same unpaved road Kent had shown them and followed the path to the old stone wall. She smiled when she considered that this was twice in as many months that a wall stood between her and a place forgotten by the passage of time. She traversed across the fields of heather and grass to the place where she imagined a grand home had once stood. It had felt good to stretch her muscles and walk about. It reminded her of Murphy and their walks together.

Not far to the east, a deep stream and a lovely, treed grotto called her. She made her way across the uneven terrain and over several patches of thick, dried grass, hoping not to disturb any creatures that might be hiding within and was surprised to discover a small, weathered marble bench scarred and worn by time tucked into the dense grove of trees. She sat and took in the space. How beautiful it must be in the warmer weather.

A strong breeze gave her a sudden chill and she pulled her coat tightly around her. The sky, an endless blue when she'd parked her car, was now dappled with grey-colored cloud cover. With the drop in temperature from the lack of sun, a layer of mist about three feet high began to form. She watched as it snaked and drifted throughout the heathered landscape. Above, a loud cawing drew her attention to a flock of crows settled around this little glen. Another gust of wind brought more birds. They swooped down and surrounded Eliza, settling into the trees above her and the ground near the bench. Her mind flashed to Highgate and the day she'd first discovered the Brown family plot.

The cawing settled into a regular rhythm, constant and cacophonous. Her head began to swirl. From within the fuzzy edges of her mind, amidst the eddy of sound, a beautiful little girl, no more than two, holding the hand of a young mother, came into focus. The air was still but frigid around them as voices hummed, growing closer and clearer.

"Come along, Honor," a soft voice said.

Eliza stood watching as the woman and her child walked past her. When they reached the other side of the grotto, the woman turned back and smiled over her shoulder.

A glowing fog passed between them, the images in front of her like a movie playing in fast-forward motion. She saw a ship, a young family, then the child became a young woman at a wedding, and then images of Rosecliff emerged from the mist. The girl, Honor, now a woman drifted before her.

She was so familiar.

The woman reached out and motioned for her to come closer.

It's her. The woman from the beach.

The apparition was one and the same, the beautiful woman she'd seen before the Wet Lady had ripped her away into darkness.

Honor bent over and picked up a small child. She settled him on her hip, a beautiful little boy with an angelic face, rosebud lips, and gleaming blue eyes. Levi.

Honor looked at Eliza and began to speak but no sound came. She stretched her arms out to hand the child to Eliza.

"I don't understand. You want me to take him? You want me to take your son?"

The fog shifted and the boy disappeared.

A throbbing pain sliced through Eliza's head and her ears began to ring. A dark shadowy mass formed behind the woman. The entity grew into the shape of a large man with no eyes and enormous deformed hands reaching out to grab her.

Honor's face twisted with pain. She reached out toward Eliza.

"Tell me what to do," Eliza pleaded. "Tell me how to help you!"

Honor's image slowly faded, in her place a green glowing orb oscillated and grew until it shattered revealing a slimy, bent, and broken specter. The Wet Lady materialized, opened her mouth, and released a hellish scream.

Eliza shuttered and held up her hands to her ears. A biting wind whipped around them, her hair slapping her skin, the cawing of the crows loud and thrumming in her ears.

The Wet Lady hovered closer, her opaque nightdress, wet and tattered, fitted tight against her bony body. Her long hair, matted and dripping, hung around mangled shoulders. Her wild eyes fixed on Eliza.

"What do you want from me?!?" Eliza screamed, the words barely registering a sound, swallowed by the wind as if by some unseen force.

The Wet Lady pressed her head back in line with her neck. Her voice snaked out on the wind to whisper in Eliza's ear.

T'is not what is wanted but rather what is needed,
A longing for her child, a mother's heartache heeded,
A soul wrongly damned, a soul in torment,
Missing her child, betrayed! I lament,
But alas, the truth revealed t'is my final plea,
Coming across this great divide, lifted from the sea,
I wander as a specter through your waking dreams,
So often, I have called, 'Help me;' all is not what it seems,
Avenge my untimely death, my tragic demise.
Unravel the secrets that lie in disguise,
Shadows from the past will emerge from the grave,
Secrets and lies are yours to enslave,
I long to be reunited with my dear kin,
Release me from this cell and shackles from within,
Honor my name, Honor my bequest,
Find the one who murdered me and give me eternal rest!

With the words spoken, the edges of the apparition softened, growing fuzzy and more opaque. The sound of the wind and the crows growing louder and louder. Eliza pressed her hands against her ears.

The Wet Lady's ghastly face flashing in and out of clarity, morphing from hard bony edges to someone more familiar. Mournful eyes and dark hair staring back at her.

In an instant, Eliza made the connection.

"I know who you are. You and Honor Brown are one and the same. You drowned off the cliffs of my home in Coventry-by-the-Sea. It was you on the beach that day."

The Wet Lady nodded and then spoke with clarity and conviction.

Bring the truth of my death.

"But how?" Eliza yelled.

The sound of her voice startled her. The wind had died, and the Wet Lady had vanished.

Eliza steadied herself. She returned to the old marble bench under the shade of the trees and sat. Above, a bright blue sky full of sunshine belied that anything out of the ordinary had just occurred.

The sound of wings whooshed around her as a dozen crows took to flight. She stood and watched them disappear over the trees and out of view. Part of her wanted to hurry back, find Jason, and tell him what she'd seen. Tell him that it all made sense now, the nightmares, hauntings, and the visions. She'd been right. Honor wanted, no needed, her help. But would Jason believe her? Would he insist that she give up the research and the story? Would it undo the delicate balance of trust between them?

As she turned to leave, she noticed a slight impression on the surface of the bench. She bent and ran her fingers along the top. The indentation was undeniably a series of letters. She vigorously rubbed the moss and dirt away to reveal four letters: L O R D.

Eliza couldn't help but take in all that had just occurred at the Lord's homestead. Reaching into her pocket, she grabbed her cell phone and quickly snapped pictures of the age-old property and marble bench.

I came here for some photos, but I'm leaving this place with so much more.

She'd already shared with Jason that she felt called to this place. The afternoon's events were her undeniable proof, whether he chose to believe them or not.

Honor Lord Brown had once played near these trees, lived on this land. This woman who had been adored by her family and who had so fiercely loved her son had not killed herself but had become the victim of foul play. Her body laid to rest as a suicide, shamed and separated from her beloved child. The family she cherished likely died believing she took her own life.

Eliza made her way back to the car, a renewed vigor in her step. Two hundred years or not, the story needed to be corrected. Jason would understand. He had to.

Honor's truth needed to be told.

20

Eliza and Jason loaded their luggage into the rental car. The sudden beep of a horn behind them caught their attention. Kent sat behind the wheel with a warm smile and a light wave. Stepping out of his car, he briskly walked toward them.

"I came by to wish you both safe travels!"

"Thank you for everything," Jason said, reaching out to shake Kent's hand.

Eliza noticed a slight shade of red color on Kent's face. "Happily done, of course." He turned to Eliza.

"Before you go, I have something for you." He reached into the deep side pocket of his jacket and pulled out a small black velvet sack with a silver "L" embossed on the front, and offered it to Eliza.

"After our outing the other day, and the fascinating story behind it, I reached out to my aunt. She was as taken with the story as I am. She called me yesterday evening, insisted I come over and see her immediately." He pointed at the pouch in Eliza's hand. "And she insisted that I give that to you."

Eliza carefully opened the small bag and pulled out an antique gold chain and an oval-shaped locket. The front showcased a gilded cross surrounded by a floral design of three lilies, each inset with a diamond. The delicately designed locket was undeniably old, yet it still held its original beauty.

"It's just lovely."

"Open it," Kent urged.

With the tip of her nail, Eliza separated the two halves and opened the locket on its hinges. Inside were two tiny painted portraits: on the left, a couple. The man appeared to be in his late twenties, very stately and handsome with thick brown hair and mustache, and the woman, in her mid-twenties, beautiful with dark eyes and yellow hair. On the right was a pretty little girl about two years old with long ebony hair and brilliant green eyes. A delicate crystal covered both portraits. When she closed the locket and turned it over, etched in the gold: *To Josette Lord Love Honor Lord 1784.*

Eliza stared at Kent, and the chain drooped through her fingers as the treasured locket sat in the palm of her hand. "This is incredible! Where did you find this?"

"My aunt received it from her grandmother, a descendant of the Lord family. After I spoke to her, she said she remembered the name Honor, but she couldn't recall where at first. And then, when she was finishing the dishes last night, she remembered. She always assumed *Honor Lord* was a biblical commandment rather than a name. Then she put it together. The year matches the time frame the family was here; she recalled the story that it was a gift from a grandchild of Josette Lord, Ashley Lord's mother, before they sailed to America."

"Truly remarkable, but I can't take this. It belongs to your family." She put the locket back in the bag and held it out to him. "Please tell your aunt thank you for allowing me to see it."

Kent wrapped his hands around hers, closing the bag back into her palm. "I am an only child, my aunt has no children. I would be the next in line to receive it and right now I choose to give it to you. And it's hard not to think that maybe you were always meant to have it. Coincidences aside, your visit helped me better understand my own family, and certainly solidified our connection." He looked at Jason.

"Besides, I researched the history on lockets," Kent said. "This kind was common; they held a space for portraits or locks of hair. Most lockets are seen as symbols of good luck, but some had more nefarious intents, to hide secret messages or even poison! Though in this case, my intent is for luck. Help my distant cousin tell her story and find out what really happened to her. Someday I hope to come to the States and see where she lived, pay my respects."

"You would be welcome any time," Jason said, shaking his hand once more.

Eliza hugged Kent. "Thank you. Thank you for everything."

The trans-Atlantic flight landed at Logan Airport in Boston late in the afternoon. Jason secured his driver to pick them up and bring them back to Rosecliff. Eliza could not contain her desire to get home, grab her car, and pick up Murphy.

Jason reached over and took Eliza's hand.

"Thank you for coming to England with me."

Eliza smiled and leaned her head on his shoulder. "Thank you for taking me."

"As nice as it has been, it always feels good to come home, doesn't it?"

"Yes. I can't wait to go pick up Murphy. I really have missed him."

Jason leaned forward, "Paul, could you stop at 444 Main Street, Coventry Veterinary Hospital, before dropping us off? We have someone to pick up."

"Absolutely, Mr. Grey."

Eliza could not temper her excitement and let out a small squeal. "Thank you!"

"The big guy shouldn't have to wait any longer than necessary. After his vacation, he deserves to go home in style."

Eliza pulled Jason closer and planted a firm kiss on his lips. "You really are too good to me, you know."

The sleek black limo pulled into the small old parking lot with its sharp incline and faded parking spaces. Eliza opened the passenger door before the driver had even put the car in park and raced up the steps and through the vet's office door.

Meredith sat at the front desk, entering information into the computer.

"Welcome home! I hope you had a great trip."

Eliza smiled. "I did. It was everything I hoped it would be and more, but I couldn't wait to get back. How is he?"

Before Meredith could respond, a loud, reverberating howl sounded from the back room.

"Pretty sure a certain someone knows you're here."

Dr. Jackson came through the back door with the blur of a white beast pushing past him.

"Geeze, Murphy! You're as big as the *Titanic* in this small office. Hard to port, boy, hard to port!

Eliza knelt as Murphy danced about her, his tail wagging furiously. He stopped prancing around every few seconds to lick Eliza's face.

"I hope he behaved himself," Eliza said laughing as she wiped away the long streaks of dog saliva.

"Good as gold, Ms. Grey. You have yourself an awesome dog there."

"Here are all of his things," Meredith said, handing over the bag of leftover food and Murphy's toys.

She came around the desk and bent over and gave Murphy a big hug and a kiss. Then Meredith escorted them to the main door and held it open.

"Thank you, both," Eliza said waving awkwardly as she tried to hold Murphy's leash and all of his things.

"Bye, Ms. Grey. See you, Murphy."

Paul stood beside the limo and held open the rear passenger door. Murphy stopped and sniffed his shoes.

"Go ahead, Murphy," Eliza said. "Hop in; it's time to go home."

Murphy hesitated and looked up at the driver.

"It's okay," Paul said and laughed. "Go ahead."

Murphy made the leap inside.

"Smart dog, you got there," he said to Eliza.

"Smart but completely unaware of how big he is," Jason called from inside the car. Eliza could hardly see her husband behind the mound of white fur that had made himself at home on Jason's lap.

Eliza climbed inside, and within a few minutes, the limo turned down Rosecliff Avenue, past the sandy beach, and up the long driveway to the house.

"Home," Eliza whispered under her breath.

Murphy licked the side of her face and offered a resounding woof.

With their luggage carried upstairs and take-out ordered, Jason started a fire in the living room fireplace. Eliza stepped outside with Murphy to the back yard and looked out over the ocean. The autumn colors had nearly all faded. Large piles of leaves gathered on the ground beneath bare branches. The wisteria tree, now completely barren, looked like a gnarled hand grabbing the arbor.

She watched the ebb and flow of the ocean waves, mesmerized by the rise and fall of the water. The sky dappled with grey clouds, and the lone call of the seagulls as they soared above added to a sense of security and peace. This was home.

Murphy moved from tree to tree, taking in all the smells, searching for anything or anyone who had entered his domain in his week-long absence. He quickened his pace and sniffed a wild rabbit sheltered under the great pine tree at the yard's far corner and gave chase across the lawn before disappearing around the side of the house.

Eliza strolled through the feathery grass, moving toward the cliff edge. She retrieved the locket Kent had given her from her pocket. She traced the cross and lilies with her forefinger, lightly caressing the locket with her thumb. A sudden pang of sadness wafted over her. The little girl in the locket had nothing but possibilities in front of her. That she'd met an untimely end, one mired in mystery, made Eliza angry. In the morning, she would call Ginny to share what she'd learned and stop in to see Marty at Highgate. She hadn't heard from Vanessa since the email notifying her of the fire. There was a jelly donut, a chai, and the latest town gossip in her near future. And if she was lucky, the documents she had requested from the town clerk had been retrieved before the fire.

She patted her leg and called Murphy. He raced around from wherever he'd been and came to sit at her side. As she neared the cliff, she stopped short near a scrub pine half a dozen feet from the edge. She leaned against the rough bark, the sound of the waves louder. She'd stood where Honor had once walked as a young wife and mother and now lingered mere feet from where she'd died.

Eliza shivered, and a crow landed on a branch above, its sharp cawing taunting and incessant.

Agitated, Murphy barked up into the tree, then spun around, staring at the cliff edge.

A low growl sounded in his throat.

In the last vestiges of daylight, as the sun sank beneath the horizon, a figure appeared. The Wet Lady. A green light pulsed in her eyes; her lips bent in a crooked smile. She pointed a bony finger at Eliza.

Remember your promise, Eliza Grey. Her voice was rough and gravelly.

Murphy charged at the specter.

"Stop, Murphy!" Eliza screamed and grabbed his collar as Murphy edged dangerously close to the edge of the cliff.

The Wet Lady disappeared, and Eliza pulled Murphy back away from the drop-off.

"Eliza!"

Jason ran across the lawn, stopping just short of the pine tree.

"What's going on? I heard you scream." He looked over at the cliff and then back at Eliza.

She recognized his fear immediately.

She thought about lying to him. Telling him Murphy had chased a rabbit too close to the edge.

He must have sensed her hesitation.

"Just tell me the truth."

"The Wet Lady was there. Murphy saw her."

"We haven't been home for even an hour, and this stuff is starting again?"

"This stuff?"

"Yeah, this paranormal stuff. Eliza, I don't care what you do, I don't have to believe in this, but it has to stop. Figure it out. Get an exorcist, cleanse the house, see a therapist, whatever. Make it stop."

"I can't stop now. She's asked me for help. I made a promise to see it through and make sure justice is done."

"You made a promise? To a ghost, you think you saw as a child? Do you hear how ridiculous that sounds?"

Deflated, Eliza shrugged. "I don't know what you want me to say."

Jason turned and stormed back to the house.

Early the next morning, she woke to the sound of Jason's car starting and backing out of the driveway.

A note waited for her on the kitchen counter next to the coffee pot.

Gone to the office for the day and will be late. I won't be home for dinner.
J

She let the tears fall as she tried to understand his anger.

Edmond had reminded her that it would take time. And during their trip, she was sure Jason was warming to the idea that maybe there were things outside the realm of scientific explanation and chance.

She sent Vanessa a text:

Eliza: Need some advice. Maybe a shoulder to cry on. And donuts. Maybe two. Or seven.

The response came back almost immediately:

Vanessa: Crazy morning rush has me scrambling atm. Come by in an hour? We'll sit and talk. ((((HUGS!))))

Out of the corner of her eye Eliza spotted Murphy standing in the foyer. A muffled whine and the rapid tapping of nails against the floor echoed through the room.

"Okay, Murphy! Tell me what you are thinking. I can't hear you with the leash hanging from your mouth."

Murphy made a high-pitched bark and pawed the front oak door.

Eliza smiled and hugged him. "I'm up for a walk if you are." She grabbed her coat, gloves, and woolen cap and the two set out into the cold salty air. The cloud cover was thick and gloomy, the waves rough and choppy, much like her mood.

Before long, they had made their way to Highgate and passed under the large wrought iron archway towards the main gravel road that led to the Brown family plot.

Murphy knew precisely where to go and, aside from a few stops to sniff, pulled her in a direct path to the old stone fence. As they approached, Murphy started to bark. His massive plume of a tail wagging feverishly. Holding a pair of branch trimmers, Marty stood clipping branches that hung over Levi's headstone.

"Hey, Marty! How are you?" called Eliza from the gate and let go of Murphy's leash.

Murphy ran through the entrance and Marty bent down to pet him.

"Hello, Miss Eliza. Welcome back!"

"Thank you. It's good to be back." She smiled. "I wanted to thank you for visiting Murphy and taking him for walks. I appreciated it so much, though not as much as Murphy, I'm sure."

Marty stood back up. His long-legged appearance now emphasized even more by the height of his Stetson hat. His thin stature looked lost in his oversized cargo coat, his eyes modestly downcast as he nodded.

"My pleasure. I let the big fellow wander around the cemetery with me, and he liked to come here. Probably thought he'd find you here or something."

"I imagine so. Thank you for all you've done to clean up the place. There's a part of me that wishes we could do more. Honor deserves to be next to Levi."

"She knows you're trying."

"Yeah, but will it be enough?"

Marty pushed his Stetson back farther on his head. "There is a reason you have taken such an interest in this place. A reason you've been called to live where Honor lived. My momma possessed the same gift of speaking to the dead. She knew things too. Just keep your mind, heart, and ears open. Messages and clues come to us often when we least expect it."

"Like from well-intended groundskeepers?"

Marty shrugged. "Could be." He smiled shyly.

Eliza waited and hoped he'd take the hint and share any news since she'd been gone, but when it was obvious that he wasn't offering anything unprompted she asked, "So have you found anything else you think I should know?"

Marty hesitated, then glanced over his shoulder before shuffling half a step closer. "The mayor has been by a couple of times while you were away, asking about Honor's grave back there."

"I wonder why?" Eliza asked.

"Could be because he owns the land behind the plot. I'm not certain, but I think the cemetery property line stops at the other side." He tapped the stone wall with his hand.

"You don't think he's considering moving her, do you?"

"Can't say. Could be. Be a shame. Her stone is already so damaged. I don't think it would survive a move."

Eliza stared at Marty for a long moment, a *knowing* sensation tingling in her gut. She had no doubt the mayor was planning on moving the grave, but why? To what end? She needed to hurry and figure all of this out.

"Thank you, Marty, for everything. I appreciate the care you have put into the Brown family plot, visiting Murphy, and supplying me with these bits of information."

"My pleasure, Miss Eliza."

She called Murphy and grabbed his leash. She needed to talk to Vanessa, now more than ever.

"Feel like having a donut?" she asked Murphy.

Nose to the ground, he led her out of Highgate and up Main Street toward his namesake.

"Murphy Grey, you are too smart for your own good."

She waved at Vanessa as they stepped inside.

Vanessa immediately moved around the counter and hugged her tightly.

"It is so good to have you back! I missed you! Go sit down. I'll grab your chai and we'll talk, yeah?"

Eliza nodded. "Yes, please." She managed a small smile and led Murphy to their regular table. "Are you still okay with Murphy hanging inside the bakery with me?" Eliza asked, pointing to her sidekick.

"Absolutely! He's our "little" namesake after all!" Vanessa said assuredly.

Vanessa made her way over, a hot mug of chai and a plate stacked with donuts in her hands.

As she sat down, the bell over the door rang and Eliza smiled when she caught a glimpse of an unexpected duo making their way to the front counter.

Ginny stood arm in arm with Althea Wickham, or Thea, as nearly everyone in Coventry knew her. Thea was even more of a Coventry celebrity than Murphy and could claim to have seen the inside of nearly every home in town. Following in her father's footsteps, she'd been the most prominent real estate agent in the area before handing off the torch to her daughter and retiring to Boca Raton. She'd been the agent who had helped Eliza and Jason buy Rosecliff. Her once fiery red hair was now completely white. But she still wore the same bright coral-colored lipstick, the only shade sufficient to keep up with her bold fashion choices.

"Be right back," Vanessa said, blowing her bangs off of her face. "It never ends."

Eliza waited for Ginny and Thea to place their orders, then snuck up behind them to say hello.

"Thea! It is so good to see you!" Eliza opened her arms for a hug and the feisty older woman embraced her full force.

"My goodness, Eliza Grey. You look fit as a fiddle and as beautiful as ever."

Eliza ran her fingers through her hair. "I'm not so sure that's true, but I'll pretend I believe you." Eliza hugged Ginny. "You were on my list of folks to call today! How have you been?"

Ginny patted her back. "I am doing just fine. Thank you. Welcome back, dear. I can't wait to hear everything about your tales from England. Would you like to join us?"

"Oh, I wouldn't want to impose."

"Rubbish. Life's too short, impose," Thea said and laughed. She nodded to a table in the corner of the bakery. "Pull up a chair, and let's catch up."

"What brings you here for a visit?" Eliza asked Thea, once she'd fetched her chai and Murphy.

"Good gravy," Thea said as she sat down in her chair. "Who is this magnificent beast?"

Murphy sat up tall, his tail swishing on the floor as Eliza introduced him. "This is Murphy. Fluffy fur monster and protector extraordinaire."

"May I?" Thea asked, breaking off a piece of her croissant and motioning to Murphy.

"Yes. He'd never forgive me if I allowed him to miss the opportunity for a treat."

Thea tossed the piece of bread up in the air. Murphy caught it and swallowed. Then rested his large head in Thea's lap.

She stroked his soft fur as she spoke. "I'm here for a couple of weeks. Mainly to visit my daughter for Thanksgiving and the Founding Town Jubilee. I've seen, lived in, and sold so much of this town, seemed only right to come celebrate this kind of milestone."

Eliza laughed. "I couldn't agree more. I wouldn't be here if it hadn't been for you."

"Me either," Vanessa added, coming to stand beside them, her arms out, indicating the bakery. "Never in a million years did I think I'd own this place, but you made it happen."

"And the town is so much better for it," Thea replied, taking a bite of her croissant. "It's delicious! Reminds me of the ones I devoured by the dozen in my youth in Paris."

The bell over the door rang again. "I'll take the best croissant this side of Paris," Vanessa said as she scurried off to help the customer at the counter.

"It seems like only yesterday I helped you purchase Rosecliff," Thea said turning to Eliza. "But then again, that real estate deal had the making of Providence. You almost didn't get it."

Eliza couldn't hide the surprise on her face. "You're kidding. I had no idea."

"What a hubbub that sale made," Ginny added, sipping her tea. "I remember it clearly now. I'd taken you to lunch right after closing," Ginny said, touching Thea's arm. "Thea and I once had a regular mimosa and pancake brunch every time she closed a big sale."

"That's why I always insisted closings happen in the morning," Thea added. "Barclay Winthrop, the mayor's father, what a snob. So busy trying to play politics all over town, he left the management of the estate in the hands of his attorneys, who I'm sure saw Rosecliff as nothing but a financial burden and a potential source of quick money. I'm not even certain Barclay knew the house had been put on the market until after the contract had been signed. But as you recall," she said to Eliza, "said attorneys were all too happy to accept your offer not an hour after you made it."

"We had just bought our second round of mimosas when he stormed in demanding Thea nullify the sale. 'My son is entitled to that house. It must stay in our family.'" Ginny said, her arm raised, her finger pointed at the ceiling as she imitated the man.

"He had the nerve to call me a hustler," Thea added with a giggle. "Little did he know." She snickered. "I sold you that house because I could and because something told me you'd take better care of it than he ever would."

Thea took a sip of her tea. "They didn't call me the 'Historical Home Matchmaker' for nothing. You were meant for that house, and it was meant for you."

Eliza didn't bother covering her smile.

You don't even know the half of it.

"The Rosecliff sale was one for the Wickham Reality Record Books! A win-win. You bought the perfect house for you and your family, and I preserved a historical house for the town." Thea took another bite of her croissant and a quick sip of tea and finished with a victorious smile.

"I had no idea that sale was so tumultuous," Eliza said. "From our point of view, it was a breeze. We love Rosecliff and can't imagine living anywhere else."

Thea smiled. "And from what I hear from Ginny, the story of that house is getting curiouser and curiouser. Tell me about this piece you're working on."

As the two older women sipped their tea, Eliza shared the workings of her story, from her "accidental" adoption of Murphy to the discovery of the Brown family plot and even Kent's connection to the family and the locket he'd given her. She removed it from her neck and passed it over to Ginny for inspection.

"I told you when I met you that old houses call to their owners," Thea said. "I knew the moment we met, you possessed the power to bring that poor house peace. I still believe that."

"I appreciate that," Eliza said, taking the locket back from Ginny.

"It's a remarkable find," Ginny said. "It will pair nicely with a surprise I have for you," Ginny teased. "Thea and I have a few errands to run, but maybe you could stop by this afternoon? Say maybe one o'clock? I promise it will be worth your while."

Eliza felt the tingle of *knowing* in her arms and hands. "Something tells me I won't even believe what you've found."

"I suspect not," Ginny said, offering no further explanation, her smile growing wider.

"Well, I will leave you, ladies, to your errands and try not to let the anticipation get the best of me," Eliza said, standing.

"C'mon Murph, let's go see what Vanessa's up to."

"Will we see you and Jason at the jubilee?" Thea asked before Eliza stepped away.

"Absolutely!"

Behind her, Vanessa handed off two boxes of baked goods and no fewer than eight coffees to a young couple in suits.

Vanessa fanned her face with her hand. "Let's step outside; I need some fresh air."

Eliza followed Vanessa; Murphy followed her.

"Those two ladies could give Lana a run for her money when they get together," Vanessa said, glancing back at Ginny and Thea through the front window. "Looked like you were getting the skinny on something juicy."

Eliza giggled. "Thea just filled me in on some interesting tidbits about the original sale of Rosecliff. You know, that's gonna be you and me before too long."

"Yeah, sign me up. Don't get me wrong, I love this place, but retirement sure has a sweet sound to it." She plopped down on the bench that sat under the front window and patted the seat next to her.

"Sit, my friend. Tell me what's going on. What has you so upset? No less than seven donuts to ease your mind?"

Eliza sat. Murphy laid down by her feet.

"Let's just say Jason is angry with me and wants me to stop this hunt to solve the mystery of Honor Brown."

Eliza told her about the night on the cliff and her subsequent visions, including the last one that had nearly sent Murphy over the ledge.

"We hardly spoke last night, and he left early for work this morning without a goodbye. But the thing is, I can't stop. Not now. I just figured out that the Wet Lady is Honor Brown. She's been waiting for me all this time. It's like she knew that day on the beach that I'd end up in that house."

Vanessa whistled. "That's a lot to take in."

Eliza couldn't hide her crestfallen expression.

Vanessa touched her hand. "I believe you. I can just imagine that it probably scared the wits out of Jason. Maybe he just needs time."

Eliza nodded. "I get that. I don't want him to worry. I haven't told him, but that night, when I woke up and realized what had happened, it scared me too. I wasn't in control of my own body, but I saw it all happening. I just didn't realize it was actually physically happening. And I can't help but feel I'm running out of time."

"It's been a mystery for over 200 years; why the hurry now?"

"I don't have any definitive proof, just a feeling. The mayor has been talking to Marty Evans about the land behind Highgate, right behind the Brown family plot. Turns out Honor isn't buried on Highgate property. And you want to guess who owns that land?"

"Let me guess, our illustrious mayor."

Eliza nodded. "Part of me is worried if she's moved, we may never find her again. That she'll never be reunited with her son. I just can't figure out what he's playing at. Why does he even care?"

"I don't know, but if Mayor Winthrop is involved, it's probably something seedy and slimy. Vanessa glanced up and down the street before dropping her voice. "Remember my email? Patrick confirmed his suspicion about arson, but he's keeping the investigation under wraps for now. The mayor sold his faulty wiring theory to the public despite there being no factual basis for it. Patrick doesn't know what to think, but it's all a little too shady for me. I mean, what was in that building he didn't want anyone to find?"

The *knowing* burning in her gut. "Court records."

"What?" Vanessa asked. "I mean, of course, lots of court records. Pretty sure most of the building was nothing but files and old evidence boxes."

"No, you don't understand. The day before we left, I saw the mayor at *The Gazette*. I told him I was digging into his family history. That I had requested the old court cases from a lawsuit back in 1904 where his great-grandmother was named the lost heir of the Elijah Brown estate."

"Lost heir? Tell me that doesn't sound shady. So, you think there was something in there the mayor didn't want you to find?"

Eliza shrugged, then nodded. "I think so, yeah. To quote my worrisome husband 'coincidences have become strangely coincidental as of late.'"

"Just be careful," Vanessa warned. "I may not like him, but the mayor has pull in this town. 'Connections,' if you catch my drift."

Eliza nudged her shoulder. "I'm starting to sound like a broken record, but I'll promise you like I promised Jason, I'll be careful."

Eliza knocked on Ginny's front door. Since she'd left her historian friend at the bakery, Eliza had hurried home, finished unpacking, fed Murphy, and checked her cell phone a million times in hopes of a text from Jason.

The door opened, and Ginny welcomed her inside. "What, no furry sidekick?"

"No, not this afternoon," Eliza said, stepping into the foyer and pulling off her coat. "He was pretty beat after our long walk this morning. I left him snoozing on the couch."

Ginny looked lovely, dressed in a simple turquoise cardigan and black pants. Eliza noticed an exquisite gold pin with three pearls adorning her collar.

"That is a beautiful gold pin, Ginny."

"My 30th wedding anniversary gift from Mr. Burke. The man did love to surprise me. A stickler for tradition, too. He wanted three pearls for each decade and designed the pin himself. My husband, always the romantic," Ginny said. She took Eliza's coat and hung it in the closet.

"I've been trying to guess all morning what you've discovered."

"Ah, ah, ah, a cup of tea and all the details about your trip first," Ginny said as she led her into the kitchen.

Two china cups with a matching teapot on the trivet and a small dish of banana bread with homemade marmalade sat waiting for them.

"You always know how to make a girl feel right at home, Ginny."

The older woman laughed. "If I've learned anything in this life, it's that friendship is always sweeter over something fresh from the oven. And secrets are always juicer over a cup of tea."

Eliza sat and waited for Ginny to pour the tea, then reached into her leather bag and pulled out a folder with the passenger list from the ship, The *Friendship*, and pictures of the Lord homestead. She explained the relation Kent had found to his own family, then produced the locket once more for Ginny's examination.

Ginny's eyes went wide and dark as she peered at the miniature portraits inside. Her reading glasses low on her nose as she inspected the pictures, beautiful floral design and gems, and the inscription on the back.

"What a remarkable find. I can't believe this has come to you, Eliza. I am speechless."

"I agree. The parallel is uncanny. I live in the home of that little girl, and my husband works with her distant relative. It's truly unbelievable!"

Ginny perused the records before her, first the photos with the fields of heather that once held the Lord's estate, then the other documents.

"The ship's manifest is very basic. It doesn't say much, but it confirms that the Lord family did leave their home and settled in Ipswich before coming to Coventry-by-the-Sea. It also leads us to the fact that Ashley Lord became heavily involved in merchant sailing and that he did start the Lord Shipyard in Salem, Massachusetts," Ginny said with affirmation.

"I also made a small discovery before I left for England. About the mayor. Or about his family, anyway."

"Really? Do tell," Ginny said, sipping her tea.

"You likely noticed that Elijah's second wife and his two daughters died young, as did Honor and her son, Levi."

Ginny nodded.

"As it turns out, Elijah had another child, the result of an affair while married to Honor. A child he claimed on his death bed, and to whom he left the entirety of his estate."

Ginny shook her head in disbelief. "Illegitimate children were hardly unheard of, though for a man of his rank and stature to admit to it is unusual. I wonder what would motivate him to do so?"

"That I haven't uncovered. But it gets even better." Eliza shared the details of the court case, the interviews that alleged any claim to be the lost heir would prove to be fraudulent, and the subsequent flooding and death that left the case uncontested. "The woman in the suit is the mayor's great-great-grandmother and her son, Wendell Winthrop, is the mayor's great-grandfather."

"Interesting," Ginny said, her lips pursed in thought. "I remember reading something about a court case, but it all seemed on the up and up."

"I requested the court records from the city clerk's office before I went out of town –"

"Let me guess," Ginny interrupted. "They were destroyed in the fire?"

"Actually, I'm not sure. I'm hoping the clerk managed to retrieve them beforehand. I planned on stopping by the courthouse tomorrow, but maybe I'll call this afternoon. Fingers crossed."

"I'll keep mine crossed too. What a delicious bit of history that would be."

"I don't think the mayor is too fond of the direction I'm taking my investigation into the Brown family's past."

"Yes," Ginny said, with a concerned look on her face. "I meant to mention that the mayor stopped by the other day unannounced and a bit frazzled. Seems he, too, has become extremely interested in his forefathers. He asked for my help in locating the deeds of all the properties from the late 1700s into the early 1800s. The town gave them to the archives several years ago. I told him I would be happy to help and that he only needed to submit an official request in writing for the documents. Then he started asking questions about our work together."

"Oh boy. Oddly enough, he's been bugging Marty too, asking about property lines and surveys of Highgate. Now, I know we are onto something! If the mayor is making house calls, we have struck a nerve."

Ginny nodded. "I have to agree."

Eliza took a sip of tea and smiled. "So, you have a surprise for me as well?"

Ginny rubbed her hands together. "All right, you've met my terms and shared all the good bits; now it's my turn. Ready to see what you came for?"

Eliza nodded. "Yes, please."

"Follow me, then."

Ginny rose from her chair and ushered Eliza towards the stairs to the second floor. There, off to the left of a narrow hallway, she led them to a tiny bedroom decorated with a soft pink floral pattern and pointed at an ornate maple writing desk under a bank of windows.

"My daughter, Emily, and I recently brought furniture down from the attic. I always knew this writing table was from the late 1700s, but I had no idea from whom or where it came. And the drawer remained locked, and I had no idea where the key might be. I always intended to have one made but never got around to it." Ginny bent down to her knees, pulled a brass solid shank skeleton key from a ledge underneath the thick tabletop, and handed it to Eliza.

"As it turns out, my daughter had used this desk in her own room when she was a girl. And though she never told me, she actually discovered the key." Ginny pointed to the key in Eliza's hand. "Hidden underneath. She told me she'd never said anything because she liked the idea of a secret hiding place that no one else knew about." Ginny laughed. "Can't say as I blame her."

"When we moved the desk in here, and she told me she knew where the key was, I almost didn't believe her! Go ahead, open the top drawer."

Eliza did as she was told. The old brass shank key slipped into the lock and turned more smoothly than she would have expected for a desk this age. A metallic clicking sound came from inside the mechanism, and the lip of the drawer popped out slightly from the desk. Eliza pulled it open. Inside, the drawer was empty, divided in half by an inlaid wooden partition.

"I was delighted that the lock and key still functioned, but then Emily did this." Ginny gently grasped the partition and lifted. "It's a false bottom."

Eliza nearly gasped when she saw what lay beneath—a leather-bound journal.

"That isn't even the best part." Ginny lifted the book with worn and yellowed pages and a ribbon around it. "I am surprised the ribbon hasn't torn. It's fragile but still in good shape." She opened the cover and gently turned to the first page.

"When I saw the first entry, I could hardly wait for you to return." Ginny turned the book so Eliza could read.

January 1, 1808

I have been given this journal as a gift from my dear mother-in-law, Mary Lord. I am honored by her kindness and generosity. She has often shared her thoughts and says I have a gift for words and script. Niles is her son and my husband. He is an incredible man filled with righteousness and goodness. I have been blessed to be a part of this austere family.

Eliza stared at Ginny. "This journal belongs to –"

"Charlotte Lord," Ginny said triumphantly.

Eliza glanced back down at the page. "This passage was written in 1808. That's the year Honor and Levi died."

Ginny nodded. "Yes, and our girl Charlotte is true to her word and uses her gift for writing to capture many of the events of that year."

With careful hands, Eliza took the journal from Ginny and scanned the remainder of the passage. Honor's name caught her eye.

My sister-in-law, Honor Brown, is a beautiful and gentle soul. Her son, Levi, is the most handsome boy. Unfortunately, he has been ill for quite some time now. Although his complexion is pale, he has wisps of curly blond hair, bright blue eyes, and the sweetest smile I have ever witnessed. Fortunately, Levi possesses his mother's temperament. His father, Elijah, is handsome but hard and cold in personality. He is very strict with Levi, and I can see that it vexes my dear sister-in-law, Honor.

"Can you believe it? All this time, this desk and that journal have just been collecting dust in my attic. I can't be entirely certain, but with the age of the desk combined with the journal, I fully believe that I possess Charlotte's writing table."

"I can hardly stand it; I'm so excited," Eliza said, handing the journal back to Ginny. "I want to read every word."

"Why don't we bring it downstairs and look at some of the pages together?" Ginny suggested. "I've already scanned through it, but I wanted you to have the same experience I had at its discovery. There is more evidence of a troubled marriage between Elijah and Honor. The family appeared not to be too keen on him and his ways. Nonetheless, it is a fascinating account of the Lord family and shares some insights about both the Browns and the Lords."

"I am still in awe," Eliza said, taking the partition from the top of the desk and placing it back in the drawer.

"Did you notice the last page is torn out? Just a little piece remains. I wonder if it matches the page you found loose in my family Bible. Maybe Charlotte regretted recording Niles's accusations of Elijah? We may never know why."

"I believe you may be right, Ginny! Something to check into for sure!"

A thunderous thump made both of them jump.

A shade over one of the windows directly above the desk quivered as it suddenly rolled up by itself.

"I swear, this old house!" Ginny exclaimed, her hand on her chest. "It'll give me a heart attack one of these days."

A familiar tingle spread through Eliza's hands and arms. In her gut, a queasy sensation set off her alarm bells. The air around them began to cool.

"Shall we head downstairs?" Eliza asked, hoping to hurry Ginny from the room.

When they got to the kitchen table, Ginny poured them each a fresh cup of tea.

Here, with the late autumn sun streaming through the kitchen window, any feelings of unease Eliza had felt upstairs disappeared.

Ginny's phone rang. "Be just a second, dear," she said and stepped into the hall to answer the old-fashioned phone mounted to the wall near the kitchen door.

Eliza took a moment to check her own phone. Still no text, call, or email from Jason.

Ginny stepped back into the room. "That was Thea. She has invited me out to grab dinner and a movie with her tonight. It's so nice having her home again. I wish her stay in Coventry wasn't so short."

"Oh, please don't let my visit delay you from spending more time together. We can certainly pick this up on another day. I need to get back to Murphy, anyways," Eliza said, standing and gathering the documents she'd brought to show Ginny. "I'm glad you two have time to catch up."

"She might be my oldest and is certainly my dearest friend. Between you and me, I'm trying my hardest to convince her to move back."

"I hope you manage to persuade her."

Ginny picked up the journal and handed it to Eliza.

"Take this with you. Read through it. Do your research and write your piece. Then, when you return it, we will place it back in the desk where it belongs."

Eliza hugged her.

"Thank you for all of your help, Ginny."

"You are most welcome," Ginny said and pulled Eliza's coat from the closet. "You know me; nothing gets me going quite like a bit of history. Add in some mystery, and it's a wonder I'm not dancing in the street."

"Mysteries aside, I think I may have rattled the mayor's cage a bit by mentioning I was looking into the court case. Hopefully with the help of Charlotte's journal I can unravel more of the secrets surrounding the Brown family."

Ginny frowned. "Maybe just be a bit cautious then?" She reached out and took Eliza's hand. "Politics and power can make men do horrible things."

Eliza sighed. "You're the third person today I've had to reassure, but I promise. I'll be careful."

21

WHEN ELIZA RETURNED HOME, Murphy waited for her by the front door. Kicking off her boots, she headed for the dining room and unpacked her notes, the locket, and Charlotte's journal from her bag.

She checked her phone. Still nothing from Jason. She tapped out a text:

Eliza: I know you're worried and upset. Can we talk about this when you get home?

A minute later, her phone buzzed:

Jason: Yes. Late afternoon meeting. Will be home after supper.

Well, he isn't exactly Mr. Talkative, but at least he's responding.

She'd extended an olive branch; now, all she could do was wait. Hopefully, after he calmed down, he'd agree to at least talk to her about everything. She'd help him understand. They were so close to figuring it all out. Eliza rubbed her neck and did a quick search for the city clerk's office phone number.

She found the office number and tapped the "call" button.

"Good afternoon, Coventry City Records Department; how may I help you?"

"Hello, this is Eliza Grey. I was in not too long ago and requested some records for a court case settled in 1904. Any chance they're ready for pick up?"

"Oh, Ms. Grey. I'm the clerk who assisted you, but I have to apologize. Unfortunately, our office suffered a catastrophic fire the day after you stopped by. I hadn't yet pulled those files. I'm afraid any records we did have on the case you requested were lost in the fire, along with most of our older documentation prior to 1950. Only a handful of Coventry's old records were salvageable."

Eliza let out a breath. "Yes, I heard about the fire but hoped maybe I'd gotten lucky. Glad no one was injured, but what a loss."

"Yes, a huge loss. But I hear the mayor has made it his mission to make sure all the remaining old buildings here in town are up to code so this kind of thing doesn't happen again."

Eliza was thankful the clerk couldn't see her roll her eyes. "Yes, I've heard the same. Thank you for your help."

She hung up the phone and returned to the dining room table to sit and read more of Charlotte's journal. The tingling sensation in her hands and arms had been nearly constant since leaving Ginny's. She read passage after passage, marveling at the beautiful descriptions Charlotte had taken the time to capture of her home and her daily activities. Charlotte also penned a descriptive account of the abusive personality of Elijah.

August 28, 1808

I had a lovely visit with Honor and Levi today. We drank lemonade under the veranda at Rosecliff. The weather was so pleasant, and we could gaze at the ocean and enjoy our time. Levi seemed to have improved from the last time I saw him. He is such a sweet boy. He displayed a hale and hearty physique and a rosy complexion. He is much more talkative and shared stories from his favorite book, Robinson Crusoe, by Daniel Defoe. I marvel at such things. He made the story so magical as he told it. Honor, for a time, was relaxed and seemed in good spirits. We were all so happy until Elijah came home from the shipyard. He seemed suspicious of our laughter, and upon his arrival, I watched my dear sister-in-law change. She and Levi became nervous and tense. Elijah unsettled us all. He speaks in such a syrupy and condescending way that it makes me feel unwelcome. It is as if a dark cloud had come over our lovely time together. Later, Honor shared that she is having difficulty dealing with Elijah and his expectations for Levi. It is causing tension between them, and she fears it will affect Levi's well-being.

It pained Eliza to think that Honor had worried about her child's safety. Earlier passages had mentioned a conversation about the boy's health and how he'd nearly died from scarlet fever.

From the foyer, she heard the sound of the front door opening.

Murphy barked and raced out into the room.

"Hey, Murphy. Did you miss me?"

It was Jason.

Eliza glanced at the time on her phone. It was well after six. She'd lost track of her day.

She stood and hung back in the doorway between the foyer and dining room and watched him hang his coat.

He turned to face her and took a long breath in through his nose.

"I've been thinking...about everything. About all the strange coincidences...you adopting Murphy, the cemetery, your concussion, Kent, and the uncanny family connection." He stopped and looked at her pointedly. "About that night on the cliff and about last night with Murphy."

She took a tentative step toward him. "I know you're worried, but –"

He held up his hand. "Let me finish. I've thought about it, and I can understand why you want to do this, but I just don't know how I am supposed to trust that you'll be okay. I think about it all the time. What if I hadn't woken up? What if I hadn't gotten there before you jumped?"

Eliza could see his fear, but defensiveness bubbled in her chest. "I understand that you're worried, scared. Hell, I'm a little scared myself, but I can't stop. Not now. Not when I am so close to figuring all of this out. Jason, it's not just curiosity. It's something deeper. A calling. I'm being led by someone or something, and I can't switch it off even if I wanted to."

Overhead, the heavy ornate chandelier above the entry table flickered wildly. An icy gust of wind blew the front door open. The heavy oak and glass panel smacked against the wall, and a torrent of damp, cold air raced into the room.

"What the hell?" Jason turned to face the door. "I just closed that door!"

The chandelier blinked off and on and then began to swing on its chain. The wind howled, sending bits of leaves and twigs onto the floor and up into the air around them.

"She needs our help, Jason. The Wet Lady and Honor are one and the same, and we can't just abandon her now."

Murphy stood rigidly in the corner near the staircase growling, his gaze fixed on the light fixture.

From the other side of the foyer, Eliza had a clear view of the living room. A dark mist pooled near the fireplace. She covered her ears, as the sound of the wind was deafening. She watched the fireplace poker and shovel shake violently in their wrought iron frame. The brass mantle clock began to toll, the delicate sound nearly swallowed by the wind as it chimed again and again.

She reached out to Jason.

He pulled her to him and held an arm over their heads to keep the leaves and debris from hitting them in the face.

The fireplace tool holder fell over with a thunderous boom, and the poker slid across the room with an unearthly force, stopping just short of Eliza's feet. Above them, the chandelier's dangling crystals clanged against each other, sending a few prisms crashing to the floor.

"Help me figure out what happened to her," Eliza yelled over the noise. "Help me, and when we know the truth, all of this will stop."

Jason stared at her incredulously. His eyes darted up to the light and down to the poker at their feet.

"It's the only way," she added.

His eyes locked on hers. He nodded.

In an instant, the wind died down, and the room fell silent. The gentle clinking sound of the crystals continued until the massive light fixture came to rest.

Murphy whined and hurried to stand beside them. He licked Jason's hand.

Jason patted Murphy's head, "What just happened?"

"Jason, don't you see? I need to see this through."

"I know, but"—Jason's voice trailed off—"does this mean our whole house is haunted now?"

"Honor lived and died here. Our house is connected to all of this."

"I need a drink," Jason said, stepping over the poker and disappearing into the living room to pour himself a scotch from the bar.

Eliza picked up the fireplace poker and followed him.

He turned to face her; his hands shook slightly as he lifted the glass to his lips. "Is it like that all the time?" he asked after a hefty swallow.

Eliza offered him a sympathetic smile. "No, not always. I see a lot of things in my dreams, and sometimes she appears to me while I'm awake too. Usually, it's whenever I'm onto something. It's like a metaphysical game of warmer-colder. If I'm headed in the right direction or the wrong one for that matter, she sends me a sign."

He poured another two fingers of scotch into his glass. "Are you certain it's her? I mean, if her husband killed her, how do you know it's not him jostling the chandelier and throwing pokers across the room."

Eliza paused reflectively. "You might be right." The energy in the room had been stronger, colder than when Honor had appeared to her. She'd seen the darkness hovering near the fireplace. Was it possible that Elijah was here too? That he was still tormenting Honor beyond the grave?

"But if it is him, it only makes me believe that we're close to finding out the truth of what really happened." She took the glass from him and put it on the bar, then took both of his hands in hers. "I'm not an expert at this. In fact, for most of my life, I've pretended that the little moments of intuition were harmless, inconsequential. A bit of luck played out in everyday life. So, I only have slightly more experience than you, believe it or not. Especially when it comes to wild gales of wind wreaking havoc in our foyer."

She saw the corners of his mouth twitch up in the briefest smile.

"And you think once we figure this out, then she'll move on, and life can get back to normal?"

Eliza shrugged her shoulders. "I'm not a hundred percent sure there won't be other things, but I am entirely certain that she won't let us be until we've done right by her."

Jason took a deep breath and relaxed his shoulders. He picked up the glass and swallowed the last of his drink. "Now that the scotch has taken the edge off, why don't you show me what you've got? The sooner we get started..."

She smiled and took his hand. "The sooner we'll be finished."

She led him to the dining room and explained in detail everything she'd gathered from her research, the journal, and the documents and photos she'd brought back from England.

He tapped the journal. "And this proves that Elijah is guilty?"

"Not in so many words," Eliza admitted. "There are a couple of passages where Charlotte mentions Honor and Elijah. There's little doubt that he was a horrible man, prone to angry outbursts and abuse. Based on Charlotte's account, Elijah terrorized both Honor and their son, Levi. The poor kid had heart damage from a bout with scarlet fever and Honor suffered an enormous amount of stress from trying to keep her husband happy and taking care of an ailing child. Much like some of the horrible stories you hear on the news about mothers who just snap with no support. Suicide may have been the convenient answer, one I can't help but think was used to cover up something much more sinister. Elijah Brown was pretty much a bad guy all the way around. He had an affair with a woman while he was married to Honor. Fathered an illegitimate child that he only tried to do right by when he was dying and had no other heirs to give his fortune to."

"From what little you've told me of him, I'm surprised he even bothered."

"Me too. I get a sense that Elijah didn't gel with anyone, including his own family." Eliza fished out of the pile of research the book written by the town historian with details of the Brown estate court case. "And this book makes a more modern connection to all of this."

She showed him the pages with the newspaper clippings and gave him a summary of the court case as she understood it.

"So, after all that time, a mysterious heir is found and awarded the estate?" Jason asked, lifting the book to read the next page.

"Exactly. Strange, right? Any guesses who the heir turned out to be?"

Jason turned to another page. "It says here, the boy was named Wendell."

"Yes, the boy's mother remarried after the case was settled and the boy was adopted by his stepfather. His full name is Wendell Winthrop."

"Winthrop?" Jason asked, the light of understanding in his eyes. "As in Mayor Winthrop?"

"One and the same. Wendell was his grandfather."

Jason snickered under his breath. "Does he know you're writing this article about his family? I bet he's not too keen on having to reveal a suicide-turned-murder in his family tree."

"Unfortunately, he does know, but I think there's more to it than fear of a scandal that happened two centuries ago. He's been a little too interested in my article. And he's been bugging Ginny and Marty both about land deeds and property lines. Turns out, Marty and he are actually distant cousins. Marty is a descendant of Elijah's brother, Samuel, and it was his family the Brown estate was taken from after the court case had been settled. And Ginny, she can trace her lineage to the Lord family.

I told you before that Elijah built this house, our house, Rosecliff, and now we know that both Levi and Honor died here."

Jason sat down at the table and rubbed his eyes. "Let me get this straight, a would-be lecherous murderer with an illegitimate son built our house, and the woman he supposedly murdered is haunting us until we prove it?"

Eliza nodded. "Exactly."

"Okay, but what does the mayor have to do with any of this?"

"Nothing, directly. But here—" she searched through the folder to locate the article about the flood and the Brown family lawyer's interview later that year.

"I think there is actually something out there, some proof that the mayor's family's claim to the Brown estate was bogus. I think I'm getting close to figuring out what it is, and he's worried if I find it, it will throw his entire legitimacy, his wealth, even his position as mayor, into question."

"Okay, now I understand why you find this whole thing so intriguing, ghosts and haunting aside." He put his hands on her waist and pulled her to him. "Any chance we could table it for now, have a little something to eat, get a good night's sleep to stave off this jet lag and the scotch, and come back to it with fresh eyes in the morning?"

She smiled. "So, this means you're all in? You'll help me?"

He rested his forehead against hers.

"I shouldn't have doubted you," he said softly.

"I understand why you did. I sometimes have to remind myself that all of this is real." She kissed him. "Customer's choice...grilled cheese or peanut butter and jelly?"

"Whichever is quickest," he said through a yawn.

"PB & J, coming right up."

Jason was asleep before his head hit the pillow, but for Eliza, sleep would not come. She tossed and turned as her mind raced over the events of the day. Quietly she slipped out of bed and went downstairs to read some passages from Charlotte's journal. She hunkered in the corner chair under a throw blanket by the fireplace and continued reading where she'd last left off.

September 12, 1808

My dearest Honor shared a painful secret today, one that bodes danger for her and Levi. Elijah becomes easily angered with her and, at times, has become violent, accusing her of having affections for his brother, Samuel. He threatens to make Levi work the family farm, knowing that Honor fears a serious setback for his health. She has forbidden me to speak of this to Niles for fear of a violent reprisal from Elijah. It took all my reserve not to utter what Niles has shared with me in private. Elijah has been unfaithful on numerous occasions, but even worse, carried on a long-term affair with a local woman, Adelaide Abbott, who has born a son out of wedlock. The immorality of this man shows no bounds, but then I have learned of a greater insult to my dearest sister-in-law. To avoid a scandal, Elijah paid his mistress a handsome sum to leave Coventry and take the boy, now three years of age, and start anew. How can I burden Honor with that news? It angers me so that he accuses her of what he himself has committed.

Eliza's resentment towards Elijah grew with Charlotte's words. *So, he accused her of being unfaithful, while he, himself, was the adulterer.*

She yawned, covering her mouth, when a familiar tingle began in her fingers and quickly raced through her arms. The room around her started to fade away and in its place was a familiar yard with tall grass and wildflowers.

September 13, 1808

Honor meandered towards the cliff's edge, stopping briefly to pick a daisy from the side of the path. She twirled it in her fingers, bringing it to her face, letting the delicate white petals tickle her chin. She caught a whiff of the sea on the breeze and peered over the ledge to the rocky crags, covered in mounds of seaweed. The waves moved in and out. She tried to match her breath to their steady rhythm in hopes of finding a moment's peace for her weary mind.

She sighed and sat down near the edge and dropped the daisy. The wind carried it for a way before it disappeared out of sight. It was the perfect analogy for her marriage, a whirlwind at first followed by a quick descent. The beginning had been mostly happy. Levi had come into their world just shy of two years after their wedding, and his continued warm and gentle temperament, despite his illness, had been nothing short of a blessing. But as the years had passed, Elijah had changed. She could have borne his cold demeanor and cruel comments, though they crushed her confidence. Such was a wife's lot to bear her husband's children and his temper. But he'd turned his contempt and foul moods toward their son, a grievance she would never forgive him for.

She pulled at a line of loose stitching near the hem of her dress and thought of Charlotte. Another godsend. She'd known the first time she'd met her that Charlotte was her brother's perfect companion, and they'd quickly become friends. Charlotte was now her dearest friend and confidant. How Charlotte had railed when Honor shared the growing anxiety that crippled her mind, body, and soul. She'd insisted on telling Niles, but Honor had made her promise not to. At least not yet.

But if she thought about it, save her father, none of her family had ever truly cared for Elijah. Her mother had never wanted to see them married, and on the few occasions they gathered as a family, she rarely hid her displeasure. Niles had always seemed indifferent to the idea. But her father never had a cross word to say about him. He'd encouraged Elijah to be a part of the family shipping business and promoted him up through the ranks to a powerful position in the Lord Shipyard. Elijah's father also placed him in charge of the family farm after he brought in an abundance of wealth by way of trading their main crop, corn, and shipping it overseas. Corn had become a lucrative product for the two families, and Elijah was the domineering king of both domains.

Honor lay back on the grass, her hands behind her head, her gaze fixed up at the bright blue sky. Had she been born a man, she was certain she'd have had a keen mind for business. Niles excelled in finances and followed every cent that came and went like a bloodhound, but when it came to Elijah and the business he brought in, her father gave the boisterous risk-taker a larger stake in the shipyard.

How many times had she imagined sitting down with her father to tell him the truth. "Father, you must know how dangerous it is to trust him with your business. And with me and your grandson."

Honor took a deep breath and sighed, her mind spiraling back to last night's fight.

"You treat Levi like an infant. The boy is eight years old. At eight, I tended the fields and did man's work. He needs to spend more time with me so I may teach him how to become a real man."

His words had enraged her. Levi was wonderful, but he was not strong enough to work in the fields. He might never be able to follow in his father's footsteps in that way. She needed Elijah to understand that. It was her job to keep her son safe.

"You weaken the boy. He won't toughen with your constant coddling."

She had stood her ground and paid the price. She reached up and touched the tender spot near her ear where he'd struck her.

"I won't put up with your disrespect much longer, Honor. There are plenty of women in Coventry who would be most grateful to be in your position as my wife."

But she'd take his blow again and again if it meant Levi was safe. Her heart softened when she thought of her beautiful boy. In many ways, he resembled his Uncle Samuel, Elijah's younger brother. Elijah has little respect for him, either. She could hardly think of a time when Samuel's name was mentioned without criticism.

She sat up and wrapped her arms around her legs, resting her head on her knees. Their struggle had left a mess in the dining room. His violence had come so unexpectedly she hadn't braced, and a single blow had sent her careening into the buffet. She'd knocked over the crystal vase her parents had given them as a wedding present. It shattered on the floor into a pool of water and crushed rose petals. She felt a heat rise to her face. The servants would know if they didn't already.

Later that night, she'd sat with Levi. His cough had returned, and she rubbed his back until the fit subsided.

He'd touched her face, ever so gently, where the bruise had begun to form.

"Mother, did Father hurt you?"

"No, my love." Honor pulled back. "Why would you ask that?"

His bright blue eyes stared back at her. She could see he knew the truth.

"I'll do my best to get better. To be stronger. To be more like Father. Then maybe he won't be so angry."

The words cut her to the quick. "Levi Brown, you are everything to me. You are getting better and soon will be able to do everything healthy boys can. But if you do nothing else, promise me you won't become your father. Be your own man. You are hardly a fifth his age and already carry more of my respect."

The floor creaked behind them, and Levi stiffened.

Honor, still seated on the side of his bed, turned slowly to face her husband. She didn't care if he'd heard. He'd struck her. There would be no hiding her disdain for him now.

Elijah stepped aside and held out his arm, motioning for her to make her leave.

She rose slowly from the bed and placed the covers over her son Levi, bent down, and kissed his forehead. "Go to sleep Levi," she whispered.

When she reached the doorway, Elijah's beefy hand grabbed her upper arm and squeezed. "Let's go to bed, wife."

Honor had not pulled back in fear or anger. Instead, she'd gone with him to the bedroom. As she relinquished her body to him, she had promised herself she would find a way to escape, to leave him and take Levi with her.

She renewed that promise as she sat looking out at the ocean waves. To simply leave would bring scandal and potentially tarnish her family's reputation. She loved them too much to do anything to bring shame to the Lord name.

But she would find a way. For Levi's sake. She would find a way.

Eliza jolted upright in the chair, the journal open and resting in her lap. The last remnants of the vision faded. She could feel Honor's energy still tingling in her arms. And more than anything, the love for her Levi in her heart. She rose from the chair, shut off the hall light, and crept back upstairs to bed. She couldn't fight the sense that the visions were getting more intense, more real. With each vision, she felt more like Honor and less like herself.

"We'll get to the truth," she murmured as she snuggled down under the covers. "We'll find a way."

22

O VER THE NEXT FEW days, after dinner each night, Eliza and Jason read and re-read all of the information she'd gathered about the Lord and Brown families, and Charlotte's journal, in hopes of finding some clue as to the truth behind Honor's death. Nothing stood out.

The Brown family article ran in *The Gazette* on Halloween and, as she'd expected, had many in the town buzzing about the possibility of a 200-year murder cover-up.

In the days following the article's publication, she'd been surprised and delighted to see bouquets of flowers left on both Honor's and Levi's graves. The story had touched many as it had her. She was glad that others now knew of the woman who had suffered at the hands of her husband and of his notorious business dealings. A few comments online mentioned the mayor's family being related to Elijah, but they were quickly removed. As Thanksgiving approached, the buzz had died away as readers turned their attention to recipes for side dishes and the perfect pumpkin pie.

Eliza was no closer to unearthing the evidence needed to prove Honor's true cause of death. As Rosecliff would, as usual, host the Grey family Thanksgiving gathering. The day before the holiday, Eliza boxed up all of the notes, journals, and books that had taken up residence in her dining room and moved them temporarily to the upstairs hall closet. She sighed as she pushed the box up onto the shelf. This time of year always flew by, and while she was looking forward to seeing her family and having Bella home for an extended holiday, she worried about the timing of it all. The Town Jubilee was days away, and Eliza had promised Vanessa that she would help with the food prep and distribution of bakery goods at the parade and town green.

Her family would offer a much-needed distraction. Her parents had agreed to bring the pies – pumpkin, pecan, and apple strudel. Both her parents and Edmond and Leah would arrive on Thanksgiving morning and spend the night. Edmond, as usual, made himself in charge of the annual Thanksgiving cocktail. And Bella was due home at any moment, having arranged a ride from a friend who also lived in Coventry.

Any frustration or reservation about their lack of progress in uncovering Honor's truth was soon lost to the diversion of bread making and turkey brining.

By the following afternoon, as her family sat, full from their meal, she felt the itch to fetch the box and re-read through everything again.

"El, that might be the best meal I've had in a long time," Edmond said, patting his stomach. He gave Leah a side-eye.

"Don't look at me. I'm not about to argue," she said, wiping a bit of gravy off her plate with her last bite of roll. "I know I've been entirely absent from the kitchen as of late. A full partner's gotta do, what a full partner's gotta do."

He leaned over and kissed her cheek. "And I couldn't be prouder," he said. "I've been hungry but proud."

The table erupted in laughter.

"Shall we retire to the living room for some Thanksgiving cocktails?" he asked.

The family followed him, and soon he and Leah passed each of them a high ball glass full of their elaborate concoction.

"This is called an Apple Harvest," Leah said. "Apple cider, a bit of cinnamon whiskey, pumpkin pie spice, and a little Bailey's to give it a smooth, sweet finish. For Bella, our traditional 'mocktail' created especially for her."

Jason flipped the switch to ignite the fireplace, and they huddled around it for pictures, with Murphy and his snaggle-toothed grin right up front.

"How is that story coming?" Leah asked after dozens of pictures had been snapped. She plopped down on the couch beside Eliza. "Did you ever solve the mystery of the woman who owned this house and died on the property?"

Eliza looked up at Jason. He nodded, and she updated her family on the latest discoveries, including Charlotte's journal and the connection to Kent.

Eliza glanced around the room, took a deep breath, and continued. "And there's one last thing I wanted to make sure I shared while we are all together again."

Eliza locked eyes with Jason.

He nodded again, in reassurance.

"Edmond knows, and Mom, I'm sure you do too," she said looking at Jane, "And Jason knows, finally, so it's time to share my secret with you."

Eliza told the story about the day on the beach when she'd first seen the Wet Lady. Leah's and her father's expressions had been hard to read. Bella stared at her, her reaction one of obvious curiosity.

"And while I didn't see her beyond my late childhood, she reappeared in my life a few months ago. And thanks to our trip to England and dreams that you wouldn't believe if I told you, I now know that the Wet Lady is actually Honor Brown."

Bella clasped her hands together. "And she's reached out from beyond the grave to ask for your help, right Mom?"

Eliza blinked her eyes. "Well, yes. I can imagine that sounds strange, even a little scary. Does that creep you out to live here now?" Eliza asked, trying to read her daughter's reaction.

"I mean, sure, it's a little creepy, but it's also kind of cool. Like we are helping a spirit find peace."

"I believe you, honey," Jane said. "You would tell me about the 'people' visiting you as a small child. You knew things early on, things you shouldn't have. When you were little, every time we passed a cemetery or family plot where folks were buried, you would wave at the gravestones from your stroller. I asked you once who you were waving to. You told me about the people who lived there. You actually called one by a name, Smiley Face. One scared you, and you called him the 'Fraid.'"

"Mom! I have no recollection of that." In her mind, she thought of Marty. She owed him an apology for giving him any grief about calling them residents. She'd given them nicknames.

"You have a gift, Eliza. I knew it early on. After our vacation years ago, I remember you talking about the Wet Lady," her mother added.

"Me, too," her father agreed.

"And how are you feeling about this?" Edmond asked, looking at Jason.

Jason scratched his head. "Well, if I told you the things I've seen as of late, you'd call me crazy if I didn't believe her. I'm still a little unsure, but I'm here, and I'm doing what I can to help her solve this thing." His eyes darted to the fireplace poker. "For safety's sake."

Eliza stifled a laugh.

"That's good to hear," Edmond said and patted Jason on the back. "I was a little worried about the two of you."

Jason looked lovingly at Eliza. "I'm stubborn as they come, but I've got a hell of a wife. And she hasn't even told you what I think is the best part. There's a modern-day political twist to all of this."

All eyes in the room returned to Eliza.

"Oh," she said playfully. "You mean you want me to tell them how the town mayor is wrapped up in all of this?"

By the end of the night, everyone agreed that Honor had not jumped from the cliff. And that the mayor had something to hide.

"Do you think the evidence is here, somewhere?" Bella asked, stroking an almost-asleep Murphy who lay beside, head in her lap. "Hidden like a buried treasure?"

"It's possible," Eliza said. "Though where to begin looking, I'm not sure. I haven't a clue."

"Maybe Honor will send you a clue, another dream," Bella replied.

"Maybe so."

As their conversation began to dwindle, Edmond stretched and yawned loudly. "Well, fam. It's been a Thanksgiving for the history books, but we've got an early morning. Time for your favorite son to hit the hay."

"Yeah, me too," said Bella. "I'm beat, but I plan on sleeping in, so we should say goodbye now."

Jane stood up. "Good food, good company, goodbyes, and good night," she said and hugged her son and then Leah. "I suppose we should all turn in."

Edmond and Leah said their farewells, and Eliza hugged both of them, her parents, and Bella in turn.

When it was just the two of them left in the living room, Jason put his arms around Eliza's waist. "You know what just occurred to me?" he asked, holding her close. "If I understand things correctly and remember what I've read, though that second Apple Harvest may have made my mind a bit fuzzy, if there is evidence that proves the mayor's family committed fraud, he'll lose the estate. And our resident gravekeeper, Marty Evans, will inherit it all."

23

THE FOLLOWING EVENING, ELIZA and Jason had the house to themselves. Her brother, as promised, had left just after six a.m., and her parents had followed shortly after lunch. Happy to be back in town, Bella had made plans to catch up with old friends.

Eliza had spent most of her day cleaning up the kitchen and returning her house to its normal state, but the box of her research had been calling to her for hours. It was a lot like not being able to scratch an itch. She started a load of laundry and headed upstairs. She needed to satisfy that urge.

Returning the box to the dining room, she laid everything out, hoping to catch sight of something new. She called to Jason, "Up for a little research?"

He made a face. "I was hoping that with the house all to ourselves, I might persuade you to watch a movie with me. In bed?" He wiggled his eyebrows at her. "A little fire, a little wine. What do you think? You can pick the movie."

Since the incident in the foyer, and his willingness to take the leap of faith into the realm of the unknown with her, she felt closer to him, maybe more than she ever had. She looked down at the table. As much as she felt their next breakthrough was imminent, she wasn't about to turn down wine and a movie.

"Twist my arm and entice me with a black and white movie, and I'm yours. But let's make a plan to get up early. There's something we're missing. I can feel it."

As Jason brushed his teeth and talked about work, Eliza drew the drapes, her mind still focused on Honor.

Jason poked his head out the bathroom door, toothbrush still in his mouth.

"Did you hear what I said?"

"I'm sorry, honey. I was off in la-la land, and the toothbrush in your mouth didn't help. What were you saying?"

He held up a finger and tucked his head back in the bathroom to spit and rinse.

He returned to the room with a hand towel in hand, wiping the corners of his mouth.

He wore a tee shirt with blue striped pajama bottoms, his thick wavy hair mussed about his head. It didn't matter how old they got; she still found him crazy handsome.

"I said, I forgot to tell you that I got an email from Kent this afternoon. He found a few more tidbits to share with you about the Lord family. Something about a document that showed some sort of business dealing between the Lord Shipyard and another shipyard in Liverpool and the purchase of an additional ship to add to the Lord fleet. It would have been purchased for trade explicitly between the two ports. He found the name of the ship. And you'll never guess what it was."

Eliza waited for him to continue, but he paused to pick up the two empty wine glasses and place them next to the wine bottle atop the fireplace mantle.

He grabbed both the tv and fireplace remotes and simultaneously shut them off.

"And the name of the ship was...?" she asked, staring at him expectantly.

"The *Eliza,*" he said. "The largest of the merchant ships. Much larger than the *Trade Winds* and the *Zephyr* and would have been explicitly used to trade Sumatra pepper."

"The *Eliza*?"

"Yup, crazy, right?" He shut off the light and headed to his side of the bed.

Murphy settled between the two great windows on his large dog bed and sighed.

Eliza leaned down, patted his head, and crawled into the bed.

"The *Eliza,*" she repeated. "I suddenly feel like I'm getting punked. Like the universe has a very long memory and a strange and wonderful sense of humor."

"Kent said he found a small passage written about the impending deal. Pretty expensive endeavor, especially for a moderately small shipyard like the Lords'. But it never happened. The deal fell through, something to do with finances."

"Do you know when this all took place?"

"No, Kent said he'd put it all in an email and send it over to you later this week. Mentioned something about it being in a random section of the archives department where Katherine's cousin works. He did say, though, that the deal wasn't the work of Ashley Lord but of a certain Elijah Brown."

"You're kidding," Eliza said. "I'll watch for his email. I still can't believe it's true. What are the chances?"

"Fathomless, my love. Your discovery in the graveyard has sparked an international investigation," Jason said with a wink.

Eliza let the details of another coincidence roll around in her mind. She wondered what had happened to make the deal fall through. She was about to ask Jason if Kent had shared any other details, but Jason snored softly beside her.

How does he do that? Just put his head down and then off to sleep?

She glanced over at Murphy, completely out cold, intermittently snoring.

Even my dog can do it.

She stared up at the high ceiling for several minutes, took a deep breath, opened her mind, and called out to Honor.

Show me what's next.

Her arms began to tingle, and the edges of her vision blurred, and she gave into the sinking sensation that pulled her under.

In her mind's eye, she could see herself lying in bed, Jason beside her. The Wet Lady stood in the doorway, a long bony finger curling in the air, beckoning her out into the hall.

Follow me, Eliza.

Eliza pushed off the covers and followed the specter through the door and down the corridor.

Drops of water pooled beneath the woman's dripping white gown. Eliza could feel the cool water between her toes as she walked behind.

They stopped at the entry of the spare room, and the door creaked open. Inside, a black marble mantle clock ticked away the seconds with a steady, deafening staccato.

Eliza put her hands over her ears and stepped into the room.

The Wet Lady, eyes glowing, stood in front of the small fireplace.

Give me your hand.

Eliza shuddered but obeyed.

A sharp icy sensation danced over Eliza's skin and made her teeth chatter, but she refused to let go. The Wet Lady lifted her arm, and pressed Eliza's fingers behind the ticking clock to a half brick, partially covered by the wooden mantle.

This fireplace hides the key to the answer you desire,
Remove this mantle and quench thy fire,
Lift this clock and stop the horrid tick,
For once you do so, you will find the loose brick,
Dislodge the brick for what it blocks,
Within thy grasp awaits a hidden box.

A series of heavy footsteps and clicking paws called Eliza from her subconscious.

"Eliza!! What are you doing?" Jason demanded from the doorway.

Eliza jolted from her trance and shivered in the moonlit room. A raw cold rushed from her body as her breath froze and lingered in the air as she spoke.

Jason rubbed his arms. "And why is it so cold in here?"

She pointed at the clock. "The Wet Lady, she led me here. There's something hidden in the wall. We have to get it out."

Jason flicked on the light, and the brightness made Eliza squint and shield her eyes.

"It's 1:30 in the morning. If you promise to get into bed and stay there for the rest of the night and let me sleep until at least seven, I'll bust down every mantle in this place if it will make you happy."

Eliza rubbed her eyes. "And if I don't stay in bed?"

"Then you'll have to let me sleep in later. C'mon, it's cold in here."

He led her back to the bedroom, and she snuggled up against him under the covers.

"Maybe if I hold onto you, I'll actually get some sleep," he said and kissed her head.

Murphy jumped onto the bed and laid down across Eliza's feet.

Jason lifted his head from the pillow to look down at Murphy. "I like the way you think," he said.

"Now, go to sleep."

24

ELIZA CAME DOWNSTAIRS EARLY the next morning to find the coffee on and a cup waiting for her on the counter. Jason came through the garage door, stubbled face, wide grin, a crowbar in one hand and a chisel and hammer in the other.

"Good morning!" He paused to kiss her. "I don't know about you, but it feels like a good day for a little spare room renovation."

Eliza filled her cup and motioned for him to lead the way. "Ready when you are!"

He waited as she removed the decorative items from the top of the mantel. Setting her coffee cup down beside it, she turned her attention to the antique clock with inlaid black marble adorned with gold scrollwork. It was different from any of the other clocks in the house but beautiful, nonetheless. Heavy yet fragile, she would need to take great care to move it.

She ran her fingers over the glass cover of the face and along the edges. She'd found it in the deep recesses of their attic when they moved in, cleaned it up, and it had lived in this room ever since.

"Everything okay?" Jason asked.

"Yeah, there's just something about this clock I can't quite put my finger on."

"How about instead of a finger, you just lift the whole thing out of the way." He angled the crowbar at the wall. "I'm itching to rip this mantle off and see what all the late-night buzz is about."

She laughed, lifted the clock with both hands and carefully placed it on the side table.

"Ready?" Jason asked.

"Wait, wait, let me get my coffee." She wrapped her fingers around her mug and stepped back to get out of his way.

Jason stuck the crowbar behind the corner of the top of the mantle plank with a loud crack, splintering wood broke loose, and before long, Jason had removed the nailing board and dislodged the tiny mantelshelf from the wall. He took a step forward to examine his handiwork. "Huh," he said. "The brick we see here isn't real; it's just a veneer." He ripped away a large section of fake brick paneling. But this," he pointed to a section of newly revealed brickwork, "is actually brick, and I'm guessing it's original to the house."

Eliza moved closer to get a better look. "Maybe we should rip off the rest of the fake stuff and try to return this to its original state. It's a beautiful color."

Jason nodded in agreement and hauled the mantle into the hallway.

Bella appeared in the doorway, Murphy at her side. "It's official, Murph," she said, looking down at him. "My parents have lost their minds. Why are we tearing apart the walls this early in the morning? Looking for buried treasure?"

Eliza smiled. "I had another vision, and I don't know about treasure, but I do think there is something buried in the wall." She pointed to the brick on the wall and began picking away at the loose mortar.

"I've got a tool for that," Jason said, stepping around Bella and Murphy, this time with the chisel and hammer in his hand.

The sound of crumbling cement as the chisel hit the brick-and-mortar made Eliza dance in place. "This is so exciting! I feel like a treasure hunter!"

"I feel like this is going to cost a pretty penny to repair, but yeah, demolition is fun!" Jason exclaimed as he swung the hammer again.

"Jason, it's moving!"

Jason slid the brick right out of its slot, revealing an open cavity in the wall.

"Would you like to do the honor, El?"

"Seriously?" Bella asked from the doorway. "This is like HGTV meets Indiana Jones!"

Eliza shot her a smirk over her shoulder as she reached her hand in to the opening. She felt...nothing.

"It's empty. There's nothing there."

Jason came behind. "Let's remove a few more bricks, see if that helps."

"I don't understand," Eliza said. "It can't be empty. Why would she lead me here for nothing?"

"We've come this far, might as well go for broke," Jason said, banging the hammer with precision against the chisel.

Eliza waited for him to pull a few more bricks loose, then reached back into the opening. Stretching her arm as far as it could go, she moved her fingers gingerly against the rough edges of the brick.

"I hope there aren't any spiders! Wait! I feel something!"

"Good, carefully pull it forward. We don't want it to fall behind the wall."

"I have it!"

She pulled a dusty mahogany box with beautifully carved edges and a shiny brass lock into the morning light.

"Whoa," Bella said, taking a step forward. "That looks old. Is this missing evidence?"

"I have no idea, but somebody really went out of their way to hide it," Eliza said.

"What are the odds it's unlocked?" Jason asked, his fingers hovering over the edge of the lock. He pulled the lid gently. It didn't budge.

"Any chance the elusive Wet Lady told you where the key was?"

Eliza elbowed him. "No, she didn't. But it's the 21st century. We'll just find someone who can open it for us."

"Yes, but that will have to wait a few days. The locksmith is closed for the holiday."

Eliza frowned. "It's been here for who knows how long. It can wait a few more days."

Later that evening, after the three of them had made a dent in the leftover turkey and mashed potatoes, Eliza sat at one end of the table, reading Charlotte's journal. Jason played a game of checkers with Bella at the other end.

She paused at a passage she'd read nearly a dozen times:

September 25, 1808

Today I visited Honor. What was meant to be a happy visit has upset my conscience. She fears Elijah, who is abusive to both her and Levi. Her face bore a bruise, a result of his hand, and he dared to make light of it. I did not care for the way he spoke to Honor nor how he talked to both of us in a condescending and sweetly sickening manner. I shudder at what is going on in that house. My mother-in-law is deeply worried for her daughter, but Honor has become very secretive and distant. I believe it is to protect her son, whom she loves more than life itself.

Levi is very frail and ill. I worry for him. Niles sensed that something was amiss when I returned home earlier than expected. I promised Honor I would not disclose our conversation, but my husband is an intelligent man and knows I am reserved in my responses.

He did not press me, but he did something unlike him. He shared concerns about the shipyard and some oddities he attributes to Elijah. He would not say it plainly, but I now know he suspects Elijah of stealing from the shipyard and plans to address his findings with his father in the coming days.

I had hoped our entire family would come to our house this Sunday for dinner, but Elijah said they would not be able to attend due to Levi's health. I fear something terrible is brewing at Rosecliff.

Eliza glanced down to the end of the table. How lucky she was to have a husband who was kind and gentle, who would step in front of a bullet to protect their child. Her heart ached that Honor hadn't known such a man.

The familiar tingling sensation prickled from her fingertips to her arms as the vision of Jason and Bella became fuzzy and distant. Eliza watched as her dining room morphed into another time period.

September 27, 1808

Levi's thick heavy cough reverberated down the hallway as his tiny body struggled to expel the fluid in his lungs.

Honor carefully slipped out of bed so as not to awaken Elijah and made her way down the dark corridor to her son's room.

She found him sitting up, hunched over, coughing hard.

Levi looked up at her, his face reddened and his eyes bloodshot.

"Sorry to wake you, Mother," Levi said between gasps as he continued to rail and cough.

She poured water into his tin cup from the pitcher near the bed and sat beside him, her arm wrapping around him for support.

Her heart ached as she watched him gasp between swallows. Stroking his back until the worst of the coughing subsided, she was more than a little relieved to see some of the crimson colors fade from his face.

"Feeling better?"

"I am, Mother. I am sorry. I couldn't stop."

"My darling boy, no apologies necessary. I simply wish for you to be well. Shall we go down and see what Susannah has made for breakfast? Are you hungry?"

"Yes," he said, though she wondered if he was simply trying to please her.

She wrapped him in his bed jacket, and together, they made their way down the stairs to the dining room, already warmed by a fire.

"Good morning, Mistress Honor and Master Levi," Susannah, their house servant, said with the slight bob of a curtsy.

"Good morning, Susannah. A bit of warmed milk and honey for Levi."

Susannah nodded and returned with a tray of porridge, hard-boiled eggs, warmed milk, honey, and tea."

Honor watched the orange slips of dawn appear on the horizon as Levi sipped his milk.

The sound of boots on the stairs made her stomach lurch.

"Good morning, Father," Levi said with a weak smile when Elijah stepped into the room.

"It might have been a better morning if not for all that racket. Have you nothing to say for yourself, Levi?"

"Yes, Father. I am sorry if my cough woke you."

"Levi meant no harm, Elijah. He isn't well."

"Stop coddling the boy! He will never get well if you continue to indulge him!"

"He needs a doctor's care, not his father's disapproval."

Elijah's fist hit the table, and the silverware made a clanking noise against the wooden surface.

"Excuse me, sir," Susannah said from the doorway. "A letter arrived for our good mistress."

Elijah straightened and smoothed his waistcoat.

Susannah scurried to Honor's side and handed her the sealed letter.

Honor immediately recognized the script and red wax seal.

"It's from my father. Thank you, Susannah." She quickly broke the seal and read the letter in silence.

"What is it your father wants?" Elijah asked suspiciously.

She quickly reread the letter, then looked up at her husband. "He and my mother will be coming for a visit tomorrow."

She fought to hide her smile when she watched the worry and concern wash over his face.

He cleared his throat. "Your parents are always welcome here. Your father raised a son, and perhaps I shall ask him to impress upon you the same techniques in childrearing since my demands are unheeded." He snapped his finger at Susannah. "Send word to the stables to prepare my mare. I will ride into Salem today."

Honor let the satisfaction of his discomfort roll through as she led Levi back upstairs to dress for his daily lessons. She could see the weight of his illness and his father's cruelty on his slender shoulders.

When they were alone in his room, she hoped to put his mind at ease. "Don't fret. As soon as your father is off, we'll send for Dr. Williams, and Schoolmaster Higgins will be here later to check on your studies. Why don't you rest for a bit? I'll come back for you once I've dressed."

"Yes, Mother." Levi smiled weakly. "Someday, when I am better, I shall take you on an adventure."

Honor smiled brightly. "And where shall we go? Under the sea to find monsters and mermaids? Or into the forest where the fairies live?"

"Wherever you most want to go," he said. "Wherever makes you the happiest."

She hugged him tightly so that he could not see the tears that threatened to fall.

She prayed a silent prayer that her parents would come and see the state of things and insist she leave with them.

She kissed the top of Levi's head. "Rest now."

With Susannah's help, Honor dressed in a jade satin gown with gold embroidery. The dress, the latest fashion from France, with a high waist and black satin sash, made her green eyes sparkle. But it could do nothing to hide the bruise on her face that had lightened from purple to a sallow yellow.

I wonder if my parents will notice this tomorrow, she thought to herself.

"Thank you, Susannah," she said, reaching for a gold necklace with cascading emeralds and pearl clusters Elijah had given her on the first anniversary of their marriage. "Will you ask the cook to prepare some of the tea the doctor left for Levi on his last visit? I'll be down to fetch it shortly."

"Aye, mistress," Susannah said and scurried from the room.

Honor was startled when she caught a glimpse of Elijah in the mirror. He stood in the doorway, admiring her.

"I haven't seen you dressed up in quite some time, Honor. You look almost beautiful."

Honor knew his tricks, and chose her words carefully. "Thank you, Elijah. A wife likes to hear she is pleasing to her husband's eyes."

He put his arm around the front of her and touched the fleshy center of her neck with one hand. He let his fingers glide up towards her lips.

Her body stiffened involuntarily. There was a time when his touch would have set her skin ablaze. But along with his tenderness, her affection for him waned. He turned her slowly to him, looked deeply into her eyes, and kissed her lightly then squeezed her upper arms until she winced.

"A husband responds to his wife positively when she makes herself available to him and no other. Do I make myself clear?"

She nodded; Levi did not need to hear another argument erupt between them. But his accusation was nothing more than his own insecurity. She'd never so much as thought of another man, let alone gone out of her way to catch anyone else's attention.

"I'm to Salem but expect to return by nightfall. See that our boy finishes his lessons. And have Susannah order one of the geese slaughtered for our dinner tomorrow with your parents."

She watched him ride away from their bedroom window, then bounded down the stairs to the kitchen, where she found Susannah cleaning the dishes and preparing a stew.

"Susannah, leave your chores. Ride into town and fetch Dr. Williams. Make haste. He must see Levi at once."

"Aye, mistress."

Dr. Williams arrived an hour later. A handsome man with a furrowed brow, he carried his walking stick in one hand and his brown leather satchel in the other.

Honor brought him at once to Levi's bedside and sat in her watch chair praying for good news.

"Good day, Master Levi," the doctor said with his usually congenial bedside manner. "Let's take a look at you."

When the exam was complete, Dr. Williams patted Levi's shoulder and motioned for Honor to join him in the hall.

"As I am sure you are aware, your son is most decidedly ill. His breathing is labored, and he is pale in color. I recommend bed rest, a letting of blood, and a tonic of seawater and tar juice for his moist asthma. I will return tomorrow to perform a bloodletting and will leave more of the tea that should help him rest and sleep."

"Thank you, Dr. Williams, for checking on him. I should expect you again tomorrow, then?"

"Before noon. Forgive me for saying so, but you look rather tired. And..." He tapped the side of his face, indicating he had noticed the fading bruise on her cheekbone.

Honor felt her cheeks flush with shame.

"Far be it for me to say what is right between a man and his wife, but your father is a particular friend of mine, and I dare say he would not approve. Take care of

yourself, my dear. Levi needs you more than ever, as I fear his condition will only worsen if his mother is not nearby to care for him."

"I understand and appreciate your concern Dr. Williams. Here are the two shillings for your care. We will go to see Susannah for the remainder of your compensation with an allotment of salt pork, brown sugar, and butter."

Honor escorted the good doctor to his carriage and stood in the warm morning sun until she could no longer see or hear his horse. Anxiety surged inside her like the crashing of the shore against the waves.

The heavy thud of horse hooves against the dusty gravel made her take a breath. Had Elijah returned so soon? Had he passed Dr. Williams?

She let out a sigh of relief when the rider drew closer, and she recognized the tall, broad-shouldered form of Samuel, Elijah's younger brother.

Although he often wore work clothes from tending the fields and managing the cows, he was a handsome man with soft sandy brown- hair and kind blue-green eyes.

Honor waved as Samuel's horse neared the dirt drive.

"Good day, Honor. You look lovely in green," *Samuel said as he tied his horse to the hitching post.*

"Good day, Samuel. What brings you to us on this glorious morning?"

"I came to speak with my brother about the corn crops. We are in the midst of harvest, and I believe we will be on target."

"I am sorry to say that he's not at home. He's gone to Salem and won't be back until this evening. Why don't you come in? I'll have the cook put a plate together for you. Perhaps a bit of ale while you wait?"

Samuel looked disappointed. "I can't stay for long, but what kind of uncle would I be if I didn't at least stop in to see my dear nephew?"

"I would be much obliged. Levi has not been well and would dearly love a visit from his uncle."

They entered the house together, and Honor sent Susannah for lemonade. "We purchased an abundance of sugar cane this year," *Honor said as she led Samuel upstairs to Levi's room.* "There is nothing better to quench your thirst on a day such as this."

They found Levi resting in his bed, reading a book.

"Levi, you have a visitor," *Honor said, stepping to the side.*

"Uncle Samuel!" Levi's face beamed.

"What are you reading there, nephew?"

"Robinson Crusoe, by Daniel Defoe. I wish to go on such adventures."

"Ah, and so you shall, Levi," Samuel said gently.

By the time the last of the lemonade was finished, Samuel had promised to come again and bring Levi a copy of his favorite book, Gulliver's Travels by Jonathan Swift, and Honor had convinced Levi to put his book away and sleep until his afternoon lessons.

She followed her brother-in-law back down the stairs.

"You and my brother are blessed," Samuel said, stepping outside. "He is an incredible boy. I will pray that he is soon recovered and in full health once again."

"Thank you, your prayers are most welcomed. Be they enough to see my boy healthy now and for the rest of his days."

Samuel reached out and turned her face into the sunlight.

"My brother did this to you?" he said so much as asked.

Flush with shame, Honor looked down at her feet.

"I will speak to my mother; she will talk some sense into him."

"No," Honor begged, touching his arm. "You mustn't say anything to anyone. I angered him intentionally if I am to be honest. His temper will not be thwarted by you or your mother. For now, he is content to direct his anger at me, and for that, I am grateful, for it keeps Levi safe."

"You deserve better," Samuel said softly.

She offered him a sad smile. "Travel safe. I will let Elijah know you came to see him. I pray your harvest meets all your expectations."

She could tell he wanted to say more, but he simply bowed and mounted his horse, waving before nudging the mare into a steady pace back toward his family's farm.

Watching the dust settle as his horse rode off, Honor battled against an overwhelming sense of loneliness. Samuel's kindness was both a blessing and a curse. It reminded her that some men could be gentle and kind while others, like her husband, could be cruel and hard.

It was well after dark when Elijah arrived home. He stomped through the house, yelling at servants, ranting his dissatisfaction before slumping down in an armchair in the parlor, a bottle of whiskey in his hand.

"How was your business in Salem?" she asked, knowing full well that whatever he had gone to accomplish must have ended in utter failure to see him so angry.

"Your brother is a thorn in my side. He chooses to fight me at every step to expand the trade with England."

"My brother has always had a keen mind for figures and budgets. If he fought you, it is likely he thought your proposal too risky."

Elijah took a hard swig of his drink and slammed the bottle on the side table.

"And what would you know of figures and budgets?" he snarled at her.

"Nothing, husband. Nothing at all." She kept her tone contrite, but inside, she bubbled with glee that her brother had put a stop to any plans Elijah was so determined to see through.

"Samuel came by to see you today," she said, changing the subject. "He mentioned the harvest is looking well. He was kind enough to check in on Levi. Said he will be back tomorrow."

Elijah sneered at her. "So that's why you've put on this dress and your pretty baubles. Not for your husband but for his brother? Or perhaps it was for the doctor you were so quick to call for when you should be heeding my advice. I am very aware of what is done behind my back."

Honor said nothing. She had seen him this way before, knew that tone. She had made her way into his sights, and he would twist her words no matter how she responded.

"You dress for other men, Honor. You spend time primping when my brother or the doctor comes to visit. But what have you done for me?"

She met his gaze and held it firm. "What do I not do for you, husband? I keep your house; I care for our son. Shall I speak to my brother on your behalf that he may give his blessing to whatever venture he has thus denied you?"

In a rage, Elijah lunged from his chair towards Honor, grabbing her wrists. He twisted her tender skin until he saw the pain register on her face.

"Don't test me, wife. Or I'll slice that tongue from that pretty mouth of yours."

He forced a kiss on her lips, his teeth gnashing against hers.

She tasted blood, but she did not cry out. She would not give him the satisfaction.

He shoved her away, picked up the whiskey bottle, and stormed from the room.

"I loathe you, Elijah Brown," she said under her breath. "When Levi is well enough to travel, I will take him away from you, far, far, away from you."

She hurried to her room and found it aglow with a warm fire and several candles. From her desk, she took both ink and paper and drafted two letters: one to her mother, the other to Charlotte. She then blotted the ink on the letters and folded them in half. Quickly, she tucked them into the pages of her Bible.

Far, far away.

Eliza jolted awake to the sound of laughter.

Bella sat opposite Jason, a game of checkers between them at the other end of the table.

"I win again; pay up," Bella said, holding out her hand. "Did you see that, Mom, a quadruple jump to win the game?"

Jason winked at Eliza and pulled a twenty-dollar bill from his wallet. "You win every single time."

"Don't let him fool you, Mom. I know he lets me win."

Eliza rubbed her eyes. "Well done, Bella."

"Hey, you okay?" Jason asked.

"Yeah," Eliza said, the tingling in her arms subsiding and her vision sharpening. "I think I just zoned out there for a minute."

Bella snatched the bill from her father's hand. "I'm headed out for dinner and a movie in a bit. Catch ya later."

"Oh hey," Eliza called after Bella. "Don't forget, the jubilee is tomorrow, and your dad and I will be helping Vanessa most of the day. You'll be on your own for a bit; you good with that?"

Bella hugged her mom. "I'll be fine. Plan on sleeping in and then coming down to check out all the festivities. It'll be my last hoorah before heading back to school."

Eliza held Bella's hand. "I hope this was a good getaway for you. I know we, well, I, have been a bit preoccupied with all of this." She motioned to the stacks of books and papers on the table. "But it's been good having you home."

"This was exactly what I needed," Bella reassured her. "And Christmas is only a few more weeks away. I'll be gone and back before you know it." She kissed her mother's cheek and waved the twenty-dollar bill at her father.

"Have a good time," Jason said. "Love you. Seatbelt."

Bella smiled. "Love you both."

Jason came down to the other end of the table, and Eliza handed him the journal. "Could you just look over this one more time? Maybe I am missing something. I've read through this a dozen times, but I still feel there's more. Something I'm not seeing."

"You sure everything is okay? You looked a little flustered."

"Yeah, yeah, I probably do." Eliza rolled her neck. "I had another vision, a glimpse into Honor's life. It feels like I get sucked into a time warp. Like I'm there, seeing it all happen as she lived it."

Sucked in. That's a good description. But now it's getting harder to get out.

"Anything I should be worried about?" He gave her a sly smile. "Am I going to have to get involved and kick Elijah's ass?"

She swatted at him. "No, I don't think so." She paused and looked at him.

"What?" he asked. "Do I have food on my face?"

"No," she said with a smile. "I just love you and appreciate what a great dad you are."

He leaned in and kissed her. "I love you too, and you are, by far, the best mom I know."

Jason settled into a chair, whipped his reading glasses out of his pocket, and opened the journal. "I'll read it cover to cover if you bring me some coffee."

"Deal," Eliza said, happy for the change of scenery, even if it was just the kitchen.

She filled the water, turned the coffee pot on, and waited for it to brew. Her eyes drifted to the box they'd found in the spare room. Half of her was ecstatic that her vision had proved true, and they'd found something hidden exactly where she'd known it would be. The other half of her struggled with frustration. To find it and not be able to open it was more than a little aggravating.

She poured Jason's coffee and carried it back to the dining room.

"Well, my love," he said, taking the mug from her. "I think I found something."

"Already? Seriously? Show me," she insisted.

He flipped the journal open to the back cover. "Look along the page seam here." He pointed to a small line of handwriting she hadn't noticed before.

Eliza moved the book into the light and lifted it closer to her face so she could make out the words.

Susannah Watkins, faithful servant at Rosecliff.
Letter

"How did we miss this?"

Jason looked at her befuddled.

"Why on earth would a servant at Rosecliff be writing to Charlotte?"

Jason shrugged. "I have no idea, but what are the chances that the letter is in the same place you found the journal?"

"In Ginny's desk?" Eliza shook her head. "I looked inside the drawer; there was nothing else, just the journal."

"We didn't think there was anything behind that brick at first either. It had been pushed back. Maybe the same thing happened to the letter?"

A slow smile spread across Eliza's face. "Mr. Grey, have I told you today how much I love you?"

"Only about five minutes ago, but I don't mind hearing it again and again."

"I need to find my phone. Call Ginny."

"What? Now?" he asked.

"Yeah, right now. We found that box, and I can't open it, and it's driving me crazy. If that letter is in that desk, I need to see it. Tonight."

She left him in the dining room and found her phone.

Within seconds, Ginny's sweet voice answered her call.

"Hello?"

"Hi Ginny, It's Eliza. I hope it is not too late to call."

"Eliza. Why not at all. What can I do for you?"

"We found another clue in Charlotte's journal. We've learned quite a bit about what Honor experienced in her final days, but Ginny, what do you know about Susannah Watkins?"

"I'm not sure I recognize that name. Is she mentioned in the journal?"

"Yes. Jason noticed a notation at the end of the journal. It referenced Susannah Watkins and a letter she'd given to Charlotte. I believe she was a maid in Honor's household. She lived and worked at Rosecliff."

"Hmmm...I don't recall ever coming across a letter from Susannah Watkins. Besides, why would a servant from another household be writing letters to Charlotte?"

"That is an excellent question. Ginny, is it possible the letters were with the journal but maybe got pushed back, maybe stuck in the rear of the secret drawer? We never pulled it out completely."

"I mean, it's entirely possible. That desk has been moved up and down from the attic and various rooms in the house since I was married. Why don't you come by, and we can search together."

"Can we come now? The suspense is killing me," Eliza said.

"Of course, I can hardly wait to see it for myself. I'll put the porch light on."

"See you in about fifteen minutes!"

Eliza called for Jason. "Let's go; she invited us over to check the desk."

"Right now?"

"Yes, right now. Get a move on." She smiled and tossed him his jacket. Murphy whined and tugged at his leash on the hook.

"Why not? Come on, Murphy. But you'll have to wait in the car."

Eliza could feel it in her bones, the answers were close, and Honor wasn't going to disappoint.

Jason drove the speed limit to Ginny's house, a fact that Eliza had to bite her tongue to keep from commenting on. As promised, the porch light awaited their arrival.

Eliza slipped out of the driver's side and told Murphy to stay.

Ginny's silhouette cast a shadow from the front door. "Nonsense, Eliza. Bring Murphy inside."

"Oh, Ginny, that's very kind, but he sheds. *A lot.*"

"It's fine, Eliza. I own a vacuum cleaner. Bring him in."

"Okay, but you might need a lint roller or two, as well."

Eliza opened the door and took ahold of Murphy's leash. "You better behave yourself."

He licked her face and jumped down, and pulled her up the steps. He sat in front of Ginny as she petted him, then followed as they went inside.

"I appreciate you letting us come over tonight," Eliza said, her voice practically buzzing with excitement.

Eliza pulled the journal from her inner jacket pocket and opened it to the last page to show her the entry.

"It is beyond puzzling," Ginny said, handing the journal back to Eliza. "Why would Charlotte go to the trouble to make such an odd notation without anything definitive to explain it?"

"I don't know," Eliza said. "I'm hoping we find the letter, and it somehow helps all of this make sense."

"Lead the way," Ginny offered.

Murphy pulled Eliza up the stairs and down the hall, stopping at the door into the room with the desk. He sniffed the bottom of the door and let out a low growl.

"Is this the right room?" Jason asked over her shoulder.

"Yes."

"Go on in," Ginny said, coming up behind them.

Eliza pushed open the door and flicked on the light.

Murphy pulled into the room, his growl growing in intensity, his gaze fixed on the window next to the desk.

Eliza caught Jason's gaze.

"Let's look and get out of here. Something or someone may not want us here," he whispered in her ear.

She nodded and bent to pull the key from its hiding place and turned the lock. The drawer made a popping sound, as it had before, and released. She lifted the slatted dividers to display the false bottom and placed her hand all the way back, feeling for any loose paper or envelopes.

"There's nothing here," she said with deep disappointment.

"Let's pull it all the way out," Jason suggested. He turned to ask Ginny, "Is that okay if I promise to be careful?"

Ginny shooed him on. "Of course, of course."

He knelt down in front of the writing table and carefully pulled the drawer out to its full depth, then lifted gently until he felt it slip from the track. The drawer glided out, and he carried it away from the desk.

Eliza reached back inside and felt around. Still nothing.

Ginny moved toward the desk. "Jason, would you mind setting the drawer on top of the desk?"

Jason complied.

"Just as I thought," Ginny said. "Look at the desk and the depth of this drawer. The desk is much deeper. Eliza should be able to reach back to nearly arm's length, but she's barely into her elbow. I think this desk is full of surprises, including a false back."

Eliza stared at Ginny incredulously, but after looking at the drawer, she had to agree. "Jason, any chance you've got your cell phone handy?"

Jason nodded. Turning the flashlight on, he handed the phone to Eliza.

Still kneeling, Eliza flashed a light into the dark cavern of the writing desk, and to her surprise, she spied a short lever. She lifted the handle, and the back wall of the desk dropped, exposing a small section farther back. In the dusty cavity, folded neatly, lay a letter and what appeared to be a necklace with a broken chain.

She retrieved the items and handed them immediately to Ginny.

Murphy began to whine. "What is it, boy?" Eliza asked.

"I'm going to take him downstairs and outside," Jason said and bent down and patted him on the back. "C'mon, Murphy!"

"Let's take these down to the kitchen, Ginny," Eliza suggested; the air in the room was noticeably colder than it had been when they entered.

"Hurry," Jason mouthed and led Murphy down the stairs.

Eliza and Ginny followed them to the first floor.

"I can't believe we just opened a portion of that writing table that has not been exposed for hundreds of years," Ginny said as she sat at the kitchen table. "Most likely, the last person to know of its secrets was Charlotte Lord."

"But what is it exactly that we've found?"

They sat side by side at the table, and Eliza gingerly unfolded the yellowed and extremely fragile letter and read aloud:

November 10, 1808

Dearest Mistress Lord,

I must unburden my soul of the guilt that fills my days and nights. Guilt I carry for the loss of Mistress Brown and her dear, sweet Levi. I loved them with all my heart and pray to Almighty God that he forgives me for any role I unwillingly played in their deaths.

You must know Mistress Brown suffered dreadfully in this house, as did Levi. He ailed terribly the week he died. One morning, his father demanded that he be woken and prepared for the fields. I wanted to wake my mistress, but he forbade it and waited as I helped the boy to dress. I knew it was wrong, he was too sick to labor so, but I obeyed my master. I will forever wish I had not.

My Mistress was inconsolable the hours after Master Levi's death. Master Brown had taken to his whiskey. I fretted leaving my Mistress, a sorrow I now carry, but the staff was dismissed to our homes early. Upon my return the next morning, I learned of Mistress Brown's death and found Rosecliff in disarray.

I send, with the letter, my lady's necklace, which I found broken whilst sweeping under the upstairs tea table the morning after my Mistress died. I would never steal my mistress's possession, that I swear to you. I am returning it to you, whom I know she dearly loved.

I have since told Master Brown that I will no longer serve as a house servant to Rosecliff. I have taken my leave and have accepted a position in Salem with a prominent family. If you must find me there, please do so discreetly, as I fear what Master Brown will do should he find out what I have told you.

I finish with this: I knowest my Mistress best and beg you to believe as I do, that she did not kill herself.

Susannah Watkins

Eliza finished reading the letter and set it down gently on the table.

"There you have it," Ginny said. Ginny's blue-grey eyes looked even more prominent as she stared at the words on the page. "I think this letter leaves little doubt that Susannah Watkins didn't believe Honor killed herself."

Eliza turned her attention to the emerald and pearl necklace on the table. Its double-link gold chain broken near the main cascade of emeralds.

"I can't believe that lay inside that desk all these years!" Ginny exclaimed.

Eliza picked up the beautiful intricate 18th-century necklace. The delicate stylized floral and scroll-designed pendant was set in gold and silver with clusters of pearls embellished with white, pink, and blue enamel and adorned with four table-cut emeralds. The craftsmanship was nothing short of spectacular. The gold chain with annular ropework and curbed linking lay heavy in Eliza's hands. "It must have taken considerable force to break such a thick chain."

After a moment, Eliza realized the time. "It's getting late; we should go. Any chance I could keep these with the journal for further study? I want to go back through, see if Charlotte ever mentions a necklace like this."

"Of course, if you and Murphy hadn't discovered Honor Brown's story, that necklace would have remained within that writing table for another century if it were ever found at all!"

"If we do find that Honor was murdered, what do we do then?" Eliza asked as Ginny walked her to the door.

"We can petition to have her cause of death amended. Set the history books straight officially."

"Do you think the historical society would be willing to foot the bill to have Honor's grave moved? Her and Levi? To put them together, maybe closer to her parents?"

Ginny patted Eliza's shoulder. "I'd say we've already uncovered enough to at least ask. I will do what I can to persuade the council to grant the funds to do right by Honor and her son."

Eliza put her hand on top of Ginny's. "Thank you."

Back in the warmth of their dining room, Eliza added the letter, journal, and necklace to their growing body of research on the table.

She read the letter to Jason, and he leaned on the arm of his chair. "We know the necklace belonged to Honor, and it would seem she was wearing it the night she died. I'm no jeweler, but it looks to be expensive. And it's such a distinct piece of evidence. Why would he leave it there for someone to find?"

"It was found under a table, so maybe he didn't see it? Susannah also mentioned he was drinking. I suppose it's possible he didn't even realize it was there."

Jason rolled his neck and rubbed his eyes. "It's late, and we've got the jubilee in the morning. This took us a huge leap closer." He nodded toward the foyer.

Murphy was stretched out, dead asleep on the entry rug.

"How about we take a clue from Murphy and call it a night?"

"Fair enough," Eliza said, letting Jason pull her to her feet. "I should text Vanessa, make sure the plan is still the same." She pointed at the box. "Please help me to remember to take a break tomorrow morning and call around for a locksmith. The answer to our other mystery could be just a lock away."

While Jason turned down the bed, Eliza sat at her vanity, brushing her hair. Her disappointment over how their morning had started was nothing compared to the exhilaration she'd felt watching the false back panel drop away from within Ginny's desk. Surely the letter would be enough to prove that Honor had met with foul play at her husband's hand.

As she pulled her hair up into a bun, her arms and hands began to tingle.

Her reflection in the mirror clouded, hidden behind the frostiness of her breath as the temperature around her grew cold.

The Wet Lady called her name.

Eliza.

Eliza struggled to focus. Her brush felt heavy in her hand. The bathroom grew darker and began to spin.

You found the box, its secrets dear,
The key once held in death's grip no longer here,
But another item exposes more lies,
A seal of green with secrets of my demise,
Find it in a hiding place where the light cannot see,
High above a cupboard wall where a larder be.

The ghostly apparition disappeared. Jason stood behind her, staring at her in the mirror.

Eliza nodded and tried to stand, but her knees buckled.

Jason reached out to steady her.

"Whoa, sit back down. You okay? Another vision?"

Eliza nodded. "The Wet Lady was here just now. The key we need for the box isn't here." Her head swam, and her thoughts felt muddled. "I have to find the 'seal of green.'"

Jason lifted her in his arms and carried her into the bedroom.

"I have to find the seal of green," she said again, the room spinning at the edges. "In a cupboard or the larder, I'm not sure which."

"We'll figure it out in the morning," Jason said softly.

She felt the pillow beneath her head and the warmth of the covers as Jason tucked her in and she fell asleep.

25

THE SUN HAD RISEN above the ocean's horizon when Eliza tossed Murphy's bag into the back of the SUV the following morning. She'd promised to meet Vanessa at her booth on the town green at 9 a.m., which would give them a solid hour to prepare before the 10 a.m. Jubilee commencement.

Jason lumbered down the porch stairs with a tote filled with blankets and supplies.

Murphy, with a festive red, white, and blue bandana tied to his collar, trailed behind.

"I think that's everything," Jason said, setting the tote next to Murphy's bag and closing the back of the SUV. "If we've forgotten anything or think of anything else, I can always run home. You ready?"

Eliza hesitated. Something gnawed at her intuition.

"You're going to think I'm crazy, but I feel we should take the box we found in the wall with us."

Jason gave her a look. "Why, have you arranged a clandestine meeting with a locksmith in the parking lot?"

"No," she said, rolling her eyes. Her sense of humor was still sound asleep upstairs in their bed. "I just have a feeling." She put her hand on her stomach. "My gut is screaming for us to take the box with us."

"I don't know, El. There's going to be a lot of people in town today. Residents and out-of-towners. What if the car gets broken into?"

She waved off his concern and hurried up the porch steps to retrieve the box from the dining room table.

When she returned, locking the door behind her, Jason still stood in the driveway, looking skeptical.

"I can't help it, Jason. Something is telling me we need to keep the box close. So, I am bringing it. We'll hide it in the back of the car under the blankets."

He held up his hand. "Far be it for me to argue with your gut feelings. You want it close? We'll take the box."

When they arrived, the large parking lot near the town green was already buzzing with activity. The booths, strategically arranged in a circular fashion around the perimeter of the green, gave easy access to all those attending. Banners of red, white, and blue and the town flag – a white panel with an anchor in the center and waves all around it – fluttered in the wind. The high school band, donned in full uniform, warmed up their instruments at the corner of Main Street near where the parade would begin.

In the center of the green, the town gazebo already sported the podium set for the day's sequence of guest speakers. The scent of apple cider donuts, fried dough, and coffee filled the air. Children ran about holding pennants, and the townsfolk congregated in large groups, chatting away.

Even though it was the last weekend of November, the cold temperature didn't keep the crowds away, and the sun peeked up over the horizon, promising a bright, sunny day for their little town celebration.

Eliza searched for Vanessa and her bakery booth, spying both of them across from the front of the gazebo.

Jason carried the tote with their supplies, and Eliza carried Murphy's bag and his leash. Halfway across the green, Murphy gave a loud bark and darted to the left, pulling his leash from her grip.

"Murphy," Eliza scolded, turning to chase after him, Jason right behind her.

Murphy stopped short of the parking lot and jumped up on a tall man in a Stetson.

Marty Evans.

Marty's hat fell off his head and landed in the grass behind him as Murphy licked the man's face from chin to forehead.

"Is it just me," Jason asked as they closed the distance, "or does this look like a case of the cowardly lion attacking the scarecrow?"

Eliza snickered and shoved his arm. "Be nice."

When they reached the edge of the green, Marty bent to retrieve his hat and brushed bits of grass off its felted surface.

"Good morning, Miss Eliza," Marty said, putting his hat back on his head.

"Good morning! Marty, this is my husband, Jason." Eliza bent to retrieve Murphy's leash. "Jason, this is Marty Evans."

Marty shook Jason's hand.

"I've heard a lot about you, Marty. How you have helped Eliza with the gravesite and uncovering clues. It is a pleasure to meet you."

Marty nodded, obviously uncomfortable.

"Marty, Jason and I found something." She leaned in closer and dropped her voice to a whisper: "A box hidden behind the wall in one of the rooms at Rosecliff."

Marty's eyes grew wide.

"I think what's inside could potentially have an impact on you, on your family, I mean."

Marty's eyes lit up. "I can imagine, Miss Eliza, that the only reason you would find a buried box in a wall at Rosecliff is because Honor led you to it."

Jason looked surprised. He nudged Eliza. "Does everyone in town know about this whole Honor/Wet Lady thing?"

"No, not everyone," Eliza said, surprised that she didn't feel compelled to hide her gifts. "Marty knows. He knew before I was even willing to admit it."

She smiled at him, and Marty smiled back, shifting from one foot to the other.

"And Vanessa knows. Other than that, just my family and you."

"Well, then, since you know how this works," he said, looking at Marty, "you have no idea the lengths this ghost has gone to expose the truth," Jason said emphatically.

"There's just one problem," Eliza added. "I don't want to get your hopes up. I don't know exactly what's inside the box yet; it's locked. I didn't find a key, and I have no idea where it might be. I am hoping to locate a locksmith who might be able to open it for us without damaging the box or anything inside."

Marty looked at her pensively, quietly for a moment, then rubbed his neck.

"Miss Eliza, I think now would be a good time to tell you a little story. When I was a small boy, my grandfather used to grumble and complain about losing our family fortune. Don't get me wrong, he wasn't caught up in the money part. Like me, he was a simple guy, didn't need much. But whenever he got going, he would go on and on about how my great-grandfather hid the evidence that would prove our side of the case and then died without ever telling anyone where he stashed it."

"Oh, Marty, I'm so sorry," Eliza said, reaching out to touch his arm. "I can't imagine how hard it must have been on your family. To lose everything like that, with a gavel strike and a signature, everything just given to a stranger."

"He also told me another story about how when they found my great-grandfather lying on the floor after his heart attack, they found a key gripped in his hand. Had to pry it out of his fingers; he held on to it so tight! They always assumed it had something to do with the evidence he hid, but they had no idea what the key was for."

Eliza could have sworn her heart skipped a beat. She squeezed Marty's arm. "Please tell me you know what happened to that key."

Marty's face split into a wide grin. "My father gave it to me before he died. He told me to hold on to it. Said it might come in handy someday."

Goosebumps raced up Eliza's arms; she glanced at Jason, hardly able to contain her excitement.

"Any chance we could talk you into dinner at our house tomorrow night? A little steak, a little dessert, and a little box that could change everything?"

Marty nodded, and his face looked visibly lighter.

Out of pure excitement, Eliza hugged him.

He surprised her by hugging her back.

"I'd like that, thank you." He reached out and shook Jason's hand again.

"Let's say six," Jason said, shifting the weight of the tote.

"Six it is," Marty replied.

"See you tomorrow." Eliza waved and tugged Murphy's leash.

Together, Eliza and Jason hurried across the green to Vanessa's booth.

"I thought I saw you coming, and then you disappeared," Vanessa said, shaking out a tablecloth and spreading it out over a long narrow table at the back of the booth.

"I have so much to tell you," Eliza said, "but first, put us to work."

By noon, Eliza was certain they'd served up a croissant or jelly donut to every resident of Coventry and most of their extended families. Murphy had made himself at home, moving between a spot near the front of the tent to greet customers and accept treats, and his travel bed, which sat beneath the booth's front table.

Eliza marveled that despite all the people moving in and out, Murphy could still fall asleep. She caught the soft, buzzing sound of his snores in a lull between customers.

"What a turn out," Vanessa said, adding more water to their coffee and hot chocolate carafes.

Jason tied off a bag of garbage and pulled it from the can. "Gonna go toss this in the dumpster, be right back."

When he was out of earshot, Vanessa nudged Eliza. "Things going okay with you two? We haven't talked much since the big blow-up."

Eliza added more cocoa powder to the tall heating tank and stirred it with a long wooden spoon. "Oh, yeah. Actually, we might be better than we've ever been. He knows," she said, putting the lid back on the carafe and flipping it to heat.

"He knows?" Vanessa squealed. "As in, he knows you *know* things?"

"Yep, and about the Wet Lady, the visions, all of it."

"How'd that go over?"

Eliza smiled. "Could have gone better. I had a little paranormal assistance in convincing him."

"He actually saw a ghost? I mean, *the ghost*? He saw the Wet Lady?"

"Oh no, I'm not sure he could have handled that. Just a massive swinging chandelier and a fireplace poker fly across the room by itself."

Vanessa shook her head, then mouthed the word "Wow." "Oh my gosh," she said, covering her mouth with her hand, "I can just imagine the look on his face. I'd have run straight out of the house!"

Eliza laughed. "But seriously, he's been a big help. We've uncovered so many clues and hints about Honor and her family. And about a certain local politician."

"Yeah, hold that thought," Vanessa said and nodded toward the green. "Said certain local politician is out making rounds, and it looks like he's headed this way."

A few moments later, Graham Winthrop stepped under the awning of the bakery tent.

"Good afternoon, Ms. Grey. Ms. Murphy."

From beneath the table, Murphy let out a snarl. He stepped out from below the table, teeth bared.

The mayor took a step back.

"Murphy, come," Eliza said.

Murphy ducked back under the table and reappeared on the other side next to Eliza and stood, glaring at Graham.

"Nice dog, Ms. Grey."

"What can I say, Mayor? Murphy usually has such impeccable judgment when it comes to people."

"Yes, so long as you keep him in check. We wouldn't want anyone to get bitten. Town ordinance would require such an animal to be put down."

Eliza's eyes narrowed, and she bit her tongue.

Graham, I'm the wrong woman to threaten.

Jason reappeared and cleared his throat. "Everything okay in here? Good to see you, Mr. Mayor." Jason offered his hand.

Graham looked down at Jason's hand, huffed, and turned and walked away.

"The mayor just threatened Murphy. But he's messing with the wrong woman," Eliza hissed through gritted teeth.

"I don't trust that man," Vanessa said, kneeling down to offer Murphy a pumpkin donut hole. "Even Murphy knows that, don't you, boy?"

"I'd have to agree," Jason said. "Maybe we'll get lucky, and folks will finally vote him out."

"If Patrick has his way, he'll be locked up before the next election," Vanessa said quietly. "There's no doubt now that the fire was arson. A street camera caught a certain green sports car speeding away from Main Street about ten minutes before the fire alarm went off. Can't prove anything definitive yet, but it's just a matter of time."

Jason put his hand on Eliza's back. "We should try to steer clear of the mayor. He's got a lot to lose."

Eliza leaned against Jason's shoulder. "I'm not afraid of him. Like Vanessa said, it's just a matter of time before the truth comes out."

Any further conversation was lost to a surge of new customers, the scent of fresh coffee and hot chocolate proving to be the perfect lure.

After the rush of patrons brought out by the parade and live music, the line at the bakery tent remained steady but slowed.

"I'm going to take some of these empty trays back to the bakery and pick up some fresh goodies for this afternoon. You two okay here on your own for a few minutes?" Vanessa asked, pulling several empty trays from under the table.

"Yep, I think we can handle it," Eliza said.

Jason stepped up beside her and took Vanessa's place behind the table.

"It's almost two," he said. "Can't believe how fast the day has gone," wiping up a small spill on the table before adding more napkins to the dispenser.

"Hey, look," Eliza pointed to two women approaching the tent. "It's two of my favorite people."

"And here are two of mine," Thea echoed, coming around behind the table to hug Eliza and then Jason.

"What a perfect day for our 250th Jubilee celebration!" Ginny remarked, examining the sweet offerings on display.

Thea made a face. "I'd prefer the Florida sun and a mai tai to hot chocolate, but hey, it's tolerable."

Ginny leaned closer. "I hope you don't mind, but I shared a bit of the excitement of last night, the letter and the necklace, with Thea," Ginny whispered.

"Not at all," Eliza assured her. "So, what do you think, Thea? Have we added another member to our Honor's truth club?"

"Without a doubt. I still can't believe that stuff was just sitting at the back of the desk, waiting for someone to find it. I told Ginny years ago she should sell off all that old antique furniture, but she ignored me. Guess keeping all of it was the right choice after all."

Thea bent down to pet Murphy then settled into a game of twenty questions with Jason about his business and any updates to Rosecliff since she'd last been in town.

Ginny pulled Eliza aside. "Any movement on the other little mystery? I saw Marty a while ago. Thea and I went to go check out the movie schedule for this evening, and the mayor had poor Marty cornered between the gazebo and the sound equipment. Whatever they were talking about, the mayor looked angry. We were afraid he might strike Marty, but in the end, he just stormed off. We thought of checking on Marty, but when we got to the gate, he'd disappeared."

Eliza huffed. "The more I learn about our good mayor, the more I'm convinced he's a snake in a tailored suit. The morning after we found the necklace, Jason and I found a locked box hidden in the wall at Rosecliff. We can't open it yet, but Marty thinks he might have the key. I can't be certain, but my gut tells me it's the missing evidence proving the mayor's family fraudulently stole the Brown estate."

"I'm sure you already know," Ginny said, her face awash in concern, "but Graham Winthrop is the kind of man who uses his money to get whatever he wants. He's bullied the town's historical society on more than one occasion." She pursed her lips. "I suppose now we know why."

"What are you two gossiping about over here?" Thea asked just as Vanessa stepped back into the tent, several boxes of freshly baked goodies in hand.

"My plan is to convince you to give up all that warm weather and move back here to keep your oldest and dearest friend company in her old age."

Thea's eyes teared up.

"Oh gracious," Ginny said, putting an arm around Thea's shoulders.

Eliza handed her a napkin.

"Oh, look at what you've done," Thea said, swatting Ginny with the napkin before blotting her tears. "Maybe you should give up the snow and come with me." She laughed. "We could do some damage; mai tais, and old ladies taking the beach by storm." She pressed a hip out. "Bought myself a neon-pink bikini last month. We could get you one. But I think lime green is more your color."

Eliza laughed as Ginny blushed.

"C'mon," Thea said, linking her arm through Ginny's. "Let's go grab one of those spicy sausages we saw on the way in."

Ginny waved and let Thea lead her out. "Keep me posted," she said, glancing back over her shoulder at Eliza.

"El, you said it before. That will be us in thirty years," Vanessa said, unloading a box of apple pie fritters onto the display tray.

Eliza watched Ginny and Thea as they walked across the green. She'd never have pinned the two to be such good friends, but they couldn't be more perfect for each other.

"I'd drink mai tais and storm the beach with you any day."

"Ditto that," Vanessa replied. "Now we just need to decide who gets the neon pink and who's showing up in lime green."

26

Eliza tossed the last bag of garbage into the dumpster and hugged Vanessa.

"If the two of you are ever looking for a job, Murphy's Bakery's got aprons with your names on them."

Sales had remained steady throughout the day, and they'd closed down the tent just after six, in time to join a crowd of their fellow Coventry residents for the mayor's closing remarks and the lighting of the town Christmas tree. It had taken all of Eliza's self-control to keep from heckling the man as he spoke about tradition and the importance of friends and community. She'd searched the crowd for Marty, hoping to make sure he was all right, but she hadn't been able to find him.

Eliza waited until Vanessa made it to her car before jogging across the parking lot to Jason.

"Ready to go home?" he asked, holding the leash of a very tired Murphy.

"So ready," she said and opened the door for Murphy to jump into the back seat.

With him securely inside, she headed around to the back of the SUV and checked that the wooden box was still safely hidden under several blankets.

As they passed the shore and into their driveway, the sun had slipped beneath the ocean's horizon, and the stars began to peek out, one by one, in the crisp night air.

"I think there's some take-out, a hot bath, and early bed in our future, Mr. Grey."

"You'll get no argument from me," he said, offering his hand.

She put her palm to his and interlaced their fingers. She'd asked a lot of him to reconsider what he believed was possible, what he considered to be true. It had taken a fair amount of convincing, but he'd come through for her. As he always did. And she loved him dearly for it.

Jason parked the car and popped the rear hatch, and they quickly unloaded the back.

Murphy bounded up the porch steps but stopped short, just shy of the front door, and began to growl.

"Oh, I know how this ends," Jason said, dropping the tote next to the door and fumbling for the keys. "If the chandelier starts swinging, we're going out for dinner."

He nudged her with his elbow, a goofy grin on his face. His smile disappeared the moment he opened the door and flicked on the foyer light.

"What the hell!" he exclaimed.

Murphy tugged at his leash, pulling away, barking as he tore through the foyer, then raced to the kitchen.

Before them lay a house in terrible disarray. The Tiffany lamp smashed on the floor; its delicate shade shattered into dozens of pieces. From the foyer, Eliza could see into the living room. The cushions had been torn from the couch, drawers turned upside down, their contents scattered across the room.

"Oh my God, Jason!"

"Eliza, call the police. I am going to check the house." Flicking on the living room lights, he grabbed the poker from the fireplace.

Eliza grabbed his arm. "Wait, what if whoever did this is still in the house?"

"I think we're alone. If someone were still here, Murphy would have them pinned by now."

Eliza dialed 9-1-1 on her phone and followed Jason into the kitchen.

Every cabinet drawer had been pulled open and dumped. Contents of the cabinets tossed onto the floor. Tears sprung to her eyes at the sight of a few treasured pieces of her wedding china, pulled from her glass cabinet and broken across the top of the kitchen island.

"This is 9-1-1; what is your emergency?"

"Hello, this is Eliza Grey, 1 Rosecliff Avenue; someone has broken into our home."

"Two units are on their way to you. Is anyone hurt? Do you know if the perpetrator is still on the premises?"

"No, no one is hurt, and no, I don't think whoever did this is still here. Our dog would have found them by now."

"Help is on the way. They are five minutes out. Try not to touch anything. So sorry this happened to you."

Eliza thanked the woman and hung up the phone.

Glass littered the floor in front of the open French doors. The evening winter air drifting into her kitchen.

Murphy sniffed the glass.

"No, Murphy. Come," Eliza said, and Murphy trotted over and followed her into the dining room.

With one glance around the room, she no longer tried to hold back the tears.

All of the research they'd amassed was strewn across the room. A large scrape marred the top of the table. She searched the floor; the letters, Ginny's family Bible, and Charlotte's journal were nowhere to be found. And there was no sign of Honor's necklace or the locket Kent had given her. She instantly regretted not locking it all up before they left.

Jason called her name.

Eliza hurried back into the kitchen and found him staring at the floor.

"Come tell me what this looks like to you."

"Stay here, Murphy," she said and hurried over to Jason's side.

He pointed to the first in a trail of muddy shoe prints.

"I'm no detective, but these aren't sneaker prints or boot prints. In fact," he squatted down for a closer look. "I'm pretty sure I recognize that sole pattern. It matches a pair of dress shoes I bought last year in New York. If I were a thief looking for a quick score or your everyday rabble rouser just looking to make trouble, I'm fairly certain these are the last shoes I'd put on to do it."

They followed the trail, being careful not to disturb the prints. When they reached the stairs, she shivered at the thought that a stranger had been in her bedroom.

Jason took her hand, and they climbed to the second floor. The footprints, though lighter, were still visible down the hall leading to the spare room. The black mantle clock remained safely on the side table, untouched. Additional bricks had been ripped from the wall and tossed in a pile on the bed.

The sound of sirens approaching grew louder until they screamed in unison with the flashing red and blue lights from the driveway.

"We should let the cops take it from here," Jason said.

The police spent the next hour taking their statements and searching the house. The first officers on the scene asked them to wait outside, so they sat in their SUV, out of the cold, waiting. Murphy made himself at home in the back seat, whining every so often, and he watched all of the people coming and going.

Chief Coleman approached the car, and Jason rolled down his window.

"We found these in the backyard, near the French doors, which is where, you probably guessed, whoever did this, got into your house." He held up the emerald necklace and Kent's locket.

"With these recovered, do you feel like anything of value is missing at this point?"

"I think some of our research is missing," Eliza blurted, once again on the verge of tears. "A large family Bible, several old letters and a handwritten journal from the 1800s."

The chief took out a pen and notebook and jotted down some notes. "Whoever broke in was obviously searching for something particular. No regular thief would have left this behind." He handed Jason the two necklaces. "We've dusted them for fingerprints and came up empty, so you can have them back for now. Do you think whoever did this broke in to steal your research?"

Eliza wiped her nose with her sleeve. She wanted to insist that the police go immediately to the mayor's house and arrest him, but they didn't have any real proof. She glanced at Jason. He shook his head ever so slightly.

Eliza returned her attention to the police officer. "No, I mean, I can't be sure. Few people even knew I had those things."

Chief Coleman made a few more notes, then climbed the porch steps to chat with two other officers before returning to their car. "We've wrapped up inside, taken pictures, and dusted for fingerprints. Unfortunately, we didn't find anything other than some muddy shoe prints, but we'll keep you posted. If anything else turns up missing, let us know." He handed Jason a business card. "If you need help, I can have a couple of my guys help you secure those French doors for the night."

Jason put the business card in his pocket. "No need; I've got plywood already cut to fit as part of our storm supplies. I can take care of it."

"One question, Chief Coleman," Eliza said abruptly.

"Yes, Ms. Grey?"

"Is there still an ongoing investigation into the courthouse fire?"

He gave her an odd look. "Well, I can't comment on any active investigations, but Fire Chief Murphy's report will be made public by the end of the week. Out of curiosity, why do you ask?"

"I work for *The Gazette*. Always looking for the next story," she said, hoping he wouldn't press her interest further. "Thank you, Chief. For everything."

"It's what I'm here for." He tipped his hat. "Sorry this happened to you. Take care and stay safe."

The exhaustion that had promised a bath and early bedtime evaporated, and Eliza set about picking up the living room, returning cushions, the contents of drawers, and things from shelves, back to their proper places.

The house echoed with the sound of hammering as Jason affixed their storm plywood over the broken doors in the kitchen. She'd tackle that room next.

She sank down on the couch and let the tears flow freely. Not only did she feel violated, her beautiful home a wreck, but she'd lost valuable artifacts, the evidence she needed to prove Honor had been murdered. She'd have to call Ginny in the morning and let her know. She'd be devastated at the loss of her precious family history.

Jason found her sitting in the dark and sat to put his arms around her.

"There is one silver lining in this whole thing," he said, wiping her tears with his thumb.

"Oh? What's that?" she asked, reaching across him to pull a tissue from the box on the side table.

"You were right about taking the box with us. I'm guessing you and I both know who did this, and after our dinner with Marty tomorrow, everyone will finally know that Mayor Winthrop is a fraud."

27

T HE HOUSE STILL LOOKED half a wreck when the doorbell rang.

Marty stood on the front porch, with a bouquet of red chrysanthemums and white carnations.

"Why Marty, you clean up rather nice," Eliza said, taking the flowers. His sandy brown hair had been neatly combed to the side. He wore a beige wool jacket, a pair of navy blue dress pants with a crisp white shirt, and his usual Stetson held tightly in his free hand.

"Come on in, but please, pretend you don't see the mess."

Eliza had done her best to make her home look presentable. The living room looked mostly normal, and she'd covered the damage to her dining room table with a tablecloth.

"I heard about the break-in," Marty said. "Glad no one was hurt."

"Not physically, anyway," Eliza said. "But I am devastated and heartbroken that the letters Ginny and I found, her family Bible and Charlotte Lord's journal were stolen. They were priceless, and I'm worried we'll never get them back."

Marty stepped into the foyer and took in the room. He spun slowly, looking up to the ceiling.

"I've only seen some pictures of Rosecliff when I was small. This is spectacular. What a beautiful home."

Jason rounded the corner from the kitchen and held out his hand, "Hey Marty, welcome!"

"Thank you, Mr. Grey."

"Please, Marty, no formalities. Call me Jason."

A sudden thumping came from above them on the grand staircase landing. Murphy came racing down the stairs and almost knocked Marty over.

"Hello, big fella!"

Eliza led Marty into the dining room. The wooden box they'd found in the spare room sat on the table. "You wouldn't believe the mess we discovered when we got home last night," Eliza shared as she motioned for him to take a seat.

"Can I get you something to drink?" Jason offered. "Water? A beer? I've got some eighteen-year-old scotch that really takes the edge off."

"A beer sounds good," Marty said shyly, putting his hat on the table.

"Ms. Eliza, I feel like I should apologize. I think I know who broke into your home and I'm pretty sure I know why. I'm also certain it's my fault."

"We're pretty convinced we know who did this too, but it's hardly your fault."

Jason returned and set a beer on the table in front of Marty.

Marty adjusted his posture, reached for the beer, and took a long sip. "The mayor cornered me yesterday at the jubilee. Started questioning me about what I'd shared with you, if I'd told you about him asking for the land survey. Told me my side of the family was nothing but garbage and that my great-grandfather was a nut who had died spouting lies about evidence of fraud."

"That man is a piece of work," Jason said, taking a seat next to Eliza. "The sooner our town is rid of him, the better."

Marty continued. "Then he started calling you all kinds of names, Miss Eliza, and threatened to have Murphy put down, and I just lost it. I told him what I thought of him and that the truth about his whole family was about to come out. He got so angry, and then he just walked away. I think he realized you'd found something and came here looking to find it."

Marty hung his head and stared down at his hands.

"But he didn't find it," Eliza said and pushed the box across the table. "How about instead of blaming yourself for something that is in no way your fault, you just show me a key and open this box. Let's see if your great-grandfather got it right."

Marty offered a weak smile, his eyes fixed on the box. He reached into his jacket pocket and pulled out an old shank skeleton key.

It slid perfectly into the lock. A resounding *click* soon followed, and the spring-loaded mahogany box top sprang open. Inside, a folded piece of

parchment lay atop a deep green velvet-lined base. Underneath were two folded
death records, recorded by a Seven Valleys, Pennsylvania, local church in 1812.

Eliza unfolded the paper and read it aloud:

August 23, 1842

*Upon the request of my brother Elijah Brown, who left this world on May 31,
1842, his lawyer, Horatio Adams, and I set out to locate his only living heir, an
illegitimate son, David Abbott.*

*We traveled extensively looking for both he and his mother, Miss Adelaide
Abbott, and tracked her origins and family to Seven Valleys in Pennsylvania.*

*Together, Mr. Adams and I sat down with Miss Abbott's surviving relative, a
sister. She explained that Adelaide and her son, David, perished in a house fire in the
summer of 1812 when David was just seven years old. At that meeting, she provided
the necessary death documents sufficient enough for Mr. Adams to settle the estate.*

*As I am now confirmed as my brother's last living relative, his estate, left in my
care, shall revert fully to me.*

*This is my sworn statement and acknowledgment, signed and notarized on this
day, the 23rd of August 1842, as requested by Mr. Adams to record the events as I
have laid them out here as a record that I have fulfilled my brother's dying wish in
locating his lost son. May they now both rest in peace.*

Samuel J. Brown

She handed Marty the letter.

Marty's head hung down to his chest, and his shoulders shook as he cried.

"My family searched for this document for years." He wiped his face
with the back of his hand. "My great-grandfather died trying to expose the
Abbott/Winthrop lie."

Eliza touched Marty's arm. "This means you are the rightful heir, Marty. This
letter and the death records prove it. All of it belongs to you."

"I just so happen to know a great estate lawyer," Jason said. "He's one of my
clients. Let's reach out after dinner and see what he has to say. It's time to correct
this mistake."

Though she served dinner on a set of mismatched dishes, the table looked beautiful.

Martha Stewart would be proud.

Marty was chattier than she'd ever heard him. He and Jason talked about everything from baseball to their deep-sea fishing adventures.

Eliza was incredibly happy for Marty but still heartbroken over the fact that she might not ever be able to set the record straight for Honor.

"It has been quite an eventful two days. Between the fight with the mayor, the break-in at Rosecliff, and now my family finally exonerated, it feels like everything is settling into place. Don't you sense it too, Miss Eliza?"

"I feel some of it is coming together, but with the robbery and all my research gone, I don't know how I will be able to give Honor the justice she deserves."

"It does feel that way, doesn't it? But then again, she hasn't failed you yet. She'll show you a way, I'm sure of it. You'll seal the deal...."

Eliza sprung up from her chair. "What did you say? That's it! A seal. A green seal. I forgot to look for the green seal."

Marty stared at her, obviously confused.

Jason wore a similar expression.

"Miss Eliza, I don't understand."

"The other night, after we got home from Ginny's, I had a vision." She held a hand to her forehead. "Honor told me the key wasn't here at Rosecliff, but that box would reveal the truth. But she said there was more—something about a cupboard or a larder. I don't even know what that is. What's a larder?"

"My grandmother used to call her pantry a larder," Marty said.

Eliza snapped her fingers. "Of course. That has to be it. It's one of the few practically untouched spaces in the whole house. I knew there was a reason I kept it intact!"

Eliza darted from the dining room into the kitchen.

Murphy barked and chased after her.

She made a beeline for the pantry, threw open the door, and pulled the light switch. A dull yellow light lit the shelves and cupboards inside, all original to the house. She pulled out drawers and ran her fingers along the shelves, pushing canned and dried goods out of her way, looking for some kind of green seal. Her fingers fumbled as she picked at crevices and crannies.

"It has to be here, whatever it is. But I don't see a green seal anywhere."

"Miss Eliza, stop for a minute and listen with your heart," Marty said from the doorway.

Eliza nodded, stopping her frenzied search.

"Good idea." Eliza took a moment to clear her thoughts, closed her eyes, and placed her hand over her heart. She took a deep breath.

Inhale. Exhale.

A familiar chill and cold tingle rose up her arm, and a cloud of mist from her breath formed in front of her.

Honor, help me.

She felt a slight push against her back and moved deeper into the pantry, stopping when the cold pressure against her shoulder blade released.

She stretched her hand up to where the last beam connected at the corner. Her thumb brushed against something soft. Dusty particles floated down and tickled her nose.

She stood on tiptoes, reached up and pulled down a small package wrapped in a worn piece of cotton fabric.

"Whoa, what do you have there?" Jason asked.

"I'm not sure. It feels like a book."

Eliza's heart raced in her chest as she unwrapped the fabric. Inside, she found a journal, similar to Charlotte's, and a letter. An unbroken green wax seal held the letter closed. The initials HB pressed into the wax.

She carried the journal and sealed letter into the kitchen and set them down on the granite island. Her hands trembled as she stared at the tea-colored paper. She turned it over to read the addressee "Mr. Ashley Lord," she said aloud.

Ever so gently, she removed the wax seal and unfolded the letter.

September 30, 1808
Dearest Father,

My heart is heavy as I write this letter. Charlotte confided in me that Niles suspects that Elijah is embezzling funds from the shipyard account. Though I know you don't believe a woman has a place in business, I nonetheless feel compelled to ensure your success in whatever manner I may. I found proof to confirm Niles's suspicions. My husband plans to use the stolen money to purchase another ship and rob you of your most loyal customers.

What's more, my beloved Levi has fallen seriously ill in no small part due to my husband's continued disregard of Dr. Williams's orders. His willful hatred of me makes me believe my life is in danger. I cannot stand by and allow this man to harm my son or my family.

Please come to Rosecliff at your earliest convenience. I await your arrival.
Your Loving Daughter,
Honor

"He was stealing from them," Eliza said, her eyes scanning the letter, her mind whirling with this new information. "And she found proof. I wonder if he knew. Maybe that's why he killed her."

"The fact that the seal is still intact makes me think he never found this letter. But I guess he could still have figured it out somehow," Jason said.

"And what's that?" Marty asked, pointing to the journal.

Eliza opened the cover and read the first passage.

January 1, 1808

My dearest mother has gifted this journal to me and one just like it to my sister-in-law, Charlotte. I shall be happy to keep a record of my days here at Rosecliff.

Eliza sat back against the stool and wiped her tears. "It's Honor's journal. I can't believe it. Her mother gave one to both her and Charlotte."

Eliza turned the pages until she came to the last entry. It was short, and there was no date, but the whole of it took her breath away.

I am hiding from my husband, Elijah. He is searching for me even now. He is trying to kill me. God have mercy upon me.

Eliza ran her fingers over the entry. Her heart felt an unbearable heaviness for the torment Honor felt those last days and moments of her life.

"This will surely put her spirit at peace. And peaceful spirits bring tranquility and light," Marty said softly.

"Well done, Mrs. Grey," Jason said, wrapping his arms around her. "This was no small feat. You solved two mysteries in one night. The truth will be revealed."

"*We* solved two mysteries," she said, looking at him and then at Marty. "I couldn't have done it without either of you."

Later that evening, she crawled under the covers and carefully opened the fragile journal. Something nagged at her to read the entries for the last week of Honor's life.

She reached over to her reading lamp on the side of her bed and gingerly turned the knob.

Looking over at Jason, now fast asleep, she quietly flipped the last few pages. Although her eyelids fluttered and grew heavy, a familiar tingling sensation shot up her fingers and arms, pulling her deeper into the past.

September 30, 1808

"May we speak in the spare room, Mrs. Brown?" Dr. Williams requested.

Honor's throat tightened, and she could feel the tears well in her eyes. Wearily she nodded and ushered him into the next room.

"Honor, what in God's name happened? Why did the boy go out in the farm fields all day yesterday? I asked Levi, and he said his father took him."

Honor whispered, "I was not privy to that decision. He took him out before I awoke. I am beside myself. Elijah knew Levi was not well enough for that excursion."

"We will do our best to help Levi. It will be difficult, but you must be diligent in his care."

Pain stabbed at Honor's heart, but she would do as the doctor requested to save her son.

As the day wore on, Honor and Susannah waged a battle with Levi's fever. He would sweat right through his bedgown and drift in and out of delirium at times.

Susannah held the spittoon as Honor lifted Levi's frail body allowing him to release the green phlegm from his infected lungs. Each hour brought a new struggle, but finally, Levi quietly slept. Honor gently rubbed her son's forehead and prayed for relief for him.

"I will go and make more tea, Mistress, while Master Levi sleeps. Can I get you anything?"

"No, thank you, Susannah. Tea for Levi is all."

Honor watched as Susannah hurried to the kitchen.

"The time has come for me to act. I have no more chances," Honor whispered to herself.

Honor proceeded into the spare room that contained her writing desk. She quickly opened the locked drawer, removed a piece of paper, opened her inkwell, and composed a letter to her father. She quickly blotted the paper, carefully folded it, and affixed a green wax seal with the initials HB to the closure. Sliding it into her dimity pocket, she would give it to Susannah to deliver immediately.

"Susannah, I need you promptly!" Honor called from atop the stairs where she waited.

Susannah heeded her call and ran upstairs, "Aye, Mistress?"

Honor peered around the hallway, checking for Elijah lurking in the shadows. She pulled the folded sealed letter from her dress pocket and slipped it into Susannah's hand.

"Leave at once. Deliver this letter to my parents right away. I am giving you two shillings to go into town on your return to pick up more tar water and herbs at the apothecary. You must make haste for our dear Levi, is that understood?"

"Aye, Mistress."

Susannah tucked the two shillings and letter into the lined purse inside her apron and ran downstairs to the kitchen.

Honor stood from the top of the landing to make sure Susannah left quickly. The sound of heavy boot steps sent a sickening wave of nerves through her body. Her fingers clenched tightly to the sides of her dress.

"Where are you going in such a hurry, Susannah?" Elijah demanded.

Susannah stopped, her eyes cast down.

"Mistress Brown has given me two shillings to go into town to get more herbs and tar water for Master Levi." Pulling out the two shillings in her palm to show her master.

Honor held her breath, frightened that Susannah would show him the letter.

"Very well, Susannah. You seem nervous. Is there a reason?"

"No, sir. I am in earnest. My Mistress has asked me to go in haste for Master Levi. That is my intent at the moment."

"Then, go."

Susannah curtsied, casting a side glance up the staircase where she and Honor's eyes met.

Honor nodded her approval, relieved in the devotion of her house servant. She observed the quickness of Susannah's steps as she threw off her apron, placed her shawl around her shoulders, and hurried out the door.

Honor paced the floor in between helping Levi with his cough and fever, waiting for Susannah's return. My father will come at once; I know he will, and we will be saved from this horrible situation.

The pounding of horse's hooves and the wheels of a cart came to a screeching halt. Honor listened for the sound of the servant's door and the scurrying of feet.

Within minutes there was a light tap at the bedroom door.

"Come in."

Susannah came bustling through the doorway to Levi's room with a tray, a tin cup of tar water tea, and a cool cloth for his head.

Susannah approached the bed softly with the cup in hand, "How is Master Levi doing?"

"He struggles for every breath. I hope this tar water and herbs will ease his discomfort."

"Aye, as do I, my Mistress."

"Susannah, thank you. Were you able to complete all your tasks?"

"I reached the apothecary and purchased what you requested, but oh Mistress, I have failed you."

"What do you mean?"

"I panicked when Master Brown called me. In haste, I pulled the shillings out of the apron to show him, but I forgot to take the letter out when I hung up my apron. I never delivered it, my lady; it is here—" Susannah's voice cracking as she patted her apron.

"Oh, no, Susannah!" but a sudden coughing fit from Levi halted her reaction.

"I am truly sorry, Mistress. I can bring it on my way home."

"No, we won't worry about that tonight. We have to care for Levi. Please give me the letter, so it does not fall into the wrong hands. I will bestow it upon you when the time is right."

Honor took the letter and walked to the spare room, placing it inside her journal.

"Time is of the essence, and this letter and journal must be hidden from prying eyes," Honor whispered to herself.

Shortly after midnight, Honor knew she was losing the battle she waged for her son. The light of the beeswax candle created an eerie glow as the fireplace embers crackled in the silence of the room.

Exhausted and lacking nourishment, she barely noticed the creak of the floorboards in the doorway.

"How is the boy?"

"He is struggling for breath no matter what I do."

"What can I do?"

A level of contempt rose within her, but she forcibly swallowed it down.

"Go fetch Dr. Williams. Tell him it is a matter of life and death."

Elijah paused.

"Elijah, for God's sake! Get the doctor!"

Turning to her now quiet son, Honor held Levi against her breasts. She could hear the violent thud of horse's hooves riding away from Rosecliff. A pain so deep within her chest began to tear at her very essence.

Honor held Levi's head in the crux of her elbow, desperately trying to support him for air.

"Rest, my sweet; the doctor will be here shortly. Mother is here."

Levi's breath became shallow, and he closed his eyes.

"No, Levi, don't leave me."

Honor screamed a heart-wrenching wail that echoed through the empty home, permeating the very timbers of the house.

Eliza jolted upright, barely catching her breath. A shattering pain throbbed through her body. A grief so deep, she could feel the abyss of despair.

28

GINNY LET OUT A long breath and sat down at her kitchen table. Eliza sat down beside her, overcome with guilt.

"I'll never forgive myself for not keeping all of it under lock and key."

"It's a devastating loss," Ginny said and reached across the table to pat Eliza's hand. "But I hardly blame you. None of it was locked up here. It could just as easily have been my house that was broken into."

"Yes, but the reason for the break-in, the reason all of it was taken, is my fault. I've been poking the bear." She shared the details of Marty's exchange with the mayor at the jubilee.

"So that's what they were arguing about," Ginny said. "Poor Marty got caught in the middle."

"He may have gotten caught in the middle, but poor he is not, or at least he won't be for long." Eliza pulled out her phone and showed Ginny a picture of Samuel Brown's statement. "This is what was inside the box we found. We believe it's the evidence Marty's great-grandfather hid. Jason made a call to an estate attorney he works with. They feel pretty confident this will help Marty's case, though without copies of the original documents from the archive, there's a small chance the court could still uphold the previous decision."

Ginny read through the statement on Eliza's phone and handed it back to her. "Marty deserves a break. His family has been reeling from this travesty for too many generations."

Eliza reached into her bag and pulled out Honor's journal.

"And we also found this." She handed it to Ginny.

A look of confusion crossed Ginny's face. "But I thought you said the journal was taken."

Eliza offered her a sad smile. "Charlotte's journal was taken. This belongs to Honor."

Ginny's eyes widened, and she opened the front cover and read the first entry. "Identical journals, both gifts?"

"It would seem so. And sadly, this," Eliza took the journal and flipped to the last entry handing it back to Ginny, "proves that Honor didn't kill herself."

"Dear God, that poor woman."

"I know we don't have much, but do you think we'll be able to convince the historical committee to petition to change Honor's death certificate? Move her grave?"

"I have to think so. At least enough to spark some interesting discussion and a little more research on their part. I'll bring it up at our next meeting."

Eliza stifled a yawn. "Excuse me," she said. "After all the excitement yesterday, I stayed up half the night writing a follow-up article about Honor, the events leading up to her death, and about Samuel's statement and the theft of the Brown estate from Marty's family. Sent it to Art just after one. It might not change anything right away, but it's about to rattle some cages."

Eliza's phone buzzed. *The Gazette*'s main line flashed on the screen.

"Speak of the devil. Do you mind if I take this?"

"No, not at all."

Eliza answered the call. "Hello?"

"Eliza, this is Lana. I need you to come to the office. Art's got something he wants to talk to you about."

"Art wants to talk to me?" Eliza asked, incredulously.

"Yes," Lana blurted. "Right now. You should come right now."

The call abruptly ended.

"Is everything all right?" Ginny asked.

"Everything is...strange," Eliza replied. "That was Lana. She wants me to come down to the office. Right now."

Ginny's eyebrows rose. "Strange indeed. Perhaps you should go."

Eliza nodded and stood up. She put the journal in her bag. "I plan on checking with the police later today. See if, by chance, we were wrong about who broke into our house. Fingers crossed, they find everything. Again, Ginny, I'm so sorry."

The older woman stood and hugged Eliza. "History is wonderous and fascinating, but if I got upset over every artifact that has been lost or destroyed, I'd be a blubbery mess."

Eliza found a parking space across the street from *The Gazette*, her mind deep in thought as she waited for a break in the traffic before crossing the street. Part of her was terrified Art was going to tell her he couldn't or wouldn't print the story.

But he had to. The truth about Honor and the mayor needed to be made public. To set the record straight.

She hurried into the building and stopped short when she spotted Graham standing next to Lana at her desk. Standing a little too close.

"There she is," Lana said.

Eliza's expression cooled.

"Ms. Grey," Graham said. "Lana here was just telling me about your article. Said it was something I needed to come down here and see for myself."

Eliza glared at Lana. "Is that so?"

"I told you," Lana said, pushing her glasses back up the bridge of her nose. "I care about this town. Coventry deserves to know the truth about the mayor and his family. Your article is a bit unbelievable. Hidden boxes, false bottom drawers. Really, it's a bit much, don't you think?"

Eliza fumed. "Where's Art? Does he know you've been pilfering through his email?"

"It might be a bit late, but I've decided to take you up on your request for an interview about my family history," Graham said, the hint of a smirk on his face. "How about we start now, and you can quote me on this, 'Your article is nothing but false accusations and lies. And if this paper prints it, I'll sue you and this office for libel.'"

"I'm not afraid of you, Mr. Mayor. I have all the evidence I need to back up my story. This town will finally know the truth. About you and Honor Brown."

"Oh, but I thought I read in the police blotter that most of your research, most of your evidence, had been stolen in a break-in." Then he added, feigning sympathy, "Too bad."

Eliza paused and let the warm satisfaction of knowing his smug expression was about to sink into an agonizing frown. "You may want to give your legal team a heads up, Mr. Mayor. As it turns out, you're about to be sued for the entirety of the Brown estate. And everyone will finally know what I know, and I suspect you also know. That you and your whole family are nothing but lying frauds."

"I will prove any documents you have are forged. I have friends in very high places. You're in over your head, Ms. Grey."

Behind them, the bell over the front door rang. Chief Coleman stepped into the office.

"Chief," the mayor said. "Good to see you. Ms. Grey and I were just discussing the growing crime rate here in Coventry. Good people having their homes broken into."

"Yes," the chief said, moving closer to Lana's desk. "About that."

The chief lifted a set of handcuffs from his belt and pulled the mayor's hands behind his back. "Graham Winthrop, you are under arrest."

"What?" Graham bellowed, squirming as the chief locked the cuffs in place. "What are you doing? What am I being charged with, you idiot!? Say goodbye to your job, Chief. And take these off me. Immediately!"

Chief Coleman jerked Graham toward the door. "Funny thing, Mr. Mayor. We got an anonymous tip last night. Seems someone with access to your home office found some old documents, a couple of letters, a family Bible, and a journal. All of which had recently been reported as stolen."

Graham's head snapped to Lana. "You? You did this?"

Lana shrugged and leaned on her desk. "Well done, Captain Obvious, you figured it out. Honestly, you did a lame job of trying to hide them. I went into your home office looking for a pen and couldn't resist going through your glassed-in bookcase. One round of snooping, and there they were just barely hidden among your old books. Very sloppy, *Grahammy*."

She picked up her phone and showed Eliza a picture. "These are yours, right?"

Eliza recognized Ginny's Bible and Charlotte's journal immediately.

"Yes, yes, they are part of the research documents taken from my house," she said, looking up at the police chief.

Lana sighed with disgust. "And to think I actually considered letting you marry me. Chief, I'll stop by the station later and sign my statement."

Another uniformed police officer opened the door to *The Gazette* office, and the chief hauled the mayor outside.

Eliza stood next to Lana at the window and watched the chief read Graham his rights before putting him in the back of the police cruiser parked at the curb.

"Lana, I don't even know what to say."

Lana crossed her arms. "Too bad, really. Turns out he was not only a crook but a stupid one at that. I didn't even have to nose through his drawers. He literally left it all right there on his bookshelf. When I realized what it was, I put two and two together. I read about the break-in at your house. I knew he'd taken them; I just didn't understand why until I read your article. I phoned the chief early this morning. Sent him the pictures."

Eliza let that information sink in. "Art doesn't really want to talk to me, does he?"

Lana polished her nails on her shoulder. "Nope, he's not even in the office today. He took a couple of days off to go see his mom in Rhode Island." She shrugged. "What can I say? I've got a flair for the dramatic."

Eliza laughed.

"It really is too bad," Lana repeated. "That man makes a mean chicken piccata. And he wasn't a bad kisser either."

Eliza grimaced. "On that note, I'll leave you to bask in the glory of a dramatic mission accomplished."

Back in her car, Eliza phoned Vanessa and relayed the events of the past couple of days.

"Never in a million years did I ever think I'd be thanking Lana for her role in all of this," Eliza said.

"So, the hero makes friends with her arch nemesis, and together they catch a bad guy. Nice!"

"I wouldn't go so far as to say we're friends, but Graham got arrested, and I get to set the record straight about Honor's death. I'd say that's a win."

"It's almost unbelievable," Jason said over the phone later that night after Eliza had told him about the day's events. He'd stayed for a late meeting in Boston and was driving home. It was well after 9 p.m. when Eliza finally managed to get ahold of him.

"I know. This has been a hell of a ride. I'm so glad everything worked out in the end." She sat in the living room, sipping on a glass of Bordeaux. Murphy slept soundly in front of the fireplace.

A low rumble of thunder sounded.

"Hey honey, it's starting to rain. I'll let you go," Jason said. "Why don't you take it easy? I'll be home soon."

"That sounds like a great idea."

The lights flickered several times.

"Ugh. Looks like we might lose power. Drive carefully. I'll see you in a bit."

She tossed her phone onto the coffee table and watched lightning dance across the sky over the dark churning sea. The wind suddenly picked up, howling through the leafless trees. A sudden, violent sheet of rain began pelting the windows.

Murphy opened his eyes, a low growl in his throat.

A gnawing sense of apprehension sent a shiver up Eliza's spine, and the edges of her vision began to blur.

Secrets unraveled. Secrets revealed.

"I figured it out," Eliza said, her head spinning. "I'll tell everyone what really happened."

A whisper slipped through the silence.

Eliza.

A soft green glow drew her attention across the large foyer to the dining room. She rose and slowly made her way across the entrance.

Honor's necklace eerily glowed against the tablecloth.

Put it on.

She lifted the necklace to her neck. The metal and precious gems felt cold against her skin. She turned to look at her reflection in the large gold mirror above the sideboard.

Above her, the dining room chandelier began to sway mesmerizingly back and forth. The dangling crystals made a delicate, hypnotizing sound as they moved. Her head felt heavy as if she were drugged.

A loud whistling hissed through the fireplace hearth, shaking the poker in its stand.

Murphy cocked his head and bared his teeth toward the inky blackness of the foyer. He pressed against Eliza's leg.

An enormous boom of thunder made Eliza jump, and the walls shook in reverberation. The lights went out, dropping the house into darkness. Eliza stared at her reflection, now cast in a green glow. The room around her fell out of focus.

Eliza, come to me...

The sound of glass shattering in the kitchen drew Murphy's attention, and he raced from the room.

A cold hand gripped Eliza's arm and pulled her to the foyer, the French doors between the two rooms slamming shut. She turned to see Murphy, trapped, barking and scratching frantically against the glass. Unable to move, she turned her gaze back to the unearthly grip of the familiar specter.

Honor Brown stood in front of her, her hair mussed, an ashy paleness to her skin, vacant eyes, and a gash across her face.

It is time to finish what you promised.

"I don't understand," Eliza said, struggling to find the words. "I found your journal. I know the truth, and soon everyone else will too.

It is time for you to see and finally set me free.

The darkness faded, and Eliza found herself sitting on the edge of a bed. Her body was no longer her own, but she knew where she was and, more importantly, who she was. This was Rosecliff, and she was Honor. Beside her on the bed, Levi's frail body, now absent of breath, had taken on a greyish pallor.

Her self-awareness softened as if pushed to the back of her mind. She could feel the fabric of Honor's dress against her skin. Feel the weight of exhaustion in her body. She could hear Susannah scurrying around in the kitchen below.

Eliza relinquished control, her awareness growing sharper once again. There was the sound of footsteps and the swooshing of Susannah's gown as she climbed the stairs. Then a light knocking at the door, followed by a kindly voice as the door pushed open.

"Good morning, Mistress. I've brought his tea."

Honor looked up at Susannah. Her eyes swollen, her throat sore from hours of sobbing.

Susannah's sight settled on the bed and she let out a cry. "Oh no! Not our dear, dear boy!"

Honor spoke, her voice rough and raw. "Shortly after midnight, he left us."

Susannah's shoulders shook as she sobbed into the tea.

Honor stood and put an arm around the woman's shoulder.

"Oh, Mistress. I am so very sorry."

Susannah took the tray of tea and carried it down to the kitchen, Honor behind her.

"Find the stableman James," Honor said when they reached the first floor. "Send him to my parents' house and to the farm with the sad news."

"I will, Mistress, at once."

Left alone, Honor sank to her knees; an overwhelming sense of loss and grief washed over her, a deep, tormented cry escaped her lips.

Eliza felt herself grow heavy, her mind fighting to retain focus as the room around her spun, pulsating flashes of green light illuminating snapshots of time moving forward faster and faster.

Doctor Williams patted her arm. "I am so very sorry."

Flash.

Then Mary and Ashley Lord rushed up the steps. She felt her mother's arms wrapped around her, igniting a fresh crop of tears.

Flash.

Charlotte and Niles were at her side. She felt Charlotte's embrace and the growing baby bump at her waist.

Flash.

William and Abigail Brown embraced her together, unafraid to share their tears.

Flash.

Samuel. Kind Samuel pulled her into his arms and held her as she cried.

Flash.

Then Elijah appeared. His face drawn and somber.

Once again, the room came into focus, and Eliza felt Honor's energy surge through her as a well of anger rose within her gut. The voice in her ears not her own, but there was no doubt whose words lambasted the man who had taken a sick boy out into the fields.

Honor pounded on Elijah's chest.

"You killed our son! You killed my Levi, and I will never forgive you!"

Faces flashed before her. Their voices calming, urging her to rest.

And then she was alone in her bedroom, dressed in a white lace bedgown. Her family had come and gone, their concern echoing in her mind.

She is mad with grief; give her time.

She is not herself; you must let her be.

She wrapped herself in a woolen shawl and stoked the last burning embers in the fireplace. She felt the weight of a necklace at her throat and lightly touched the emeralds and filagree. She'd forgotten to take it off while undressing. She hesitated momentarily to call for Susannah but remembered Elijah had relieved the staff from their duties for the night.

A heavy sense of hopelessness washed over her.

If the sun did not rise in the morning, It would be of no matter to me.

Eliza heard Honor's thoughts as if they were her own.

I will leave this house. First thing in the morning.

I should have begged my parents to take us with them when last we saw them. My mother saw the bruises, saw Levi. She would have taken us, made my father take us home.

She wiped a tear from her eye. *Didn't I wait too long already? Had I done it sooner, my son would be with me. I thought I had more time.*

The door flew open. Elijah stood on the threshold, disheveled and hollow-eyed. The beautiful man she once adored and loved now a menacing monster.

Her throat tightened. Every fiber of her body vibrated with hatred and repulsion.

He had taken from her something more precious than life itself.

"Honor, we need to speak."

She turned her back to him, taking up the poker to stoke the fire. "I have naught to say. Your cruelty has destroyed me. Destroyed our family. I hold nothing but contempt in my heart for you. I will stay with you no longer. I'm to my father's house in the morning and pray to God, who surely now must comfort my son, that I shall never set eyes upon your face again."

She heard his footsteps, felt the heat of his hands as he grabbed her. Her grip tightened on the poker, and she spun, slashing out at him. The poker struck him at the temple.

Blood spurted from the deep gash, and he screamed in pain.

She darted around him and out into the hall.

Elijah bellowed and fell into the door frame behind her. His hand pressed against the flow of blood at the side of his face as he gave chase.

She raised the poker, ready to strike again, but he grabbed the shaft and yanked it from her grip, tossing it over the baluster.

"Leave me alone; I hate you!" she screamed.

He grabbed at her as she turned to flee, catching the necklace at her throat and ripping it away. An intense pain and pressure tore at her neck. Her feet tangled in a rug, and she fell to the floor, her head catching the baseboard trim. A cut above her eyebrow dripped blood into her eye and down her face.

"I always knew you were nothing but a spoiled, useless, stupid woman," Elijah said, pulling her to her feet by the front of her gown.

She pushed against him, then kicked him hard in the groin.

He groaned, his grip loosened, and she scrambled toward the stairs. He caught her by the hair and yanked her back, and flung her against the wall.

Her fingers reached out for a vase of flowers atop a hall table, and she hurled it at him. The base of the vase hit him square on the forehead before it crashed to the ground and shattered around them.

Blood streamed down his face, and he fell against the wall.

She raced down the stairs to the kitchen, bits of broken glass digging into her bare feet.

Outside, thunder boomed, and rain pelted the windows. She shook with fear, the adrenaline pulsing through her body. She needed to hide.

A fire still burned in the hearth, and a single lit candle occupied the kitchen's large worktable. She took the candle and stepped into the larder, quietly pulling the door closed behind her.

From atop a beam, she took down her journal. Tucked inside, a letter to her father.

Would that I have sent this to you sooner.

She found the quill and inkwell she'd hidden behind a small barrel of vinegar and squatted at the very back of the pantry.

She could hear Elijah's movement from the floor above, his heavy steps on the stairs, moving swiftly to the dining room toward the kitchen.

With a shaky hand, she dipped the quill in ink and hurriedly added a few words to the page before returning the journal to its hiding place.

She doused the candle with her fingertips and crouched down low, pulling her knees against her body and held her breath.

Heavy footsteps thundered just outside the door.

Elijah ripped open the larder, and she screamed.

"Like a child hiding in the dark." He laughed at her, his face covered in disgust.

He dragged her into the foyer and out the front door, out into the night and the raging storm.

A blast of frigid air took her breath away. Within seconds, the icy rain soaked through to her skin, pressing the nightgown tight against her frame.

His footing slipped, and she broke free of him and raced across the front lawn up toward the side yard.

He yelled for her, but she continued to run through the darkness. The rain and wind howled around her. Lightning flashed, and she caught sight of the edge of the cliff and stopped short. Her hair hung heavy against her head; the nightdress translucent as it clung to her body.

Elijah came up slowly behind her. He held out his hand. His voice dampened by the wind and rain.

"Come here, Honor. Step away from the edge. You are acting like a child."

"I hate you!" she screamed, the emotion ripping through her entire body. "You killed our son! You killed my beloved Levi, and I shall NEVER forgive you. My father will know the truth about you, Elijah. He will know about your embezzlement, your mistreatment of me, and your scandalous affairs!"

Elijah lunged forward and grabbed her arms. "Perhaps you're not the stupid woman I thought you were after all," he said. A smile spread across his face as looked at her. He touched her cheek gently, pulling a piece of her wet hair from her face. "But I can't have a wife who speaks so ill of me."

Eliza felt Honor break, the will to fight suddenly gone. She watched a cold detachment settle into Elijah's gaze. Then flashes of Honor streamed through her mind. She and her brother Niles as children, her wedding, the birth of Levi, Levi's first steps, meeting Charlotte and her last conversation with her mother.

I'm sorry, Mother. I promised you I wouldn't wait too long.

A flash of light zig-zagged across the sky, illuminating the figure that loomed before her.

Elijah's expression hardened, and he raised his arm. She barely felt the sting as his open hand connected with her jaw.

All sound and pain dropped away; time slowed as her body fell backward.

She stared into Elijah's cold, ruthless eyes and his smug grin as she clawed at the air, her feet slipping away from the rocky ledge, her white nightdress fluttering in the updraft. The sensation of the frigid air swallowing her in its embrace. The sound of the waves crashing against the rocks below as eternal darkness engulfed her in its wake.

And then the sound of barking broke through the darkness.

Eliza screamed. Her voice finally freed, erupting from her throat. The scent of wet earth and salty air filled her nostrils.

Hot breath covered her face as a frantic whine sounded in her ears.

She felt a tug at her neck, heard the sound of fabric ripping. It was only then she realized that her legs hung over the edge of the cliff. Adrenaline surged through her body, and she reached for Murphy, hugging his neck as he pulled her back.

"Eliza!"

She heard Jason's voice muffled by the rain and called out to him.

"Jason!"

The beam of a flashlight swept across the lawn, and he raced toward her, sliding to the muddy ground beside her and pulling her to his chest.

His arms tightened around her.

She sat up and stroked Murphy, "It's okay, boy. I'm okay," she repeated, consoling him.

Murphy nervously licked her face and pawed her chest.

Jason helped her up and walked her inside.

When he shut the door behind them, a sudden surge of noise crackled through the air. Light illuminated the house as the power came back on.

Jason set her on the couch and wrapped a throw blanket around her shoulders.

"Murphy must have broken through the French doors to get to you. They look like a wild beast had ripped them open. I followed the noise of his barking. Thank God I found you."

"It's over," she said through chattering teeth. "I know the truth, all of it. He killed her. His negligence caused Levi's death. She tried to leave him, and he hit her and sent her over the cliff."

Murphy whined and pressed his nose to Eliza's face.

She reached out and pulled him into an embrace. "My good boy. Good boy, Murphy."

A calm settled over them, and an undeniable peace filled the walls of Rosecliff Manor.

Epilogue

Coventry-by-the-Sea, May 28, 2022

"WE SHOULD PROBABLY HEAD out in about ten minutes," Eliza said as she sipped coffee and buttered her croissant.

"The weatherman says it is a perfect beach day," Jason said, holding one of several copies of the morning paper. "Maybe we should spend the day on our private little beach."

Bella sat down at the kitchen island wearing a melon-colored sundress and gold sandals. Murphy sat obediently at her feet. "I'm game for the beach," she said, reaching for her own croissant and tearing off a small piece to toss to Murphy.

Jason held the paper up, tapping it with his finger. "Marty made the front page! Can you believe it?"

Eliza smiled. "I'm so glad history has been set right again. The case to reinstate Marty as heir to the Brown estate had resolved in his favor quicker than anyone had anticipated. His great-grandfather's letter, along with a DNA analysis, definitely proved that Graham Winthrop was not related to the Brown family in any way and made the decision to return the Brown family fortune a no-brainer."

"It also likely helped that the former mayor had been charged with breaking and entering and first-degree arson, seeing as how the shoes he was wearing when he was arrested were a perfect match for the footprints left by the intruder at Rosecliff, and the one found outside the city archives after the fire. And now he's currently awaiting sentencing in the county jail," Jason added.

"Graham should have known better. Imported leather Louis Vuitton shoes aren't worn by the average thief!" Eliza laughed.

As they waited for Bella to get her wallet from her room, Eliza, attired in a simple white lace dress with gold accessories, stood in the dining room looking over the framed copy of the article she'd written about the Brown family, highlighting both Honor's murder and the fraud that had stripped Marty of his family fortune.

She ran her fingers over the glass along the byline. "Honoring the Past: A Story of Love, Death, Betrayal, and Truth" by Eliza Grey.

The article had been a local sensation and eventually syndicated in newspapers across the state and even across the country.

"Ready?" Jason asked softly.

"Yes, I believe I am," she said.

When they arrived at Highgate, a small crowd had already gathered around the Lord family plot.

Honor and Levi's original headstones had been carefully repaired and placed next to the graves of Mary and Ashley Lord and Niles and Charlotte Lord. Honor and Levi now lay side by side and close to her family.

Eliza surveyed the crowd. Marty Evans, dressed in his finest, stood coordinating all the arrangements with the funeral director. Ginny Burke, dressed in a pretty sky-blue chiffon dress, waved warmly at the Greys. Vanessa and Patrick Murphy broke from the crowd to stand beside them.

"Eliza, what a beautiful day. You must feel such peace," Vanessa said, hugging Eliza tightly.

"It feels so surreal," Eliza said as a tear slipped from the corner of her eye. "It's quite a little turn-out for Honor and Levi, isn't it?" Eliza scanned the many faces and caught one familiar in her periphery.

"Excuse me for a minute, Van."

Althea Wickham stood quietly in the crowd next to Ginny Burke. She was decked out in a vibrant electric blue dress with big chunky white earrings and a super-sized white beaded necklace. Eliza quickly zigzagged through the small crowd and greeted Thea with a hug.

"Thank you for coming today. It's so nice of you to travel for this occasion."

"Oh, for heaven's sake, it's nothing. I wouldn't miss it for the world. This is a big day for Coventry-By-The-Sea. Plus, I get to spend time with my daughter and grandkids, as well as my dearest friend in the world," Thea said as she pointed toward Ginny.

Eliza nodded. "True. You are a part of this journey, you know. Helping us buy Rosecliff. Believing I was the one to heal the wounds of the past."

Thea giggled. "Eliza, I have a gift. You know, putting the right person in the right house. Houses speak to me, and Rosecliff *wanted* you. I just knew."

"Yeah, I guess you did."

The ceremony and dedication began with the minister sharing a few words about a mother's love for her child and how nothing changes that emotion, even beyond death and time.

The preacher called Ginny forward to read the proclamation on behalf of the historical society. She approached quietly and stood before the crowd.

"I am here today to see justice served and to decree that the official cause of Honor Lord Brown's death has been revised and the town records updated. She will forever more be buried beside her beloved son, Levi Ashley Brown, in this hallowed ground this day, on May 28th, 2022, at Highgate Cemetery."

The crowd clapped, and Jason gently placed his arm around Eliza and whispered, "You did this, El."

The minister read a few psalms from the Bible, before finally bestowing his blessing upon Honor and Levi. Those in attendance formed a single line to approach the caskets and place a rose atop each one. Yellow for Levi and dark, dusty pink for Honor.

The two coffins were lowered into the earth and to their eternal resting place, side by side.

The edges of her vision blurred, and Eliza looked beyond the gravesite to a small grove of trees. A warm, comforting breeze blew up around her, bringing with it the pleasant aroma of lilacs and roses. In the shadow of the trees stood Honor and Levi, hand in hand. The two figures shimmered in the morning sun. Honor raised her arm and waved.

Marty was right. Peaceful spirits bring tranquility and light.

A soft voice whispered *thank you* in Eliza's ear.

The crowd began to move away, and Marty made a direct line over to Eliza and put out a hand to shake hers.

She swatted at his hand and pulled him into a hug.

Murphy barked and nudged between them, his tail sweeping back and forth, making a dust storm of dirt behind him.

"Well, hello, Murphy! How are you, big fella!"

Marty shook hands with Jason. "I can't say thank you enough. You've changed my life," he said, his voice cracking under the weight of his emotions. "And Miss Eliza, you've done something really special here." He nodded toward the gravesites.

Eliza smiled. "I couldn't have done it alone. *We* did this. Together. Remember?"

He glanced up and around at the trees that provided the backdrop to the Lord family plot.

"Not sure if you noticed, Miss Eliza. There aren't many crows hanging around now. Kind of interesting, don't you think?"

She listened and searched the tree line. Not a single crow.

"They call a group of crows a murder, you know."

Eliza smiled. "So they do."

Returning to Rosecliff, Eliza sent Jason and Bella off to their small scrap of beach with a blanket, cooler, and towels in hand. Choosing a little quiet time for reflection instead, Eliza opted for a walk along the tidepools with Murphy.

"If you two don't mind, I think Murphy and I will walk up the shoreline. I will join you in a bit."

A warm summer breeze blew her hair across her face. The wild roses her home was named for were in full bloom; their vibrant pink color cascaded down the cliff, the occasional cloud of petals drifting down in the wind. Bits of driftwood and seaweed littered the gritty sand.

She inhaled the salty air and released a deep, cleansing breath. Any remnants of the months of heaviness and anxiety ebbed away. Honor and Levi had been reunited, and all felt right with the world.

The surf rolled gently against the shore, and she let the waves swirl around her ankles as she walked along the water's edge with Murphy. She stopped near the outcropping of rocks where she'd seen Honor and her ghoulish form, the Wet Lady, all those years ago. She imagined Honor standing here as she did now, her feet in the sand, the sun on her face.

Murphy barked behind her, and she turned to find him yapping at a group of seagulls swarming around him.

"What in the world?"

She hurried to his aid, waving her hands. The birds scattered and flew out over the water.

Murphy sniffed at a small pile of rocks, pawing at it, then looked at her as if asking for help.

A small blue crab scurried out between his legs, making a break for the surf.

"Ah, we feel the need to protect a little sea creature from impending doom, I see."

Murphy whined and chased after the tiny crab, swiping at it with his paw.

"Oh Murph, let it be."

Murphy's forehead furrowed. He hung his head, then barked at a seagull that tried to swoop down and snatch it away.

"Good grief," Eliza said, her tone slightly exasperated, but her heart warmed by Murphy's instinct to protect a more vulnerable creature.

She carefully scooped up the crab and gently tossed it into the ocean, where it made a small splash into the breaking surf.

As she stepped back, a shimmering glint of something caught her eye. The shiny object was ensnared in the crevice of a rock and tumbled within the fissure.

She hurried to snatch it up before a wave pulled it from view.

She held the object tight in her grip, letting the water rinse away the sand before opening her palm. A beautiful, elaborately designed ring sparkled in the afternoon sun.

Eliza examined it more closely. The style was distinctly Victorian. A full moon face was carved into a milky white stone – a moonstone, if she had to guess – encircled by what looked to be twelve rough-cut garnets. She brought the gold band closer for inspection.

Inside the band was an inscription.

Eternity, whose end no eye can reach -ADA

Eliza felt a familiar tingle dance up her arms, and she let a smile spread across her face.

"Hey, Murphy! Let's go in. Looks like I've got a little research to do."

About the Author

Thank you for reading *The Attachment*. If you enjoyed this book, please consider leaving a review at the following websites:

www.amazon.com

For more information, please visit me at the following:

https://www.facebook.com/JudithAnnCosby

https://www.linkedin.com/in/judith-cosby-799079124

https://www.instagram.com/judy.r.cosby

https://twitter.com/cosby_judith

judithacosby@gmail.com

https://www.judithcosby.com

Also By Judith Cosby

Threads – A journey into the picture of the soul
Spirit Threads – Messages of hope and healing
Weaving Threads of Gratitude - Journal

Available now on

Amazon.com
and
Barnes & Noble.com

Made in the USA
Middletown, DE
30 January 2025

69657541R00205